MIGHTY UNCLEAN

CODY GOODFELLOW

GEMMA FILES

MORT CASTLE

GARY A. BRAUNBECK

Contents

Alive & Kicking

One of the most persistent popular conceptions is that "horror" fiction is, as a viable genre, "dead." Of course, the key word isn't "horror" or "dead" but rather "viable."

If one waits around long enough, sooner or later everything that isn't the trendiest at that particular, precise moment will be termed "dead" or "dying." Whether from an economic, popular or aesthetic perspective, the viability of almost everything is questioned and – often prematurely – declared a gone goose.

In my lifetime alone, I can recall everything from 8-track tapes (perhaps not the greatest loss) to the game of professional baseball receiving epitaphs. As I write this, daily print newspapers, paper books and even the publishing industry as we know now it all are apparently earnestly being measured for their shroud.

I'm not here to predict what will happen with newspapers or books, and I am certainly not going to enter the debate about the current state of publishing. But, what I am here to do is to try and offer my belief that, to paraphrase the quotation so famously offered by Mark Twain: the reports of the death of horror fiction are greatly exaggerated.

It is true that many bookstores have removed the separate designation of a stand alone "horror" section in recent years. This seems to trouble some folks to no end, and yet I can't imagine fully why that is the case. While it is all well and good to separate genres, do we really need a unique section labeled "horror" in a bookstore? Is it so wrong that horror books sit on shelves next to titles in "general fiction," "popular fiction" or – heaven forbid – "literature"?

Perhaps it stems from the fact that people who perceive themselves to belong to a particular genre also tend to feel fiercely protective of that genre. It is surely true that mystery writers may have a different audience that science fiction writers, and romance authors probably aren't writing specifically for the Westerns crowd, but I think perhaps such specialization is more a networking tool for the writers themselves rather than a useful guidepost for prospective readers.

If we've seen anything, it is that the 21st century is the rise of the mash-up, the genre-busting, category-challenging work that combines elements from all kinds of different sources and synthesizes it into a special, unique brew.

Which brings us to the real reason that horror fiction will continue to not only survive, but thrive. Genres wither and die primarily for two reasons: lack of interest and lack of fresh ideas.

The good news is that, from an audience standpoint, there is no dearth of interest in the dark, the macabre, the frightening. Whether it's called "horror," "dark fiction," "thriller," "dark fantasy," or "booga-booga stories," there has always been and always continues to be an audience for scary stories. Horror films continue to make money at the box office, and the same is true for publishing.

Folks tend to like to go back to the "boom and bust" period of 1980s and 1990s for referencing the rise and fall of horror fiction. Many say that the genre has yet to get up off the mat from that fall. While it might be true that publishers are creating boutique imprint lines and throwing cash at every devil child or haunted house tale, the real truth is that horror fiction continues to chug along – just like it always has. Maybe even under the guise of "commercial fiction."

But, even more encouraging is the level of talent turning their hands to horror fiction today. Not only the amazing new voices that are appearing, but also the work being done by people who have been working in the field for years. I would go so far to suggest that, perhaps, someday, when historians look back to this particular period of time, it may be regarded as the beginning of "renaissance" of horror as an archetype in literature.

There are simply so many talented authors writing stories today, and in so many different styles. And – in a very roundabout way – it leads us to why you're holding this book in your hands.

Because there are so many interesting things going on in the world of horror fiction, and so many talented folks working at creating memorable stories, it is a great honor to be able share some of that work, in all of the different incarnations that it appears.

Quite simply, Cody Goodfellow writes stories like no one else. While that sort of sentence may be a somewhat tired cliché, in this case, it really and truly applies. Descriptions like "outré," "boundary-pushing" and "extreme" might be truthfully applied to Cody's work, and "honest," "thought-provoking" and "amazing" would be equally appropriate.

From the seeming logical sensibility of the narrator in "Love to Give" to the wry social commentary lurking beneath the surface of "The Weak Sisters Break Out" to the absolutely indescribable "Venus of Santa Cruz" it is obvious that if Cody Goodfellow is a writer of "extreme" stories, then it is as a writer of concomitantly "extreme" ideas – the "thinking person's extreme writer."

If Cody Goodfellow's stories are the feverish embrace of a mad genius, Gemma Files' are the cool kiss on the forehead from the debauched intellectual. Gemma's work is once again proof positive that a writer does not have to raise her voice to make an impact just as devastating.

The quiet rationality, the gorgeously-constructed sentences, the obvious intellectual acumen all serve to lull the reader into a false sense of security – which renders the inevitable nastiness all the more powerful. The insane protagonist of "Ring of Fire" is formidable indeed – but perhaps not quite as formidable as the well-spoken narrator. In "Crossing the River" we are confronted with a dizzying array of shifting loyalties, unknown limits of infernal powers and an examination of what exactly might constitute "monsters." And, in "The Speed of Pain," we are strapped into a rollercoaster for a journey into a mystery perhaps best left unsolved – and one that we fear is going to end badly for the seekers. What makes these uncommon tales all the more riveting is an uncanny sense of timing and pace – the stories proceed in their quiet, measured manner and the reader is helpless as the sense of unease grows and grows and the sense of dread hanging over the pages becomes a palpable, almost physical presence.

Most of the folks reading this volume will need no introduction to the work of Mort Castle. If you're discovering Mort's writing for the first time, you are in for a treat from another master of deceptively-constructed prose. If Gemma Files' writing quietly insinuates itself into the reader's brain before blowing everything open like a stick of dynamite, Mort's approach is equally clever coming from a different angle.

The genial, casual language that could pass for the conversation of a close friend combined with the encyclopedic knowledge of everything from obscure jazz tunes to arcane Hollywood legends creates another comfort zone for the reader, who instantly knows he or she is in the safe hands of a true pro. And that's when the bottom falls out.

Because Mort writes about music and musicians quite a bit (and happens to be an immensely talented one himself), his work is often compared to pieces of music, and the comparisons are especially apt. In stories like "Bird is Dead," "Moon on the Water" and "Music on the Michigan Avenue Bridge,"(all related somehow to music, natch) you can see Mort doing the equivalent of tuning up – revving up his engine as he gets ready to really deliver the goods, and the payoff in each of those stories reflects that power. In "I am Your Need" Mort plays a tune about the glitter and glamour of Hollywood in an understated minor key, emphasizing the desperation and fear and outright terror in a sophisticated and wholly compelling voice. And, in "Dreaming Robot Monster," Mort once again uses his gifts in a clever misdirection – while the reader initially enjoys the amiable riffing on a widely-mocked film, he is actually setting up something much more nasty and contemplative as a coda.

It is difficult these days to find someone who combines "nasty" and "contemplative" consistently as perfectly as Gary A. Braunbeck. Gary's work continues to receive award after award – and it is certainly easy to understand why. Whether working with the unnerving, implacable unfolding of the surreal "Merge Right" or the in-your-face graphic nastiness of "As It Is In Your Head" (and here's what should be an obvious tip for readers – whenever the author begins a story with an epigraph from *Titus Andronicus*, you know things are going to get really ugly and REALLY messy…), Gary's work combines that clarity of thought and idea with the terrifying that often lurks just under the surface of such clarity. In "Bargain," he provides a different sort of surreal platform for another provocative idea. And, the increasingly urgency in the narrator's voice in "…And When It Is Decided The War Is Over" uses that uncomfortably evolving immediacy to guide the reader effortlessly to the devastating conclusion.

And, what could better declare the health and robustness of horror fiction that such a group of seemingly disparate tales from four seemingly disparate writers? But, underneath all of the different styles, there is one clear unifying thread – a fierce and curious intelligence. From Cody to Gemma, Mort to Gary, these are writers with ideas to explore. As widely-varying as the voices may be, it is still intoxicating to be included on these journeys as they follow their ideas to the very darkest places.

Perhaps most promising of all, these four writers represent only a small fraction of the talented folks exploring their own ideas via the trusty and venerable vehicle of horror fiction. If nothing else, that indicates to me that horror, as a "viable" genre, is far from "dead and buried" but is, instead, very much alive and kicking.

Enjoy.

– Bill Breedlove
Chicago, Illinois
May 2009

Cody Goodfellow has written three and a half novels: RADIANT DAWN, RAVENOUS DUSK and PERFECT UNION, and JAKE'S WAKE with John Skipp. His award-shunning short fiction has appeared in CEMETERY DANCE, BLACK STATIC, DARK DISCOVERIES and (with Skipp) in WHISPERS V and HELLBOY: ODDEST JOBS. He lives in Los Angeles.

Visit his website at www.perilouspress.com.

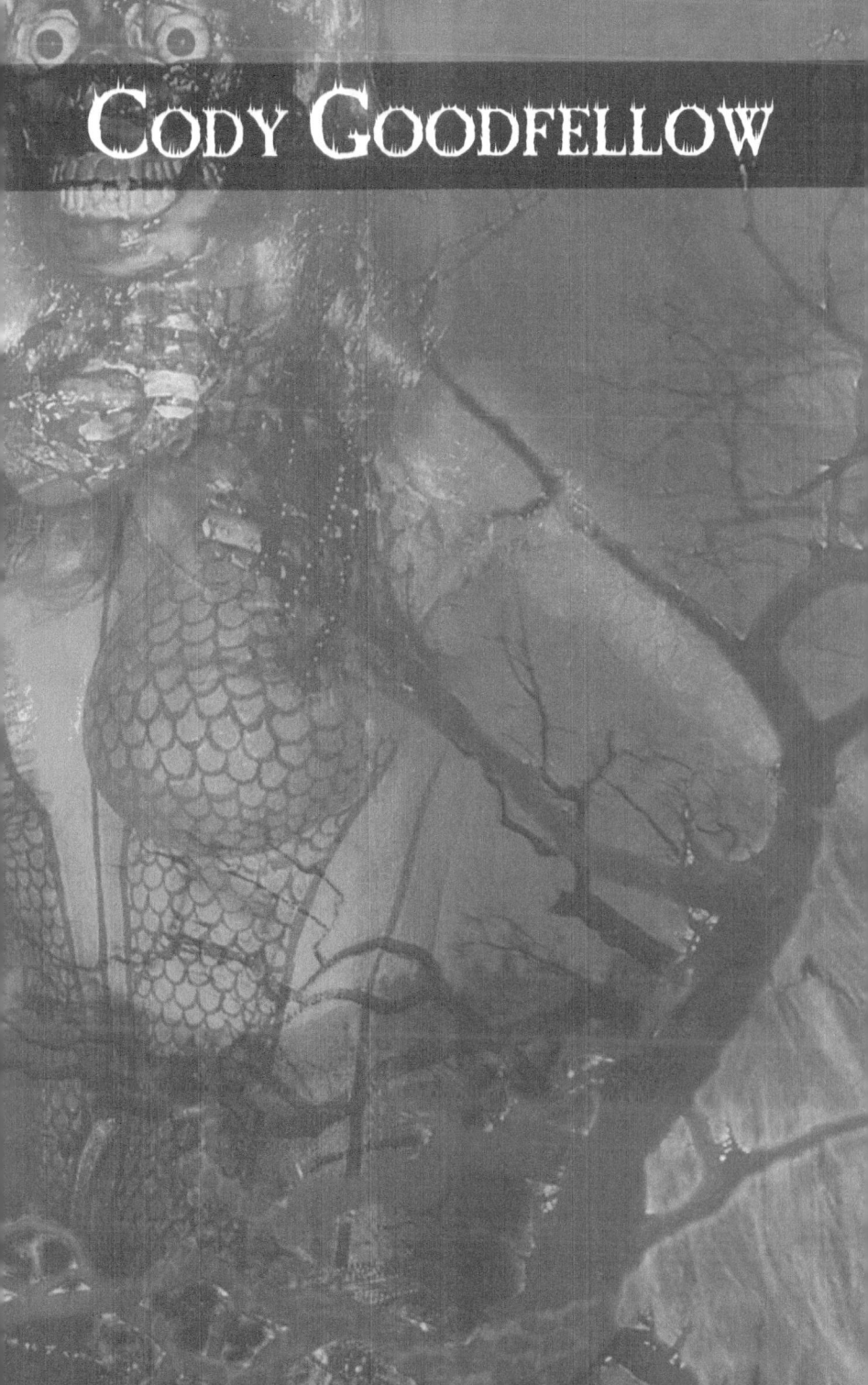

CODY GOODFELLOW

Venus of Santa Cruz

L ike the Big Bad Wolf in a city of brick houses, Officer Brad Friendly cruised the fog-swaddled streets of Santa Cruz, huffing and puffing for an excuse to be a cop. 2:37 AM on a Monday: bars already closed without incident, even the most twisted freaks had somewhere to hide.

Friendly coasted through the central bus terminal, a late night agora for drugged-out hippie kids with names like Sky and Grateful, cast-off spawn of parents who never made the jump from hip to yup, brains cooked in a congenital stew of bullshit and bad acid. The last bus from San Francisco nosed into port, disgorged a few tie-dyed freaks, a Mexican in cowboy boots seven sizes too big and a hot blonde coed with a duffel bag who looked lost and in need of a cop.

Friendly waved. "Hi, you need a ride anywhere?" The girl passed through his headlights.

"What, you're too good to say hi?" leaning out his window, flipping on his searchlight to light her way to the curb, where a blasted orange '76 Datsun rustbucket idled. A short redhead, cuter and more stacked than the blonde, climbed out, took her friend's bag and enfolded her with a deep, tongue-thrashing kiss, unpainted nails tracing a brand on the curve of her girlfriend's ass for Friendly's benefit. They got in the car and motored off.

The only thing harder than getting a good bust in Santa Cruz was getting laid. Lesbians from all over the country came to this cloistered haven of clam-bumping, a Mecca for their unfortunate lifestyle choice. Most of the police force was nominally female, big bad bulldaggers who could bench press Friendly and called him "Breeder" or "Rapeman" behind his back. Once or twice he'd tried rounding up a few of the handful of single, straight guys on the force to go to hit the strip clubs in San Jose. To a man, they'd looked at him like he'd proposed they go fuck some cows, and couldn't wait to report him.

Friendly spotted a white '70 VW microbus cruising north on Main Street, weaving the unmistakable waltz of the fucked-up motorist. He followed at a discreet distance to Western Drive, where the streetlights abruptly stopped and Main became Pacific Coast Highway, a lonely, lawless tunnel to the outside world.

The bus was probably on the return leg of a drug run, making for San Francisco with a payload of blotter acid and a bale or two of homegrown dope. Half the town grew pot to sell to the other half. His pigeon was probably stoned into orbit with a fat roach in his beard right now, which he'd eat the moment Friendly kicked the siren. To get probable cause to search the van, he'd have to spook him into reckless driving. Friendly switched off his lights and closed in, ram-bars air-kissing the VW's bumper in the dark.

Friendly glimpsed a flare of cherry on a joint in the van's rearview mirror. He snapped on his hi-beams, the siren and the sno-cones all at once. The VW bugged out like a bumblebee in a bell jar, whipping a hard right into a stand of bamboo grass and a drainage ditch.

Friendly jackknifed in alongside the bus and leapt out, hand dancing on his gun. A northbound sedan, also running lights out, whipped around the cruiser at well over eighty and took a glancing bite off the ass-end of the VW, spraying sparks and candy fragments of taillight as it fought for traction, tires screaming flayed strips flying in all directions, lost it and slewed off the road into a tree.

The silvery black night sky was pregnant with mist, individual fat droplets suspended in the air before Friendly's face. The night and the road became the whole wide world, gossamer threads and blobs of orange marking the edge of town on the horizon. With no one coming or going, the road was the eye of a cyclone.

Friendly was torn between elation at having caught two perps at a single stop and recognition of his own guilt in having caused a possible fatality accident through his LA cowboy tactics. He laid out a fan of road flares and radioed for an ambulance and backup, then approached the wrecked sedan.

It was a '74 Duster, lemon yellow under the glaze of dust, oil and bird shit that covered everything but a slit in the opaque windshield. The front end was an accordion, and Friendly knew the guy would be impaled on the steering wheel if he wasn't wearing a seatbelt.

He wasn't. He seemed to have popped most of his ribs on the steering column, breaking off the wheel. He was still conscious. Mumbling his hippie coping mantra, or something. "Gottagetheroutthetrunk!"

Friendly drew his Glock 9mm – one of the few perks of the SCPD, they let you carry your own ordnance. "Hands where I can see them, sir! Now, help is on the way, but if you're able, show me your license, registration and proof of insurance."

"Gotta get her out! She wants to get out!"

The driver's fingers spasmed and clawed at the keys, while his other hand disappeared down his pants in search of CONCEALED EVIDENCE or a CONCEALED WEAPON. His gibbering devolved into a choked growl that made Friendly feel completely justified in jamming his gun in the driver's face.

"Get your hand out of your pants, sir! Right now!"

The driver wailed, eyes locked on something closer and more urgent than the gun. "She wants out! She wants to fuck!"

Most people close their eyes and turn away from a gun, wishing themselves into a happier place and time, anywhere but staring down the barrel of the great leveler. Friendly had never before had cause to stick his gun in anybody's face, but cops talk, and Friendly listened, inwardly preparing himself for that day.

But this asshole leaned in and grabbed the gun and, opening his mouth to expose a toothless pit of terminally diseased gums, deep-throated the muzzle and proceeded to fellate it for all he was worth. He sucked three bullets out of it before Friendly even noticed it going off as he tried to get his beloved Glock 9mm free of the pervert's mouth. The recoil jerked the gun out of his gooey rictus even as the driver's head flew away on hollow-point wings.

The body slumped forwards, one spastic hand pitching the keys so they jingled and struck Friendly's washboard stomach. He stooped and picked them up, wiped his gun off on the driver's flannel shirt before holstering it.

He raced around the car. Not noticing that the microbus was gone, checking out the keys. A San Jose Sharks bottle opener, a broken Swiss Army knife with only the corkscrew remaining, a foam rubber boner with the address for a shitty grind joint in Capitola, the door, ignition and gas keys for the Duster. Friendly unlocked the trunk and stood back as it swung open. He saw A

HOSTAGE in a bundle of crushed velvet, stiff with secretions both mechanical and organic, stretched taut over the unmistakable outline of a heaving female form.

He heard it calling to him, though the air was so still he could hear his pulse. Its voice was a scent that bled into his reptilian midbrain, down to the glandular *fuck/kill* engines that drove his organism. Capping the driver was the perfect foreplay for what the thing in the trunk invited him to do now and for all time.

Friendly fell, pushed and pulling, into the mouth of the trunk. And as his eyelids gummed shut, it seemed the trunk slammed, or was pulled shut, just as headlights swept over the crash scene.

Hours later, when the wreck had been swept up and reports filed away and Friendly debriefed on the fatal shooting, they sent him home, told him to stay there for a few days. When he came to in the ambulance, they told him he passed out. The paramedic was also a sensitivity counselor, and if he wanted to talk about anything, or just cry it out, that'd be okay. Friendly felt too weak to hit him.

«« — »»

The political correctness bullshit in Santa Cruz was like pollution nobody else could see. Signs on the county line proclaimed Santa Cruz a Nuclear Free and a Clothing Optional Zone. A Mayoral runoff election next week would pit the incumbent, a gay nudist Socialist, against a black lesbian Wiccan Communist. A church group from San Jose came over every Palm Sunday to exorcise the place.

The university waffled like a battered wife, calling the cops when the brats got onto some bad acid, but always tying their hands when push came to prosecute. They kept a lid on the serious shit, like the obligatory freshmen suicide attempts every finals week, or the serial rapist who hunted coeds unopposed for three semesters because the school valued women's empowerment too much to provide them with escorts.

But the hippies needed someone to protect their bongs, so they voted two years ago to bring in more cops. Students graduated and took jobs at 7-11 so they could stay, but nobody wanted to be a pig, so the call went out and Brad Friendly, two days out of the Los Angeles Police Academy and suddenly pressed to leave town, signed on. For their part, the locals smelled the LA on him and showed him no love. On or off-duty, they treated him like a spy from a hostile nation. Looking around this place, it wasn't hard to imagine it was once the Serial Killer Capital of the world, home of Ed Kemper, the Coed Killer, Herbert Mullin and John Linley Frazier.

He drove back out to the scene of the crash, looking to make sure he wasn't followed. Just before dusk, he found what he was looking for. Stowing it in the covered bed of his matte black Ford F150 pickup, he looked around once more and climbed into the truck, drove home just slow enough not to get pulled over.

He slipped in with the bundle under his arm, looking over his shoulder at two feral kids in ankle-length tie-dyed T-shirts spying as he carried it over the threshold. He didn't have a couch, so he laid it on his weight bench and moved to the far corner of the room, arms clenched at his sides.

He was fucking off here, not as bad as LA yet, but getting there. He was CONCEALING EVIDENCE. He was an ACCESSORY AFTER THE FACT.

And it had made him do it, no it had only suggested, no, it was his idea to hide the thing at the scene and pick it up later, because they'd never understand, they'd try to take it away. And they couldn't—

He approached on his knees and pulled back the crushed velvet veil.

There was a torso.

A woman's torso, a Cro-Magnon goddess, a primordial Venus of voluptuous alabaster curves and folds, sculpted flesh describing archetypal angles of luscious succubi. Turgid skin glistening with iridescent oil-slick rainbow glow of gamy oysters. Neck, shoulders and hips terminated in sphincter-mouths, pouting lips trembling with arousal.

She needed neither head nor limbs to command Friendly to abase himself before her. She made him writhe on the floor in a mangled mating dance of broken instinct. Under her control, he descended to the abyss of Now, to the impulse that anchored his body, kept it from flying apart. Every cell strained against that impulse every moment of his life, the base ore of their lust to BREED sublimated into the ghost in the Brad Friendly machine's need for MANIPULATION DOMINATION CONTROL.

The heady aroma of the Venus short-circuited Friendly's ghost and spoke to his cells, and the voice of the aroma was all there was to SEX and Friendly was in full rut in seconds, forcing himself upon the Venus, thrusting his cock into the quivering stump-mouth where a head would have been on a mortal woman.

The other mouths attached themselves to his body and made a throbbing cock out of every inch of his flesh. He looked down at himself through oceans of red hunger and saw an undulating carpet of questing penises boring holes in the Venus, then his sight went white as cascades of orgasmic stimuli washed over his brain. He felt the millions of penetrations meld into a single vortex of force and pour down the shaft of him into Her.

He became a plumed sperm-serpent encircling the Venus, plunging into one mouth and out of another, transfixing Her and gliding through tempestuous seas of estrogen musk. Finally, he breached the pulsating core of his mate and rammed himself into it with a final surge of his last reserves of stamina, felt the furious, frail bubble of his masculine power burst and blast its message of FRIENDLINESS into the crucible-womb of the Venus, and the shockwave rent the walls of him, the consummation of his desire opened a vacuum that sucked away blood, lymph, liquefied organs and plasma-charged brain.

Wracked with galvanic spasms, Friendly's naked skeleton tried to pull itself away from the thing that sucked him dry. Then She lurched against him and vomited him back into himself, like a mother bird regurgitating into the mouth of its young. He tried to lift himself up and collapsed on the bare tile floor. His body was a billion bodies, and they were not on speaking terms. He fell asleep at the foot of the altar, one arm slung over the cooling hip of the Venus.

«« —— »»

The weeks that followed were probably, if he'd stopped to think about it, the happiest he'd ever known. As a cop, he could throw himself into the job without losing control as never before, and his performance did not go unnoticed. Men still ignored him, and women seemed to smell the musk of the Venus on him with veiled disgust, but the captain suggested that he might consider taking the sergeant's exam next time around. He liked to think it was due to his new, objective demeanor on the job, and not the lingering odor of a goddess that aroused her interest.

Friendly stopped lifting weights, yet he'd never been in better shape in his life. He moved the weight bench into the corner and made a tent of the Venus's shroud, a private shrine where he spent his nights and many lunch hours. His torso and arms rippled with starkly defined muscle like bundles of bridge cable. He got more than enough exercise, and burned off fat and loose skin so fast he worried about cancer and tapeworms. He burned with thirst, and he'd developed a serious craving for exotic fruit juices with weird supplements blended into them. He worried idly that he wasn't putting on muscle, that the Venus was merely sucking him dry, drinking up the stored resins of his mortality. Was it getting fat?

The most dramatic benefit negated all other concerns in keeping him away from the hospital: his penis, never anything to shoot a Polaroid of for Ripley's, now stood a full eleven inches out from his taut abdomen, almost every hour of the day. For this, he didn't ask himself if she was a goddess or a circus freak. He hadn't gone blind, he wasn't going insane, and he wasn't dying from any hideous disease that he knew about. If there was a God, surely he blessed their union, or was just jealous, which would explain all the bad dreams.

Night patrol takes him into an unfamiliar corner of town, where the streets have no names and the cookie-cutter houses have none of the usual hippie-follies, mini-Stonehenges and suchlike, that reflect their inhabitants' desperate need to seem unique. He's asking himself if any of this needs protecting, when snow-cone lights paint his cruiser in chiaroscuro red and a horn whoops. He's being pulled over. Friendly picks up the radio and requests an ID on the cruiser behind him, but the box squawks black static, voices breaking through like banshees incanting a pagan rosary in a nuclear blizzard.

"Virgin, Harlot and Hag, Magna Mater, the Black Goat—"

He jerks at the tapping at his window and the hand reaching in to clamp his shoulder, mag-light beam pinpricking his pupils, and he shields his eyes like a bleary drunk, sees uniforms coming out of the dark, uniforms he's never seen before. Two cops look him over, muttering words that turn fuzzy and rot before they reach his ears.

"222-stroke-87, PR-28720a, eh?"

"DW5051-stroke-8086, yep," his partner chuckles. He opens Friendly's door as the first cop pries him out of the cruiser and deftly palms his Glock, looks at it like a booby prize from the county fair. His partner rips the gold foil badge off Friendly's uniform and unwraps it, pops the chocolate surprise inside in his mouth.

He tries to pull free, tries to arrest them for ASSAULTING AN OFFICER, but the arrest turns inside out, he is IMPERSONATING AN OFFICER. He watches himself present his hands behind his back and the manacles jingle. He waits docilely to be led to the cruiser, but one of the cops squirts his hair with lighter fluid and the partner touches a lighter to his butch-waxed buzzcut and shoves him and he's FLEEING THE SCENE, a human bomb racing through the trees to its target...

At 5:40 one Monday morning, Friendly stopped in at Farrell's Donuts on his way to the dayroom briefing. Aside from two post-rave punks at the Samurai Showdown machine, the dreary dining room was empty. He ordered two assortment dozens and a cranberry smoothie and sat to wash down some vitamins while they were boxed up.

A bum slipped in the door and into a booth, picking stray sprinkles and flakes of glaze off the table. A vital foundation of Santa Cruz's ecology, bums were the town's sacred cows. It didn't pay to roust them, because as often as not they turned out to be lawyers or sociology professors. The bum cleaned off the booth and slid into the next one, leaned across it into Friendly's face.

He smelled like a rendering plant. His sickdog eyes glinted through a mastodon pelt of filthy dreadlocks. The advanced decay of his person seemed to have been cultivated to Dickensian proportions. Perhaps he belonged to one of the fringe communes in the mountains between here and San Jose, come into the valley to "tox out" and cadge a free love ride miracle ticket thirty years out of date.

"Do you know why Herbert Mullin did those murders?"

Friendly shook his head once, a first and final warning.

"Believed only the shedding of blood could stop the Big One. Little bloodshed's a small price to pay to live in paradise, isn't it? 'Materialism must die or mankind must stop.' No, that was Linley Frazier."

"Are you high on something, or just stupid?"

"Shit, fuzz, I feel at home with you because you been laying with the Lamia." The bum drew closer and sniffed greedily, like a cat trying to steal his breath.

Friendly scrambled out of the booth, drew his baton. "Get the fuck away from me."

"Hey, man, it's cool, I don't want to fight, I want to fuck. Where can a guy like me get a ride on that Night-Hag, I wanna know? Guy's gotta have cash or a badge, for some of that gash."

The Korean cashier ordered the bum out, waving a broomstick over his head. Friendly followed him to the parking lot and kicked him as hard as he could just above the tailbone.

The bum launched into a parked car without raising defensive arms or even shouting. His soft-boiled head dented the door with a leaden crump, and Friendly had his baton under his jaw before he could lie down.

"So you think you know where I spend my nights, asshole?"

"Shit, man, I'm not trying to harsh your mellow, man. We're both like, men of the world, right? Didn't mean nothin' by it…"

"You keep your filthy mouth shut about it, and show some respect. She's a goddess." Friendly went in and got his donuts.

Friendly went eight rounds with the Venus that night and staggered into the kitchen for a pineapple-kelp shake with spirulena and henbane, when he realized he could see with the lights off. Red flame shadows danced and devoured each other on the bare walls, silhouetting a nude woman standing before the stove. Friendly smelled burning hair. The flames haloed her head and obscured her face, but he saw the glint of tooled steel manacles on her wrists and knew who she was.

21

"Hello, Brad. I wish I could say I was glad you've finally found somebody."

Friendly's spine rebelled, dumped him on the sticky linoleum at the apparition's feet. "Francine," he managed to gasp, "I never thought I'd see you again—"

Though two years had passed, the unique circumstances of their parting had left Friendly without a sense of closure. The night after he'd marched in the Academy commencement ceremonies, he'd finally convinced Francine it was time to go all the way. She was saving herself for marriage; he'd made it clear that his becoming a cop was the next best thing, and a sure guarantee of the other. The sex was good; he lit candles and gave her a backrub first. She had to remind him to be gentle only six or seven times.

Somewhere in the middle of it, however, Friendly lost touch with the program and got kinked on her. He pinned her arms behind her back with his brand new handcuffs and tried to force himself in her mouth. She kicked away from him and knocked over the candles, igniting her hair. His last glimpse of Francine was in her role as impromptu Passion Play martyr, pinioned arms akimbo, hair blazing, shrieking to beat the smoke alarm. She'd bolted from the bachelor apartment before he could muster his wits to put her out. That was the last time he ever saw or heard from her until now, when she'd returned, naked and blazing, to his kitchen.

"Are you a ghost? Are you... dead?"

"I'm not here about what you did to me. You have to come to grips with what you're doing here, now."

"I don't need any shit from somebody who ran out on me. Besides, I'm not doing anything... wrong..."

"Has she met your parents yet, Brad?" Francine laughed, spitting tongues of fire at Friendly's eyes. "On some level, you've got to recognize how deeply fucking wrong this is. You tried to rape me, and look where it's got you. You confused love with dominance before and now you fuck a monster, and you're falling in love with it."

"You're not Francine. Francine never cursed. Fuck off!"

"You believe this is how it was meant to be, and who can blame you? You've clubbed one and dragged it back to the cave, and it can't crawl out again. The perfect wife for the perfect cop. You're so sure of the dominator you have to be that you can't see what's dominating you. She's using you, Brad. Think about that, for me."

The flames died away.

Friendly lay on the floor for a while before he got up. Where he wasn't numb with cold, he itched, and everything was frozen but his crotch. He hobbled into the bathroom and turned on the light, then turned it off again. Then on, off, on. Trying to see what he was supposed to see, and not what glared back at him.

His swollen penis and testicles were studded with succulent purple buds, like malignant kernels on an ear of corn from Love Canal.

He ripped the medicine chest off the wall in his haste to get the tweezers. When he pinched one, there was no sensation, but the rubbery skin refused to tear. When he tried to pull one out by the root, it popped and squirted acrid, unripe pheromones in his eyes. He reeled, clawing at his eyes as if he'd been Maced.

He saw the black room in murky shades of red, a dying solar system, and a collapsing sun in the shrine. He shielded his eyes and rushed at it, brought his fists down between its pendulous breasts and felt something give way beneath. At first, his blows rebounded like a child's fist against a punch balloon, but he made headway with one of the dumbbells under the bench. It was like a pumpkin; beneath the pliant womanflesh rind, the Venus was a sac of membranes, bloated, fibrous organs and reservoirs of fluid, some his, some Hers. He smashed and smashed until his arm became tired and he noticed the stacatto pounding from the ground floor tenant.

"Call a cop!" Friendly screamed, and smashed on.

The next morning, Friendly called in sick and prowled the strip joint advertised on the rubber boner on the driver's keychain. Knowing his name and rap sheet shed no light on the trail of the Venus, so he forgot it. He broke out the footlocker and unwrapped a Colt Desert Eagle and a .22 short-barrel automatic. He loaded each and shrugged into a shoulder holster for the Colt, an ankle holster for the .22.

Casing the parking lot from across the highway, Friendly recognized no one. He massaged rubbing alcohol and hydrogen peroxide into his crotch until he was sitting in a quagmire of eye-watering antiseptic. He got on the highway and turned around, scoping for cops as he pulled into the lot.

Dancers wobbling around the foyer on cocaine fumes, tiredly offering private shows. Feminazi students blandly took notes. A naked woman sat on a director's chair at the end of the runway, reading something with Oprah on the cover. Sad, sagging silicon ballast reminded him of the perfect curves he'd crushed, and he choked back a raw sob of longing.

Friendly paced the room, hoping to scare someone into flight. No one budged. He tossed the men's room. Three sailors sharing a tiny bindle of crank dropped their works in the toilet and bailed.

He smelled the Venus. He touched his bobbing dowsing rod, still icy from its antiseptic bath. While the chemicals did nothing to stop the buds, they stifled the smell, so he practically saw the cloying contrail wafting out of the fourth bathroom stall.

He kicked the door in. It rebounded off the occupant's knee-caps, and Friendly kicked it again. The screaming from within had barely gone into its overture when Friendly's eager hands flipped the new cripple over and dunked his head into the toilet.

"I'm going to ask questions, and then you can breathe. Cool?"

Glubs of desperate willingness to please filled the bowl, or maybe he was just trying to blow the turds away from his mouth.

"I'm going to trust you not to scream." He lifted the man's head out of the bowl, cradling him in the prelude to a sleeper hold. His intake of breath was almost enough of a scream to merit another dunk, but it trailed off in whimpers.

Friendly said, "Tell me why you smell like you've been fucking my girl."

"I didn't know she was yours, man. Blow job for blow, bitch tried to cut me—"

"You know what I mean. I'm talking about Her," driving the capital home with a quick dunk in the bowl. "Where did you meet Her? Where did you fuck Her?"

"Bullshit! I don't know who the fuck you think I am—"

"Don't shit me! I can smell her on you!" Friendly shoved his head in the bowl and flushed. A cyclone of sewage engulfed the toilet dweller's impassioned cries for salvation or death. Friendly brought him up, a fist still knotted in his thin hair. "The House of the Venus," he gurgled, punctuating *his* capitals by vomiting in the bowl. "Everybody knows where it is. Off the 17, ten miles out from Front Street."

"Address."

"No numbers out there. Just trees, and trees and trees and the House of the Venus. Three stories, no paint, bunch of fucked-up old cars and trucks and shit all around it. What, you want a map?"

Friendly rapped the man's head on the rim and seated him on the bowl. As he turned to leave, he caught a glance, out of the corner of his eye, purely by accident, at the man's dick. It was a priapic purple nightstick to shame his own, twenty inches and ribbed for Her pleasure with purple buds the size of macadamia nuts. Friendly saw himself dousing the diseased member with lighter fluid, but how could he do to another what he wasn't man enough to do to himself?

Friendly never had cause to wander the indifferently maintained roads that wound through the Santa Cruz backwaters; sheriff's deputies had that detail, and he didn't envy them one bit.

If the northbound PCH out of Santa Cruz was a tunnel by night, Highway 17 was a leap over a Berlin Wall of wilderness, a ribbon clinging to a mad jumble of rampaging ridges and valleys that time tried to forget. Forty miles of alpine hairpin tarmac christened "Blood Alley" by those damned to commute on it, the 17 claimed almost daily accidents, over half of which were fatal. Exits lurked behind glowering stands of pines, leading to hermitages for freaks who made the weirdest citizens of Santa Cruz look like Mormon missionaries.

He watched his trip odometer climb to ten, killed his headlights and slammed on his brakes to veer down an unpaved tunnel through the trees, a glory hole into the black guts of the forest. His truck shimmied and bucked on the loamy soil of the road, Friendly bolt upright and peering through the windshield, navigating by stray streams of teasing moonlight. Too narrow to be an exit, this was probably a private driveway, though there was no sign of the obligatory wrought-iron gates and TRESPASSERS EATEN HERE signs. He fought the road to a level stretch that broke out of the trees into a meadow strewn with a menagerie of rusted-out car-carrion. Across the vast expanse of junkyard and hip-high weeds, Friendly made out the derelict hulk of a school bus up on a scaffold like a Sioux warrior decked out for burial, its Day-Glo war paint proclaiming "House Of The Venus–All Suitors Welcome."

Friendly drove up to the porch, climbed out. The windows were boarded up and covered with graffiti depictions of coitus in all its forms, animal, vegetable and spiritual. The door was reinforced with steel bands and had no doorknob. A view slit rattled open and bubbled over with suspicious eyes. Friendly smiled engagingly and sidled close enough to draw his revolver.

"What do you know?"

"I've got purple shit growing out of my dick."

The door opened a crack and Friendly shouldered in and rapped the doorkeeper across the bridge of his nose with the massive muzzle of the Colt, scanned the room for potential threats.

The atrium opened directly on a great hall, the walls a shadowy smear of tapestries and incense clouds. Pallets and beanbags scattered over a crazy quilt of Indian rugs, bums and thugs spilled all over them, heads numbly turning like buds to the bright sobbing of the doorman holding his nose together.

A circle of huddled heads in the center of the room, each clutching a tube to the colossal hookah before them, inhaling and puffing out in unison like monks sucking the poison out of the world's wounds. One of them stood and came around to the door. Dressed head-to-toe in clashing tie-dye patterns, his Santa Marx beard twinkling with tiny bells like twittering thornbirds. One of his eyes twinkled merrily as Friendly's game face melted, staring fixedly at the hippie's other eye, which was gone. Out of the socket sprouted a toadstool with iridescent orange gills, like a poisonous frog penis.

"Welcome to the House of the Venus." His nose twitched and his smile went queer, bemused but ever playful. "You smell funny, friend. I smell cop, but I also smell our best kind of friend. What's your pleasure?"

"I want some answers, shithead."

"Hey, wow, you're that cop, who wasted Rafe Heenan."

"That piss you off?"

"On the contrary, dude, if it wasn't all in the line of duty, I'd owe you one."

"He got the... Venus... from you?"

"He stole it out of my cellar. He was gonna die, one way or the other. Nobody steals one of my love goddesses."

"There's more than one?"

Bells tinkled in his beard. "Shit, dude, I grow 'em."

The dealer led Friendly down into the basement, a black abyss of hothouse damp, chittering animal panic and miasmal stench. The air was syrupy with Venus musk, and Friendly bit back thunderous nausea, which redoubled at the realization that he was sporting wood like never before.

Once a wine cellar, the cavernous basement opened on groined vaults that were in turn divided into stalls with curtains of black crushed velvet. From behind them Friendly heard men moaning, gasping, growling, begging. Voices called, "Bitch!" voices cried, "Mommy."

"See, fuzz, my church welcomes all forms of worship. And when you think about it, everything we do is an act of worship or an act of rebellion against Her, isn't it? Watch your step, fuzz. Big pits of batshit."

The dealer stepped over a trench filled to the rim with tarry black bat guano. The trenches marched off into the inky darkness at the far end of the cellar. The festering excreta was pocked with clusters of flesh-colored bulbs, like a fat farm for headless Barbies. Real live Cabbage Patch Dolls, Friendly thought. Beneath the wrenching sounds of men and beasts, he could hear them growing.

A towering wrought-iron cage took up one end of the room. Bats squealed and hurled themselves at the bars. "Get it by the ton from a guy in Mexico, but it pays to have a source of fresh."

"Tell me what they are."

"It's a fungus, but in function, it's a lot like *Sarracenia*. You know, pitcher plants? No?

"Well, anyway, they secrete sweet juices to attract flies and bees, and they trap them in a sticky honey pot. Digest 'em. The Venus is special, though. It attracts an animal host and feeds off it, while implanting its spores on the host's dingus. Then he moves along, fucks another one, and the cycle begins anew."

"Why do they look like chicks?"

The dealer's bells jingled. "Natural selection, fuzz. Cavemen took a shine to the shapelier ones, started cultivating them to look the way they do. Or maybe they just knew what we liked. Kind of a chicken-or-egg question, really.

"This strain came from the Amazon. Psychopharmacologist friend of mine dug it up. But I think they were everywhere, a long time ago. You ever seen the Venus of Willendorf, or any Stone Age fertility fetishes? If you did, you'd recognize the Venus. To the ancients, I think it must have been the purest form of sexual congress–a holy communion with the Mother Goddess without the messy strings of human procreation. It probably survived as late as the cult of Astarte in Mesopotamia. Her priestesses were the first prostitutes, you know that? They had to take over after the matriarchy exterminated the Venus. They were jealous because men would rather fuck a fungus than them. These here are the fruits of original sin. Now let's see what we can do about getting those spores off your dick."

Friendly couldn't let it go a moment longer. Pointing at the dealer's infested eye socket, he said, "You know… you have something growing out of your eye."

The dealer chuckled and touched the shaft of the toadstool gently, guarding it. "Shit, dude, if I can get viable spores from this puppy, I'll *buy* a new eye."

He led Friendly back to the furthest vault from the door, and raised his hand to part the mouth of a curtain. Friendly couldn't see more than a few inches beyond it. He raised his gun to the dealer's face. "Don't fuck with me."

"Nobody's fucking with you, fuzz – not yet. The only way of getting the smut off, short of a blowtorch, is pollinating another plant."

"No way. I'm never going near one of those things again."

"Have it your way, man. Those things may just drop off in about ten years. Funny thing about the Venus is, they tend towards hermaphroditism. Big word, huh? Plain English, they may already be fertilized spores, and they could sprout. They like bat shit best, but they can grow just as well out of human flesh, when push comes to shove. I know you don't want that, and I want my spores back. So why don't you just be a man and go in and satisfy Astarte, back there."

Friendly imagined the purple buboes sprouting out of his cock and balls, singing their virulent hormone mating call to turn him into their zombie slave, turning his crotch into a raging fungoid brothel. "Okay. What do I have to do?"

"Just go in there and introduce yourself, and let nature take its course."

Friendly backed into the vault, his gun trained on the dealer. Then he heard something moving behind him and he turned. The dealer shut the curtains. "Don't be freaked out by Astarte's appearance. He's, uh, kind of a mutant."

"He?"

Friendly's dark-adjusted eyes barely made out a column of mottled purple flesh rising five feet out of the batshit trench. Its gill-frilled stalk split in a vaginal mouth to display pouting red lips like a giant calla lily, or a giant baboon's ass in estrus. The gleaming, honey-dripper lips parted provocatively as a tongue, white and eel-slick, slipped out and lapped up the cream of its own distilled overripe desire. Friendly backed away and raised the gun. "Don't come any closer—"

A trumpeting fart split the lips of the fungus and ejaculated a shower of pheromonal syrup into Friendly's face. There was no coy chemical invitation in Astarte's message. It was an undiluted masculine command to render up his seed for fertilization, and though it made a WOMAN of him, it was not to be denied.

Waves of indomitable lust tenderized him, and he dropped his gun to tear off his pants. The prehensile tongue darted out of the mouth to circle enticingly above his head as he approached. Seeking its own spoor on him, it homed in on his engorged penis, now twice its normal size. More tongues shot out of the livid mouth and buffeted him, lifted him off the ground and into the waiting, hungry lips.

The tongues greedily scoured every last bud off his crotch, then bored into his asshole and his cock, down his throat and into his stomach to retrieve spores he'd ingested during his affair with the Venus. Penetrated and transfixed, Friendly retreated into a tiny bunker in the attic of his brain and sang to himself, rode out ferocious orgasms that multiplied to critical mass when he gagged on the fungoid tongue down his throat as it met another of its kind that had come in his asshole. He exploded fluids out of every

orifice and felt them licked away by rasping tongues, MANIPU-
LATED DOMINATED CONTROLLED.

He prayed to die until the male Venus spat him out.

He lay insensate for years at the foot of the torpid Venus,
bleeding and heaving, gasping for breath enough to slip into a
coma.

Then he heard gunshots.

Friendly clambered to his feet and staggered out into the
strobing glare of flashlights.

"Freeze! Police!" A strident female voice pinned him down.
Friendly tried to cover his nakedness and hold his hands up at the
same time. He understood now the hesitant panic of the SUS-
PECT, that drove them to grope and make half-steps towards fleeing, even as they surrendered.

"Lie down on the ground! Put your hands straight out at your
sides! Do it Now!"

"You don't understand! I'm a victim! I mean–I'm a cop! I'm
one of you!" Lying down in batshit, a boot on his back, hands laced
in the small of his back and cuffed together.

"Really? Where's your ID? In your pants?" Friendly was
hoisted to his feet and steered towards the door. A line of cops,
all butch bulldaggers, stood along the wall, up the stairs and on
out the front door, waiting their turn to glare in righteous disgust.
Friendly hung his head and tried to pin his shriveled cock between
his legs, noticed that the buds were gone. His penis looked and
felt as if cats had been licking it all night long, but he was free of
its mark of sin.

In the Captain's office, rubbing cuff-burns on his wrists, studying his shoes. The Captain's eyes flinty gray buttons robbing him
of his last dignity. Her scrubbed, ruddy face pinched in distaste.

"I suppose I should say first that you are back on suspension.
Your actions, once they're finally sorted out, will be entered into
your permanent record. We don't like off-duty Dirty Harry's in
this person's police force, do I make myself clear?"

"Yes ma'am."

"Now, I have to say that without your tip on the drug house,
the raid we launched never would've been the success it was. We
were unable before today to penetrate the ring, and you provided
an invaluable source of information." Her face pinched still more

as the script she was reading from left its bitter taste in her mouth.

"It wasn't a drug house," Friendly managed.

"Not true. They were growing and distributing a controlled substance in the form of a psychoactive marital aid. We also found a number of other illicit substances, along with a cache of illegal firearms. They resisted our attempts to serve a search warrant, and we responded with force to insure your safe recovery."

Her acting stank up the joint. If this was TV, Friendly would have turned it off. "How did you know I was in there?"

The Captain's jaw worked. "You phoned us before you went in to the house."

He wanted to scream at her to stop it. "How long were you having me followed?"

"You called us, Officer Friendly. No one followed you. Ever." Tight lips pressing truth into the assertion. "We advised against your going in, which advisement you disregarded, hence your suspension. But your captivity led to a search warrant, which led to the raid. You–are to be commended. Well," closing the file on the desk before her, "your ordeal has left you in need of rest, so why don't you get yourself cleaned up and go home. You'll be facing a board of review in about three weeks, but I wouldn't worry."

"Thank you, Captain."

"We have to have men on the force like you, Friendly. You're an example to us all, an example of–what we could become."

Friendly went to the locker room, and realized just how filthy he was. Black gobs of guano under his fingernails, in his hair, and… The buds were gone, but the thing he'd had to be with to get rid of them left him unable to touch or look at himself. He'd never been able to bring himself to use the locker room showers–homophobia or fear of athlete's foot, or enjoyment of his own B.O., or all of the above–but he knew he couldn't go another moment coated in the slime of the night-hag.

He stripped and wrapped in a towel, went into the shower room. A misty steam-tunnel, the shower room curtained each of its bathers from each other, so that as Friendly tore off the towel, turned the water as hot as it would go and scrubbed the purifying stream into his crotch, he didn't see the other cops. He noticed their feet as they came out of the steam, a cordon hemming him into the corner. His eyes wandered up to their faces, but never got there, because for the first time in his life, Friendly stared deliberately at male genitalia without questioning his own manhood, and understood why the other cops all looked at him like he was some kind of freak when he'd tried to get them to go cruising.

Each cop's penis dangled down to his knees, studded with prickly-pear purple buds, swollen fit to burst.

"You smell like Her," one of them said, and came closer.

The Weak Sisters Bust Out

When the Aryans took over B Block right after dinner, everyone in the prison knew who they wanted, and got out of their way. Once the few unlucky Mexican Mafia and Bloods trapped in the block were put down, they converged on the secure cells. They carried shanks, machetes, bedspring garrotes and gasoline. They climbed to the top tier and pounded on the bars of the separatee cells, howling for the Weak Sisters to come out to play.

Yogi squatted atop a bunk to hold the mattresses up against the bars. "Come on in, motherfuckers! We'll kill you all! See if we don't!"

The Aryans barked and bayed like horny pit bulls. "Keep running your neck, foolio! When we get into that control room, you all mine…"

Yogi always trembled, but today, it was not with rage or fear, but raw, red anticipation.

"What we gonna do, Yogi?" Osmond stammered, wetting his pants, but he took the batteries out of the radio and stuffed a sock with them, like Yogi told him to. Bucky sucked his thumb and jacked off on the naked springs of his bunk.

"Show them, Osmond. Be a man and fucking show them how we roll. Show them what happens when they fuck with us blood-brothers."

"We ain't brothers, Yogi," Osmond said in a choked little voice. A stupid, all-day sissy, but he knew the score. "We weak sisters, like they all sayin'."

Outside, they splashed gas on the mattresses and stabbed through them with long steel shanks. Yogi fixed the Eye on Osmond and didn't say a word.

Osmond looked down at the spreading apron of urine on his bright orange jumpsuit. "You right, Yogi, you right." Osmond took out a shiv, a dirty icicle of melted plastic. "I am a man, ain't I?"

"You can be, Oz. Do it for Shy Girl." Yogi stared him down until Osmond stabbed the palm of his other hand.

Yogi pried open a crack in the mattresses. Osmond shoved his bloody hand through the bars. Osmond screamed and bit into the mildewed mattress.

Someone must have stabbed or slashed at Osmond's hand, because the force of the blast blew the gasoline-soaked mattresses off the bars and toppled the bunk beds. Yogi saw cartwheeling bodies wrapped in dancing white fire so hot it roared like the afterburner of a jet fighter, reducing whatever it touched to crunchy ash.

They crawled, they prayed, they melted away. Yogi crowed and danced on flaming mattresses.

The fire alarm went off. Prisoners howled to be let out of their cells. Yogi wrapped Osmond's bloody hand in a wet towel. Loose droplets of blood on the floor sizzled and burned out like phosphorous in water.

The door of their cell buzzed and clanged open. "I got it, bros!" an Aryan shouted, down below. Yogi decided not to stay in the cell until the Crisis Containment Team broke in and took over. "Come on, bitches. We're busting out."

««——»»

Yogi knew right away what the riot was about. Slocum, Jughead and a couple lesser Aryan warlords took Shy Girl in the showers, dragged the tranny into a janitor's closet that they paid for and outfitted handsomely as a fuck pad. When Shy Girl told them he had AIDS, they laughed, because they did, too. When he resisted, they cut him.

They ID'd Jughead and Slocum by dental records, but the other three had to be pegged by head count, because they couldn't find enough teeth.

As the surviving senior Aryan Brother, Thor was honor-bound to kill the Weak Sisters, but they huddled in their secured separa-tee cell. After trying to bribe and poison the problems away, Thor

34

snapped, or maybe just decided to do this for giggles, since he was serving five lives, already.

What he didn't know and was too dumb to figure, was that the Weak Sisters were not so weak, anymore. He never guessed why they were separated from general population, and probably never heard of the experimental treatment for which the four of them volunteered.

They were told it was a cure for AIDS.

«« — »»

Yogi leaned over the tier railing and scanned the black smears on the concrete below. None of them was Thor.

The other cons in the housing unit huddled under the tiers or in their cells. Yogi could see the whites of their eyes from across the block. All eyes on him, and his crew. Nobody would ever call them Weak Sisters, now.

Alarms screamed lockdown all over the prison, but no guards came through the door to the block, which was jammed open. No Aryans held it now, either. Yogi strolled down the stairs and crossed the common area as only a man with a leash of pit bulls or a vest of dynamite sticks can, as a master of his own destiny.

He went to the control room, found Thor's stooge Orvis Buchannan standing over the guards. He looked fit to shit himself when Yogi stepped into the booth with his empty palm out. "You want some, trash? You want to burn?"

Orvis tugged his long ZZ Top beard and tried to look casual. Orvis's come tasted like rubber cement, and when he got off, he liked to choke you. "Come on, Holly, we all white men, here – "

"I'm the only man here, and my name's not Holly, bitch!" Yogi's other hand lashed out, the sock with the batteries in it connecting with Orvis's jewels so hard he lifted off his feet and whistled like a teakettle.

Orvis came at him with a toothbrush shiv, but Yogi was short and wiry, and he'd been dreaming of this moment for two years. His heel sheared down Orvis's right knee and smashed it off, so the hillbilly buckled and fell on the guards. Yogi beat his head to pulp until Osmond caught his arm. "We gotta go, Yogi, gotta go – "

"Pick a guard," Yogi said. Castillo and Pomerantz lay at their feet. Castillo had a black eye and a dislocated shoulder, but Pomerantz just looked stoned.

When Guard Pomerantz fucked you in the ass, he made you call him Coach. "Osmond, get Castillo out. Come here, Bucky. You know Bucky, don't you, Pomerantz?"

Osmond hoisted Castillo up by the plastic zip-ties around his wrists. The guard grunted when his shoulder popped back into its socket, but said nothing.

"He hurt me," Bucky whimpered.

Pomerantz shook his head and tried to spit his gag out.

"Well, he won't never do it again, Buck. You show him."

Bucky's hands hid behind his back like kicked puppies. "It hurts. I don't wanna—"

"Didn't it hurt when he drilled you? He turned you out, Buck, hung the bitch jacket on you. Didn't that shit hurt?"

"I ain't no bitch."

"That's right, Buck. Show him what you are."

Bucky reached for the bloody sock, but Yogi dropped it. "No. Burn him."

Bucky looked long and wetly into Yogi's eyes. "He jumped you, too. Whyn't you do it?" Afraid of everything, a big dumb baby, but Yogi knew where the levers were.

"Army's got generals, Buck, and Indians got chiefs. Every family's got a daddy, right?"

Bucky nodded, already holding out his big, meaty hand.

Yogi took it, stroking him the way you had to, to make him let go of his fear and realize how afraid the world should be of him. He never broke the locked gaze, even when he slit the fat of Bucky's forearm. "Daddy says burn."

Bucky bit his lip. Blood drizzled all over the wriggling guard's face, and ignited.

«« —— »»

They used Castillo's keys to get off the block and down the corridor to the dining hall and the door to the yard.

Bucky walked point with a wet rag pressed to his arm. Yogi steered the guard down the hall and Osmond loped along in the rear. At every intersection, they stopped and looked around, but they saw no guards, just cons running, laughing and pointing at the Weak Sisters like they were new fish. It hurt, but Yogi ignored them. He was used to it. Scorn and abuse made the Weak Sisters a family.

The doc singled them out because they were all AIDS-positive, and because they all, by choice or grand penal design, got their shit pushed in regularly.

He told them it was an experimental AIDS vaccine. They all signed up, but Yogi pushed for favors. Got them the segregation cell, cable hookup and a little ten inch with a shitty old VCR. It was Yogi's idea to tape shows for smokes, and to boost drugs from the doc to peddle on the block.

Every week, they got injections. For six months, the doc pricked them, blood out, drugs in, but none of them felt any different. Maybe they weren't falling apart as fast as some of the AIDS victims on the block, but they'd never gone so long without getting beat up or raped.

Then one day, the doc was gone. The trustee who usually took them to the infirmary dropped a note on Yogi's bed, and split.

On a slip of prescription pad, it said, *There is no project. Say nothing. Eat this note.*

Yogi pulled sick to get to the infirmary, and grabbed the doc's files. They weren't in the locked file cabinet, but hidden in a false ceiling panel in his office. Yogi read them, or tried, because he dropped out of middle school and never looked back. The folders told him little about the project, which had nothing to do with AIDS, but he learned a lot about himself and the other Weak Sisters.

Subject 001© ("Yogi") is a classic Napoleonic passive-aggressive, short, submissive, but driven to psychotic agonism by his acute sexual panic, acting out to dominate other outcasts and "prove" his heterosexuality.

There was more, and worse, so nasty that he wished the doctor was here, so Yogi could refute his theories on abuse as a determiner in character with an unlubed mophandle. But compared to his cellmates, the stuff on him was a love letter. Abuse. Brain damage. Bedwetting.

Levers.

The doc and his experiment made them freaks. Yogi and the files made them a gang.

37

«« — »»

They stepped out into the big yard. Sirens honked and wailed. Cold white stadium lights gave them each three shadows, and the towers swiveled spotlights on them. "Go back to your cells, or you will be shot."

"Our cell's on fire, fuckers!" Yogi shouted. He jerked Castillo up by his wrists. The guard yelped through his gag. "We're going to a hotel!"

They didn't say anything for a while, sweating him out. They doubted him.

Yogi's blood surged in his ears. He got hot and itchy all over. He had to fight down panic, deep breaths and soothing thoughts like the doc taught him, or his blood might just blast out the top of his head and nuke the whole prison.

This was, all of this, God's fault. Had he been born into a bigger, badder body, he might never have had to commit a crime, to get his share in life. Nobody ever believed him, and so everything he'd ever gotten busted for, he'd done to prove a point, to get respect.

He reached around Bucky and jabbed the shiv into Castillo's ear. The guard whipped his head around, so the shiv sliced through the cartilage and skidded up his temple, laying a flap of scalp across his eye. Castillo screamed now, and he knew they heard it.

"Stop! Jesus, don't hurt him! Nothing's happened that can't be fixed, right?"

Funny, they must not have camera feeds running in the block. Thor thought of everything. He wondered how much of the prison the Aryans controlled. "We want the warden!"

"We want a Playstation," Bucky added.

"Sure, Yogi, we can get him—"

A stream like piss from a racehorse hit Yogi in the eyes. He threw up his arms and screamed, "Pepper spray," but he heard the others catch it as he fell down.

His eyes closed over and his sinuses swelled shut and blew mucus out in streamers, but the scalding, searing pain that hit his brain left him a tiny bug in a burning house, and he couldn't even look out the windows.

He lurched into someone and punched out, heard Osmond

shriek, "I WANNA GO HOME!" and then a plastic shield slammed him to the ground.

Drowning in snot, crushed under dogpiled bodies and pummeling clubs and booted feet, Yogi couldn't get breath in to curse his attackers, let alone beat them back, but he gouged with his fingers and bit something until it came off between his teeth.

Pure, flaming jungle rage surged through his bloodstream, a rush so great he wanted it to happen, for his blood to ignite and blow them all away, to leave a crater so big, they'd name it after him. The beating on him fell off, but only because he was smothered.

He couldn't tell if his eyes were open or shut, if he was screaming or coughing, if he was alive or dead, but he knew he should let some of his blood out, that would show them who they were fucking with.

Then all he could see was red and it was hot like the yard opened up and gave him to Hell. The guards on top of him flew away, whooping fireflies in mating frenzy, and Yogi jumped at the nearest one and kicked, punched and tackled him. He could hear shots in a wild volley from somewhere above, and he tried to use the guard as a shield. He screamed, "Bucky! Osmond! Where you at?"

"Yogi—"

"Oz, you alright, where are you, brother?" Yogi flailed out with his free hand. The guard crumpled from the beating. Yogi could sort of see Castillo at the end of his arm.

Osmond's hand caught his and turned him around. Osmond's piss-stinking odor choked him. "Yogi," he cried, "I'm on fire—"

Yogi let Castillo drop and wiped the foamy tears out of his eyes. Osmond's other hand was a Roman candle shooting sparks out of the slash in his palm, which he must have opened in the dogpile.

He almost laughed, because Osmond's own expression was more one of terrified wonder than pain, but then he always was slow to catch on. What wasn't catching on slowly was the spread of the flames, which ate up his arm like a fuse.

"I WANNA GO HOME, YOGI!" Osmond wailed.

Yogi shoved him away and started running for the administration gate. "Come on, Oz, let's go home!"

The guard towers were shooting at each other. The catwalks

above the yard got taken over by the Mexican Mafia, cadres of hardcase vatos with riot shotguns trading wood slugs with the snipers. Nobody thought the Weak Sisters were worth stopping.

Osmond ran right past Yogi towards the administration gate, and Yogi stopped dead, throwing his arm across Bucky's flabby torso and folding him to the ground.

He saw the hunched men with rifles through the heavy-gauge chainlink fence, and the one sniper in the tower who was very unconcerned with the Mexican problem, and gave Osmond his undivided attention.

They gave him fifty new ways to breathe with every step he took, but sheer inertia carried him all the way to the gate. Blood spouted out of him and caught fire in midair, and when he arched his back and slopped into the fence, one of the guards cried out, "My eye, it's in my eye—"

Osmond exploded.

The blast from Shy Girl getting stabbed in the heart destroyed the whole shower wing. Shy Girl was no girl, but he did weigh in at about ninety-two pounds soaking wet, anemic and raddled with full-blown AIDS. Osmond was only HIV-positive, and a robust two-twenty. When he went off, he knocked the earth out of its orbit and made the day a minute longer.

White high noon sunlight blew down the fence and bent the tower over, scoured the yard, burned the chore jacket off Yogi's back, knocked Bucky on his tubby ass. Masonry and steel hurtled through space and glass rained down, half-melted from touching the heat inside the blood of Osmond Dickson.

Gray smoke gurgled out of the hole in the prison, but Yogi could see into the gutted admin compound, all the way through to the front gate.

Was it luck? It would sure be the first time. What it was, was how it had to be. "Come on, Buck. We're walking out."

They walked across the yard like they were going to buy smokes. Stepping over a yard sale of guards and charred parts of guards, Yogi picked up shotguns and sauntered into the checkpoint for visitors and employees.

The air smelled like lightning and hot dogs. Bucky had his shotgun cradled against his face so he could suck his thumb.

Inside, there were more bodies, a mess of cons and a couple

of guards stabbed or shot, and Yogi thought how beautiful it was, that the riot had spread so far. They might not even be noticed for days. Sometimes it paid to be small fish.

Yogi made for the gray light of the front doors. He still couldn't see too well from the pepper spray, so he stepped over a big bloody corpse and never looked twice until it reached out and twisted his ankle so he crashed into the floor headfirst.

Bucky yelped, "Thor!"

Yogi tried to roll over. The shotgun was pinned under him, but he had his thumb in his teeth like the pin on a grenade.

Slow reader that he was, he could read THOR on the knuckles of the fist that smashed into his face.

《《—》》

"You tried to do me, Holly," Thor growled in his ear, and the worst part was, he sounded hurt.

Yogi threw himself at Thor, tripped on his bound feet and jerked short on the end of a choke chain. He gagged and vomited in his mouth, sagged against the desk in the warden's office.

Red and blue lights bled in through the windows. Helicopters circled overhead. Outside, the world turned on, never to know the name of Dale "Yogi" Hollis. None of it mattered. None of this was so he could escape, he figured. All of this had been to deliver him to Thor with this new gift, to even the score, even if – no, *because* – it would kill him.

Thor shucked off his bloody prison blues and stepped naked into the light from the windows. The power was cut, so harsh pools of darkness squirmed with ranks of Aryan Brothers, white trash Vikings getting psyched to storm Valhalla, and the hooded bodies of cons and guards trussed up as hostages.

Thor stood over Yogi, looked at him looking, and smiled. Thor was stupendously ugly, with a cleft palate someone clumsy must have tried to repair with a staple gun. But he towered over the other cons, and stayed ripped on steroids and gladiator battles in the yard, and his beautiful golden hair hung in plaits down to the root of his spine.

Tattoos: undead Nazi stormtroopers, hammers, wolves, lightning bolts, ravens and runes, and on the steel-belted washboard of

41

his abdomen, just above his semi-erect cock, a hot barbarian bitch crouching, prowling, presenting her perfect heart-shaped ass and slyly winking. Far too sophisticated for prison ink, and so artfully shaded you could hardly see the name hidden in the whore's hair at first glance: HOLLY.

Thor got sent to juvie at fifteen for making a skinhead traitor bite the curb. He took to it like Disneyland, and especially to Yogi, who was just Dale, back then, a thirteen-year old runaway and already hustling, sent up for peddling crushed No-Doz as crystal meth.

Thor branded Dale, rechristened him as Holly, made him wear a wig and makeup. Thor seemed to think it made him seem less queer, or maybe he just liked to humiliate Dale to get off harder. Forever after, no matter what town or county he got pinched in, going back to jail was going back to Thor.

"After all we been through together," Thor rumbled, "you sent me that nasty she-male as a peace offering? Was that supposed to go off on me? What the fuck, Holly?"

"Nobody had to cut her. Nobody had to hurt anybody…"

"What the fuck am I supposed to do? Slocum'll fuck anything, so I passed it up the chain."

"You killed Shy Girl!" Bucky moaned. He was chained to the desk, too. Blue and bloated, he lay on his side and wept into the brown indoor-outdoor carpet. They'd worked him over hard, but they were careful not to break the skin.

"You fucking liar!" Yogi roared. "You ass-raping faggot liar, I never pimped my brothers! Don't listen, Buck —"

"Your bitch killed the main man, Holly, but you made me the goat." Thor teed off and chopped Yogi in the gut, lifting him off the floor and dropping him to his knees.

Yogi vomited again, spat it at Thor, who flinched – yes, and the rest of them, too, because they feared him, now, a little.

He couldn't get his hands up to his face, but he could still burn them, or get Bucky to do it. He should do it himself for Thor, the motherfucker who turned him out.

"Yeah, you're smarter than the average bitch, alright," Thor chuckled. "You had a hell of a plan. But now the plan is, we all walking out of here, with you exploding sissies in the front. And then we gonna settle up, traitor."

"Let's do it now, punk-ass!" Yogi strained at his leash, hanging from it but not choking. The cords of his neck stood out like rubber bands in a slingshot. "Do your friends know how you like it in the ass, you switch-hitter faggot?"

Thor whirled and clapped his big broad open hand across the side of Yogi's head, cupping it over his ear so the blow sucked Yogi's brains halfway out.

The crowd said, "Ooh," but Yogi couldn't hear it. He spat at Thor, who lunged at him and throttled his skinny neck.

Nose to nose, Yogi could hear Thor very well through his undamaged eardrum. "You maggot, I fucking loved you, you fucking queer race-traitor cocksucker, I would've done anything for you, and you fucking tried to burn me. You made me do this, Holly, you made me—"

"Liar," Yogi whispered like a gas leak. "You loved my mouth, and you loved my ass, but you never loved me—"

"No, Holly… don't… please—"

On the floor, Bucky choked and sputtered and barfed out his gag. His barf was red. A fat pink goldfish flopped across the bloody rug.

Thor jumped back and shouted, "Fire extinguisher!" The blood leapt up and wrapped red dragon garlands around his legs and up his torso as he riverdanced across it.

Bucky rolled over and sprayed a jet of red napalm across the office from the stump of his tongue. Crackling splatters washed the papers off the warden's desk and sparked in mid-air into tracer-rounds and bouncing betty mines.

The brothers and their hostages scattered for the exit, but though they trampled the hostages and each other, they all got caught, consumed and fused in the deluge from Bucky's blowtorch of racial equality.

But the hungry fire traveled just as eagerly up the jet to Bucky's face. His chubby cheeks and lips peeled back, blackened teeth cracked, but he kept playing the tongue of voracious flame across the office, until only charcoal danced.

Thor tried to swim upstream to get at Yogi. Bucky's aerosolized jet fuel cremated him on his feet, oiled golden braids blazing, Viking tattoos curling up like the pages of a comic book, but he kept coming.

Yogi looked from Thor to Bucky and saw the same sick, crazy gleam in their eyes, all eyes on Yogi, until they melted away.

Thor collapsed and shattered on the floor.

Whimpering, eyeless, Bucky tried to clamp his jaws shut, but his mouth was a cracked chimney, leaking freshets of incendiary gore down the front of his chore jacket.

Bucky reached out for Yogi to hold him, to make his big half-witted ass feel small and safe in this horrible day care center, where Mommy was never coming to pick him up, because he killed Daddy. Daddy was God, and Yogi was Daddy, now—

Yogi ripped his chains free of the incinerated desk and ran for the door.

Bucky lurched up like an elephant seal, throwing his arms out in Yogi's path. When he gasped, the sound of the blood filling his lungs was like a pilot light switching on.

Yogi dove through the doorway, ran down the hall, knee-deep in Aryan barbecue, scrambling on all fours… and still Bucky didn't go off.

Yogi could hear an amplified voice from outside saying, "Prisoner Hollis, Prisoner Walters, Prisoner Dickson, there's a man here from the Army, who wants to talk to you – "

Yogi ran across the lobby. With his good ear, he still heard Bucky sobbing and drowning from the inside out, "Yogi, save me —"

Yogi almost got to the doors when Bucky exploded.

The whole prison disappeared.

The shockwave hurled Yogi through the plate glass, flensing his skin off down to the bone across his back and neck, driving thousands of needles of glass and wood and stone into and through him. He hit the ground running and didn't even notice his wounds for all the lights and cops and National Guardsmen, waiting just for him.

Yogi staggered out of the chorus of secondary explosions that flattened the remaining façade of the prison and hurled debris over the Mexican border, two miles away.

He almost tripped and fell when he saw his left hand was two fingers shy of what it should be, and smeared with volatile blood. He wobbled, but jogged across the rock garden and the staff parking lot, into the sights of the army of cops and media.

This was all he'd ever really wanted. From the first days of school, when big boys beat him because they could, and made him do things when they got bored with hitting, and he sat in the office, waiting for another paddling and lecture about his temper, what burned him up the most was how, outside his bubble of flaming rage, everything else ground on, oblivious, as if to mock him.

The sun still shone, clocks still ticked; the secretaries still breezily answered the phone like there was no emergency. The principal laughed and joked with a teacher, as if *his* problems didn't matter, as if nobody felt his pain.

Now, at last, Yogi saw the impregnable ranks of the police arrayed around the prison, the helicopters slicing up the night sky, the firemen too scared to come in and fight the raging inferno at his back, and the child in him was finally satisfied. The world felt his anger, his rage, his frustration, and the world finally got it.

His blood began to tingle inside him, and he felt as if he'd sprouted wings, and was going to lift off any second and fly away over them, could do whatever the fuck they wanted, but they couldn't run away, they couldn't ignore. At last, he was not afraid to throw himself into the wind. He flung out his bloody arms and ran.

It was not for him to escape, but only, perhaps, to escape this life a bigger man than he came in. He was bigger than all of them, inside, a master of other men. The doc saw that, when he chose him for his role in the experiment.

Far more important even than the biochemical breakthrough of this new procedure, is the impact of the psychological data collected. It should put paid, once and for all, to those naysayers who claim that Westerners are too individualistic, too egomaniacal, to serve as – I shall not demur to use the proper term – 'suicide bombers.' The perceived obstacles are, in fact, the triggers, which, with socio-engineering of the kind already mass-produced in the American penal system, make one willing to volunteer as a vindication of their selfishness.

The ultimate proof of this phase of the experiment should come to fruition in Subject 001©, whom I, as a precaution against his volatile nature prematurely setting off the experiment, pre-selected to be the Control. Acting only on the cues from his subordinate inmates and the mildly psychotropic placebo "treatment" in his system, 001© should demonstrate the true potential of egocentric fanaticism.

Yogi knew nothing about science, or what a control or a placebo was, so he never stopped feeling the fire yearning to blossom out of him as he charged at the barking guns. When Yogi exploded, he took the whole world with him.

❦

The Wet Nurse

She awoke, and the phlegm in her chest was a brittle ceramic glaze that shattered with the first coughing fit. Deanna rolled over in bed and lit a smoke before she opened her eyes. She could finish the pack, and nobody could say shit. She'd paid for her crime, and now, all alone in her body, she answered to no one.

Not that they came to check. They got what they wanted, and she left what they still needed at the door for them to pick up every morning, like a dutiful cow. It was like her mother used to joke after she threw out Deanna's father: *when you get the good stuff out, you throw away the wrapper, right?*

She found the TV remote bolted down on the nightstand, thumbed it on and flipped through the early talk shows. Prescription bottles rolled off the edge.

She still had plenty of money. She wouldn't have to do anything harder than phone sex again for a while, if she kept her wits, but she wouldn't be able to get good, legal shit like this, so even though her womb still oozed blood and her muscles felt like the floor had been torn out of her, she denied herself another pill, for now.

She would get through this. Dr. Ramos said there would be depression. She explained it like Deanna was an idiot, but it made sense. Her body had been put to its ultimate test, the task for which it was made, and for a while, it was going to try to do that job, until it sunk in that there was no baby.

It still hadn't sunk in to her mind, either. She was free. She had money, more than she'd ever make at any kind of real job. And all because she'd sold something that she would gladly have paid someone, anyone, to scrape out of her. Dr. Ramos, who steered her away from the door of the Planned Parenthood clinic, had shown her a better way.

It hadn't been easy, but Deanna had made the most of the time. Sitting in this room for six months, she'd worked as hard as the baby inside her, to grow and change. She had made plans, but she couldn't remember them right now. All she could think of was sleep, and the dream.

She rolled over in bed and muted the TV, treated herself to a bonus pill she found in the folds of her pillowcase. It stuck and slowly dissolved in her throat like a tiny glacier. The leaden morning light melted into trippy haloes around the pharmaceutical nativity scene on her nightstand, and she melted with it.

"Oh, it's beautiful," everyone said, and they were right. She could see the baby rising like a bloody sun from the valley between her legs. Her vision was all oily trails from the tsunami crash of pleasure-in-pain, flying high above her body, watching herself. And then her baby was in her arms, and she glowed in that eternal, perfect moment, anchored for the first time to her own life, to all life, to the wisdom that ran in her blood, that told her just what to do. She tugged down her hospital johnny and lifted the baby's mouth to her nipple.

Her beautiful child sucked eagerly, and she gave a sigh of relief as the unbearable pressure in her turgid breast gave way to a tickling of pure contentment, as all that she was, and all who came before her, flowed into her newborn. She forgave the world and everyone who'd made life hard on her – from her stepdad to JT Barnhardt, and all the other boys and men who might have fathered her child, then drove her out of town. She forgave them unconditionally, and begged the pardon of all those she'd ever hurt, and knew true peace.

Her heart's desire fussed and nibbled at her drained breast, twisted in anticipation as she lifted the hungry newborn to suckle at the other one. Eagerly, tiny jaws working, it fed, and all the untapped pain and promise stored up in her flowed out.

She floated out of herself again. Light gushed out of her, and she had one of those things like an orgasm that saints had in those paintings, where they looked like God was goosing them up the ass with an electric toothbrush – but these were only the unworthy words she used to try to describe it, afterward. For now, she was transported, transformed, into a mother. She would be a wonderful mother, she would clean up for good, she would change—

Cold rubber hands lifted the baby out of her arms, and she was like smoke trying to claw at the nurse who turned and presented her baby to the skinny lady and the balding man who talked on his cell phone throughout the birth. They thrust a pen into her crabbed hand and she made a mark on some papers, and then they were gone. Tears smeared the ink on her check.

She rolled out of bed, arms reflexively cradling her deflated belly.

Dr. Ramos said she'd have dreams. Postpartum depression. Pills. Her hand went up under her sweat-slick T-shirt. Her breasts were slack, not engorged like they'd been for months. She hissed in surprise and pain as she touched her outraged nipples. They felt chewed, but they resonated, rang like nervous chimes with the echo of feeding her baby. It had felt so right, so real—

In real life, she never got to touch it. She did not know its sex, had never seen a sonogram. They told her only what she needed to eat or avoid during the pregnancy, and trained her to pump her breasts and leave milk in a Styrofoam cooler outside the door.

She only saw its shadow as they lifted it out of her, heard a single thin wail as they took it to be weighed. But when she touched her nipples, she knew that somehow, somewhere, it had been real. She hugged herself, to hold in the last fleeting traces of joy.

Deanna's mother didn't raise an idiot. Taught her to know smart from stupid, if not right from wrong. Her father kicked in little of value to her blossoming maturity, though he did nothing to queer it, either. She knew him as a nice but busy man who worked hard to pay for a house he didn't live in.

Any talk show therapist would zero in on Deanna's slut act as a function of Dad's absence and Mom's indifference, but her motives were simpler. She just enjoyed sex as much as boys did.

When her period went missing, she could only curse her mother for telling her always to be smart, and not forcing her to be good. When JT Barnhardt dumped her by way of punching her in the mouth, she stole money from Mom and hitchhiked to the next state to get an abortion on her sixteenth birthday.

She told herself she was not just smart but brave, taking care of it before she started to show and the procedure got even more expensive and gross; but then the little Filipino lady from the nameless adoption agency bird-dogged her and made her an offer.

The clients set her up in the motel room and paid all her expenses, but she plugged away studying for her GED, and socked away a lot of extra cash doing phone sex. It kept her too busy to fall back into doing speed, and the damned hormones had her masturbating all the time, anyway.

Fuck it. Fuck motherhood, and fuck you, too. She had done a job, the finest form of piecework, and she got paid. She could afford to lie back and wait for something to tell her what to do with her life, and until then, there were plenty of diversions to numb the nagging ache inside her that tried to tell her life had just passed her by.

She wasted half an hour trying to squeeze milk out of her breasts. The cold plastic suction cup wrung her out, but collected only a few drops of white-gold Deanna-juice. Had she milked herself and forgotten about it? Stupid cow…

The Styrofoam cooler was empty. Dr. Ramos would be pissed. She scribbled a note and left it on the door, changed into fresh clothes, and went outside.

She went to the bank and deposited her check, pulled back cash for snacks and smokes, polished off a lumberjack omelet with raspberry jam on it at Rudford's. Dr. Ramos said the cravings would stop any day, now.

As she walked down the sun-blasted sidewalk, she avoided the stares of street trash, dirty old men and tattooed weirdoes ogling her angry tits and flabby ass, hid her flushed face that betrayed how badly she longed to take one or all of them home.

She had to get off the street and fill some bottles, lie down and rub one out; she had a hole burning in her, and if she didn't get to safety, it would suck someone in with her.

By the time she got back to her room, her billowing, maternity-sized T-shirt was plastered to her chest, and not with sweat. She peeled it off and wrung it out over the sink. Cloudy mother-of-pearl rivulets of oily human milk dripped from her fingers and circled the drain.

She got a paper to look for an apartment – she hoped the clients spoiled their new baby with all the money they'd saved keeping her in this shitty motel. Poring over the classifieds, she found and circled an interesting ad. MOTHER'S MILK: HIGHEST PRICE PAID. SOPHISTICATED CONOSSIEUR SEEKS ENTERPRISING DAIRYMAIDS.

She turned on the TV as she set to work with the pump, settled on a Mexican talk show. For extra flare, the first row of the jeering studio audience was packed with circus freaks. An obese mongoloid cyclops thumped his chest and pawed his mate, a giggling pinhead girl, as the platinum blonde hostess harangued the caged transvestites onstage.

Deanna stared, transfixed by their deformities, thinking of all the drugs she did before she found out. Shit, she thought, *maybe you dodged a bullet*. But she knew her baby was perfect.

Her fingers absently tweaked and twisted her nipples, still engorged after six bottles. She only felt wired after masturbating, so it took two pills to knock her out and deliver her to the dream.

Deanna could build a bridge of words pretty far across the chasm between reality and her dreams, but even with better than the standard four-cylinder brain, she only knew that she was feeding her baby, and it felt so divine as to make everything else she could do, drink, snort or smoke in this life seem like a waste of time.

She held all that was good in the world in her arms, and it was entrusted to her to nourish and nurture it, but something had torn her away from her charge, something was coming to take her baby away—

The phone shook her awake. She rolled over and rubbed her chest, her nipples tender and sore, her fingers wringing them as they must have done all night. Torturing herself, her body trying to drive her crazy. A forlorn little sob gargled out of her, but she bit it back, to keep herself from hearing it.

She had to stop being stupid. She could face anything. She had gone clean when she knew she was pregnant; had not, even then, succumbed to the dumb drives of her drug-hungry flesh. A voice inside her had told her to get clean and do right by the thing inside her, even as she stole the money to scrape it out.

"Hello?" she asked the phone, but only then remembered to pick it up.

Sniffling breaths and a thickly accented voice from a mouth as tight and inscrutable as a Chinese finger-trap. "Deanna, I came, and there was no milk. The baby needs milk, Deanna..."

She tried to explain, but only a strangled moan got out.

"Deanna, you sound upset. How are you feeling?"

She tried to speak, but her eyes and sinuses clotted up with tears, and nothing came out but a sob of, "Uh-huh... I mean... no?"

"This is a difficult time, Deanna, and you shouldn't be alone. You haven't contacted your family, have you?"

"I—" she gasped, "I'm all alone, Duh-duh-Doctor—"

"No, you are not alone, Deanna. I'm coming over. I want to help. You let me help you, okay?"

"Okay," she said, and hung up. She drifted off, forgetting who called.

She had to break this cycle. Hormones and pills weren't the boss of her. She was rich and young and free. She could jump on a plane with just the clothes on her back, fly to New York and shop for a new wardrobe on 5th Avenue, go to a posh nightclub and dance alone until the finest guy in the place fell under her spell, go back to his place and fuck his brains out, get knocked up and start all over again—

Her vagina still throbbed with dull pain, but it had to be taught a lesson. She slipped two fingers into her panties and kneaded the hood of her clit. It was dry and sore and dead as a wart to pleasure, but she licked her fingers and kneaded herself into a grudging semblance of arousal. It had to learn what it was for. I'm not just a chute for strangers to slide in and out of. *I'm not a fucking farm animal!*

At last, some spark of desire kindled inside her, the merest mote of light, and she thrust herself at it, plunging three fingers into herself and throttling her clit with her thumb.

The hot, soft hell of her womb opened up, cervix dilating down to meet the eager spears of her fingers, nails gouging divots of velvet meat out of her uterine wall. Her hand spasmed, wracked with cramps, but she twisted it further, probing the ticklish pucker of her asshole with her pinky, driving all four rigid digits into her holes like the torrent of swords in the coup de grace of a bullfight.

A wounded gasp ripped out of her. The impending orgasm teetering overhead like lightning gathering to strike her down, but then it melted away like an unanswered prayer. She worked even harder, until at last, there was lubrication in abundance. She didn't care if it was blood.

She had brought a child into the world just for money, she could take anything. *This is what you are for—*

Her fingers touched something that was never, ever there, before. Never, except when—

Something brushed her still, stiff fingers. Something inside her grasped them.

Deanna yanked her hand free and screamed. She was careful when she played with herself during the pregnancy, but there was nothing like that in there—

She rolled over and vomited all over the nightstand. Her pill bottles and *People* magazines washed over the edge on a pink wave with little Oxycontin icebergs in it. Her stomach rolled and heaved itself dry, but her womb rumbled and quivered like a clogged volcano. She did more than hurt herself, down there. She woke something up.

The neon light for the *Cash Fast* place outside her window came on, drenching the dark in epileptic red and gold. She lay down on the bed and prayed for sleep, prayed for the dream. And this prayer, at least, someone saw fit to answer.

She held her baby, and everything was fuzzy and heavenly white, bathed in that flattering, Vaseline-filtered light the movies used on aging actresses. She knew this moment could go on forever if she just let it, a perfect closed circuit of need and nurturing, a universe unto itself.

The gauzy light brightened and became a substance, bandages winding around her face. She saw nothing, but felt her dream baby gnawing at her breast, felt its silky skin and stolen warmth growing heavier against her belly. Something magical was happening; her dream was birthing itself into the real world.

This time, the hot, hidden parts of her that ruled in secret, the parts of her that knew all along what they were doing when she had seemed most out of control – those parts filled her with the blood-truth that she would never let her baby go, this time—

When the light died out, she felt a flood of unpleasant sensations – the crinkle of stiff waxed paper beneath her, the dull ache in her joints from general anesthesia, and most of all, the mingled relief and soreness of her breasts.

She tried to move, but she found herself restrained, pulled taut against the tattered vinyl examination table.

If you stared hard at the spiky calligraphy on the yellowed degrees and certificates on the walls, you'd find none of them bore the name Midori Ramos.

This was her office, just down the block from the motel. She wasn't really a doctor, not in this country, anyway, but in the Philippines, she was some kind of highly respected surgeon.

Deanna's baby cooed as it drank from her.

In the dim gray light that slanted through the blinds, she saw that she was no longer dreaming, and that the thing she suckled was indeed very real, but it was no baby.

No human baby—

A bloated, ghostly lamprey attached to her breast, pulsating with the rhythm of its greedily siphoning sucker-mouth. Floating in the air above her, living liquid like a jellyfish or a cloud of semen in white wine, but she could feel it rasping and throbbing and wringing the last drops of milk from her slack, flaccid teat.

Deanna screamed and tried to roll off the table, but her body was bound too tightly to lift her hands, let alone pry off the parasite. As she struggled, the agitated thing shivered and flushed deep red like she'd shamed it, or maybe it was drinking her blood.

She had fed this thing in her dreams, and it had grown fat on the flood of tears her breasts wept, the drainage from the amputation of her child. Deanna howled her throat raw, but it kept sucking at her.

The door clicked and opened. The harsh blast of fluorescent light dispersed the lamprey. Deanna felt it compress its turgid, ethereal mass into her vagina, and the violation redoubled as she realized this was the cause of the orgasmic climax of her dreams, as the sated parasite slithered back to its lair in her womb.

"I've seen this before," Dr. Ramos said. "I am no doctor in this country, but at home, I perform most respected psychic surgery. Nobody believe me, when I try to show them."

Deanna fought to brake her runaway hyperventilation, tried to ask, to curse, to beg, but all she managed was, "Get... it... out of me—"

"Every life is sacred, Miss Deanna. You did not ask to become pregnant, but the Life Force came into you. We talk about this, and you say you want to be a bearer of life. Your baby is in a better place, but this... is special."

Only hysteria gave her the strength to speak. "I don't... want it in me! Get it out, get it out—"

Dr. Ramos's tiny hand stroked the dome of Deanna's belly,

even as it seemed, once more, to swell. "Life wants to live, Miss Deanna. It fills all the cracks in the earth, large and small, for its own glorious purpose. Where there is shelter and food, there is life. Even in us, yes, especially, for where is there safer shelter?

"There are worlds inside us, and food of a kind unique in all of nature." With a soothing touch softer than moonlight, Dr. Ramos caressed her heart and head. Deanna felt her runaway pulse slow, and the short-circuited sparks of her thoughts settled into a torpid brownout.

"If the food and warmth inside us can foster a world of lower life, what kind of life could thrive on the heat of our thoughts, our emotions? All hate, all love, all wishes and dread and dreams, come out of us like waste heat, like sweat and milk and soil. These living things are as fleeting as the food they crave, born and breeding and dying in hours and days, invisible to us, as they must be, for their sake and ours."

"I— I saw it," Deanna started, but Dr. Ramos pinched her lips shut, and continued.

"In Manila, I see a lady who lived on the street whose baby died, and nursed a baby no one else could see, and they called her crazy. But when they tried to take her to hospital, they saw the 'ghost-baby' in her arms. The crowd killed them both."

Dr. Ramos touched Deanna's face, knobby knuckles and stubby fingers that looked all the more improper for their slavishly manicured and sensibly glossed nails. "I wanted nothing more than to be a mother, Miss Deanna, but I was born into wrong body. I knew it could never happen, that nothing on earth could make my body become what I was inside. I would never know the kind of joy you saw only as a curse, but in my longing, I became a mother, of sorts, as well."

Dr. Ramos lifted the front of Deanna's gown. Her hand became a blade and slid, without friction or effort, into Deanna's gut.

It was a repulsive parlor trick, yet Deanna felt the insane violation of the tiny hand groping through her until it seized on something that was *not* her, that clutched Deanna's vitals in its desperation as Dr. Ramos began to draw it out.

It slithered between her fingers, but it kept coming and coming out of the hole Dr. Ramos bored into her. It writhed in and out of her, wafting up on the stale stirrings of the air, spilling out like smoke from burning plastic, mute witness to the vastness of the void inside her. It wound round and round Midori Ramos's arm, an eel eating itself, but even to Deanna's fear-widened eyes, it was little more than a shimmering shadow, an unborn ghost that would never yield detail to closer study.

Now, Deanna at last understood the odd, eager smile that Dr. Ramos always had for her. It was a mask of admiration and hope, but mostly envy.

She let the thing squirm off her hand and retract like a molested octopus back into Deanna's womb. "The milk of my soul is sour. I can almost give it true life, but not flesh. In you, it found a home."

"Get it out of me!"

"When it has finished gestating, we will see. No specimen has ever been brought this far, so who knows what we will discover? When they give the species a name, I think it only fitting that it be *my* name, since you care only for money."

Deanna subsided in her bonds; and if something in her mind finally snapped, it was a welcome reprieve, and all she lost was a skin that no longer fit. If this was what Deanna was meant to be, then she could still prove Midori Ramos wrong.

Dr. Ramos went to the freezer and took out several bottles, dropped one into a silo that swung into place, like a hamster feeder, above Deanna's face. Golden droplets of milk – her own – drizzled into her mouth. "We see what refining your diet does, shall we?"

Deanna eagerly gulped it down.

Her child would thrive and grow in the security of her womb. It would come out to be loved and to feed on her tears of joy, and then go back inside her, where no one could ever hurt it or take it away…

She would be a good mother, and her baby would be perfect.

⋏⋎

Love To Give

You want to know about my victims. That's what you keep asking, and that's why I haven't answered. Semantics are important to the accused, you should know that. If you had asked about my *mates*, my women, or my *lovers*, you might have gotten a different answer, but we'll never get anywhere if you keep calling them *victims*.

All I can tell you is that you don't know about all of them, not by a long shot. I tried to keep records, at first – to be responsible, to keep control – but you know, don't you, how these things get out of hand?

You don't believe me, but you want to hear, because you want to know where all my "victims" are. Even I don't know that, but I do want to talk. I want you to understand. I'm not sorry for what I did. The Life Force will not be denied, right?

Last year, my doctor told me I had a year to live, at the outside. Nothing they could culture or incubate, nothing environmental, nothing they could identify in my genes; just a simple, systemic failure. I hadn't told them about my father, and I didn't know, yet, about myself. The doctor gave me brochures for hospices, and a company that froze sperm.

≪≪—≫≫

Mom and Dad found each other late in life. Dad wasn't much help on the facts of reproduction. "First time I saw your Mom, I knew, and she put her hand in mine, and the rest is history." Whenever I pressed him to explain, he would only say, "We are blessed people, son. We don't need to debase ourselves and cast our seed like other folks. Find a woman pure of heart who loves you for yourself, and everything else will fall into place."

I never saw either of them naked; I don't think they did, either. I never saw them kiss, except when they blew them from across the room. I took a lot of kidding from my few friends about their sleeping arrangements. Separate twin beds, like brother and sister, with a lacy curtain hanging between them.

Dad died when I was twelve, a precipitous six-month decline and fall that I always thought was cancer. Mom never elaborated on Dad's vague dismissal of the birds and the bees.

I was twenty-two when she succumbed to a stroke. After college, I still lived in my old room, and still got carded at R-rated movies. Puberty had struck only a glancing blow, but my attitude towards women matured without any of the glandular contortions that plagued my peers. By then, I had no friends. Left behind by nature, I was even more cruelly isolated by society, but it didn't get me down.

There's nothing of note between their deaths and the day I learned of my own appointment with fate. I lived, I worked, and I waited, until the day my urine came out the color of coffee, with the faint odor of ammonia.

The test results came as a shock. Right there in the doctor's office, I wept. I itched and burned all over. I broke out in cold sweat like my whole body was crying. The doctor excused himself and left me dripping hot, snotty tears on the crinkly paper of the examination table.

I suddenly realized that whatever was supposed to happen in my life to make it worthwhile was not coming, and I hadn't even known, until then, that I'd expected anything.

For the first time in my life, I thought about girls. (Women, I mean – I never have been a pervert, even at the end, so far as I know.) I thought about all the mysteries of love and sex and parenting that I'd never know, and I didn't care if they heard me in the next room.

A nurse came in and put an arm around me, offered me a Kleenex and said some nice things that I didn't hear. I had paid her no mind as I came into the office, but she was something else again, in that moment. Her cinnamon brown hair hung lank around her face, stricken by an ill-advised perm. Her wideset hazel eyes had flecks of gold that sparked like she had been crying, too. Her sad Italian smile made me picture her as the subject of a Mannerist portrait of Mary Magdalene washing my feet. The deep cushion of her breasts was a welcome pressure on my side, transmitting a secret heat and sleepy calm through her faded blue scrubs.

I did not even know I was doing it, when I made her my first.

You don't really want to understand, and I don't blame you. You think of it as rape, what I did, but if a rape occurred, it was invisible to all but God.

The nurse – her name was Cynthia – took my clammy hand and eased me off the end of the table, so the sweat-blotted paper stuck to my legs. She peeled it off, balled it up and dumped it in the medical waste bin by the door, opened the door to let me out. I apologized for my behavior and left the office.

Did I leave something out? Did the sordid details of my first and favorite conquest leave you cold? Is it really outrage that makes you so hot to dissect every slap and tickle, or just good old-fashioned lechery?

Dad was right. We are truly blessed people.

《《—》》

The war of the sexes doesn't cease when one combatant surrenders and lies prone for the other; it enters an invisible arena, where no quarter is given to love or beauty, and all engagements are to the death.

Inside the female, a relentless array of defenses purges unfit sperm. In many species, such as domestic hens, a uterine gate-keeper detains the suitor's seed for several days until a competitor may weigh in, at which time the inferior seed is summarily ejected. In external fertilizers such as fish, selection pressure is even more intense, shaping males into a carnal display of color and fantastic fins to close the deal.

In such an arms race, escalated by eons of rape and rejection, no organism can maintain a foothold for more than a paltry hundred generations, before some breakthrough mutation in the enemy gender's camp shatters the advantage.

I freely admit that a rape did occur, but it was the rape of her egg by my sperm, which is the universal method whereby all the animal kingdom crowns its queens. I did not physically rape her. I did not need to. Seduced by my grief, she accepted me, and all the love I had to give her.

59

«««——»»»

The true criteria that drive reproductive fitness are not the superficial courting displays that win trysting rights. The fitness of a suitor's gametes has no correlation to the organism's fitness or desirability – an ugly duckling's sperm have as much chance of penetrating the egg as the seed of its handsome rival, so the arms race of sexual selection occurs on two, almost mutually exclusive fronts.

Mayflies, of the order *Ephemeroptera*, mature, mate, spawn and die in a single day. The fierce and absolute urgency of their mating is a good model for understanding what goes on inside us, in the throes of the act we call love.

In most "lower" orders of life, production of offspring is the culmination and the end of the organism; in the most ruthlessly efficient insect species, the next generation hatches and feasts on its superfluous parents, wasting nothing. Only in advanced or social animals can any individual earn its keep after birthing, as parent, caregiver or queen. We take such a system for granted, because the alternatives have been lost to us for so long. This is why I do not feel that I am anything new; rather, what I am is very, very old…

«««——»»»

I returned in a month for a new battery of tests. My liver and kidney function were still steadily declining, and I had a year at the outside. My uncommon blood type made the possibility of an organ donor match almost impossible. That day, I did not cry.

On the way out, I chanced to overhear Cynthia talking to a secretary. She and her husband had tried for years, but no joy, his count low and motility a joke. They were looking to adopt, when out of the blue, she came up pregnant.

The secretary who took my co-pay and forms, a college-age blonde, big-boned, acne-scarred and achingly wholesome, clucking her tongue in a stage whisper that she'd missed her period, and hadn't told her boyfriend, but wasn't that a weird coincidence? I thought about pregnancy and coincidence and natural selection, and how much love I still had to give. By then, I had fallen in love with and pined for a hundred or more brief glimpses of women, and if it were within me to force myself upon one, I know I would have. I had begun to suspect that I had some effect on them, as well. The smile of every waitress and supermarket cashier was a little wider, their hands brushed mine and lingered a moment as they gave me my change. I did not kid myself that they fell in love with me, but it was the light in their eyes that first gave me an inkling of what I was giving them.

I thought about Mom and Dad with their Lucy & Ricky beds, and about how Dad took Mom's hand, and the rest—

«« —»»

Around the same time my organs started to fail, my skin cells were transforming. Newly activated glands in my epidermis began to produce sperm – or, to be more exact, viral RNA in capsules that mimicked, but vastly improved upon, human spermatozoa. When I got nervous around women and began to sweat, I was a teeming ocean of lusty, never-say-die gametes, and any fleeting contact was enough to deliver several million onto the object of my desire without arousing anything but a fleeting blush at my timid touch. Difficult to wash off, capable of surviving on the skin for a week, my sperm stood an excellent chance of being delivered into the host's eyes or mouth, and from there they swam, like determined salmon, to spawn.

I knew where I came from, and I knew I had even less time than the doctor predicted. Dad lived for twelve years after he took my mother's hand. I'm burning brighter, using myself up faster than my father, and won't last even the few weeks they say I have left. My father never touched the bare skin of any woman, not even my mother, after I was born. And I have touched so many...

«« —»»

Fewer than six hundred specimens of the giant squid, genus *Architeuthis*, have been discovered in the last four centuries, and not a single one has been captured alive. Its mating rituals are an enigma, a primordial sex crime reconstructed from autopsies. The male adult giant squid may grow to six meters in length, and its penis is longer than its body, but down in the lonely dark of the ocean deeps, its quest to slake its burning lust and perpetuate the species is a suicide mission.

The solitary female giant squid is a third larger than its suitors, and viciously repels any amorous approaches with its sucker-studded feeding tentacles and razor beak. The male *Architeuthis* organ is a high-pressure hose, which injects its packet of sperm from a distance, hopefully into the thrashing tentacles of the female, where it will migrate to the sex organs internally and fertilize the target. These submarine mating battles often result in the male, badly damaged and often dying, haplessly inseminating itself or a hapless rival, wasting its fleeting chance at some sliver of immortality.

What would drive such a magnificent creature to sacrifice life and limb for such a cold exchange of passion with a deadly enemy? What empty mote of hopeless pleasure must it take from such a bitterly hostile transaction? I, alone, can truly say that I know.

«« — »»

Determined to make the most of my remaining time, I went out on the road. I went courting.

Just a few for-examples: I was a greeter at a Wal-Mart in Oklahoma City for a week. I was a towel boy at a country club in Albuquerque for two weeks. I have been a masseuse, a door-to-door salesman and a bartender's assistant, all over the eastern states.

My most fruitful jaunt was as an ordained minister at a quickie wedding chapel in Branson, Missouri. I was there just long enough that the place got a reputation. I touched at least a thousand fertile women before I moved on to Reno, and then Las Vegas.

On the strength of that social custom whereby an extended hand must be shaken, I have seduced multitudes. Bony, pale, bird-like hands with immaculately manicured nails; robust, mauling, mannish hands the color and texture of pot roast; palms soft and supple as the belly of a newborn hare, or horny with calluses from hard labor; the tattooed hands of biker chicks, prostitutes and circus freaks, and the meek, plain hands of nuns and veiled Moslem women whose faces I will never see.

Obviously, I try to sow my investments among Catholic and

conservative Christian communities, and I've found that warm climates work best for conducting my genetic material. I suspect that my viral sperm aerosolizes and travels under hot, humid conditions, for I have had to leave more than a few jobs and apartments, after discovering that I had impregnated multiple women I never once touched or shared facilities with. An elderly spinster landlady whom I avoided for multiple reasons made the news when she died in childbirth, but every one of her octuplets survived.

You look at me like I'm a lunatic, a liar or a freak, but in a handful of generations, they'll teach that my reproductive system gave me a competitive edge, so my appearance was predestined, my conquest inevitable. Schoolchildren will wonder, as they snicker and fondle repulsive museum exhibits of internal fertilization with antiseptic mittens, how humankind ever endured the dark ages of sexual reproduction.

It's one of the things I wonder about as I lie alone in bed, when I'm not wondering how many more nights I'll be alive to wonder: how many of them know? And if they knew, would they tell? Or would they just kick the dirt over it and walk away? Or would they steal into the cribs of twenty or thirty thousand helpless babies, and snuff them out? And how could they know if the babies in those twenty or thirty thousand homes – or fifty or a hundred thousand, for all you know – are even half of my children?

I only regret that I'll never to get to see them all grow up, to tell them what they are; but I know it's best that they will find out as I did, and make the most of their daylight.

I sincerely hope you will make the most of yours.

Born in England and raised in Toronto, Canada, Gemma Files has been a film critic, teacher and screenwriter, and is currently a wife and mother. She won the 1999 International Horror Guild Best Short Fiction award for her story "The Emperor's Old Bones", and the 2006 ChiZine/Leisure Books Short Story Contest for her story "Spectral Evidence". Her fiction has been published in two collections (KISSING CARRION and THE WORM IN EVERY HEART, both from Prime Books), and five of her stories were adapted into episodes of THE HUNGER, an anthology TV show produced by Ridley and Tony Scott's Scot Free Productions. She has also published two chapbooks of poetry. In 2009, her short story "Marya Nox" will appear in LOVECRAFT UNBOUND, a new Lovecraft-themed anthology edited by Ellen Datlow, while her story "each thing I show you is a piece of my death" will appear in CLOCKWORK PHOENIX 2, from Norilana Books.

GEMMA FILES

Ring of Fire

Late June, 1857:
"The sepoys themselves, strangely enough, have a phrase which describes my current state of mind to perfection: 'Sub lal hogea hai' – 'Everything has become red.'"

«« — »»

Unlike most madmen, Desbarrats Grammar was debatably lucky enough to be gifted with an enduring understanding of the exact instant when his sanity had collapsed. The moment in question had occurred shortly after the retaking of Calcutta, during what his commanding officer had then referred to as "the mopping up", post-Indian Mutiny – a process of justice which, in keeping with the usual British reinterpretation of Biblical tradition, required considerably more for the price of an eye than payment in kind. Correspondingly, a method of retribution had to be improvised which would be both impressive and educative.

And this was how Grammar, then a mere twenty-two years of age, soon came to be standing next to a cannon across the mouth of which a lucklessly uprisen native soldier of the British Army had been strapped, briskly dropping his sword in one neat arc in order to visually indicate that the order to fire had been given – upon which the cannon bucked, swinging a bit to one side on the recoil, and enveloped him in a halo of molten blood before his attentive native second-in-command even had a chance to get him out of the way.

Grammar stood a moment, suitably frozen, only his eyebrows – still lightly sketched in gold – indicating that he had not been born with red hair.

His second-in-command asked him something, presumably in Hindi, which Grammar spoke quite well; his service in India had soon revealed an unpredictable facility for languages. But the man's voice, usually so clear and strong, had apparently dulled to a scanty murmur in the brief space between order and result. Grammar narrowed his eyes at him, straining to read his lips.

"Repeat that," he said.

The second-in-command did. No enlightenment ensued – until frustration brought him around the other side of Grammar's blood-soaked head.

"...thee, art thou hurt? *Sahib*, I have asked thee—"

Grammar nodded, slowly. He was beginning to form a theory, but knew it would have to wait some while yet to be confirmed.

"Keep by that shoulder, I pray thee," he replied, "that I might have the benefit of thy protection a little closer to hand, in the future. And bring on the next one."

Hours later, when the work was done, a physician reported that, yes, the cannon's concussion had blown out one of Grammar's eardrums, causing him to consequently lose all hearing on his right side. Grammar nodded again, thanked him, and left the tent – refusing, gracefully, the doctor's offer of a pan and cloth to wash himself with before he saw his commanding officer to ask that his duty be extended to finding and executing those remaining sepoys who had fled beyond Calcutta's limits.

Grammar wore his mask of sepoy's blood until it flaked and ran, until his own sweat washed the worst of it away. Only then did he accept a handful of rice from his second-in-command, with which to rub away the flies which had gorged themselves and died in his sanguine crown. Because he could not shave, he avoided mirrors; occasionally, however, the unexpected sight of his own stained face would waver momentarily in streams and puddles, or grin at him from the broad surface of a rain-soaked leaf. And he would pause, obscurely flattered to recognize – once again – how well this red dust suited him, redefining all those subtle undercurrents which had once swum invisible beneath his honest British skin. Reminding him of who – and what – he had always been, in truth as well as unvoiced dream.

This was the beginning of it.

The two mental games he had kept to for most of his life, Home-face and Acting-as-though-one-were-Away, had suddenly been discarded in favor of a third, less well- remembered play: Don't-Care Island. For madness had always lain dormant in him, the hidden loot in his genetic plum-pudding – generations of half-lies and after-the-fact explanations for inexplicable behavior, as when his grandfather had suddenly thrust his Aunt Myrtle's forehead down against a lamp during the playing of a game of cards, causing her hair to blaze up like a torch. Or unknown facts, like the layers of mutilated bird- and mouse-corpses which had, for so long, fertilized Strait Gate Hall's incomparable gardens. Now, due to a combination of circumstances no Grammar had ever faced before or ever would again, that madness had been given whip-hand.

And thus it remained.

It was perfectly easy to be mad in India, Grammar soon found, as long as one were British, with some rank, some breeding and – most importantly – some money to prop one up. After all, his madness made no particular outward show (at least, not in civilized circles); he did not rave, or make insane gestures. He did not shirk his duty – on the contrary, he embraced it whole-heartedly, always tasting the wind for any trace of slaughter. And this was because the smell of incipient tragedy whipped his madness into a fire that made his pulse pound like a singing, liquid drum. It made him grind against himself in a frenzy of excitement. And once, when the battle was safely done and his group had all had their way with a certain woman of the sepoys, it made him smile at her in such a warm and reassuring manner that she wept to see him, thinking him an angel – before cutting open her belly with his bayonet, and thrusting his penis inside the slippery bag of her bladder until both their groins were stiff with urine, blood and semen.

To you who listen, meanwhile: I do not tell you these things to make you hate Lieutenant Desbarrats Grammar, o my beloved, and neither do I tell you them to make you fear or pity him. I tell you only what is true.

«« — »»

July, 1857:

"Another body burning on the ghat this evening; as I stood to watch, there came a sudden flood of bats, as big as crows, flying over our heads. Beyond, the river was covered with odd-looking boats, and a copper-colored sky bent over all, vivid and still as some frieze from the Arabian

Nights. (Memo: Romesh Singh reminds me that I have a riding engagement with the Misses Mill tomorrow.)"

Romesh Singh was Grammar's second-in-command; they had exchanged full names long before, at the outset of Grammar's posting, though Romesh Singh had never since been forward enough to ever suggest Grammar actually USE his when addressing him. The Misses Mill, meanwhile, were called Ottilie and Sufferance: One tall, one not, both equally dishwater-plain and more than financially equipped to compete for the hand of Calcutta's most eligible potential bridegroom. Their coordinated flirtation, polished and hollow as an acrobatic troupe's routine, stirred nothing in Grammar beyond a dim contempt – as was, perhaps, only to be expected. But he was between atrocities at the moment, and in need of diversion.

"Were one to report today's weather accurately in one's correspondence," said the Miss Mill at Grammar's left hand (tall, therefore Ottilie) – her head swathed with soaked gauze under a big straw hat, hooped skirts well-spotted at the hem with mould – "no person at Home would ever believe one did not exaggerate."

"Especially since it is so very *hot*, one would not know how to spell the word large enough," the other – Sufferance, presumably – murmured.

Grammar made some slight noise in reply, vague enough to let either Miss consider it confirmation of her acuity.

It was mid-July, and the rains had just begun. Large stains rose like veins from the bases of pillars, while green ones spread darkly down from wherever water cascaded off the roofs of British-owned Calcutta's fine, white lime-coated buildings. The rooms grew high with blistered drawings, damp-cracked books, mildewed daguerrotypes. Silverfish were everywhere, and the cream of the Raj were already eating off of white marble tables covered to some depths by a frail, crackling layer of wings discarded by flying ants. The aforementioned heat, meanwhile – undiminished, even in the teeth of such humidity – had split the ivory frame of Grammar's only miniature of his mother, allowing white maggots to eat up the paint.

(I was there as well, of course, as an unseen extra darkness in the blur of their horses' shadow. It was my face that made the beasts shy an hour or so later, throwing both Misses to their respective injury and death.)

Down by the riverside, an age-bent man lay fetally curled in a palanquin sprawled almost directly across their chosen path – blanched and sallow beneath his tan, half-lidded eyes too full of blood to close, his friends and family hovering in patient attendance as death grew palpably nearer with every shallow gasp.

Grammar reined in. "What do they do here?"

"He dies, *sahib*," Romesh Singh replied, shrugging.

Ottilie, generally a fraction quicker on the uptake than her sister, had already realized as much; gulping back bile behind one lace-gloved hand, she whimpered a genteel prayer, drawing Grammar's glance.

"Apparently," he agreed. Then, taking Ottlie's other hand – much to Sufferance's annoyance – and kicking his horse a step or two further on: "Suggest to this lot that he do it somewhere less obvious."

(Because it was only yet another scene of life under the Raj for all of them, o my beloved: A world of colorful shadows, glimpsed as from a great distance, as through the wrong end of binoculars – with no emotional response roused but that of the most casual interest as to whatever flat, exotic, meaningless vista might present itself next.) Romesh Singh, ever compliant, barked some Hindi curses at the party, who drew back in quick and respectful silence – all but one woman in a red-and-gold sari, who hoisted the child on her hip a little higher and told it, beneath her breath:

"Be calm now, my darling, that thou dost not draw his gaze – only turn away in quiet, and think no more on what he is. *Rhakshasa araha hai.*"

Grammar paused a moment, staring at her. His blue eyes dimmed to slits, so narrow they could only take proper stock of her flash by flash, a visual piece-meal: Red cloth draped loose over lithe brown skin, red dab of fixed bindi between her level black brows. Round curve of thigh flexing beneath red folds, enticingly graspable; flatter curve of belly stretched taut under the child's whimpering grip, inviting perforation. The whole of her lapped in red-tinged afternoon shadow and a sudden red wind that blew his own scarlet uniform jacket briefly open and shut, then open and shut again, rhythmless as a diseased heart's liquescent flap.

Through a rising hiss of arousal, he noticed – without even much anticipation – that his hand had already fallen, reflexively, to the hilt of his sword.

And Romesh Singh stirred uncomfortably in his saddle, sweat starting up on every limb, as he caught an improbable whiff of old blood – the death-inflected musk of British madness – from Grammar's clean blonde halo of hair.

"*Sahib*," he began, delicately.

Beside him, Ottilie Mill gave an equally well-modulated cough of pain. Suggesting, without rancor:

"You will bruise my hand if you continue to hold it so tightly, Lieutenant."

Grammar – abruptly remembering he and Romesh Singh were not, after all, free to act as though they were alone at this particular moment – nodded, politely, and let her go.

"My most sincere apologies," he told her, in English. And meant it.

(For she – and her sister as well, wide-eyed and silent behind the unfurled screen of her fan – were both so very little to him indeed that they deserved such meaningless courtesies.)

Then, switching back to Romesh Singh (and Hindi): "*This...*"

...indicating the woman, who stood stock-still before him, her eyes downcast...

"...has named me unfamiliarly, perhaps insultingly, as 'Rhakshasa'. Hast thou some idea of what she means by it?"

"No, *sahib*," replied Romesh Singh, his own eyes busy on the river's muddy bank – now thoroughly vacated, but for his country-woman and her child.

"I do not think thou art being entirely truthful," Grammar said, sweetly. "But no matter, for I do not care enough to inquire further."

To the woman: "As for thee, let us not meet again; for I tell thee truly, if ever I behold thy face within these city walls, I will certainly rip thy child's head from its throat and wash my face in its blood."

He urged his horse on, gesturing to the Misses, who followed, gratefully – along with Romesh Singh, keeping his usual careful distance. The woman watched them go, hugging her child to her, and heard the distant cries of a pack of children playing age-old games with forced confinement and flame: A scorpion in the dust, under the pitiless sun; a sloppy circle smeared first with saffron, then further limned in lamp-oil; a spark, falling. Simple pleasures.

Up and down the river, meanwhile, servants waited on the green lawns of British estates, their only duty to push any bloated corpses which might come floating by a little further on, so as not to spoil the view.

Later that night, after the accident, I was to complete my role in the day's events by appearing to the surviving Miss Mill – Sufferance, cheated of her chance at precedence yet again – in the guise of her dead sister, naked and desirable. Her resultant suicide by hanging, from a peepul tree by the very stretch of riverside where she and Ottilie had listened (all uncomprehending, neither being particularly fluent in Hindi) as Desbarrats Grammar threatened to bathe in baby's blood, only lent the Lieutenant further social cachet, increasing his glamour as Calcutta's resident homme fatal – a turn of events which struck me, surprisingly enough, as not entirely to my liking. For though I am many things (all things to all people, as the phrase so aptly goes) I had never before thought myself vain.

It is from this point onward, then, that I enter into the narrative fully for the first time, o my beloved – making myself known, initially more through rumor than deed, but with an ever-increasing sense of proximity.

Any given human being is, under even the most reassuring of circumstances, a frail and awful thing: A far-too-crackable ivory nut stuffed full of addictive meat, a bag of scented blood, a walking fever. But since it is so patently in the nature of the British to haunt, as much before their own deaths as after them, I now understand just how predictably suited the mantle of my well-earned reputation was to fit Grammar, once mass opinion had mistakenly assigned it to him. The whims of a beautiful (and mortal) monster are, in their own way, often more fearful a threat than something inexplicable can ever be – especially for those unlucky enough to stand directly in his way.

We seemed fated to be namesakes, he and I. So, to seal this undeclared liaison, I began a series of elaborations on my usual theme – variations in the tone of red, involving our mutual chosen prey (unrepentant and uncaught sepoys, whores and beggars, low-caste Indians of all descriptions). The credit for which was inevitably laid directly at Grammar's increasingly bemused...and more than slightly flattered... door.

Obviously – though it was really then long past the time for such small pleasantries as introductions – a meeting was in order.

My plans towards this end were aided greatly by the nature of Grammar's next posting, which would send him upriver – to a tiny, jungle-bound village named Amsore, outside of which a last, lone outpost of sepoys was rumored to still be in hiding – and away from all the "civilized" influences which conspired to keep him sane.

The continuing presence of Romesh Singh, already more than half in worshipful lust with his chosen British "master", promised to be similarly useful, as he remained one of the few who did not fear Grammar enough to desert him. His potential impact on the situation could in no way be underestimated, since – the innate idiocy of his desires aside – he was a wholly upright Sikh, a career soldier, no prude, and (above all) no fool. He knew that wanting Grammar was both morbid and perverse on his part, but the freak-ish glamor of a berserker must always hold its own attractions, especially for a military man.

He was also the only person near Grammar who not only *knew* exactly what the woman had meant by calling him Rhakshasa... but might actually be counted upon – eventually – to *tell* him.

All people of Hind – educated as they are in the laws of *dharma* – know both of the Wheel, which pulls them up or throws them down, and of enlightenment, whose attainment offers them es-cape from it. But for the Rhakshasa, whose forms are as many as their hungers are simple – with whom I may, respectfully, stake my claim of kinship – there is no escape, and no need of one. There is no Wheel for us. Nothing changes. From the moment we elect to leave it, everything stays firmly tied to the same crooked track of appetite and deception.

Novelty, however brief, is the only thing we have left to wel-come.

I had smelt Desbarrats Grammar coming from as far off as his landing at Calcutta-*ghat*, wading up through the river's muddy shallows, as the bearers struggled with his gear: A pale blaze of frustrated heat with nothing but itself for fuel, too quenchless for remorse. There was a hole inside of him that demanded either light, ever more light, or an equal and engulfing darkness. Romesh Singh still quietly offered him the former, which he spurned; it hurt Grammar's terrible British pride, I venture, to think the solution for his many sins could have been something so simple as love.

So he remained alone: A promise of sport, on my part.

And a possibility – however scant – of danger.

«« — »»

August, 1857:

"Some unidentifiably rancid stink seems to hang over everything I touch these days, always rising, though already thick enough to swim in. This morning I woke feverish as ever, boots on and my clothes stuck fast to me, my own sweat so hot against my skin it made me wonder whether I had slept in blood. I am also running out of usable paper, a fact which does not disturb me overmuch, since I no longer know who I might possibly be writing this for."

Amsore had been one of the last places to succumb to the Mutiny, long after the boats at Cawnpore had drifted away on a bloody tide, and the well of the Bibighar was stopped with the beaten corpses of British women and children. But even as Amsore's settlers dithered in their punkah-shaded homes, a preparatory whisper had nevertheless gone up and down the nearby river's banks, borne on the dust from Meerut and running deeper than its own mud-sluggish current: A promise of support, of like-mindedness; of loyalty kept carefully unvoiced, and weapons kept hidden but ready. It was the old, old cry of the surreptitious sepoy-sympathizer, soon to become Grammar's adopted mantra: *Sub lal hogea hai* – "Everything has become red."

In this particular case, however, the signal had never been given time enough to go any further than that first glad acknowledgement. The Mutiny was a failure, a frenzied knot of rage without the necessary guidance to keep it from strangling itself in its haste to stem the "White Plague"'s spread. Calcutta fell again, its Black Hole found and emptied, and the few stragglers remaining fled – most straight into the British army's vengeful hands, some of them to Amsore...and beyond.

Into the jungle.

Outside of Amsore's limits, everything familiar falls abruptly away into a green abyss: Screaming monkeys, unseen eyes, filtered rays of feeble, leaf-washed sun. Snakes hang dappled and silent as vines, sectioned by their most muscular areas, and here and there – stumbling half-blind through an endless funnel of foliage – one trips headlong across knots of roots from which erupt bright, fleshy flowers, big enough to drink from. The *Ramayana* calls forests home to wind, darkness, hunger and great terrors – a poetic description, but not entirely inaccurate. Jungle-swallowed, one must eke out direction; one finds one's way with senses other than those most usually given or employed.

Outside Amsore, the trees hide miles of ripe, interlocking tracklessness: Verdant ventriculation, sap-fed growth, a living maze. A wholly fitting provenance for lovers, or for madmen.

They found the camp at sunset, through a hazy glare of red already half-deepening to grey as twilight retook its nightly portion, adapting all it touched to darkness. Insects still hung thick around the ash-heap of a dampened fire, on which a brass pot full of half-cooked rice sat abandoned. Further still, a few hastily-improvised huts of mud and fallen wood vomited scraps of clothing or the odd rusty weapon, spoiled supplies and broken crockery. Deritus lay everywhere, the spoor of retreat, scattered and rank. Grammar's party – the bulk of them barefoot, and thus more likely to consider where they chose to step – picked their way carefully through it, stabbing at every heap and corner with their bayonets. Except themselves, nothing moved but those few small creatures one occasionally heard rustle in the grass, and – just above – three lone kites (barely visible, through a bald patch in the jungle's roof) which dipped and cawed in a slice of red-grey sky.

At the crotch of one overhanging tree's trunk, a wet, red, knotted rag of some not easily identifiable substance glittered. Under the tree was something else, equally red, but moaning; this proved – after Romesh Singh was so good as to kick it gingerly over – to be what remained of a man who had been partially flayed. It was a portion of his forcibly donated hide, apparently, that gave the tree its surreal extra coat.

"How long since is he dead?" Grammar called across the clearing, idly running his sword through a sack of dried beans that soon proved both soaked enough to rot, and full of maggots.

"He lives yet, *sahib*," Romesh Singh replied.

Mildly impressed by such resilience, Grammar stooped to examine the man, who lay gasping – long, low, shallow gulps of liquid air, the humid foretaste of approaching rainfall – but inert, a thin line of bloodshot ivory just showing under each eyelid. Using the flat of his blade, Grammar scraped lightly over the man's denuded chest, flicking the bright half-circle of raw flesh where his right nipple had once been back to full, painful life.

The man reared up with a scream, then back again. His eyes, all white around their irises, fell on Grammar – and immediately widened further in horrified recognition.

"Where are thy fellows, offal?" Grammar asked him.

The man coughed, wetly. At Grammar's nod, Romesh Singh kicked him lightly in the head, forcing him further sidelong into the mud. The man doubled up, vomiting earth mixed with blood on Grammar's boots. With a little moue of disgust, Grammar put one shiny black heel to the back of the man's neck, pinning him down, and leant again to rephrase his initial request, this time a bit more insistently. Adding:

"It will do thee no good to lie. Remember, thou hast some skin yet left to lose."

The man drew a fresh gulp of air, mixed with a fair chunk of his own waste.

"Thou...knowest," he managed, at last.

Grammar frowned.

"I fear," he said, "that thou art mistaken."

Even he, however, could see that the man was clearly far beyond dissembling.

Grammar looked to Romesh Singh. Behind them, someone gave a nervous little step backwards, crushing something not particularly loud, but obviously breakable.

"Thou knowest," the man repeated, dully.

"Then it can do no harm to tell me again."

The man spit, a weak, retching stream of pink, which Grammar easily avoided. His dying eyes took on a blank gleam of un-satisfied malice.

"Human tiger," he said. "Blood-drinker. Evil *thing*. Why dost thou return? Why bring thy lackies, when you needed none upon thy first visit? We were many; now my fellows are gone I know not where. And it was thee that brought us to this pass, white corpse-eating dog, thou mocking horror. It was *thee*."

(And here occurs a mystery you city-dwellers cannot hope to know, o my beloved, especially without the benefit of personal ex-perience: The sheer, shocking speed with which light drains away when sunset has ended, here in the jungle's heart – in one bright gush, like blood from a slashed throat, leaving nothing behind but a certain stillness; the hush of drawn breath, or the barest of un-voiced sighs.)

On Grammar's deaf side, one of the company blurted, all un-thinking: "Rhakshasa!"

Grammar did not hear it, of course – but caught Romesh Singh's brief little jerk of reaction from the corner of one eye, and whipped quickly around, following it to its trembling, rooted source. His pistol had already appeared in one hand, amusingly enough; primed, aimed and ready, almost before he had conscious-ly thought to draw it.

"Who said that?" he asked.

No one answered. Undeterred, Grammar shifted only slightly, sighting down the barrel at the soldier he judged most clearly in range.

"You, I think," he said, coolly. And pulled the trigger.

Romesh Singh shut his eyes. There had been a bazaar boy the company had adopted, not long since – silent and tensile with near-starvation, good mainly for scouring pots, packing kits (but only when there was time to watch him do it, for he had never quite gotten over his early habits of casual thievery), and running those few small errands his shaky command of English would al-low for. Grammar – stalking restlessly around camp, quietly ablaze with his usual nimbus of potential lunacy, as everyone took care to stay out of his way – had not even seemed to notice his existence, until the child made the understandable mistake of laughing at a whispered joke while still within Grammar's eyeshot. Without breaking stride, Grammar had swerved to scoop the boy up and carried him into the cooking tent, where he ground him face-first into an open cask of chili powder for some long moments, then dropped him. To stand, watching patiently, as the boy thrashed and huffed awhile at his feet – nose, eyes and throat all swollen shut, the rest a tight, red mask of burns – before suffocating on what later proved to be a flood of his own shocked mucus.

And he, Romesh Singh, had shut his eyes then as well, so as not to have to see Grammar's scarlet-coated back draw up all at once like a shaken snake, straightening with pleased arousal at the spectacle of his own cruelty.

(Thinking: *Oh*. Like a bell. *Oh*, a heart-beat's sharp-soft squeeze between rib and gut, tolling. This is so wrong. I am so very wrong to even be here, with him.)

Gunshot and thunder blended, signalling the torrent's arrival. And before this one (now forever nameless) soldier's corpse had fallen to earth, the rest of Grammar's company simply broke and ran in the face of Grammar's insanity – always no more than a reputable quirk, until it had finally turned their way.

The flayed man gave a laugh, drawing Grammar's second shot. The pistol jammed; Grammar swore and threw it after them, as the soldiers' shadows faded like ghosts under a curtain of warm monsoon rain, leaving officer and second-in-command alike behind, entirely at the forest's mercies.

Grammar snarled, a tiger's half-cough.

"Cowardly bastards," he said, in English. Adding, contemptuously: "'Rhakshasa', am I? Hardly an opinion worth dying over."

Romesh Singh, wisely enough, said nothing – his own eyes kept firmly shut – as a long, wet, green moment passed over them, darkening both their scarlet coats to rust.

Grammar laughed, and let the sheath drop away from his sword, falling point-down. It quivered by one foot, mud-supported, forgotten.

"Well, come then, my shadow," he told the curtain of underbrush before him (having, without even noticing, slid fluidly back into Hindi). "Or shall I haste to meet thee? For either way, you will find me as I find myself: Ready."

And still Romesh Singh stood, feeling the rain seep down through his clothes and lave his trembling body abruptly to life, every nerve set winking in the gloom like unseen stars above.

(Thinking only: *But now we are alone at last, thou and I. Together.*)

They were both wrong, of course. Grammar, all his impressively flaunted rage aside, was nothing near to ready – as Romesh Singh might have told him, had he cared to solicit a second opinion – and neither was alone, with or without the other.

For I was already here. As I always had been.

≪≪——≫≫

The rain, the mud, the dead and cooling bodies, the silent trees. I was present and accounted for in all of it at once, a speck of me everywhere the eye might care to light, pixilating slowly to fruition. In the very air itself, between every falling raindrop – sub-dust, sub-viri, void-breath on the back of the neck, a shadow on the face of the whole. I spread out around the carcass of the dead former sepoy like a stain, over the clearing's seared floor, so fragrant yet with ash; and ah, but that fire had burned brightly, for all it was only a heap of corpses doused in lamp-oil. Brown corpse melting to black, black rivulets twining like veins across the soaked earth, black snakes rising in their wake. A black river, abruptly, in full flood, lapping the British soldier's remains in as well with no visible distinction – rearing, seeping, clotting – knitting both together like some prescient scab, the kind that outlines itself before a wound has even been opened.

One hot whiff caught on the wind, a brief, intestinal stink: Eau de massacre. One sentient platelet left swimming in a sea of blood, shed and unshed alike.

Beyond the fire's sodden ring, Desbarrats Grammar had already slashed the first layer of leaves aside and forged on ahead into the jungle (bent on finding any kind of explanation for the night's work, or his sadly smirched reputation, that did not involve the word Rhakshasa), leaving Romesh Singh to plead vainly after him – sick to heart and increasingly cold, with his empty hands ineffectually raised against the drumming rain.

(For the bell tolled in him still, o my beloved – fluid, subterranean. Mateless, but crying for its mate. And this suited me so well I would have smiled to see it, had I but the lips to smile with – or the eyes to see.)

Such a lack, however, was easily remedied.

"Romesh Singh," I called him, softly. He turned.

Upright now, a loosely wavering column of matte black against the clearing's larger blackness – hollow, scarring, extruded from the space between all things – I drew myself in tight, and called Grammar's all-too-familiar face to me, simultaneously making myself both a spine to hold it up and a skull to hang it on. I let flesh drip over me, pore by pore.

Over the flesh, I drew skin; over the skin, blood.

Naked under the rain's caress, I opened Grammar's eyes – so blind, so pale, so very, very British, in the raw mask that was his truest reflection – and raised them, meeting Romesh Singh's.

"My good soldier," I said.

He swallowed, pupils wide, his dry throat grating tentatively back upon itself.

"Thou..." he began. "Thou art..."

"Oh, *I*." Stepping, cat-sure on Grammar's smooth-soled feet, to print the mud between us. "A wandering minstrel, I," I said. "A knight of air and darkness."

"...Rhakshasa," finished Romesh Singh.

He said it with a sigh, so soft the word was part of his exhalation. That fatal – that *only* – name. I nodded at the sound. To prove the truth of his assumption, I spread my hands – my fingers – on which the claws bend back so far they are not really claws at all, but twisting knives of sharpest horn.

"Shreds and patches," I said. "Dead man's fingernails."

And I peeled back Grammar's lips, to show how my teeth arced up from his narrow British jaw like some ill-timed jest, sharp and yellow as a carrion dog's.

Yet Romesh Singh held his ground, back straight, like the warrior he was.

(For we both knew Grammar was too far ahead now to hear him, even if he chose to call for help. But no man really wishes aid at such a moment, o my beloved – not when his longest-held dream finally stalks towards him on nude white feet, arms out, and smiling.)

"Let down thy hair, my brother," I suggested, "that I may feel its weight."

Lightly, surely, I laid my claws on either side of Romesh Singh's jaw and worked the muscles like hinges, pinching his lips open – and though I had hoped (if I could) to grant him a gentle exit, my hunger soon betrayed itself in their sharpness, rimming the corner of his mouth with blood.

He gasped, swallowing it.

"Be merciful to me," he whispered. "As... he would be."

Oh, loyal, loving, deluded man. A born victim, if ever there was one.

"Ah," I said, gently. "But we are the same, he and I. So I cannot promise you what *he* would never give."

A flash of moon, bisected, fell over us through the trees; the blood caught its light, sparking a hot copper flare of lust that made my own lips abruptly wet. To compensate, I licked his clean.

Our tongues touched.

This distracted him enough, hopefully, to make what followed only a brief (if, no doubt, rather unpleasant) surprise – as I suddenly forced the rest of my head through his mouth until his head cracked like a wishbone, rupturing his throat, making his face my collar, spraying teeth. Hugging him to me, *into* me, as I rooted for brains in the blind, red ruin of his skull.

I suppose I had foreseen – somewhat faintly, considering the Lieutenant's continuing capacity for unpredictable behavior – that the sound of this process would draw Grammar back to the clearing. Not that it mattered much either way, at this point, though forgoing a prolonged chase (wearing Romesh Singh's now-uninhabited skin, perhaps?) would certainly have saved me a little time. But just as the consumption of a long-desired object tends to erase whatever wait one may have had to put oneself through in order to attain it, so strategy must inevitably dim in appetite's shadow. Blood filled my eyes; I drank deep, and gave myself up to ecstasy.

Presently, however, I felt Grammar's blade graze the back of my neck – wing-sharp, a dragonfly's delicate needle – and knew my plans had not been laid in vain.

Popping Romesh Singh's remaining eye between my teeth (just in case, should intelligible conversation yet prove necessary), I turned – grinning – to show him his own face: Red from brow-line to Adam's apple, chin slicked with fresh overflow. And a jolt passed between us, starburst-quick – not one of shock, so much, as of recognition. The Lieutenant's prim British mouth crumpling like an insulted cat's, ludicrous with embarrassed amazement, to find his unsought namesake's pleasures were so very like his own.

The sword, however, did not waver.

I smiled at the sight – and swung Romesh Singh's carcass like a dancing partner, dipping it towards him, as if offering him a bite.

"You must be hungry," I said. "Please: Do not hesitate to indulge yourself."

Grammar snarled again (his sole response in such circumstances, it seems) and stabbed me through the throat; I flexed, and sucked him further in, immersing him up to his armpit. For one endless moment, too paralytic even for struggle, he felt my internal organs stroke him seductively, and gagged. At which point I interrupted his train of nausea in mid-heave, just as gorge met gullet, and assured myself of his complete attention by thrusting my own arm (up to the elbow) inside his armpit – cracking ribs, perforating lung, expelling a warm rush of half-digested food from the lower esophagus, all in quest of that wildly-fluttering knot of muscle he called a heart.

Grammar coughed, and went rigid. His eyes turned up. But it was not my intention to let him die quite so quickly, now that we had finally met.

My fingers closed fast around left and right ventricles, pumping him awake. Saying, solicitously:

"Oh, no. Be so good as to not leave me just yet, Lieutenant."

With an effort, Grammar forced his eyes to focus on me. A rictus pulled at his cheek. Words formed, along with a bright new bubble of blood.

"Do... your... worst," he replied, carefully. "I... don't care."

I gave him a wide, blank smile – and chanted, singsong:

"Don't-care didn't care. Don't-care was wild. Don't-care stole plum and pear, like any beggar's child."

Sucking him closer – the maw that had been me (and him as well, come to think of it) now covering almost all of him below the shoulder, sprouting a fine interior coat of teeth that pressed and teased, unable to resist sampling at the anticipated feast; here a shaven fingernail, there a beheaded nipple.

Looking down, I could see his genitals begin – all unnoticed, for once – to stiffen.

"But Don't-care was *made* to care," I continued, blithely. "Don't-care was *hung*. Don't-care was put in the pot, and boiled 'til he was done."

And I gave his heart another little squeeze, for emphasis.

Oh, yes, his Empire might well linger far into the next century. But *he'd* be going home much sooner – and not to London, either, where he might at least occasionally be able to buy someone to kill. Back to some dreary Suffolk estate, to take up the middle child's portion, dazzling idiots behind the hay-wains with a fading grab-bag of exotic memories, doomed to forever wear the mask of respectability. To marry, to breed, to be buried and rot. And all in a dim, small place that no longer held anything but potential boredom for him, where no one would know to stiffen at his scent, or whisper his name in fear as he passed by.

Well, we were in the jungle now. And the law of the jungle is universally understood: Eat, or be eaten.

"Have no fear, Lieutenant," I murmured. "For you may count yourself assured that, even if no else does, I will take care to always award you a place in my memory."

Grammar blinked, his eyes already red-lined and darkening, as the cilia slowly hemorrhaged. His mouth worked, but words failed him. I brought mine closer, in case a final sentence might yet be forthcoming.

Then he gave a gushing whoop, and laughed out loud, spattering our mutual visage with liquid viscera.

Whereupon – with no regrets to speak of – I bit the mad bastard in half.

≪≪——≫≫

And so at last we come to you, o my beloved – little raggamuffin, would-be tourist district date rapist. You, with your fresh-cut fade and precious Apache Indian concert tickets, with barely enough real Hindi under your belt to tell the demure Calcutta girl you once thought I was – when first we met, you all swagger and chatter, spinning yourself a man-sized noose of lies as you steered me towards this oh-so-deserted alley – a dirty joke. Here in this bright, drunken, filthy place, so full of neon and flies, this overhanging crush of shacks where one open window lets slip a lick of the latest Bollywood duet, another the drone of Johnny Cash falling down, down, down. The ring of fire, the endless Wheel, spinning.

You thought me merely a bumpkin to be robbed of her virginity, and yourself the true synthesis of Anglo-Indian culture, post-British Occupation. But I believe you now know better.

The Mutiny of 1857 marked one whole turn of the Wheel for India and Britain alike, replacing up most firmly with down; it gave the British (via the East India Company) a perfect excuse to stay in India, to seize control, to cut down the guilty and the "loyal" alike in their lust for gain. They imposed their own system of values on everything they met: Breaking apart clans, ransacking treasuries, erasing whole villages, disinheriting heirs because they were adopted rather than biological, and deeding the lands involved to a plump little Queen, more concerned with the state of her marriage than with exactly whose bleeding hands all these exotic gifts had been ripped from.

Soon enough, Army replaced Company – but nothing really changed. The British swept in like a tide of cockroaches, mating and killing as they willed, forcing themselves in at the top of our caste system in order to escape their own. They stayed until they had outworn their welcome a thousand times over, until those brought up in India – but still calling an England they had never even seen "Home" – were immune to even its most enticing charms. They maintained their stiff spines upright against heat and dust, forgetfulness, sensual excess and nonviolent protest alike, clinging to their Indian holdings even as the rest of their duskless Empire crumbled – slowly but surely – from within, until their provisional government here was nothing but a skeleton at the feast, last guest left at a singularly unpopular party, still busily stuffing food down its denuded jaws and protesting all the while (whining like a spoiled child, even as the bouncers edge it towards the door) that it is not sleepy, that it has hours yet to revel, wishes yet to make, and room for much, much more.

At last, however, the British *did* leave – freeing us to return to the long-postponed business of slaughtering each other over differences of race, creed, history. The Wheel had turned again, as it always will.

Yes, it burns, burns, burns, this ring of fire. It keeps on spinning. And I hope you find it hot enough for your liking, o my beloved, just as the Lieutenant and I do – and have, ever since that night in 1857, when his mad appetites mingled so very surely with my own immortal ones, along with his stringy white meat. That night, when I bit through him at one swallow – rind to pulp, red juice spurting, like an overripe piece of fruit – only to have the taste of him linger not only in my mouth but in every other part of me as well: Infected, infectious, infec*ting*.

Before that night, I had no "true shape" to speak of. It was my curse, and my strength – this restless formlessness; this unstinting, innate empathy pulling me forward through the centuries, making every new thing I touched my potential refuge. This much, at least, has never altered. I can still be anything I choose, if I choose.

But now, whenever I relax my hold, I flow back – relentlessly – into *him*.

Namesake to namesake: The mask and the mirror. Desbarrats Grammar usurped my title, so I made him my prey; I consumed his flesh, and it engulfed me. What was an accidental mislabeling has become a complex truth. Here in the ring of fire, Lieutenant Grammar and I twine tight as mating heartworms, joined at the supernatural equivalent of DNA – the Mutiny that walks like whatever it chooses to. We catch and claw. And at last, almost two hundred years later – as the Wheel, in our case, fails to turn – between the two of us, each only half-there to begin with, something has finally evolved resembling a coordinated whole. *Sub lal hogea hai*, with a vengeance; so much so that neither of us – former occupier or former occupied – can truthfully tell where we once began, or where we now end.

For were we ever so very different, really?

Liars both. Madmen, cannibals. And monsters.

Ah, but I see you yet stir in my embrace – so slowly, so feebly. Your lips move. Do you wish to refute my words? To confirm them, perhaps?

Lean closer, then, o my beloved. Do not be shy, but do choose your side wisely. Lean closer, closer. And speak up, I pray thee – for I am still quite deaf in this one ear.

Crossing The River

> *...dreaming evil, I have done my hitch*
> *over the plain houses, light by light:*
> *lonely thing, twelve-fingered, out of mind.*
> *A woman like that is not a woman, quite.*
> *I have been her kind.*
> – Anne Sexton

Here's how it probably happens, that first time, if you're anything like me...

Your Momma wakes you in the middle of the night, takes you up on the mountain. Says she has something fine and secret to show you, something that sets you and her apart from all the rest of the common herd. *This here is our'n, baby girl*, she tells you, *gifted by Him who made us to the whole of our blood – and you more than most, darlin'. You more than any.*

And what is it you see once she's got you up there, anyhow? Maybe a dog with horns or a black cat bigger than a bull, a goat with women's breasts and owl's eyes, some sort of beast having ten horns, ten crowns, and on every head the name of blasphemy. Or maybe just a pale man with a black beard and a sad face, like the ghost of Osama bin Laden, who lays one hand on the top of your skull, the other on the sole of your foot and laughs, saying: *Shall I really take you for gift on only your mother's word, all of you, everything which lies between this hand and that? What true mischief could I ever possibly do in this world with such a little one as you, Gley Chatwin's gal?*

If you're anything like me, which most just ain't. Because my Momma was a witch, same as hers, and so on; it's from their side of things that I can't stand the touch of salt, can't cry real tears. But I sure ain't no hill-woman like her, either, out hollering to Old Scratch every full moon – and I never did kiss any man's ass but for money, horns or no. I got my pride.

So: I can throw out a fetch, given time, and dirt enough to build one from. Bring anyone my way and keep 'em long as I

87

want, using nothing but a drop of their blood, a drop of mine and a hank of my own long hair to tie the knot with. Spread out a pack of cards and tell you your future; knock a rag against a stone and raise up a wind, then write nonsense words on myself to whip that same wind into a Force Three twister; make doors slam, tables tap and call up a ghost to talk through me, just like that woman of Endor who got old King Saul in so much trouble with the Almighty.

I've read some books, too; Montague Summers, Scott's *Discoverie*, Stuart's *Daemonologie*. The mighty Hammer. I know my history, such as it is. My culture is different than yours, older still than the Travellers with their tricks or the Injuns with their anger – ain't just moonshine and trailers, back where I come from. And I got but two things to blame for everything I've done since, I suspect: Gley Chatwin and the Daddy she chose to get me on her, her cold witch blood and his hot demon seed. Or three, maybe, if you choose – like I do – to also count my own bad self.

But if any of the above meant I could witch myself right in and out of prison anytime I felt like it…well, we wouldn't have too much to talk about, now, would we?

'Course, biology does count for something, at least in terms of execution. If I was a man, they'd probably have to keep me in Ad Seg 24/7, for fear of me trying to stick my dick in anything that moved close enough past me for me to grab at it. Being I'm not, though, my "unrepentant serial sexual offender" sins always tended to err more on the side of *knew I shouldn't've, but I went on ahead and did it anyways:* It, her, him, them. Whatever.

I mean, sure – my not-Daddy messed around with me some, just like everybody else's. But I'll gladly own the rest.

Sometimes I feel like I must've been drunk, high, picking up trade and robbing folks blind for a straight year before the Powers That Be finally got around to slinging me right back in where I so obviously needed to be. Seems like I looked up the once and I was in custody, looked up twice and I was in court, allocuting before sentence. Looked up the third time and I was already dug deep down here in Mennenvale Women's Penitentiary, Block A, max security – sweating hard, getting clean; not such a bad place to do it, either, when all's said and done. Certainly does concentrate the mind wonderfully.

Getting *into* Hell, that's the easy part, always; people do it every damn day, though far more often by accident than by intent. It's getting out that's harder, 'specially on demand – though it's not like *that* can't be done either, exactly.

Not so long's you can only make yourself patient enough to wait for just the right sort of...leverage.

One way or the other, what you maybe need to know most about me is this: I don't think of myself as a monster. Never have. Never will.

But then again, I guess most monsters don't.

«« —— »»

Now, leverage comes in many different forms, by many different methods. I mean, if you're looking to understand just how somebody like me ever came into partnership with two kick-ass do-gooders like Samaire and Dionne Cornish in the first place, much can probably be made of the plain fact that Cornish and Chatwin lie almost right next to each other come roll-call, alphabetically speaking...but then, there's really no earthly reason I wouldn't've noticed them anyhow, eventually – Samaire, in particular. And not for the reasons you might initially assume, given my record.

That same morning, just before the fish-truck pulled in, I was lounging at the cell-door with my pretty little Maybelle already all ground up against me, one thigh slung so tight over mine I could fair feel the heat of her through my pants (sweat-moist, or what-have-you), over my hip-pocket. Murmuring in my ear, as she did it:

"They got the Cornish sisters comin' to call in this batch, Alleycat. Pulled life plus nine-nine between 'em both, mainly 'cause of the three strikes rule." Pause. "Well, that, and they had a whole car full'a concealed weapons, when the Feebs finally caught their asses at the Border."

She was mainly putting on a show for rubes like that new C.O., Brenmer, who threw us a full-gawk double-take as he went by, pulling at his crotch like he'd suddenly noticed someone slipped ants in his shorts.

"Oh, you're so bad, baby girl," I told her, and watched her pout, more in confirmation than denial. "But I guess you aim to be."

"I do."

"Thought so." I pulled her closer, adding, in a murmur: "Hell, ain't like *I* mind."

And oh, didn't she just perk up and glow at that? 'Cause May always *was* easy to please…just as well, what with her being Grade-A born victim meat thrown straight into the lions' den, rare and bloody as any potential bitch-turned-butch might hope for. Her ability to enjoy herself under pressure was probably pretty much all that helped keep her sane, given the circumstances.

Was a time when I could do sweet (if not innocent) fairly well myself, but prison ain't exactly conducive to that. Oh, I guess I could glamour up now and convince you my skinny stringbean bones were sleek and foxy, this hillbilly hatchet-face of mine "interesting" rather than offputting, my many visible scars fascinating rather than freakish. But one of the few things I like about lockdown is how you can breeze by on half-speed, or even quarter-, you just know how to play it right; talk people in and out of things like a human would, fuck and fight to a stand-still without ever even having to use your own full strength.

That's how I got myself my pocket-money business, running mail and brokering favors; how I snagged May right out from under M-vale's former baddest Daddy-miss of all time, Verena Speller, who – after an extended turn in that extremely locked-down part of Ad Seg known as the Finishing School – eventually decided that having only three super-stacked blonde groupies with Nazi nicknames in her Aryan harem was probably impressive enough.

No magic involved in either case, nor (in fact) did it need to be…just like with fishing in Head C.O. Guard Erroll Curzon, King Prick in a whole jailhouse full of corrupt hacks, and so in love with his own piggy self that I sure didn't have to raise any Hell but the usual in order to convince him he was the one raping *me* every so often, not the other way 'round.

"I ain't afraid of you, Chatwin, you goddamn witch," he'd say, not even knowing how right he'd got it. And I'd just nod along, smiling. Thinking: '*Course not, boss. Not like I scare most folks, after all.*

Hell, sometimes? Sometimes, I even scare myself.

So he'd lumber on and off, huffing hard. And every time he did, I'd inject just a hint more of my poison in him, to keep him firmly on the hook; never did have to worry about falling pregnant, which was a mercy. Going by past record alone, I don't really think I can conceive – not with a human man, anyhow. Not with the legacy of what my Momma conjured up coursing through my bloodstream.

Holler magic – blood, tears, sweat and spit. Bodily fluids of all descriptions. The good part is, it's very direct. Bad part...well, *one* bad part...is, it sure won't get you out of jail, not once you're already in. Not when any given escape scenario means you gotta beguile each and every one of the hundred-some people between you and the front door individually, one by one by one. Daily penal system grind aside, ain't no one has *that* sort of time to waste.

And: "Here we go," Maybelle said, jumping off of me, while the P.A. simultaneously crackled and Guard Curzon's voice rang out: "*COUNT*, LADIES! ALL ASSES TO THE RAIL!" A general stomp and shuffle, a screech of contact locks; the gates slid open, admitting our newest members. And here was where I finally saw the Cornish sisters for myself, as they stepped onto Mennenvale Block A, with my very own eyes: Caul-touched, always slightly narrowed against the light.

And just like that, not even a minute gone, I knew Samaire Cornish – the younger, taller, even blonder of the two – was my sister. Not just a sister, a fellow practitioner of the Art – like Gioia Azzopardi, Dom the Cop's *stregha* widow, or that gal they call Needle, over in Psych – but a true something-sibling, with Hell's own mark spread all over her too-calm face like an invisible stain. I think I know my own bad blood well enough to recognize the taint of it in others, even when it's hid inside their veins.

I also noticed that while both of 'em were cute in their own particular ways, all their (many, inventive, enticing) tattoos were strictly magical in intent. Tough little Dionne had the Gran Tetragrammaton on the back of her neck, Solomon's Seal overtop her heart and the holy name of Saint Michael Archangel girding both arms, just like the warrior she was; Samaire's whole rangy body, on the other hand, seemed inked up with spell-script specifically designed to not only keep things out but keep things *in*, as well.

Those images looped above and beneath her skin, buzzing against each other like rot.

Not that anyone but me could have told, by either witch-sight or plain-sight. But then again, that is precisely why they call such things "occult". From the Latin, *occultus*, "to conceal". Because their true meaning, their real story is…

…a secret.

≪≪──≫≫

What I knew about the Cornishes before I met 'em boiled down to what everyone else did, albeit with one very important difference. In a nutshell, the sisters' act had kept 'em criss-crossing backroads America for upwards of seven years now, laying a trail of odd mayhem that'd grown into sketchy legend. They robbed gun-shops and places of worship, desecrated graves and left arcane graffiti behind; kicked ass, too – an unholy lot of it. And told the FBI that the people they'd killed along the way weren't people at all but demons in human form, preying on the innocent. That they'd *had* to kill 'em, along with anybody those demons'd touched, to keep Armageddon far off and little children safe at night. Which was why, in the main, they were in here now.

Digging back, what seemed to've kicked it all off was the State-assisted death of the man whose name they both wore, Jeptha Cornish. Their paper trail started where his finally went to ground: Raised off the grid by like-minded outlaw parents, a demon-slaying cult of two, up 'til Jeptha was popped by the law for killing his common-law woman Moriam, somehow managing to reduce her body to a flesh slurry so fluid its provenance had to be back-traced through her daughters' DNA. Local constabulary thought he might'a used a woodchipper, though they later had to admit they couldn't find *that*, either – along with much of a motive, beyond the usual hit parade of *well, he's weird* and *well, so was she* and *since when's a damn domestic get this complicated, for shit's sweet sake?*

Money, sex and/or parentage, the Jerry Springer trifecta. Maybe she'd been cheating, or maybe he'd just thought she was; maybe he'd figured out Samaire might not be his after all, not to mention the basic difficulty inherent in some self-taught backwoods exorcist's wife popping out hellspawn on the down-low, no matter *how* that circumstance might've originally come about.

The girls went into foster care either way, separated for most of high school; Dionne did a tour in Iraq, then rabbitted after she got tapped for stop-loss turnaround, taking a load of Army weaponry with her when she did. Samaire, armed with a sprinter's scholarship and a panel of genius-level I.Q. scores, managed to make it into law school by twenty, but dropped out just before finals of her second year. Her neighbours in residence said she got a visit from some woman looked almost exactly like her, except for being half a head shorter, about a week before she packed up and hit the highway. And the rest, as they say, is history.

Like most history, though, the really *intriguing* bits are always those ones which rarely get written down. Like the difference between the official version, say, and mine: Where most probably considered Samaire and Dionne Cornish either crazy or faking, I knew they were right. Didn't necessarily mean I approved of their methods, let alone their raison d'etre – they did kill monsters, after all. Awkward.

Yet that, more'n anything, was what made Samaire's potential heritage issues so very…interesting, might be the word. Especially within context.

≪≪——≫≫

Back in the now, meanwhile, the new fish got 'emselves all lined up, "yes sir"-ing quick-smart in turn, as Guard Curzon checked their names off his print-out. "Ahmad, Zaidee. Burch, Lisanne. Cornish, Dionne. Cornish, Sahmeyer…"

"SahMEERah," the Cornish in question corrected, quietly.

Curzon frowned. "What'd you say there, convict?"

"That it's pronounced SahMEERah. Boss."

"Oh, really. And what is it makes you think I give a good Goddamn about cross-checking the correctness of all your little biographical details? I look like Oprah friggin' Winfrey to you, cupcake?"

Others might've met this sort of dickery with a similarly harsh word, or even a punch, and ended up in Ad Seg for a month as of Day One for it; Dionne sure as Hell looked like she wanted to kick him where it counted, from the way her fists balled up. Samaire, though, just shrugged, and made herself look somehow small –

small as a gal who loomed over Curzon by a good two inches while slumping ever could, at any rate. Projecting, if not saying right out loud: *Nope.*

"Thought not," Curzon shot back, and flounced off to finish count, Guard Brenmer hot on his heels. Which left us all alone together, free to get acquainted however we felt most inclined.

«« — »»

But I didn't approach 'em right then, no. I watched 'em a while instead, from long-range – across the yard, passing in the halls, two tables over in mess. Sent Maybelle to do fly-bys; she told me how they'd been split up for work (Samaire got library, Dionne got workshop), but stuck together as cellmates (no surprises there). Kept my eyes peeled for whatever scuffles might arise, so's I could confirm for myself both what quarters said scuffles might come from, and how the Cornishes might deal with 'em, if and when they did.

Now some fools will speak from hubris and say that we women are too frail to fight, and some'll speak from rosy innocence and say we're too compassionate. Neither of these is true. What is true is that unlike men, women – *most* women – don't fight for *fun*. A woman throws down with you, she wants you either dead, or beaten bad enough you'll never look her in the eyes again. Two women throw down, it don't stop until it stops for good, or *gets* stopped. Which is why women mostly don't start a fight unless we're either damn sure we'll win it or we got no other choice, and why we learn right quick to tell the fights we can win from the ones we can only hope to survive.

Even the dumbest of M-vale's denizens, it seemed, could see with a single look neither Cornish was a winnable fight. Around them the subtle vicious swirls of violence roiled on, while they floated through it like pumice in a Yellowstone caldera, untouched, untouchable: Model prisoners, 'cause they could afford to be. And because... they needed to be.

No, it was the *guards* they had to fool, not us; it was the men with the keys they wanted to be overlooked by, the watchdogs they had to bore to sleepiness. That extra edge of alertness Maybelle reported, that I saw for my own self, whenever a bluebird came within hearing of their constant low mutters to each other: The tension, the flickering eyes, the expert balance of submissiveness, dullness and sullenness, thrown over that spark of sharp defiance like an oil-rag wrapping carbon steel. That it took me so long to realize what it all meant is some embarrassing, in full honesty.

Once I *did* realize, though…well. I never have been one for wasting time, once the course of action is clear.

«« — »»

"You two're thinkin' on escape, ain't you?" I said, sliding in between both Cornishes without any fair warning, as they leant up against their usual staked-out corner of the prison yard. Dionne reacted pretty much just like I'd expected she might to this display of unmitigated gall: Shifted back into fight-stance and fisted one hand, while the other went on the sly for that shank she kept shoved down the back of her pants. But Samaire just drew herself up to full height and shot me the downwards cut-eye, before asking, calmly—

"And…you would be?"

"Oh, just another poor victim of stunted parental creativity." I stuck out my own hand, so fast she almost couldn't help but take it, if only for a second. "Allfair Chatwin – Alleycat, they call me; looks like "all-fair", sounds like Ah-la-fAHr. Kinda like bein' named Cinderella, back where I come from."

Dionne glowered at me, and snapped: "Don't say word one to this bitch, Sami. I've been askin' around; she's nobody we need to know."

"Oh, I'd say that probably depends, pretty gal."

"On what?"

"On whether or not it's true your li'l sister's Daddy wears the same set of horns mine does." She flushed a bit at that, but didn't argue; though it might still be a sore spot, the concept obviously wasn't really up for debate. So I simply smiled, and continued. "'Cause if he does…"

"*If*," Samaire put in, raising a brow.

"…well. Then I think we might be fit to do some business together."

Dionne and Samaire traded looks; Dee's seemed to read like

she thought she could probably stab me quick and walk on 'fore the guards noticed, but Samaire's half-shrug, half-headshake seemed less for than against. So Dionne let out a breath, and stepped back just far enough to let me get between her and her sister – metaphorically, at least. Especially considering exactly how little wiggle room she'd left me to work with…

(For now.)

"I mean, you *do* need to get outta here too, am I right? Go back to savin' the world, and all." Now it was my turn to get looked at. "So…how's that goin' for you, anyways?"

Dionne: "Like it's any of your damn—"

But: "Not as well as I'd hoped for, considering," Samaire replied, cooler than cool, at almost the same moment. "But I take it you have suggestions."

'Cause she could see it on me too, 'course; no way she couldn't. We *all* know each other by sight, if nothing else.

I nodded. "Now, don't get me wrong," I began, "I hear you're an educated woman, so I know whatever sort of craft you practice probably got to have mine beat all to Hell and back, just on the reference material. But I been in here long enough to learn this much: Craft in itself ain't gonna get you through gate one, let alone out those front doors without anyone puttin' a bullet through ya…or better still, through *her*."

Dionne snorted loudly at the very idea, naturally – but Samaire's eyes flicked over nonetheless, automatic as a skipped heartbeat, like she was already checking for damage. And: *Well-a-day*, I thought to myself, wonderingly, as I so often had before. *Ain't family something SPECIAL?*

Best earthly way to get an otherwise smart person to do somethin' stupid under pressure that I ever have tripped across, inside jail or out of it, hands damn down.

"I'm listening," was all she said in return, though. Which was more'n good enough.

I walked her through what I knew about M-vale's various pitfalls, as gleaned from tales of other past break-out schemes (sadly truncated in their execution, most often), then sat there while Samaire walked *me* in return through what she'd decided on when she first heard the verdict read out on her and Dionne, and why it wasn't quite coming together the way she'd thought it would.

"I usually practice hierarchical magic," she said. "But that's pretty tool-heavy for in here – not least since they took all my supplies away, before we even went to trial…"

"Uh huh. Good luck gettin' hold of 'a hazel-wood wand new-peeled' on the black market, not to mention the steel caps, lode-stone and virgin cock's blood you'd need to consecrate it." Adding, as she stared: "What? You think just 'cause I ain't been to university, I don't know my basics?"

She kept on staring a second, then shook it off. "Okay," she said, finally, pointing to a sinuous double line of text snaking up around her right-side humerus. "If you're really up on your *rituale magiciae componentum*, then – what's *that*?"

I just grinned: Man, *far* too easy.

"Why, that there'd be protection against demons if you read it one way and a binding on your own demon blood if you read it the other, written in the language known as Crossing the River – *Transitus Fluvii*, as the dead Roman tongue would have it. Y'all don't know everything just 'cause you read a book or two got written before Gutenberg made up his first Bible, Princess."

Dionne, impatiently: "Look, so you know some shit, and she obviously knows some of the exact same shit…was there gonna be a plan in here somewhere, or what?"

"Like you say, wizardly workings tend to take the sort of accoutrements our current position renders pretty much inaccessible," I told Samaire, ignoring the unsolicited commentary from the peanut gallery. "So why not go the opposite route?"

"Such as?"

"Holler magic. Y'all might have heard of it."

"Sure. That's the tradition where every spell involves wearing your materiel in your crotch for a day or so."

I nodded, unoffended: "Ain't fancy, I'll grant you, but it's simple, cheap—"

"If you don't count the boiled-down human body parts you usually build it from," Dionne muttered.

"—and it *does* work…'specially so when you got *two* qualified people doin' it, 'stead of just the one. And that's my main point, Princess: You ain't ever gonna get where you want to by exactly *when* you want to, not without help from another worker. But if you was to lay your high-class hexation next to my gutter witchery and let 'em cross-pollinate – feel on each other awhile, or such – might be they'd both end up movin' a tad faster, to our mutual improvement."

"Like a sort of a...really *skanky*...feedback loop."

"Well, I never did go too far through school...but metaphorically, sure. Why not?"

The Cornishes exchanged another glance. "Look, Sami, you already know what *I* think," Dionne said, at last. "Witches are witches. Plus, word on the yard is, banking A-Cat here'll do anything more'n lie right to your face, then kick you down and fuck you ain't gonna get you anything but kicked down and fucked even harder. But we both already know you're gonna do what *you* want, just like always."

Samaire nodded. To me: "So, assuming everything she's said is true – how could I ever trust you to hold up your end of the bargain? What do you want to get out of here for, anyhow?"

Never you mind, kin-killer, I almost snapped back. But said instead, out loud—

"You kiddin' me? I want to be out of here to be *out* of here, Princess, same's anyone else. 'Cause it's cramped, your options for fun are substantially limited, and I been here more'n long enough already. 'Sides which, you sure don't have to *trust* a person to *work* with 'em. That's half the fun, ain't it?"

She looked at me then, long and level, eyes hard.

"Tell you what," she said, at last. "If if turns out I *do* find I need you for – anything – I'll go ahead and have Dionne let you know."

I nodded, thinking: *That's all I ask.*

«« —»»

That night, in the slice of space between count and lights-out, Maybelle'd already laid there pouting for quite a bit before I finally wised up enough to look over and notice. She'd seen me getting what looked like up close and personal with Dee and Samaire, and that made her nervous; guess she *was* a bit too well-used, at this stage of the game, to think goin' back on the market was a good idea, particularly if she wanted to trade up (rather than down) from where she was right now. So she wanted some token show of reassurance she really wasn't in immediate danger of bein' being thrown over for a newer model, which I – truth be told – was more'n happy to provide.

"Them Cornishes got each other, darlin'; they ain't plannin' to be in here long enough to need anybody else, even *if* they either of 'em swung that way. Not like I need you, anyhow."

"You need me, A-Cat?"

"Let me demonstrate."

After, while she dozed – all replete, with dreamy dreams of how the two of us were both gonna squeeze, hand in hand, through whatever magickal escape hatch Samaire and I ended up cobbling together dancing in her empty blonde head – I studied the darkened ceiling and thought yet once more about that no-contact buzz I'd gotten just from standing *next* to (not-so-) little miss Princess; how she couldn't helped but've felt it too, rippling up and down those carefully tattooed limbs of hers, the shiver before the quake. And how it'd probably only get stronger yet, the longer we stayed in proximity – ratcheting up unstoppably as we drew ever closer, like the static charge hum just before a flashbulb's flare, or the filament whine as a lightbulb bloomed to full incandescence…

Dee might not be able to *feel* it, bein' what she was, but she'd sure made certain I knew she didn't like what she almost *thought* she saw going on: Protective, like some five-foot nothing Mama Bear with her claws out, ready to fight to the bitter end. Which I guessed I could understand, though only in principle. 'Cause me, I never did know what it was to have a sister, not even half of one… but then again, the pull I felt towards Samaire wasn't entirely familial, as Dionne could no doubt tell; things always were a whole lot slipperier down in Hell than they were here up top, 'specially in the bonds-of-kinship department.

I did need to know what-all they were planning to do next, though – about me, as much as anything else – and the surest way to find out was to send something to listen at their keyhole. Which I could certainly do, for all I hadn't in quite some time – and like any other muscle, a witch's craft does tend to get a mite…tight, if she doesn't let it out for exercise on the regular.

So I shut my eyes, said a few choice words under my breath, bit my own lip 'til it bled and took a deep old swallow. And a few moments later, I coughed out a little red glob of sickness onto the cell floor... dirt from my insides, stuck together with Hell-juice and ill-will. A fetch, just like my Momma taught me to make way back, long before I ever saw any Dark Man on top of any hill.

A beat more, and it opened two tiny black jewels to look my way, stretched out its spun-glass wings (still tinged pink with spray) and rubbed its delicate stinger-legs together in greeting. Its voice rose up drily, echoing off the concrete walls – a thin, companionable, whispering vibration.

Let me do thy will, Lady? the fetch asked, eager, inside my skull.

Gladly, I replied.

«« ——— »»

Over in their own cell, meanwhile, Samaire sat cross-legged on one bed with her eyes all rolled back like she was meditating, while Dionne paced the floor, one hand on her shank. Announcing, as she did—

"Look, this is just a *bad* idea, Sami, twenty years or not – that bitch is everything we ever fought, all wrapped up in a hag-ridin', Devil-worshippin' bow. Even layin' aside what we already hear about how she conducts herself on the strictly human tip, she's the sort of witch who probably takes names and steals babies – and we're gonna let her back *out*, where she can get at the next given normal comes along, just to serve *our* interests? That ain't buddies."

I never stole a baby in all my life, I thought to myself, huffily, as the fetch hovered inside a vent above them, watching their debate through dim, colorblind eyes. Then added: '*Course, I never really HAD to, just 'cause I needed the parts. There's abortion parlors all over the great state of Alabama, after all...and they dump out their trash like clockwork, twice a day.*

(Ah, the conveniences of modern living.)

Samaire, unmoving: "*Not* helpful, Dee."

"Right. 'Kay." A beat. "Seriously, though, Chatwin's Hell-bait; we've killed enough like her to fertilize a car-park. A witch is a witch is a—"

"—witch, yeah, I got it." A pause. "So what's that make me?"

Dionne stopped, mid-stride. "Not *her*. You get *that*, right?"

"Except...I am."

"But you *use* this shit, Sami. You don't let it use you. That's the difference."

Samaire opened her eyes at that, and raised a doubtful brow; she looked down at her hand, studying that wrap-around ribbon of Transitus Fluvii circling the arm it attached to, like she could see things movin' underneath it.

"Six of one," she said, half to herself. Then: "You *hear* that?"

"What?"

"That…buzzing."

Okay, time to go.

They both turned towards "me", then, and I knew the fetch had almost reached its expiry date. So I peeled my consciousness back from it in long, sticky strings, letting its sight grow ever fuzzier, bleeding away pixel by pixel. 'Til the bond between us finally grew so tenuous I barely even felt a thing when Guard Curzon swatted it from the air as it flew from vent to vent, and crushed it messily beneath one boot. I could hear Brenmer through the wall, muffled, as he blurted out—

"Damn. How those things get *in* here, anyways?"

Curzon, stomping on: "Fuck if I know. Maybe they can smell all the pussy."

Which was crude, as ever. Yet not entirely inaccurate.

I turned over, wondering if Samaire would bother sending a fetch of her own to watch me sleep – or if she even knew how to *make* a fetch, considering who'd raised her. One way or the other, I wasn't about to lose a good night's shut-eye over it.

Things learned so far: Cornishes don't want to work with me, but too bad, 'cause they ain't exactly got another choice to switch to, I thought. *So let 'em sweat on that a while; hell, I got time.*

Nothin' but.

«« — »»

That was Friday. And a day or so later, I come 'round a corner in the library – mail-cart in hand – to find Dionne waiting on me between the stacks, arms crossed and scowling, with Samaire looming right behind.

"…we might need your help, after all," was all Samaire had to say, after a moment.

And: "Oh, Princess," I said, "tell it to me again, will ya? *Slower.*"

《《—》》

"What do you know about Abramelin the Mage?" Samaire asked, as she pumped a thirty-pound barbell in the southmost corner of the weight-pile, with Dionne spotting. I sat down nearby, took up a pair of ten-pounders and started doing curls, to cover my reply:

"Abramelin? He thought all worldly phenomena were produced by demons working under the direction of angels; we all come with a guardian angel and a demon attached, the one liftin' us up, the other suckin' us back down, like gravity. Thought initiates could make 'emselves into angels, for as long as it took to control the demons…"

"…by using spell-squares. Five-line palindromes that read the same up and down, forward and back. The most famous of which being…"

"…the SATOR box? 'SATOR, AREPO, TENET, OPERA, ROTAS: Hold this in thy right hand, ask what thou wilt, and it shall be delivered.' No tools nescessary, 'sides from pen, ink and willpower. But the thing also repels witches somethin' fierce, so too damn bad we can't either of us use *that*…"

"That's right, we can't." She pumped up one more time, shelved it, and lay there a moment, sweating. Before adding—

"But Dionne can."

We both shot Dionne a glance, like we'd been choreographed that way; Dionne – who'd been watching this little back 'n' forth of magickal esoterica like it was a Satanic tennis game – flushed deep, looking uneasy for maybe the very first time since I'd made her acquaintance.

"Hey, man," she said, "I don't…*do* magic. Ain't my style. I just don't got it in me."

Samaire nodded. "You're not trained, no – but seriously, Dee, once it's *made*, this item's pretty much idiot-proof." A beat. "No offense."

"None taken. If it repels witches, though, then how are you guys supposed to make it?"

"Take turns. A-Cat does a character, I do a character, out of order. You hold the paper, so we don't even have to pass it back and forth. Easy."

Dubious: "Oh yeah, sounds it."

For once, I had to agree. "Yeah, it's a neat little concept – 'cept we'd have to shield ourselves, somehow, just to stay in the same damn room while Lady Di here worked her will on the thing. You got any bright ideas about *that*?"

"…not yet. I thought, though, with both of us going full-bore—"

"Princess, I can't shield *myself* from the SATOR box, let alone you too."

And there it sat, for a minute; I could see her thinking on the problem – hard, straight white teeth just denting her lower lip – which was a sort of pleasure in itself, for all it went on just a shade too long for comfort.

"We'd need a jolt, then," she said, at last. "Some sudden extra burst of power, like jump-starting a…car battery, or whatever – "

"Sacrifice, sure. So kill somebody."

Dionne, without even thinking twice, like she'd just remembered she was the *big* sister here: "We're not gonna do that."

I looked right on past her, straight to Samaire, the more innately practical of the two. "Let *me*, then; you know *I'*d do it. Do it in a damn minute, I thought it'd get us outta here…"

"Well, demonstrably, Alleycat!" she snapped back. "But *we won't.*"

"Okay, then: *Fuck* someone, that'd work almost as well. Or are you too damn good to do that, either?"

Now it was her turn to blush. "Not with you," she said, shortly. Adding, as I looked back at Dionne, cocking one eyebrow: "And not with her, either – I mean, Jesus! Just what the Hell is wrong will you, anyways?"

Quantifying that one'd've probably took us all night, so I just shrugged. "Does sort of limit our options, then don't it?" I pointed out, instead.

"I can still figure something, given time," Samaire muttered.

Time. Which we had, again, and didn't have, in justabout equal measures – but I knew enough not to push.

"Well, okay; you just go on ahead and do that, then. I need a couple of days to myself, anyhow."

"Why?" Dionne asked, suspiciously.

I shot her a smile. "Oh, nothin' too strenuous. Just gotta wrap up some…unfinished business."

«« — »»

Obviously, it had already occurred to me that trying to tote Maybelle on top of everything else would be a tad – difficult, at best. So while the Princess dicked around trying to figure out some slightly less morally suspect way to render her otherwise brilliant escape plan's kicker fully functional, I went ahead and got my pretty May to help lay the seeds of its other components – conceal Abramelin's SINAH box (SINAH, IRATA, NANIR, AX-IRO, HAROQ) somewhere in her regular haunt, the laundry, so's it could buy us the sort of violent yet short-term distraction we needed to slip the rest of our business past the C.O.s, while they were a bit too conveniently caught up in something else to notice.

According to Abramelin, SINAH meant "hatred". The SI-NAH box was thus most often used "to create a general war" – a riot, say – which, because the square wasn't perfect, wouldn't go on forever. It'd start slow, working on whatever threads of conflict were already there, 'til the conflagration finally bloomed into full effect...and really, M-vale was (by definition) just chock full'a people who couldn't keep it in their pants for long, literally or figuratively, on *both* sides of the uniformed divide.

"Like yourself," Dionne supplied, when I suggested this tack. To which I simply smiled, freely admitting—

"My impulse control *can* be somewhat inconsistent, dependin' on circumstances."

"Yeah, I hear that happens a lot, with people who end up in jail."

"It does. Welcome to the curve, ladies."

Naturally, though, there was a second element to trusting Maybelle with the SINAH square – mainly, that it got her out of my hair long enough for me to go through her stuff, and get some of *her* hair. Then get naked and take a steamy trip through the shower-room, where I rifled the discarded brush of the next long-haired woman I saw: In this case, a hot little Latina Queens baller named Felicia Suarez who saw me hovering near her stuff and scowled like she would've happily thrown down with me right there and then, if only the floor hadn't've been so damn wet.

"Stay on your own side, *mami*," she told me. "I ain't lookin' to switch teams."

I shrugged, thinking: *Hmmm. Too bad for you, then, darlin'* – *'cause you may be in for somewhat of a surprise.*

By chow-time, when Maybelle drifted back my way, I'd already had more'n enough opportunity to tie the two of 'em together by those two locks of hair in a classic holler lust-knot. And sure, she was just as attentive as ever, 'till she glanced up to see Felicia comin'. A stammered excuse later, Maybelle went off to get "another chocolate milk", and didn't come back 'til count; the two of 'em disappeared under the stairs for maybe half an hour, re-emerging with disordered hair and their shirts tucked back in wrong only to head in opposite directions, fast, and blushing; sort of cute, when you thought about it. Though probably a bit offputting for them.

"That was…really crude," said Samaire – who'd seen me snickering to myself, and obviously wondered what the joke was – after she'd finally figured out what just happened.

"Could'a just made 'em *kill* each other, and solved both our problems," I pointed out. But she kept on shaking her head, like a damn looming metronome.

"You don't *have* to do things like that," she said, finally. "To be like that. You just…don't."

"Probably not; I just *am*. You too, gal. And one of these days, you really gonna have to start to relax, lay back and enjoy it." I paused. "'Sides, you *do* kill your own. Don't you?"

Dionne, quickly: "They're not *our* own."

"'Course not, Lady Di. But then again…I wasn't talkin' to you."

Another head-shake, but slower this time. I saw something nasty bloom in back of Samaire Cornish's too-calm eyes, and felt my heart leap in recognition – a shark ill-hid under blue water, sniffing 'round for blood.

"We kill monsters, not people."

"Not even people who *are* monsters?" When she didn't answer: "And what about the half-monsters, Princess – the low-down dirty 'breeds, like you 'n' me? But I don't suppose you wanna look too close at *that* one, now, do ya?" I laughed out loud. "Gal, you got issues."

And now Samaire was watching me *really* close, like she was studying hard on how good my head would look, severed and stickset. Took her a beat yet just to collect herself far enough to say—

"My Dad killed my Mom for getting raped by demons, Ms. Chatwin. So yes, my feelings about heritage are... complicated."

"Uh huh? Well, *my* Momma killed my not-Daddy for bein' human, pretty much. That, and he owed her money."

Dionne stepped in between us, then, clowning hat on firm. "See?" she said, lightly. "It's like I always told you, Sami – *never* lend to family."

Good save; even Samaire had to smirk a bit at that, boiling off the tension. But it didn't surprise me much, even so, when – later that same afternoon – I stepped into the mailroom supply closet pushing the cart before me with one hip, only to find Dionne's shank suddenly pressing up against my carotid.

"Listen up, bitch," Dionne began, a bare voice in the dark, low and grim and even. "I know how you think I'm some kind of dead weight 'cause my blood's a hundred percent human, but here's the deal – we get out, we give you a head start, and that's all. You're a monster, we're monster-killers. End of story. Nod if you understand me."

I did, quick-smart. "Won't happen again," I managed, voice thin with effort.

"Good." The blade drew back – but she leaned forward nevertheless, whispering right in my ear: "Oh yeah, and by the way...try to fuck with my little sister again, and I'll cut your damn tits off."

"Message received, loud and clear."

"Better be," she told me. And was gone, into that same darkness, long before I could get up the nerve to look 'round.

«« — »»

On some level, I truly do think I believed I was doing May-belle a favor – but I also know *she* didn't see it as such, because for the next couple of days she followed me around, alternating frantic make-out sessions with Felicia with equally frantic apologies to me. On the surface, she seemed genuinely horrified both to have "cheated" on me in the first place and by her utter inability to not keep on doing so, any and every chance she got; at base, she was scared shitless I might kick her to the curb, so's she'd be back out on the market again, with no one to protect her at all.

"Think you might be doin' Felicia somewhat of a disservice

106

there, darlin',"I pointed out. "She seems a loyal sort, from everything I've heard; I'm sure she'll stand by you."

"Don't make fun of me, A-Cat! I just…why did I *do* that? I just don't *understand*…"

"Well, c'mon, gal: Seriously, it's okay. You two seem very happy together."

"But I'm *not*! A-Cat, please don't cut me loose, please. *Please*."

And there I was, still trying to be nice, but really; this was all getting somewhat ridiculous.

"Maybelle," I said, "you just need to *step off*, right now. Stand on your own two. It's pitiful."

I just walked away and left her standing there, lips trembling, with nary a backwards glance. And the very next time I saw her was when Guard Curzon came by our cell, as per the Warden's request, to take me to the morgue.

It's harder to kill yourself in M-Vale than you might think, 'specially if you're dumb. But she'd managed it, nonetheless: Drank a bleach cocktail, industrial-strength, and crawled in between two heavy machines to wait it out, making sure nobody'd find her 'til the worst was long over. She didn't look too kissable, afterwards, what with her mouth all gone blue and vomit in her long, blonde hair. Still, I bent down so we were nose to nose, shooting Curzon a glance that penetrated even his rhino skin; made him step back, shut the door halfway behind him, and give us some time alone.

To this day, I'm not all too sure what I really felt for her, if anything – though I certainly did appreciate the effort she put into things of an intimate nature, 'specially where I was concerned. But at the time, all I could think was—

Guess she really did LOVE me – how 'bout that. I mean…fancy.

Turns out, Maybelle didn't just stay with me 'cause I made it impossible for her to be elsewhere; she was mine 'cause she *wanted* to be, all along. Unlikely. Surprising.

…depressing.

Yet potentially useful, all the same.

I rummaged 'round in my bra for an empty aspirin bottle I'd found on the infirmary floor one day and managed to keep hid, a secret bit of inexplicable contraband saved for just such an occasion, through all the subsequent strip-searches in between. Slid my thumb to line both triangular childproof seals up, and popped the lid. After which I leant down to the china-pale curl of Maybelle's ear, closed and dumb now as any empty snail-shell, and murmured into it:

"*O lenti, lenti curite noctus equii*...come back to me but a spell, honey, 'fore you go gentle into that good-night. Shed that cocoon on your way to wings. Break off just some tiny unnecessary bit of yourself and leave it here, for me, to remember you by."

Took but a second or two for my words to reach her, trailing down the snarled and fading synapses of her dead brain. And then I saw it right at the back of her throat, a dim light flickering between her stained teeth, on the necrotized black skin of her tongue – some merest fragment of sweet Maybelle Eileen Pine's soul, like a fluttering luminous moth, snared in her very last wisp of earthly breath; dull as a sub-molecular Los Alamos half-spark, powerful beyond Oppenheimer's fondest dreams yet struggling still against death's inertial pull, its foul gravity. Trying blindly to force its way up to me who loved it, against all hope, or logic...

I sucked what was left of Maybelle's pathetic little soul in hard, lip to lip, so close I felt the bleach yet left there start to crisp my skin. Then spat it right back out into the aspirin bottle, along with a smear of my own black blood, to keep it trapped there 'til I needed it.

And: "Thank you muchly, baby girl," I sang out, briskly, straightening again. "Never think, wherever you do end up, that I'm not grateful for your sacrifice – because I really, *really* am."

Like I said – didn't seen that one comin', though maybe I should've. But I surely did appreciate the gesture, all the same.

"Your jolt, Princess," I told Samaire, much later, as I placed the bottle in her hands.

«« — »»

The riot broke out on a Tuesday, over in the mess hall – something about somebody either encroaching on somebody else's territory or looking a bit too hard at someone else's woman, which soon enough swelled to embrace the shank-wielding triple-header of all good prison conflicts: Race, face, personal space. Not that I was there to witness it first-hand, of course...since I knew enough to avoid getting myself inconveniently locked down before all the fun began, I'd already made sure to turn Guard Curzon's piggy eyes firmly back on me, long before that particular storm ever started to break.

So here we were instead, in that same supply closet, deep in congress – his version thereof, anyhow – when the alarms went off; he jumped for his gun and stick, only to find 'em suddenly both in my hands, instead. Then went backing away from me at an awkward half-shuffle, with his pants down 'round his knees and his dick flapping free, 'til he ended up just where I wanted him – right overtop the most sinister of Abramelin's squares, which S.L. MacGregor Mathers says 'should never be made use of', and must be buried in a place where the intended victim will walk over it in order to work to fullest capacity:

CASED – overflowing of unrestrained lust;

AZOTE – enduring;

BOROS – devouring, gluttonous;

ETOSA – idle, useless;

DESAC – to overtake and stick close.

The CASED square can render its wielder invisible, under the right circumstances (along with gaining them access to all nearby hidden treasures, works of art and statuary), so at first I'd thought of that…'til the Princess herself had pointed out a peculiar secondary characteristic of the square which might be just as useful to our cause, given the restrictions we were laboring under. Or even more so.

As Curzon's foot made contact, he froze stock-still, unable to shift a quarter-inch further either way. "Uh," he said at the feel of it, intelligently. Then: "Oh, my God. What the good Goddamn shit Hell?"

I just smiled, feeling my own skin ripple as his form flowed up and over mine, from face to naughty parts and everything in between. "'Lo, Erroll," I said. "How's it hangin'?"

He gaped at me a while, not even resisting when I unbuttoned his shirt, shucked the rest of his pants down and gently encouraged him to kick his boots off, too, like some five-foot-ten toddler. Finally, he observed – with the stunned yet slightly self-pleased air of somebody who's just figured out what the word hidden in that big Saturday morning paper jumble must be—

"—you really *are* a witch."

"Yup. Now, how 'bout takin' one last ride on the ol' skin snake, just for luck?"

"...what?"

"Aw, don't fret, cupcake – you ain't actually my type, anyhow. Sleep."

Thus, all tricked out in Guard Curzon drag, I hiked up "my" key-belt and headed for the workshop. Passed Guard Bremner on the way – ensnared by a howling knot of women, caught in the very manhood-destroying act of getting beat down and having his shit took by unarmed vagina-bearers. "Erroll, help!" he yelled at me, as I went by; I shot him the double finger, and kept right on going.

The Cornishes I found backed into in a corner, shoulder to shoulder, kicking and punching at all comers like some well-trained Ultimate Fighter tag-team. And: "You two, warden's of-fice!" I yelled, discharging "my" weapon into the air, only to barely avoid being flattened in the resultant rush for the door.

Which is how we finally came, at long last, to the point of the whole damn exercise: Trading letters forth and back, each to each, like some calligraphy lesson from Hell, while Maybelle's captive soul-fragment flickered and spat and flared in sympathy like a late-night TV-blue bug-light. While that same static charge buzz tuned up and down our bodies, meshing us together in a true witches' cradle of probability strings, drawing sparks. I could see Dionne's back-muscles twitch with tension, as the free ends of her hair started to lift; saw Samaire's blue eyes darken yet once more as her bad blood rose to meet mine, studying me like I was some book she had to strain just in order to read, and wasn't even sure she really wanted to, when all was said and done. But it wasn't ex-actly like she could *stop*, either...

And me looking right on back, thinking: *Oh, you wanna think you're like HER, that you're NOT like me...but truth is, Princess, it's the whole other way 'round, 'cause the only thing you and Miss Di really got in common's the pussy you both slid out of. You just want to be normal, so bad it keeps you up nights, taste of it like a mouthful of blood; Hell, I can't blame you for that. But one day, all those restraining tattoos, all that save-your-soul script you got all over you? They're gonna just flare up and crisp off, like paper in fire…*

(Like a tower falling, struck by lightning, now and forever more. Like Babylon. Like Charn.)

…yeah. JUST like that.

And then, then – that's when we're *really* gonna get to see some fun.

Charging each other up, winding that phantom winch of combined power ever higher, higher, higher. 'Til our fingertips met across the paper and our heels began to lift, describing a slow, concentric circle in the air like we was two antimatter planets drawn into orbit, an incipient black hole twisting reality's fabric 'til it bent and broke. A paradox waiting to happen.

A howl of wind from nowhere, brisk and bleak and bone-stripping, as the lights pulsed and the sirens wailed on; it was completed, as that poor Daddy-betrayed fool Jesus Christ would say. The SATOR box was done.

I laughed out loud, hair cracking like a whip. And heard Samaire yelling to Dionne even from the very depths of her frenzy, over it all: "*NOW*, DEE, NOW – NOW NOW NOW NOW, DO IT DO IT DO IT – *DO* IT, *DO* IT GODDAMN *NOW*!"

Dionne raised the square, snug in the whirling widdershins circle of our arms, and spoke the words, her merely human voice near to cracking with strain. And we were off, gone, spiralling fast through time and space, hovering through the fog and the filthy air – out of M-vale at last, chased and dragged by Abramelin's devils and angels alike, while Maybelle's soul blew/boiled off in the other direction with a thin, despairing cry…

Samaire had her eyes closed, but Dionne had hers open; I made sure of that. So when I hove in to kiss Samaire, before either of them knew enough to protest – sudden as rape, my tongue hook-probing deep, scratching on hers like oh-so-voluptuous velcro – there was no way Dionne could stop herself from doing just what she would have under any other circumstances: Lunge to thrust herself between, SATOR box forgotten in her haste, still trailing from the same fist she was aiming for my jaw.

It touched us both at once – repelling factor back on full, with no Maybelle for protection – and hurled us to the four winds' tornado-churned quarters, faster than thought; Dionne one way,

Samaire and I the absolute opposite. we came down hard, falling fast into black. Then awoke later – much later – all on the cold hill's side...

...with no one left near to hold onto, in this dim twilight world, but each other.

«« — »»

Samaire looked over at me, head hung down, her eyes like bruises. "Where's...Dionne?" She managed, at last.

"Dunno," I said, fighting my own fair share of post-spell-travel nausea. "Could be...anywhere, really."

She shook her head. "The SATOR box...must've touched us. Thrown us...ugh, *Jesus.*" Rolling onto her knees, she heaved upwards, gained her feet and stood there, weaving. "Where...?"

I shrugged – then spat, and wished I hadn't. "Damn if I know. Sorta looks like...Alabama, I had to take a guess." Clawed my own way to standing, using a handy tree, and tried a weak version of my normal charming grin out on her: "Aw, but don't you worry none, pretty gal – given all that excitement we left behind us, I'll bet you five bucks she already must've dropped it."

"You don't *get* it, Alleycat. I need my damn *sister!*"

And: *For WHAT, exactly?* I could've said. *'Cause you feel guilty you can do things she can't, and never will? 'Cause you're so all-fired hot to get back to killin' things that're more like you than she'll ever be, just 'cause your old man taught you to? Same old man ended up turning your Momma into hash, as I recall, 'cause he couldn't stand having another creature's fingerprints left on her...and that was just too bad, by Dionne's standards, wasn't it? Too bad for your Momma. Too damn bad for YOU...*

If this actually *was* Alabama, I knew a hill somewhere 'round within walking distance where I could surely introduce her to the Daddy we both shared, for what I knew would be the first time. Put his one hand on the crown of her head, the other on her ankle, and know he'd answer each and every question she might have for him in between. We could be true sisters yet, dance at the Sabbat in our naked skins and sup on broiled corpse-flesh; ride the night astraddle like those carrion storm-birds of old Greece, seeking always for prey, and scour this land of any fool who dared think fire, or salt, or a whimpered prayer to some unhearing God would ever keep him and his safe for long from such as she and me.

But: Looking at her now, I knew it was far too late for that. Her hands were clenched against me, closed and hard like her heart; them ropes of Crossing the River were dug in too deep between the layers of her skin for anything short of a roadside conversion to ever disarm 'em – though it'd have to be one gained on the way to Dis, Hell's own lead-walled capital city, 'course, rather than on the way to Damascus.

Ah well, I thought. And said, out loud—

"Suppose you probably oughtta go back for her, then. While you still can."

She knew what I'd done, then, without a doubt; got it all in one, like the brilliant bitch she was. And kept on looking at me nonetheless, appraisingly – less with hate than a vague sort of sorrow, albeit one which came liberally admixed with a caldera's worth of barely-veiled, magma-hot rage.

"...I'm gonna find *you*, too, Allfair Chatwin," she told me, without much affect, as the air between her long fingers began to spark and whine again. "Eventually."

To which I nodded my head, briefly, in what probably looked – from her angle – like acceptance. And replied:

"Oh, but not *too* soon, I hope. Princess."

«« —— »»

Took half a second for the rift to pop open again, behind her, and the other half to close once she'd stepped back through. Then I was all by my lonesome in the dark, dark woods once more, a state of affairs which sure did seem to call for immediate relocation – so I started out walking, whistling softly; an old holler tune my Momma always used to sing me, back in the day, on empty nights like these...

Don't the moon look pretty, shining down through the trees...
Said don't the shining moon look pretty, Lord,
shining down through the trees...
Oh, I can see my baby, Lord Lord Lord...but he can't see me...

113

I went looking around for a highway, found one. Started walking. And after a while—

—well, that's when *you* picked me up. Didn't ya?

Turn in here, darlin'.

The Speed of Pain

Five o'clock A.M., and all's DEFINITELY not well.

That's the thought to which Nimue Ewalt wakes, more or less, as she pulls herself headlong from the shreds of her latest Valerian-influenced nightmare. She reaches for her nightstand sketch-pad before the connect-the-dots "narrative" behind that cold hand in her sternum can dissolve into complete uselessness, shivers plucking up and down her arms as she scrabbles for a pen in the half-open drawer, while Veruca Luz snores asthmatically on the futon couch across the room…

…and shit, what *was* it, now? A hazy wash of images overlaid like bad Flash on an overburdened browser, shucking files Trash-bound right and left and spiralling headlong downwards towards the final Big Freeze…

Out on a deserted beach at night, maybe Cherry, maybe not; the Island's polluted shore spread out behind her in a blur of garbage, rocks cold against her naked back, black lake-water lapping at her toes. No stars above. And this sensation of being watched by something hidden, maybe from above, maybe below. Of laying herself open – physically, psychically – to wait for an unseen enemy, already settling down upon her like a cloud: Entering by the mouth, leaving by the sex. Splitting her from stem to stern entire, in a sudden spray of heat and blood and waste.

Then being buried in the beach's wet sand, spade-full by hideously slow spade-full – broken, paralyzed, yet somehow still alive, a turtle's egg stewed fast in its own leathery shell. A chrysalis, waiting to hatch.

But with that, Nim abruptly finds herself shaking all over, so hard she can't hold the pen straight enough for legible notes anymore. So she lets it go instead, pulls the covers close around her, while Veruca sleeps on. Keeps her unspectacled eyes front, focus lost against the far wall's blurry stucco veneer, and waits for morning.

《《——》》

There's an early frost in Toronto this August; no big deal, a few black tomatoes here and there, but try telling that to somebody who's used to running on California time-slash-weather. So Veruca wraps herself up like Im-Ho-Tep every time they set foot outdoors, complaining endlessly about how the cold could affect her septal piercing, how if it goes below a certain temperature it could set off one of her migraines. How since of course she left her medicine at home, or maybe lost it in transit someplace, that leaves her prospectively SOL when the hypothermic muscle tension comes a-callin'...

So: "Just take the fucking thing *out*, then," Nim snaps back at her, finally – not exactly wanting to be too much of a bitch on wheels, but not willing to seem too sympathetic, either; this *is* Veruca we're talking about, after all. And with Veruca, there's always *one more thing*.

She feels bad about it almost immediately afterward, though, especially when Veruca looks down and sniffs, bolt swinging. Saying, quietly:

"Dude, you don't have to be like that. I mean...I'll be fine, totally, I'm sure. For tonight, I mean. I'm just, y'know..."

(Just what? But for the love of God, please please please don't say)

"...just...sayin'."

And here endeth the lesson, Nim finds herself thinking, for neither the first time or (probably) the last: *File under Truism 'cause it's true, and never again let yourself think that because you like somebody online, you'll like 'em in person. Or, say—*

(at ALL)

Because virtual friendships should stay just that: Virtual. Or risk spawning prospective justified manslaughter charges, on BOTH sides of the equation.

Nim takes another sidelong glance at Veruca, bundled well beyond the tenth power, with the very roots of her bleached-blonde skater grrrl-cum-faux chola cornrows visible where her hoodie meets her hairline; eyes with a semi-epicanthic droop peek out from under boxy black-rimmed glasses, half-squinted against any light brighter than that of a screen set on PowerSave. Doesn't help that Veruca seems to revel in the same chin-to-chest geekslump Nim's spent hours trying to yoga away, either, or that her voice constantly ricochets back and forth between whine (when upset) and monotone (when anything else), like she's never even taken the time to consider how she might sound to other humans.

It all makes being near her familiar and dreadful in teeth-grittingly equal measure, cringe-worthy the same way flipping through your Mom's hidden stash of high-school snapshots is – Veruca's everything Nim used to be, back before Nim wised up, *grew* up. Back before she knew, or cared about knowing, any better.

The funny thing being…in e-correspondence or chat-rooms, on ICQ or her blog, Veruca's one seriously impressive cyber-chick: She can actually spell, for one thing, which helps sort the wheat from the chaff straight off; got a strong grasp on punctuation and sentence structure, can debate without degenerating into Flame-War territory, always backs up even her oddest points with quotes or links, or both. A delight to "hang" with, no matter the URL occupied, and somebody Nim's always considered one of the closest non-RL friends on her friendslist.

But in person, Christ Almighty, in *person*—

– in person, Veruca is shy, awkward, adenoidal to the point of incoherence, scarily opinionated, possibly hypochondriac. Inside Nim's apartment, she's barely communicative; outside, she exhibits all the fine interpersonal skills of Kaspar Hauser.

She's also so obsessed with each and every facet of (say it with me now, in unison) The Late Timothy Darbersmere's life and work as to literally talk of very little else, no matter the context or circumstances…a fact, Nim is forced to admit, that she A) certainly can't say she hadn't already known, given the two of them first hooked up when Google directed her to Veruca's Darbersmere fanlisting (*A Man of Wealth and Taste*, for those who like their Stones references so old as to be practically crunchy) and B) once considered far more a plus than a minus, way back when. I.e., in those halcyon days before she'd actually met her, or been forced to squire her around in public, where they might occasionally collide with those few people whose good opinion Nim truly cares about keeping.

Still. After tonight, after the Speed of Pain opens its doors and Veruca walks through them – eyes darting 'round like she's on crack, continually peeled for any brief glimpse of The Late Tim's mysterious heir/nephew Tom, The Speed's new co-owner – Nim's probably (hopefully) never going to have to see, talk to or think about her again. She'll have served her purpose, gross as that sounds. And if, a second past the Speed's midnight, she tells Veruca to lose her number – along with her addy, her ICQ handle, and any other bloody thing Veruca can remember about her – well, to be frank, Veruca will have only herself to blame.

But that prospective relief, either cutting contact with Veruca for good or finding an environment where she's once more bearable, is still hours off. If pain really has a speed, then right now Nim would have to call it pure glacier: Heavy, cold, creeping. Going out only seemed like a good idea in comparison to remaining trapped in Nim's tiny no-bedroom; she's since been forced to settle for the Second Cup three blocks away instead of the Starbucks two doors down, because Veruca (surprise, surprise) considers the funky green mermaid logo Ground Zero for the Evil Empire of Globalization, and refuses on principle to contribute Dime One to it.

So here Nim is, making do with the second-class blends Second Cup specializes in, while Veruca's green tea cools untouched on the table in front of her – unable to compete for even a second, in terms of interest, with Veruca's latest Darbersmere monologue.

"You see the same threads running through every story," Veruca rambles. "Like, if you look at the first couple of stories Tom came out with, it's pretty obvious he's picked up where Tim left off: Human relationships are based on deception, people adapt to crisis by cannibalizing their own minds for parts, run rampant 'til sooner or later, God cuts 'em down. His word choices, his phraseology, all lifted straight from Tim's." She leans forward. "Know what happens if you take the profanity out of Tom's story 'Starfucker', though? I did that – transcribed the whole thing, dropped all the swears and translated all the automatic street cred shit back into, like, 'proper English.' And guess how it comes out?"

"Two thousand words shorter?" Nim's dry response fails to adequately cover the profoundly nonplussed, almost frightened, bemusement she feels.

"Sounding exactly like Tim."

"And you know 'exactly' how he sounds because…?"

"He spoke to me." For a minute Nim thinks Veruca's being metaphorical, but no. "On his last tour, for *The Bodiless and Embodied*. I might've been the last person to see him alive."

Oh, riiight.

Because now Nim remembers this story…she's only heard it half a million times before, after all. How Veruca sold her first motherboard to get down to St. Louis in 1999, so she could get her '79 first-printing copy of *Jaguar Cactus Fruit (a Novel in Slices)* signed in person, and tell the Late what "a babe" he was as he did it. To which stalkerish infringement of personal space he apparently smiled, and said – Veruca's treasured imitation sliding quickly into *Withnail & I* territory here, every vowel a languorous string of same, sing-songing happily like she doesn't even get how pedophile-creepy its actual content is—

—*You should have seen me when I was twelve, my dear.*

Tim isn't exactly available anymore, though: Took a header off the interstate two days after and went up in a classic Bruckheimer-movie fireball, along with his driver (some Chinese-British guy hired for the tour) and all his prospective works. Aside from whatever was in his rhetorical bottom drawer, all of which Tom now has V.C. Andrews-style legal access to…

That's the rumour, anyhow.

"People say he'd just sent 'The Emperor's…' off to the print-er," Veruca continues, rapt and hushed. "Like, he might've finished it *that same night*. People say – "

"People say Pop Rocks and Coke melt your insides, 'Ruca. 'The Emperor's…' is a myth."

"I've read excerpts."

"You've read fanfiction. Shit *you* could've written – hell, *I* could've written. Any Darbersmere groupie with a keyboard and an internet connection."

Veruca's lower lip pooches out. "You're wrong, Nim. It's not just hosted text somewhere, okay? I've seen *scans*, I've seen—" She stops, resets herself. "Besides, it's classic Tim," she goes on, weakly. "His life, pulled out further – like that thing he wrote about that accident he had, or how his first wife left him stranded in Kiev with no papers, or how he got diagnosed with cancer and thought he had six months to live…"

None of which is anything like provable, Nim wants to counter. None of which stands up to even the slightest real scrutiny. *None of which we have anybody's testimony for but HIS, in the final analysis – THAT stuff, right? i.e, FICTION?*

"Great, sure, okay. So maybe *Tom* wrote it," Nim says, finally. And leaves it at that.

In her crappier moods, Nim now sometimes doubts she ever really liked Tim Darbersmere's writing at all; never in the same way Veruca does, anyhow. She spends a moment musing over the relative merits of "coolness" for coolness' sake, as Veruca drones on…how when you're fifteen or so, something can seem really great simply because it's really alien, but that's a reaction you eventually (hopefully, if you're lucky, or *normal*) grow out of. It sloughs off relative to your own RL experience: The more you rack up, the less you feel the need to surf through somebody else's consciousness, especially when all you get out of it is feeling cool by osmosis.

That sick glamour, that *Fin du Monde* decadence, that faker-than-thou exoticism. It's the sort of classic Art School "push-pull" you get from certain Cronenberg movies – like "ewww, gross!" mixed with "show me more, show me more!"…and definitely the exact kind of creepy high you'd have to be riding, in order to make reading about pledging your true perfect love in some kid's still-living flesh a plus, rather than a minus.

(Because yes, Nim's read the spoilers; she knows damn what "The Emperor's…" is *supposed* to be about, thank you very much, just like everybody else who claims to have seen the thing itself does. Or everybody else who'd willingly sell their soul to do so.)

Still: *This is yet another thing that she's never going to get*, Nim finds herself thinking. *Because to Veruca, her own tiny opinions about irrelevant crap like this is as close to "RL experience" as she's ever going to come.*

Thus this whole trip, potential chance to hit up Tom, Darbersmere 2.0, the exact same way Veruca did his uncle: Autograph, anecdote, squee! And when Nim first volunteered (*let's not forget that: you DID volunteer*) to host her, the over-the-top delirium of gratitude Veruca's responded with had been as endearing as it was gratifying – all now, in 20/20 hindsight, nothing but a bright red warning sign.

Why do you even need to meet him, anyhow? she keeps on asking Veruca, even now; idle curiosity turned psychic self-defense, news at eleven. T*OM, not Tim, right? Dude…he's just a guy.*

To which Veruca always replies, simply: *No. He's not.* The sheer weight of faith behind her words so scary-blind, it drains Nim of any sort of satisfactory response.

Strictly speaking, she can't deny Thomas Caudwell Darbersmere carries his own cloud of intrigue: Sole executor of the Darbersmere estate and Trust, he runs the family Import/Export business, even though he's less a straight-up nephew than a sort of half-cousin once removed – illegitimate son of the dead drug-addict daughter of Tim's Dad Eustace Darbersmere's first wife, with her second husband. There's speculation that since Tom didn't pop up until after Tim kicked it, maybe he forged his name on the will somehow in order to get hold of the business and/or the books… after all, he does apparently make part of his current dough from a publishing deal allowing him to "complete" any of Tim's unfinished manuscripts, extant or conveniently hitherto-undiscovered.

Does bear a scary resemblance to Young Tim, though, from what Nim can make out by comparing recent 'Net-snaps of Tom-and-his-wife (Alicia, social-climbing-American-former-nobody-turned-instant-somebody, The Speed's real ringmaster) with those awful 1970s photos Veruca dug up. For an otherwise sleek Christian Bale clone, the dude had some seriously funky polyester fetish, and unfortunately, bad fashion sense seems to have *not* skipped Tom's generation.

But like most digital snapshots taken by overexcited amateur paparazzi, the majority of Tom's pics tend to be caught in mid-motion, too smeary to make much out, his face flashbulb-haloed, back-lit, blurred equally often by laughter or the smoke from Alicia's ever-present cigarette. It's possible that in person Tom may look disquietingly unlike his revered uncle, and be nothing like him in personality, either.

"Y'know, V," Nim says now, all casual, "I was thinking, just for tonight, we—"

(meaning you)

"—should maybe go easy on the Tim stuff."

Veruca blinks, mid-sip; puts her cup down. "How do you mean, 'go easy'?"

"Well…the club, the launch, this whole night, I mean—" She hesitates. "Given who's running the show, it might be kind of, I don't know – rude."

Nim lets a heartbeat tick by, bracing herself. But Veruca, surprisingly enough, nods.

"Listen," she starts, so quietly Nim has to strain to hear, "I get that. I just need to…figure something out, and I think if I could only see Tom, hear his voice, it might all come clear for me. Plus – I might have something for him."

"Like what?"

"…something," she replies, mysterious to the Nth degree. And it makes Nim want to—

(laugh, cry, puke, punch her in the mouth, *hard*)

Sitting there with half a muffin in hand, rehearsing comebacks she'll never quite have the balls to make; Nim huffs out, angry at her own cowardice, then tries to cover the sound with a cough. Then looks up, reflexively, to find Veruca staring right at her.

"You okay?" Veruca asks, the very pitch of it enough to make Nim snap:

"Do I seem *not* okay?"

Veruca flushes. "Uh…well…"

(get to it, get to it, get to it)

"…you seem really pissed off, actually. Is something wrong? Are you…not gonna take me there, tonight, or something?"

Yeah: 'Cause that's the deal-breaker, right there. Isn't it?

"Of course I'll still take you," Nim snarls, eventually. "Jesus fucking Christ! Couldn't get there on your own, that's for sure. Besides which, I already Goddamn said I would, didn't I?"

"Yeah, you did." A beat, then: "Why?"

(Why indeed?)

"Because I didn't know you, back then," Nim says. And gets up to pay their tab, back stiff, turned flat one-eighty to Veruca. Like she's shutting a door in her face.

«« — »»

From Scarwid and Ffolkes' *Overview of Millennial Fantasists* (Coldwater Flat Press, 2000)—

FFOLKES: I'll begin with a few of your late uncle's more noteworthy reviews, if I may…

TOM DARBERSMERE: Oh yes, please.

FFOLKES: "The bloody meat of Tim Darbersmere's stories is always the exact opposite of the soothing, reasonable tone in which he communicates it." "Never has such beautiful and clever prose been suborned to the service of such decadent and puerile ideas." "Solipsistic to the point of sociopathy. Darbersmere is the sole protagonist of every story he's ever written…the hero, the villain, and (most certainly) the love interest." As you begin your own writing career, does the potential after-effect of these remarks disturb you?

DARBERSMERE: Not at all. I aspire, one day, to a similar critical impact.

FFOLKES: And "Ellis Iseland", what about her? Why has she become central to your fiction, too – carried over from your late Uncle's work, for continuity's sake? Or does she represent some more personal archetype, perhaps?

DARBERSMERE: Ellis who? Oh, you mean the chainsmoking war profiteer *femme fatale* from that last story Uncle Tim's supposed to have written, the one no one's ever reliably found a copy of?

FFOLKES: "The Emperor's Old Bones", yes.

DARBERSMERE: Where we find out the secret key to eternal life and renewed youth is making a meal of filleted ghetto child? Well, that's a bit like quizzing me on a viral Internet meme, one of those things that seep into the creative community's groundwater with anyone noticing how, and wondering why you don't get more of a distinct response.

FFOLKES: But she turns up here too, doesn't she, in Tim's own "Echidna Comes Rising" – he calls her Lisha Illen, granted, but each version is described using much the same language. Or here, from your novella "Copshawholme Fair": Elfis Isham. Essa Highman in *A Dull Wind Blows from the North*, Ester Smallwater-hame in *Safe in Their Alabaster Hives*...

DARBERSMERE: Does she? I suppose she must. How extraordinary! You know, I never read my own stuff once I'm finished with it, no more than I *re*-read his. I really must start.

FFOLKES: Everyone's got a type, I suppose.

DARBERSMERE: Oh, certainly. Every woman I write is my wife, to one degree or another.

«« — »»

The package is waiting for them when they get back to Nim's. As Veruca trudges past, still sunk in the same kicked-puppy misery haze that made their silent walk back so excruciating, Nim unlocks her mailbox and frowns at the result: A flat rectangle wrapped in subtly-striped brown paper with a registered-mail barcode in one corner, poking up out of the rest of Friday's bills. The return is a name she doesn't recognize, in Australia; scrawled across the front in letters two inches tall, meanwhile, is—

ATTN VERUCA LUZ c/o NIMUE EWALT

"*Veruca!*" Nim's a little startled by, but not really sorry for, her own shout's volume; Veruca skitters back down, eyes wide, as she holds up the parcel. "What the hell? You gave my mailing address out to *some guy*, without even asking me? You—"

But Veruca throws herself headlong to rip it from Nim's hand, tearing at the paper, all the while emitting such a fast high-pitched squeak it takes Nim a second to decipher it: "Ooh, owemjee owemjee owemjee owemjee owemJEEEE!"

Owemjee, equalling O. M. G. As in Oh My God, in 'Net-compacted typespeak for terminally lazy hunt-and-peckers. As in—

Let's get this straight...you can't be bothered to fill in four extra letters, like you were actually saying something out loud? Like a GENU-INE FUCKING ADULT?

"What is it?" Nim makes herself ask, at last. And Veruca turns it towards her with a *Prestige*-y flick of the wrist, showmanlike, conspiratorial: Ricepaper cardstock cover, deep Chinese red, embossed carp design. Pretty classy, actually, for some cheap little one-story printing...

"Read the title," she says. So Nim does.

(Oh.)

For a moment, she's back on that blackwater beach, under that starless sky. It sort of hurts to breathe. The letters swim in front of her, drunken and dripping, pixilated in some almost tidal way – twenty characters if you count the apostrophe, letters slightly raised, DomCasual BT script at 22-point font. The Late's name underneath, silver-stamped; his real signature or a very good imitation, probably traced from a treasured memento, by somebody like Veruca.

Because: There it is, the thing itself, its lacquered cover slick like skin under her increasingly sweaty fingers. And she can't take her eyes off it.

While Veruca watches, her own green gaze reflective, serene. Almost sad.

"You see why I had to come, now?" she asks, gently. To which Nim can only nod, once. And then—

«« — »»

Flash-cut to later, as Nim logs on to CreepTracker.org while Veruca cat-naps, getting herself good and charged for the full-frontal assault on Darbersmere Central. CreepTracker's Nim's favorite chat-hangout of choice, not to mention run by another "friend" she's yet to meet in the non-virtual flesh (and man, is she starting to think that may never seem like a "good" idea again, no matter *how* calm and reasonable Ross Puget may seem when he's just text on a screen, plus a blurred icon that's all crested prematurely-grey hair and wide, crooked smile...)

Word on the 'Net, and it's not like he denies this, is Ross used to co-run a three-way haz-mat cleaning service – Glouwer-Cirrocco-Puget, currently defunct due to one of the founding members being kind of dead, the other kind of nuts – that was either a total scam or less about asbestos removal than scouring sites of "psychic fragments". <not ghosts, there are no ghosts. just, stuff.>

With a space/pause between <just,> and <stuff> that's somehow more convincing than the most detailed explanation could *ever* be – in person, or otherwise.

Nim's fingers fly over the keyboard, 60-words-a-minute speedy, more sure than she's felt since she first touched "The Emperor's…" fabled frontispiece. Asking—

GirlInTree: <the speed of pain, whats the deal? hear anything?>

KirlianPhotog: <how so?>

GirlInTree: <like psychic fragments etc.>

KirlianPhotog: <aaah. comprehension dawns, hold on> <clicky-clicky>

Her server sings its "you have mail!" song, and she keys the link Ross just sent her: More like link salad, actually – different sites, different names, different angles. But the key-words stay the same: BODY FOUND…C.O.D. NOT APPARENT…NO CHARGES…WITNESS TESTIMONY LATER DISCOUNTED… INTOXICATED…UNDER INFLUENCE OF DRUGS…EXTREME COLD…BRIGHT WHITE LIGHT…

KirlianPhotog: <got it?>

GirlInTree: <yup:)>

Seven people over three years in two separate clubs – one in New York, one in San Francisco. OWNER ALICIA DARBERSMERE HAD NO COMMENT…

KirlianPhotog: <thats tom ds wife right?>

GirlInTree: <the very same>
<taking veruca to the speeds opening tonite, just wanted> <uknow>

A pause: *Know what, exactly?* Then—

KirlianPhotog: <ok, sounds dicey 2 me>

GirlInTree: <cmon>

KirlianPhotog: <u asked man>

And then there's another chime – another email. Man, Ross codes almost faster than Nim can read…

(but not quite)

GirlInTree: <radiant boy?>

KirlianPhotog: <horribly murdered kid turned harbinger of death; the bright white lights a big giveaway. also, in the emperors>

GirlInTree: <that whole cannibal dinner thing?>

KirlianPhotog: <i got eaten alive just so 2 freaks could be young again, id be pretty pissed>

GirlInTree: <good point>

"Saying" it ultra-cool, a throw-away snark-snap, old-school Buffy-style. But feeling the hairs on the back of her neck go up nonetheless, oblivious to cliché, as her stomach clenches and flips: The disgusting gastronomic concept from which Tim's notorious "memoir" takes its title playing itself out behind her eye-sockets, utterly unwanted, bad enough when done to a damn fish. Let alone a *child*...

Except, he didn't. No one did. It's a frigging STORY, Nimue.

GirlInTree: <so>

<whats the 411? according 2 the monster manual>

KirlianPhotog: <on what, the radiant boy? like>

GirlInTree: <2 stay safe>

<if u have 2 get near it>

A *long* pause, this time. Long enough for Nim to remember the last time they "spoke", when she spilled on Ross about Veruca's RL nutsiness. Only to get a similarly wry line in return: <u do know ur probly no RL treat urself, right?>

And thinking: *Yeah, granted.* Which may well be why she and Ross keep it strictly between the lines – why they've never thought to hook up for real, even though they live in the same city. Like they're afraid to meet each other in the flesh, for fear of being disappointed that their "soulmate" might come attached to tics they can't stand: Veruca, all over again. Thinking...

Shit, am I THAT easy? That HARD?

But all things must come to an end, even this. And so the pause breaks at last, with Ross's final post—

<if u have 2 get near it>

KirlianPhotog: <dont>

<just>

<just dont>

«« —»»

Hours later, meanwhile...

...they're already through the door, inside the Speed of Pain, where the bass is loud enough to blow your hair back, bottom-heavy enough to sound like an Abyssal snake coiling and uncoiling in some parallel dimension. Up on stage, two women gyrate in a black-lit go-go cage, each using a hand-held buzzsaw to strike sparks off the crotch of the other's metal bikini. Posters are plastered everywhere, blurring together in the changing light; there's a livid yellow flyer on the floor at Nim's feet, one of many, piled in clumps so high they brush the ankles. It reads:

TONIGHT, GRAND OPENING, AFTER MIDNIGHT. NO COVER. DEEJAY CEMETERY OX 'TIL DAWN. FEATURED BANDS – FUDGETONGUE, DUST-GOWNED, PLUS RANCIDULCET (THE SOFT SOUND OF ROT).

Nim looks around, throat already raw with stray pot smoke and heat, vaguely recalling what it used to be like, back when this was still something else. But now it looks somehow darker and bigger, offputtingly so – a huge overhanging ceiling strung with lightbulb stars, a dance-floor inset intermittently with stained glass and lit from beneath, to weirdly patterned effect. Everything swims, hypnagogic, dream-sick.

And it's at this point, naturally enough – when she's already off-centre, and the noise conspires to render her all-but-unintelligible – that Nim sees Veruca's face assume an awful look of slack hunger as somebody she can only assume is Tom Darbersmere appears in the middle distance, near one end of the room-long bar: That man-shaped thing with the laughing white null for a face, arm wound around the shoulders of a woman (Alicia?) whose long brown hair hangs heavy, interrupted only by a rising dragon's tongue of smoke.

Veruca surges against the crowd, chapbook already in hand, but Nim grabs her by the arm before she can quite start to move.

"You know there's no way any of that actually happened, right?" she bellows over the roar.

"What part?"

"Like, any of it? Holy crap, Veruca, get a fucking grip. I mean, this is some *sick* sort of shit right here – "

Veruca purses her lips, a disappointed *moue*, like: *Oh, Nim.* And says, only:

"I have to go."

"Veruca, *look* at them!" Nim has to scream now, feeling her face distort with the effort. "Does he *look* seventy? Does she look, what, a fucking *hundred*?"

"Not any more."

"They couldn't get away with it. Not today. They *couldn't*. Veruca!"

But she's gone. Vanished into the crowd, a salmon slipping effortlessly beneath the rapids, heading upstream.

And it's stupid, but Nim keeps on glitching on that…story. "The Emperor's Old Bones", which she finally read in full on her way up here, under streetcar-light. That scene in the kitchen, that last phone conversation between "Tim" and the Head Chef at the Precious Dragon Shrine…

Sure, the author makes it sound "plausible" enough, in the moment – that's his damn job. Even if you accept "The Emperor's…" as Tim Darbersmere's work to begin with, though, all the Wiki'ing in the world won't let you skip over the fact that he did this exact same sort of shit before, a *couple* of times: The case-study for a disease that didn't exist, that 1960s piece where he convinced everybody who was anybody he'd lost his arms to gangrene, after a car accident outside Cannes… And yes, glamour and exoticism turns tarnished if it's revealed that the gruesomeness is factual, not just squeamish, gleeful metaphor – but it doesn't matter, does it? After all—

– things like that *aren't true*. Thankfully. Because if you thought, if you even suspected, even dreamed they were, then it'd be time to—

(bury yourself in the sand, face-down)

And besides which: How *could* it go unnoticed, even if? How could such a price be paid over and over again in a world of SINs, DNA and GoogleEarth, of YouTube and datamining, a world drowning in celebrity poon-shots and political blowjobs, where nothing stays secret for long?

Yet: *That's* exactly *why*, Nim suddenly realizes, silent and unmoving amid the rave, completely unconscious of the odd looks she's getting from the crowd. *Veruca thinks she's stumbled across the greatest story never told, so she wants in.* Not to take part, never that – but just to know, to be certain, to be on the Inside, for once. If only the once.

So either Veruca's just batshit and about to get thrown out for spouting craziness all over the host, or...

But Nim shies away from the *or*, on principle; She doesn't believe it, doesn't need to. Forcing herself into movement, shouldering her way through the crowd, sliding between bodies where she can't force them apart, ignoring the passing gropes and the leered invitations; nothing matters now except heading Veruca off, before she can render both their chances at a genuine life even more remote.

Then – thud, stumble, recognition: Anticlimax. Veruca stands (more accurately, sways) at the edge of a small circle ringing the good-looking man and his smoke-wreathed wife. Her face is pallid, her eyes wide and bright, and she clutches the chapbook to her heaving chest like a shield.

A second later, Tom Darbersmere can't help but see her; his eyes widen, ever so slightly. Almost as though he—

(*recognizes* her)

He leans towards her, lips moving. Something that might be: *My dear.* And Veruca, Veruca...

Recoils, falls back. Goes whiter than white. Then backs away 'til she hits somebody, blunders further, turns tail—

—and flees.

《《—》》

Nim follows after, into the maelstrom. Past couples dry-humping up against the door-frames, through room after room of excoriatingly loud music of every possible type, a thousand-song playlist set on infinite shuffle. In one of them, people toss wreaths of lit sparklers back and forth, like they're putting on some carny magic show. In another, a man hangs from the ceiling by Sundance hooks, a softball stuck with nails held tight in either hand; his friends stand underneath, videotaping the ordeal, as blood drips onto their camera's lens. Each successive room is hotter, louder, stranger—

Nim wipes sweat away and checks her watch, only to find she's lost more than an hour. Thinks: '*Cause time works differently, in here.*

Then catches a flash of blonde up ahead, ducking through yet another doorway, and heaves forward again, trying to bridge the gap between them. Ending up somehow caught inside what seems like ten or so feet of bead curtains strung one behind the other, instead – she swims through them, their warm plastic leaving a sticky trail behind everywhere it touches, and spills through to the other side: A cool, dim room so insulated she actually can't hear the music playing in the rest of the club anymore (though she can still feel the sheer erratic pulse of it coming up, floor acting as a remarkably efficient conductor, even through the three-inch soles of her shoes). The sudden contrast makes her heart slam up against her ribs, beating fast. She pauses, long enough to take it all in—

Dim and spare and hung with red, everywhere Nim looks. And it really must be later on, because the only people in there are Tom, Alicia (lighting a fresh cigarette with a flourish, then flipping her antique silver lighter shut) and a squat woman Nim doesn't recognize at all: Thick glasses behind which her eyes swim like tiny fishes; a courderoy jumpsuit with purple irises printed all over it; beige hair, beige skin, beige voice.

She carries something small and squishy-looking in a baby-harness slung tight over her massive bosom – *not* a miscarriage that's been dug up and somehow laminated, as Nim horribly assumed at first sight, but a plush creature of some weird derivation, with a gaze as hooded and squinty as her own. It jiggles back and forth with her breath as she stares down at the table, a tealight candle slopping dangerously between her palms.

Tom, to Alicia: "Not *this* again."

And: "I need to know," Alicia replies, her voice nothing like Nim night have expected – flat, Midwestern, abnormally "normal". "Especially now. Think you'd feel the same, *tai pan*."

"Would you?"

"Yeah. You saying you don't?"

A spark passes between them, chased with a sigh. "It is *your* club," Tom points out, finally.

Alicia grins. "Well, okay, then." To the woman: "Is it here, right now?"

The woman gives a long sigh, lips twitching feebly, as though she doesn't want to answer. At the same time, beneath the frame of

Nim's gaze, something stirs; she strains to focus on it for a second, before realizing—

(oh GOD)

—it's that *thing*, that mockery, the woman's snug-coccooned un-child, kicking out slightly in all directions, like it's testing uterine waters. While the bulgy eyes blink and the mouth pulse in and out, stop-motion slow, like it's clearing its throat…and from the woman's own mouth, a slurred voice issues, hissing:

"…alwaysss herrre."

(Like it's puppeting *her*. Not the other way 'round.)

Oh MAN, I need to get out of here.

Nim backs up, praying Tom and Alicia won't notice; thankfully, they don't seem to. Not Alicia, anyhow – who leans forward, brows knit, and keeps on quizzing.

"Is it dangerous?"

"Nottt ttto youuu."

"How do we get rid of it?"

"Youuu can'ttt."

"Why not?"

A pause. "Becaussse…" the thing says, at last. "Itsss yoursss. Bothhh offf youuu. Yourrre…"

"…part of it," Tom fills in, softly.

Alicia snorts. "Like fun, *tai pan*."

(That phrase: Chinese? Nim knows she's heard it before, just can't think when, or how – then feels the down on the back of her neck go up again, ruff-stiff, as she suddenly recalls exactly where.)

More snore-y breathing. The "doll" speaks on, ignoring them both. Says:

"Ittt…*hhhe*. Knowsss youuu aaate himmm. Hisss liiife. Hisss… paiiin."

"Well," Tom says, softly, "he would, wouldn't he? Can't really miss it while it's happening, not even if it's done expertly."

Alicia shoots him a look. "Enough of that crap," she says, warningly, which gets her nothing but a single arched brow in return. As Tom points out—

"Really, Lish: You're the one who *asked*."

And all through this, Nim is backing away, her face and body held equally rigid. She feels the plastic bead curtain hit her spine, stroke up her back, then collapse together in front of her; Tom,

Alicia and the puppeted puppeteer blur and distort between the strands, as they fall into place. Step by step, Nim forces herself through, drowning in plastic. The music's getting louder again, still reverberant with distance and distortion, and underneath it there's a strange cross-current of sound; phantom cellos, sawing up from below.

Recognition's a jolt of ice and adrenaline to the spine: That second layer, the Apocalyptica version of "Until It Sleeps," is her ringtone. Nimue fumbles in her purse and digs the phone out, the muffled tinniness of its repeated music refusing to fade, like it's wrapped in invisible cotton. She puts it to her ear.

"Veruca?"

Static, broken by arrhythmic crackles that might be words. Nim feels her balance going out. She can't tell if she's pushing or falling. Her feet have gone numb. The plastic beads trail slowly alongside, kelp fronds in a nightmare sea that cling, and clutch, and—

Give way.

Nim stumbles back out into the Speed, the noise disorienting for half an instant. Then her mind seizes on Veruca's voice – now obscured by nothing but the ordinary background roar – echoing in her ear. *"Nim, where are you? Nim, please, talk to me – "*

"On the floor!" Nim shouts. She casts about, futilely seeking blonde cornrows or lens-distorted green eyes. "Where the hell are you? What happened? Why – "

"I couldn't do it. God, I was so wrong – sorry—" A hiss and a coughing huff follow, sounds Nim finds almost welcome in their previously-infuriating familiarity: Veruca's taking a stress-triggered blast off her inhaler. *"But I was right, too, you saw – had to see – tell me you saw—"*

"V., where the fuck *are* you?" Nim yells back, jamming a finger past her naked tragus. "Your voice sounds weird."

"It's HIM, Nimue. Looks exactly the same, just...young."

"*Who* looks the same?"

Another huff. Then, even fainter – like Veruca's talking through a mouthful of cotton—

"...im..."

Nim scans around again, frantically. Eventually, something – some light-sliver glimpsed from the corner of one tearing eye –

133

suggests where Veruca might have gone. "Dude," she says, "listen to me, okay? Are you in the john?"

A fizzle-click "s"-slur is her only reply; might pass for "yes", on a bad day. Nim takes it as her cue to head for the pertinent sign at speed, a flickering Georgia O'Keefe rubyfruit done in flickering neon. As Veruca keeps on chattering, between white noise waves:

"...said, it's him. Them. They DID it...like the story says, not made up, it's all true. All of it."

"I'm comin', man. I'm almost there."

Puts her hand on the door, poised to push. And hears Veruca's voice from inside, twinned: Once via phone, once through the wood itself, but shit-scared either way. Suddenly droping to a dull, tiny whisper, cold inside and out, as she breathes—

" – Nim, stop, keep out. Somebody's *here*."

The phone gives a half-silent pop!, drained battery abruptly dead. Yet Nim hears another voice fading in, nevertheless – well, not hears it, exactly. More like remembering what it must have sounded like when somebody else heard it, a long, long time ago. A juvenile voice, pitched high, with that wandering edge that usually means drink, or drugs, or particularly high fever, saying...several things at once, it seems like, each sentence butting up against the one before, overlapping slightly. Like so:

I'm COLD...Where you goin', man? You said I could watch TV... Can't move my legs...Why won't you look at me? I'm right here, man... Just LOOK at me. Please...

Nim can't stop herself from applying her full weight against the handle, leaning steadily inwards. The door flaps out and back, spitting her into a washroom so ultra-cold and bright it's practically Kubrickian – and as Nim looks up into the mirror, for one split second, she thinks she sees somebody standing behind her, a shadow quivering against the crack between jamb and post on the nearest stall's door. So she turns, finds it gone; turns back, and finds the room is suddenly properly dim. All except—

—that other stall, the one within easy arm's reach with its own door swinging half-open, a single black Nike trainer-encased foot...

(Veruca's)

...wedged between hinge and jamb, not letting it rebound, let alone come to a full entropic stop.

And: *God*, Nim thinks again, though it's not like she believes in one. Not officially.

Because Veruca's inside, of course. Propped up on the toilet, pants securely fastened, *that book* wide open in her lap. But Nim can't think of much to do about it except take "The Emperor's..." from her, gingerly, holding it up by the corner like it's sticky; let the spine flop open to expose its ill-glued core, its cracked and fraying threads. Or press 911 on speed-dial, hoping she was wrong about her phone, while simultaneously averting her eyes – resolutely determined not to look down, not to try and read over her dead friend's shoulder.

Kneeling there, touching the book with as little of one fingernail as she can manage, like she's afraid it'll rub off on her somehow, its rough cover slick and dirty as dead scale under her hand. And then there's this sound from behind her, from the corner – somebody who doesn't really need to breathe doing it anyway, deliberately clearing their no-throat, so she won't crap herself with fear.

Child-light footsteps approaching, wetly, from behind her. A skinless little hand, slimy on her shoulder. An unwavering, pitiless light like a fifty-bulb night-shooting rack igniting with no perceptible warning, back-haloing the floor, the stall, Veruca's sprawling corpse...

...while the voice, that voice, repeats every one of the phrases Nim heard through the bathroom door over again in an endless, profane loop: No ending and no beginning, just – pollution, ripples spreading outwards. Curdling everything in its path.

Just LOOK at me, man. I'm right here. So...LOOK.

(No. Not gonna.)

Can't move. So COLD.

(I'm sorry for that, kid. I really, really am.)

Yeah? Then turn around, right now. And look.

(You can't make me.)

Oh no?

(Is that what you think, little geeky girl?)

You'd be amazed what I can do, I only take a mind to.

Heart bruising itself against her sternum from the inside, a

muscle-and-valve jackhammer. As the voice keeps on, never raising, never falling. Never slowing. Never stopping

He said…he was gonna take…care…of me…

Nim sits there on the bathroom floor with her eyes closed and
two fingers jammed deep into the book, still automatically holding Veruca's place for her, as hot red tears run down her face to
drip on the bright white floor below. Sits there until it stops talking, until she's *almost* certain it's gone away for good. Then keeps
on sitting there anyhow, hips and knees burning, cold creeping up
through her pant-legs; her eyes still downcast, still shut lid-tight,
afraid to open them again, in case.

Until, at last, somebody else comes in to pee. And the screaming finally starts.

«« — »»

Though the cops get there surprisingly fast, by the time they
arrive, the Speed's already cleaned itself up (and out) with alarm-
ing efficiency. No more bloodsports in the corners, no more pot-
stink or bad behavior. Even the soundtrack manages to reel itself
back a notch or ten, so nobody has to shout to make themselves
heard while they give their deposition.

They let Nim go at 3:30 AM, waving her briskly past the same
ambulance they loaded Veruca's bag-clad body into. And there,
beyond the yellow tape, she finds Tom Darbersmere waiting for
her.

"Your friend…" He begins. "…the girl with the glasses, same
one who came up to me, 'round midnight?"

"Her name's Veruca," Nim finds herself telling him, mouth
suddenly too numb to quite form every syllable. A fact he doesn't
really seem to notice, observing only:

"Veruca: Was it really. How absolutely marvellous."

A statement, not a question, odd to the point of insult. It
stings enough to make her look up, into his eyes—

—where she *does* see sympathy, of a kind. But only like a shallow sheen: All surface, china-cerulean, pale and dry and faded.
And *not* young, when you come to look at them this closely – in
no fucking way young, not at all. Not even a little, tiny bit.

"My dear," Tom Darbersmere says, pressing her hot hand between his two smooth, cool, dry ones, "I am so very sorry for your loss."

Sorrowful and civil, utterly archaic. And so much like Veruca's treasured imitation of his late uncle, it brings sick to Nim's mouth. Something burning in her nose, behind her teeth, choking her. Something deep down in her gut and lower still, sinking to where it makes her groin ache and her muscles flex, burning, burning, burning to cut and run.

("He's exactly the damn *same*..."

Who, Veruca?

"...*im*...")

Him: Tom. Or, rather—

– *Tim.*

(The not-so-Late.)

With Alicia – *Ellis*, Iseland – standing right behind him, at a middle distance, puffing away. Her smoke-colored eyes boring into Nim, slow-motion bullets. As though she thinks if she just does it long enough, she'll be able to read Nim's address off her DNA.

And: "Thanks," Nim husks, at last, dropping his hand like it's radioactive. Before running off into the night, away from the Speed of Pain, never (hopefully) to return.

Later, she's over half the way home, sitting on the Vomit Comet with tears running down both cheeks – unsought, unstemmed – before she feels the edge of it touch her thigh as she shifts, and realizes she still has the only known copy of that nonexistent fucking book of his right there in her purse.

Thinking: *Something needs to come of this. This needs to COME to something. Bite your ass. Bite BOTH your asses, you lying, dream-killing, kid-eating, unspeakable fucking, FUCKING...*

Thinking: *Because Veruca's dead, and that thing, it's dead too. But you're alive, still.*

You always will be.

Thinking, thinking, thinking: Nothing relevant, not really, aside from the dreadful half-sob that racks her now from head to toe, epileptic. Because it's late, and she's tired, more tired than she's ever been in her life. Because her only friend in the world is gone, and – stupid fixations, obsessive eccentricities, annoying vocal inflections aside – the world she has to live in now, alone, is oh so much the poorer for it.

Nim hugs "The Emperor's Old Bones" to her chest with both arms, tight like she gave birth to it, and shuts her eyes once more, knowing she'll have to keep moving now, but not knowing for exactly how long. Certain she won't sleep 'til dawn, at least. Or, maybe—

—ever again.

Mort Castle has over 600 publications to his credit: You'll find his work in classic men's cheesecake mags like CAVALIER *and* MR. *to literary publications like* RIVERSIDE QUARTERLY *and* BOMBAY GIN, *from the confessions magazines* TRUE SECRETS *and* INTIMATE ROMANCES *to agricultural publications such as* HOG FARM MANAGEMENT, *from ... Eclectic, okay? You get the idea. He's published seven novels, with* CURSED BE THE CHILD *having sales of near 100,000 and* THE STRANGERS *optioned for film. His third short story collection* NEW MOON ON THE WATER, *Full Moon Press, will be released later this year.*

Castle's been nominated for a number of awards, including the Bram Stoker (six times), the Pushcart Prize (four times) and the International Horror Guild award (only once). Cited as one of "21 Leaders in the Arts for the 21st Century in Chicago's Southland" by the Sun-Times Newspaper Group, Castle is finding new success in Poland (You like me, Mr. Walesa, you really ...) where two of his books were among the "Best of 2008" according to Newsweek *magazine.*

Writer-in-residence for Chicago Heights (IL) High School District 206 and a teacher in the fiction writing department of Columbia College Chicago, Castle has 12 feet of book shelf filled with the published work of his students and former students. Married to Jane for 38 years, Castle lives in Crete, Illinois, plays acoustic guitar like an un-reconstructed (if balding) folky, and has no plans to buy any digital book device until, like a real book, it can be dropped in the bathtub and easily if wavily set right with a microwave or clothes dryer.

MORT CASTLE

Moon on the Water

Jazzmen make it 10 or 20 years after they die. Fats Navarro, Yardbird, Coltrane ... Sure, there were people who dug them while they were here to lay it down, but it's now, years after the final bar, and gangbusters, right?

So I'm thinking it's soon going to be Breeze's time. The past year, there've been a couple reissues of sides we cut years ago, decent sales and good reviews in *Downbeat* and even – hip to this? – *Rolling Stone*.

And Breeze's trip is the stuff that makes for a cult following. He was a junky, you see. Good box office there – check with Lady Day. And Bird and Chet Baker.

And they did fish Breeze out of Lake Michigan one cold autumn day in '59, found him with his fingers on the keys of his sax.

≪≪—≫≫

Any city's a rough-old, tough-old dues paying time for a jazzman, but Chicago was better than New York for Breeze and me. That's why we blew the Apple Major, where cool and post bop and hard bop pretty much ruled, and where, pre-Coltrane revelations, if you were into something new, and you were Ofay besides, it was guaranteed nowheresville.

And Chicago was a better scene, too, if you were in "the life." If you kept your cool, the heat did not jump all over you when you went on the prowl in search of white powder.

And Chicago had the lake. First time he saw it, Breeze said, "Yes." I knew what he meant. Looking one way, all you'd see was city. Then you could turn your back on it, forget it, and there was endless water, frozen in two a.m. moonlight, making you understand loneliness and eternity. And maybe you had the kind of thought that's like smoke, curling and disappearing, thinking about magic and just how small we all are and maybe you even dreamed the kid-dream of dream monsters that swim and slither

143

just under the surface of water and just out of sight.

Yeah, for the good solid citizens of Chicago, the city that works is also the city that sleeps and when the square johns were doing Morpheus, there were many times when you could find Breeze and me by the lake. Breeze would have his horn. Most everywhere he went – then – the sax was with him. Sometimes when it was really right, the heroin rushing through you and turning your vision incandescent, you could see the radiance, the notes shining on the water, perfect and pure for an instant before they shattered and changed into foam.

So, for us Chicago did indeed make it. We had a two room dump just off Wells Street. We scored scag, did not get strung out, did not get burned, did not get beefed and we swung enough gigs to pay the freight.

It was Chicago that we found Micah and really started to get it together. Micah was stand-up bass. He was shadow-skinny and yes, he had the hands, long, long fingers and fast. Micah was younger than we were, a dude who'd dropped out of college to do the jazz thing, but there was a monkey on Micah's back, too, so we got music-tight, junky-tight and it was like it was all supposed to happen.

And we were working on and getting to and sometimes touching, really *touching* – close to the sound.

Uh-huh, the sound. What was it we wanted? What we were after?

What we did not want: tired-out, straight ahead swing. Not spit-it-out all flash and fingers be-bop. Not thud and boom and stretch it so they think you're saying something when you're only blowing smoke.

A moment for metaphysics, okay? A moment to direct your eyes on what those Impressionist painters, Renoir and Monet and Degas and Caillebotte and Cassatt and Manet, the masters of the moment, were doing with hay stacks and rivers and sunrises and railroad stations.

We wanted morning light coming through the clouds the second before the sun goes orange-pink. We wanted not a dream but the way you feel when you almost remember the dream. We wanted it be a little bit like you think maybe God is.

And looking back and thinking back and sometimes, oh, way

down there, really going back, I wonder if we didn't want the moon on the water?

Maybe that.

Maybe.

Breeze played alto. I was guitar. Micah, on the bottom, was the heartbeat. We didn't have drums, didn't need them with Micah. Here's the root, here's the core, here's the *center*, that was Micah on bass. No reason to make a clash and clatter.

Of course, Mulligan, the Jeru, with his quartet gigging out in Citrusland, did not have drums, either, but he was going his very own horn-rimmed academic glasses way and we were into something entirely else.

There were times when we laid it down, the calm and the ease and the gentle. There were times when we found the song inside you that you didn't even know was there.

There were good times.

«« —— »»

And then she came out of the lake.

«« —— »»

It was summer, around three in the morning. There were "No Trespassing – Keep Out" signs, but there was also a six foot section of chain link fence that was down. We'd left Micah at a restaurant, soothing his junky craving for sweet with Danish and coffee with lots of sugar. It was just Breeze and me and his horn.

It was not a beach for people. Rocks, great lumping boulders, and smaller ones, smooth here and jagged there, making walking something entirely else, an unearthly experience best appreciated when seriously high. Ahead of us, the beach curved. A long, falling-down pier stabbed into the moon-gleaming water like a giant, arthritic finger pointing your way to nowhere.

We drifted, the two of us and the muggy quiet, our steps taking us close to the waterline. We stood on the rocks. Spray splashed our shoes. Breeze squeezed the mouthpiece between his lips. He shut his eyes, doing some key-flipping to clear the horn. Then he let a few notes slide out of the bell, full of breath, just on the verge of breaking. There was no set time to what he laid down. It was just this shaky, brute insistence to continue, like an old man marching heavy-footed to the end.

Then he went to this riffing thing, kind of a squeak-jump-around, like the feeling you get when your arm's tied up, you've got the bubbling hit, *your* bubbling hit, in the dropper, and you know in just one eye-blink you'll spike that vein for the big rush.

That was when I saw something in the water and that was when Breeze's tune changed. Way out there, way beyond the pier, someone was swimming.

Breeze's horn was going slow, notes rounded with a tired moan edge, like a bad morning when you've got to reach for the white port to kill the pain. Sure, I knew Breeze's stuff – knew where he was coming from and how he got there – but he was putting down a sound I had never heard before. It went way back to the beginnings, to swirling fog of wishes and visions. His sax was luring and welcoming. It was the curved Viking horn bringing the far-traveled dragonship into the bay, to safe harbor and warm greeting and balance.

What was out there was a lady, a lady in the lake. She came swimming toward shore in rhythm to Breeze's music. Behind her was an ever-vanishing trail in the water. From second to second, the connection from where she was to where she had been was disappearing.

When she reached the shallows, she stood up, came walking out. She moved sure-footed on clicking pebbles, like a dance.

Breeze lowered the horn, let it swing on the cord.

She did not look frightened or surprised. All she looked – here's a word so tired it sags – was beautiful.

The moon was a halo behind her head. Her long lake-gleaming hair hung tangled like tree snakes on jungle branches. She had magic-cruel eyes and her mouth was the soft passion of a bitch-goddess.

And I remember thinking she should have been naked. Oh, she wasn't, had on bra and panties made translucent with wetness, but she should have been.

She came up to us and, in the moment before she spoke, I felt it. You get tight with a dude, hang with him, do good times and bad, there are flashes when you know you're touching just what the other cat feels. That was how it was with Breeze and me.

She was working on Breeze, doing a real number.

How? Cannot say. The old bluesmen sing about the hoodoo. The square heads write songs for square heads about enchanted evenings and crowded rooms. But, when it all comes down, who the hell can really say?

"Hey, what are you guys doing here?"

The spell – and that's no real word for what it was – was gone. I heard the over-control in her voice that hipped me she was pretty well juiced confirmed by a heavy slash of booze on her breath.

"We're jazzmen," Breeze said, like that explained everything. In a way, maybe it did.

"Jazzmen… You know what I am?"

"A chick." I shrugged, always cool, even though, well, you never did feel cool around her.

"I'm a chick who got in the car and went cruising. I was looking for something, God knows what. I don't, not anymore, if I ever did. But you know, it seemed to make sense that I'd find it in the lake, so I went swimming. There were a couple times when I nearly reached that place where the moon was right on the water. But then it moved. It always moves just when you're there."

"That's the way it goes," I said, thinking about drunk talk and crazy ladies, neither of which is supposed to make sense but both do if you think about it when you're not really working at thinking.

Her eyes did three beats on me, then triple that on Breeze; she was deciding something. "Jazzmen," she said. "I want you to come with me."

Maybe this is just "years later" wisdom talking, but I think I was a little afraid. But hell, cool means you go the way it goes and you flow the way it flows.

She'd left her clothing under the pier. Without any attempt to dry off, she slipped into a beige dress, and then we followed her to her car, parked not too far away. She had a dark blue Lincoln.

We went to an apartment building on the Gold Coast. The doorman lamped Breeze and me with a look that said it wasn't his business what kind of whatevers rich people hung with but that didn't mean he had to dig us.

She lived so way up there in the ozone that she could have

gone next door to borrow a cup of flour from God. Massive furniture that made you feel like you'd disappeared when you sat down. Windows providing a view of the city that half-convinced you everything was all right down below. And the bar at the end of the living room was a juice head's dream of heaven.

The three of us, two jazzmen and a crazy lady, sat sipping wine, and on the hi-fi set – she had a solid classical collection – was Respighi's *Pines of Rome*. And then the mood, whatever it was, was broken by the click-click of the closing grooves of the record. The crazy lady smiled and said, "Which one of you is going to bed with me? Or is to going to be both?"

I shook my head. Sorry, lady, but even before H kills your ability, it knocks out your interest. But Breeze nodded and he went off down the hall with her, leaving his sax on the sofa.

I drank more wine. I put Vivaldi's *Four Seasons* on the turntable. I listened to that fine baroque sound from that time when music and the world were tight and structured and I heard something else. Breeze and the crazy lady were definitely getting it on, the old push-rub-tickle.

Weird, huh, because, like I said, dope is guaranteed to *un-do* your ability to *do*. All I could figure was that the chick had really gotten to Breeze and that no chemical negativity could out-do what she had done to him.

Think enchantment or conjure or sex magic or as Screamin' Jay has it, put a spell on you.

The solid truth? The *emmis*?

In the end, it doesn't much matter.

«« — »»

Who was she?

Some of this I picked up pretty quick and other stuff I only fell onto later.

Name: Lanna Borland. Heiress of a family that made many, many coins mainlining their chocolate bars into America's supersweet tooth.

Occupation: Full time fun-seeker, liver of the good life, from Port-au-Prince to the Riviera. Three divorces. Notch the bedpost to kindling with all the affairs. A bullfighter in Madrid, a member of the Dutch royal family, a sometime starving charcoal artist in New Orleans, a Hollywood alleged actor who never did figure out if he dug women, men, or both.

Goals in life: Something new. Something different. Kicks.

Philosophy of life: Get what you want.

Call it the classic poor little rich girl riff: You get everything, you get it all, and none of it really does it to you, nothing ever quite manages to knock you out, to wig you, zonk you, and knock you over and so, maybe after a while, nothing means anything and you just keep on looking for something.

This time around, figures me, Lanna Borland's something was A Jazzman.

And, man, she had him. Righteously. Breeze was solid gone on the crazy lady. Dead solid gone.

She just started being there, being there all the time. She was a bringdown and a hangup to the music. Breeze and Micah and I trying to work up new charts, she was there. While we were blowing on-stage at the Fickle Finger, she was there at a stage side table, those eyes lamping and vamping, doing a back beat on Breeze and his style. And when Micah and I tried to put it back together, to get it right and tight and true like it had been – sometimes – just the three of us grooving to the sounds inside we used to share, uh-uh, it wasn't three of us – it was four.

No. Not four. Split that. It was two and two. Micah and I. Breeze and Lanna.

She had Mr. B, one hundred and two percent, had him so that she was it – and there was nothing else.

There are women like that.

And sometimes I'd get into this off-the-wall mind *shpritz* about her, how she came out of the lake, and how, oh yeah, every little kid knows it before you teach him otherwise, way, way out in the water, way deep in the water, that's where the real monsters live.

Lanna drained Breeze. She zombified him. And she slipped this dream into his head and blood to take the place of everything that was meant to be there. "Lanna's Song." He was going to write a tune for her. His mind was exploding with it, that's what he said, but that song didn't happen for a long time, and for sure not then.

Breeze tried, tried like hell. And sometimes he thought he had it, asked me to do a minor slide-and-drift thing behind him. Then he'd shut his eyes and lay down a few notes. But those notes were never part of a song. They were always unconnected and alone.

Fact: The music went to hell. We fell into routines, repeating ourselves, re-tracing paths we had already worn out. When jazz is making it, it's as real an exploration as what Christopher Colombo pulled off; it's a voyage to a new world. But when you are not making it, uh-uh, you've got a nowhere trip on the city bus.

It was wrong. It was wrong for Breeze and Micah and me.

And naturally, Micah and I wanted Lanna Borland *G-O-N-E* – Gone. We did not hate her or anything like that. When you're cool, you do not hate.

Gone was just the way it had to be for her and for her to be gone was cool, okay?

«« — »»

Take it to the starting days of cold autumn. It was a Saturday afternoon, the kind of dragging-slow time when you don't feel alive because most of you isn't. We were at the pad Breeze and I still shared but where he was spending less and less time.

We were there.

Micah and I.

Breeze and Lanna.

She was next to Breeze on the Salvation Army reject sofa. She wasn't wearing makeup and she had on jeans and a black turtle-neck. Maybe she thought she was a beatnik.

"Look," Micah was saying, "we've got to get it set, and get it down, and soon." He was moving jerky all around the room, staccato steps and twitching. He wasn't long for needing to fix.

"Okay, man," Breeze said. "Stay cool, okay?"

"Cool is cool and fool is fool," Micah said. A junky will say something like that and another junky will take it for profound.

The A and R man at BACA Records had been riding us for a while, pressing to get us into the studio to lay down some new sides. This time around, looked like there'd be real distribution, thanks to a push we got from a critic at *Metronome*.

But Breeze was making bad kibosh on recording. We had to be ready. We wouldn't be ready, so sayeth the Breeze, until we had "Lanna's Song."

"Go slow, go slow," Breeze said. He stayed cool, but Lanna came on mucho cooler. She was turned toward him, knees up on the couch, and she was eyeballing him like the Amazing Kreskin.

"Go slow," Micah said. Indubitably.

"Hey," Breeze said softly, "you're like some strung out. Why don't you unlax yourself?"

It was a good idea. Micah looked as though he were ready for the crawly-shakes. He was in need of a calm-down, slow-down trip to the no-nerves-a-jangling Beyond.

Micah nodded. "Yeah."

He said to me. "I'm carrying but I'll need your works."

Call me your Eagle Scout with a merit badge in Heroin: I was prepared. He started to follow me into the bedroom, but Lanna said, "I want to watch." There was something pretty wild working in her face. It was more than curiosity. Maybe it was hope.

Sure, she had known all along that the three of us were in the life. That's not a number you can hide from someone who's always there. But she had never seen any of us fix.

You see, it was different then. The needle and you, that was a private thing, your time of prayer with your private god.

Breeze shrugged and said, "So she sees. So?"

So she saw. And dug what she was seeing, you could tell.

Micah was one smooth and careful user. He did the cooking slow, the tip of the flame caressing the bowl of the spoon. Dr. Kildare couldn't have been more precise drawing up the junk through the thin, sterilized needle.

Micah had me tie up his arm with my belt. He worked his fist to pump up the vein. I kept glancing at Lanna. The princess watching Rumpelstiltskin spin straw into gold.

"There we go. Nice one," Micah said when a clean and fat vein popped up, ready. He dabbed the inside of his elbow with an alcohol wet cotton swab. He raised the needle. He hit perfect the first time, and the fiery good news was on the way.

He didn't even have the needle out when it hit him.

"Christ," Micah said. "*Beau*-ti-ful." And you could see the transfiguration.

"Yeah," I said. I was getting a sympathetic rush off him. He began bobbing his head, drifting with music only he could hear.

"That's what I want," Lanna said.

"Uh-uh," Breeze said.

Micah came out of his bipping-trance scene. "What you want, baby?" he said. "Huh? You tell Papa Micah what you want."

She pointed at his arm where a drop of blood was a ruby on the blue river of the vein. "I want you to fix me up."

Nothing had to happen. I mean, there's no script in the skies that shapes your life. Lanna Borland did not have to suddenly come up with a new want, did she?

Or maybe she did. Maybe she had to because of the same reason she went swimming way out in the lake, trying to reach the place where the moon lay on the water. Maybe she thought the needle had that promise – and could deliver.

Breeze got up and walked to the window. He stood with his back to us. "How about it, Breeze?" Micah said. "She's your chick."

On the couch, Lanna was rolling up her sleeve. Breeze said nothing.

"Come on," she said.

"Right," Micah said. "Initiation time." Then he said to me, "The works, if you please."

All the time we were getting the fix ready, there wasn't a word from Breeze, not even a glance from him. We tied her up and watched the vein rise, bulging and ready.

"Give it to me," she said.

"You got it," Micah said. He swabbed her arm and my eyes met his.

The thing is, I think I knew. I think I could have stopped him. Maybe.

But the other thing, the bigger thing, is that I did not want to.

And so he popped her. And then he said, "There you go. Now, kinda walk around and feel it."

She stood up and Zoop! Oh, yeah, she felt it. Her face went white. Her eyes rolled back. She dropped to her knees. She made one short sound that was not a word, and she flopped down hard on her face, and she was dead.

Breeze had turned around by then. Mouth hanging open, he just mechanically shook his head from side to side.

Nobody did anything for a minute, and then it was time for somebody to do something, so I did. I got Breeze seated on the sofa. It was like moving a dude with a brand new lobotomy. I told him to stay put, not to move muscle one.

The way he was, I was sure he wouldn't.

And then Micah and I straightened up. I had to fix before I could get thinking the way I had to think, but we took care of it.

«« — »»

Life is not *Dragnet* with the cops solving everything just before the last commercial. Lanna Borland was found a week later in a forest preserve near one of the city's northwestern suburbs. It was not front page, prime-time news, not in those days. Back then, if you had money, you could buy "hush," and so, when a chocolate bar heiress makes an OD exit, there are things happening behind the scenes to guarantee, ultra-cool, no muss, no fuss, no scandal – and what we have here is "death by misadventure."

Micah split for the coast.

And Breeze and I stayed together. That is, we kept the pad. But the way Breeze was, I could have been the oily character in the turban taking care of the mummy in one of those antique Universal flicks.

Like you might figure, music was out.

Until one night, a few weeks later.

The temperature had dropped, not yet winter, of course, but a promise of certain winter. It was down in the 20s and there was that knife slice of wind that is exclusively Chicago's own.

Breeze left our place at midnight. His horn was with him. I was with him. I don't know if he wanted me, but there I was.

We went to that rocky beach that belonged to the summer. With the wind doing its work on the lake, the water looked as jagged and tearing as the rocks we stood on. I kept my hands in my pockets, wished my jacket were warmer. I wondered if I'd ever be warm again. I was high. I had the feeling I knew everything that was going to happen, everything that had to happen.

"She is out there, you know," Breeze said. His voice and the wind were one.

I started to say something. I didn't.

The moon was full. Far out there, where the world ended, the moon lay on the water. It was a place where you could maybe find monsters down deep in the lake, or maybe the exact spot on the earth where dreams died, or maybe the one point where you'd expect a crazy lady to be.

Then Breeze had the mouthpiece between his lips and he was playing. And he played warm as your own breath when the blanket's up over your chin. Then he turned it cold, and his cold was the midnight cold when you're alone in the house and every tick-tick of a pipe and the slow drip of a leaky faucet remind you of that aloneness.

And finally, he played a curling mist that was every dream that never will be.

He was playing a song. And I knew it was "Lanna's Song."

He was still playing, variations on an end theme, as he walked stiff-legged into the waves.

That was how it had to be. So I let it be. And it seems I heard "Lanna's Song," the echoes of it, even when there was no reason to hear it anymore.

There are times I know I hear it still.

I Am Your Need

I

August 4, 1962
The Brentwood Section of Los Angles

Marilyn Monroe lies naked and dying.

You can see it there, at that spot on her forehead where electrolysis permanently removed her widow's peak. Just beneath the skin's surface, a blue black flower grows.

It is Death.

There is the promise of finality in her every tentative breath, the sporadic sighings, the intimation of ending.

Marilyn Monroe is dying.

I am her death.

And I will die, too.

That is, when she dies, I have to assume I will also cease to be.

Marilyn Monroe. She was born in the flesh and of the flesh.

Like you.

And I?

I was born of her need.

I am her need.

II

February 6, 1961
New York

I could not bear it. I could bear no more, anymore. I wanted to die.

No, I *need* to die. That is what I thought.

The address of the Lonesome Capitol of the world is East

Fifty-Seventh Street: The Millers' apartment, now my apartment. His typewriter was gone, his Oxford Unabridged was gone, his leather bound copy of *Madame Bovary*, the first "quality book" he ever bought, his underwear, his Schick electric shaver, the silk tie he wore when he testified before HUAC… He did not take the picture of me I had given him, the one in which I wear white gloves (hiding my ugly hands, my ugly, ugly, ugly hands) and a hat that Mamie Eisenhower might have worn. I looked "demure" in the picture, he said. I looked regal and contemplative and lovely, he said. I kissed him regally and demurely and even contemplatively, and then I fucked him until his eyes rolled back in his head and he screamed some things none of his characters will ever be allowed to say on stage.

I stood at the living room window. Below, the city. (The Asphalt Jungle! The Naked City! Broadway, the busiest and loneliest street in the world! All the clichés of popular culture are true!) It was a perfectly cold, perfect blue sky February afternoon. You cannot be more alone than that.

It seemed Death was summoning me. My marriages were dead. My marriage to Jim Dougherty, Just Plain Jim, the sweet Irish merchant marine. To the jealous and sweet and mean Yankee Clipper, my slugger, my Joltin' Joe.

And now, to the New York Jewish Liberal Intellectual, Arthur. I called Arthur "Pops" or "Popsie." I consider *The Crucible* his best work. He was surprised, you know, that I understood the play so well, that anyone as blond as I could possibly comprehend metaphor and symbol. I got mad when he told me that. I cried. I told him I wasn't stupid. I told him I understood metaphor and symbol, understood better than he, because I goddamned good and goddamned well was metaphor and symbol and the way he looked at me then, the way he looked at me, that clever observing way, I knew the bastard someday would use what I had said in a play.

I loved Arthur Miller. Arthur Miller loved me, but, when you realize something like that, no, you cannot stay married to a man.

There were other voices beckoning me, calling me to the Nation of the Dead.

My children. I don't know how many had been scraped out of me, poor little blobs, you have to force yourself to lose track of statistics like that, but all those children died and they cursed me:

They cursed my tubes so I could never have sons or daughters. They left behind a dead womb.

The dead call out...

There, the insane contralto of Della Monroe, dear old Gram, who muttered she smelled strange smells in the house that nobody else could smell, burning silk, fish oil, lye soap, and something she called "the putrid stink of black flowers," There were men in wool suits, men with gray hats and well shined shoes, they had to be men from "the agency, that's who they were," and they followed her. They sat behind her on street cars. They held the door for her when she stepped into a department store. They had accents, but the accents kept changing, French, Spanish, Eastern European...

You know, it's weird, but if you really try, I bet you can remember everything, everything, no matter how young you were, and I can remember Gram's lopsided determined smile as she pressed a pillow down on me (I can still summon that wet feather taste – in my nightmares I taste it) I was maybe 14 months old or so when Gram tried to kill me.

Someone stopped her. Mama? That I can't remember for sure. Maybe I have not tried hard enough. I might need more analysis. It might have been my mother. Poor Gladys, and sometimes you think she had to be doomed because she was named Gladys (I chose my name, I choose my names, Marilyn Monroe, Zelda Zonk, Journey Evers, but I cannot run away from the what I am!); not all that long after Gram played "Baby want pillow," my mother went crazy herself; one day, instead of just looking nervous, with her hands flying this way and that, she sat down and started crying. "I can't, I can't, I just can't..." She kept saying that and she went off to the asylum and that's where you will find her today.

Family tradition: Gram got packed off to the insane asylum and died there.

(Was the Monroe Madness my inheritance? I've frequently discussed that with my psychiatrists. We talk about "nature and nurture," genetic tendencies, then they prescribe new drugs – I give the Demerol four stars, but forget that Seconal: leaves you with a cotton brain and the flavor of a day old Dr. Scholl's corn pad in your mouth – but mostly my therapists want me to talk about fucking. A couple have wanted to do more than talk.)

Oh, and by the way, my movie was dead.

It was/had been called *Something's Got to Give*. I had insisted on a tasteful swimming pool nude scene, so tasteful that tasteful stills had tastefully been carried in the always tasteful *Life* magazine, pictures which tastefully showed my tasteful tits, the top of my tasteful tush crack (a far cry, don't you think, from such digest size stroke mags wherein my image used to appear as *Caper, Dizzy Winks*, and *Hotcha Babe!*) but the production was all shut down, boomthudboom. Studio lawsuits against me. Countersuits against the studio.

All right, the script was dreck a la dreck. That did not matter. *Some Like It Hot* is the kind of "filmic vehicle" that might have starred Gale Storm with Moe, Larry, and Curly, had they had a better agent, some luck, and the ability to read. As it is, *Hot* was perfect for me: I became a respected comedienne (accent it properly, if you please), a "luminous and gifted comic actress with impeccable timing and commanding presence," said Archer Kellbourne in the *New York Times*.

Something's Got to Give could have been my salvation.

No. I did not want salvation.

Something's got give and the something is me.

Okay. Grandiose, I know. Self-pitying shit.

Solipsistic.

Does it surprise you that such a word is in my vocabulary? I have, after all, despite its aging, what has been appraised as a "million dollar ass" by no less an authority than Hollywood raconteur and celebrated ass connoisseur Groucho Marx. With an ass you can take to the bank, why, mercy on my Pie O My, why ever would you even need a brain?

Pay attention, *s'il vous plaît* (she said multilingually, which has nothing to do with giving you a blow job): Here are other words I know and can properly use: insouciant, ontological, nonsequitur, dialectic, moribund, phlegmatic, truculent...

May I not say, "Seurat's pointillism never descends into perfunctory technique or mannerism"? Do you think, "That guy sure painted pretty with those little dots" is the MM style?

Maybe you are right. Maybe I am a dumb blonde. After all, I did give Yves Montand a blow job.

The hell with it.

The hell with it already.

It was time to die, time to stop concerning myself about what I truly was and what people thought I was and…

It was time to die.

My first thought was to step out onto the ledge, to take that deepest of breaths as I sucked in clean winter air, to look up at the sky and to see it with the utmost clarity and then to leap.

Step out onto the ledge…

My god, that would be like a scene from *I Love Lucy*. "Loo-seeee, choo get back in *la casa muy pronto*! You got some 'splainin' to do."

I wanted to die.

I did not want to be ridiculous.

So I opened the living room window as wide as possible. And then I backed up.

I would run and hurl myself out. A swan dive (just like Esther Williams – to her credit, she never attempted to act – or think), only sans water. I had heard that jumpers lost consciousness before they landed and there was an appeal in that.

I clenched my fists.

I licked my lips. They were dry and rough. My mouth felt cottony. Nembutal and Dom Perignon and chloral hydrate, an always interesting aftertaste.

I could hear my heart beat but not feel it. That was curious, I thought.

And then I ran but it was not so much running as floating, and I didn't know if I could really do it, if I had the force of will to kill myself.

Then just before the jump, I looked down, and there was someone out there, someone down below on the sidewalk, someone looking up at me

—and I knew him, I could see his face, despite the distance, and I knew him even though I did not know who he was

—Daddy?

—(you have had the feeling, haven't you, maybe just once in your life, but you have experienced it and so this is not a delusion of mine or a paradox for you, is it?)

—and I said, "N…Nuh-No-No."

(I stuttered as a child. Sometimes, even though I am now all grown up, I still do.)

I changed my mind.

I made a rational decision: I did not have to die. I was meant to live. I was a survivor.

But momentum or destiny or something worse carried me on, carried me toward the cold and the window and then I thrust my arms out, locking my elbows, and the heels of my hands smashed hard against the window sill and the shock went all the way up into my teeth and I went reeling backward.

I did not die.

A day later, I checked myself into the Payne Whitney Psychiatric Clinic at New York Hospital, where I was classified as suicidal, which was neo-Jungian, post-Freudian, Harry Stack Fucking Sullivan bullshit.

Fuck that, Freddy.

Marilyn Monroe is a survivor.

III

If it can be said that I am capable of surprise, I am often surprised by all that I know and by all that I do not know:

For example, I can intelligently discuss existentialism, possibly win an argument with Jean Paul Sartre himself if need be. (Existence before essence, yes, albeit not in my case.) Let the subject turn to the aesthetics of cinematography, and I will explain the importance of the Eisenstein montage and the Gance panorama. Shall we focus on the universal themes of Osip Mandelstam's modernist poetry or the immensity of suffering in Picasso's "Guernica" or the myriad subtleties of vocal shading in the performances of June Christie?

Marilyn needed me to be smart, to be intellectual and artistic. You were no dunce, Marilyn, no dimbulb bimbo, no sackready starlet with a VACANCY sign on her forehead and HOT TO TROT on her round heels. You needed intellect and that is what I became (in part!) and what I am.

I am your need.

Yet I have no idea how to write a check. That is because you had others to take care of that. On an afternoon kiddy TV show, I heard the word hygrometer; I have no concept of what it is, what it does, why it is needed, anymore than do you. You thought Sukarno was the president of India, not Indonesia; you had no idea of the history, the culture, or even the location of either country and so, neither do I.

And of course I had to be "political" because you were involved in your own way in politics. I guess you would have to call me a Democrat. Here I always aver, Marilyn, to your reasoning:

Jack is a damned clever politician and progressive thinker and not such a bad lay, say a six or seven, but he's more in love with himself than he could ever be with anyone else (poor Jackie, poor, poor Jackie), or with the country for that matter and Bobby Kennedy is a good man, usually, even if being Catholic has made him nuttier than most Catholics, and he is so smart that he doesn't feel threatened by a smart woman and so it's good to talk to him and he is a good politician and maybe he will be able to help people the way he wants and maybe Jack can help him, if Jack's ego will permit, and you know what is really nice is that he really does love his wife and kids, so no matter how bad he wants to put it to Marilyn! Monroe! and wants to even more because Big Brother has greased the gears, no matter what, Bobby probably won't do it – and you do have to respect a man who won't fuck you...

Here is what else I know, Marilyn.

You needed me.

And when the need was powerful enough, when it was pure ferocity of need, then, like magic, like dream, like aneurism or lottery, like the roll of the dice, the whirl of the Great Mandela.

I am.

With no burden of personal history, with no more clue to my beginnings than had any fleabite scratching caveman, there I am!

I am

your need

I AM

IV

September 4, 1958
Early afternoon

San Diego is the best city in California and perhaps in the United States. The weather is always so near to perfect that you do not think at all about the weather. The youth are golden and smell of sea water and lotions and if you see one of them frowning it is noteworthy. Old cars have no rust, no wrinkles, no dents, nor do old people. Dos Picos Park is the favorite park of San Diego's residents. The oak trees are majestic as only oaks can be and the shadows cast by their limbs are not frightening. And there are the ducks waiting in the pond. The ducks like visitors.

She liked being here, squatting at the water's edge, tossing oyster crackers to the appreciative ducks. She should have been in makeup and costume, should have been on the set at Coronado Beach, but she had decided to be difficult, a star turn and how do you like it, you assholes. She could not stand to be with Mr. Billy Wilder, a certified prick (figuratively speaking) but without the sensitivity of a prick (literally speaking); and she couldn't stand to be with Curtis, who told her, "The script says I kiss you, but kissing you is like kissing Hitler."

Curtis probably would delight in kissing Hitler. The uniform and the leather boots and all. Curtis definitely thought he could out-beautiful her. She thought he'd look like a mummified drag queen when he got old, and that wasn't in the least ironic because…

Oh, God, she was so afraid, she was so afraid. The mind was going: Tilt! That's all, Folks! Right into the Mad Mad Monroe Maelstrom.

"It's me, Sugar." That was her part, her only line, for yesterday's scene. "It's me, Sugar."

Here is the Reader's Digest Condensed version of what she said:

I.. i.it's sugar, me.

Sugar me

It is I! *Cigar*!

It's just me, sugar pie.

It's just fucking sugar shit fuck fuck…

It required 37 fucking takes for her to say, "It's me, Sugar," 37 takes to synch brain with mouth to get out words that Lassie could have managed with one hand cue from trainer Rudd Weatherwax and the promise of two Gaines biscuits.

And there was Billy Wilder, looking like he hadn't had a dump in three weeks and had no hope for the future, and Mr. Tony "I Feel Pretty" Curtis throwing his hands in the air.

She had to get away, had to, had to be alone—

—did not want to be alone, so alone—

Incognito time. Easy, surprisingly easy. Forget Max Factor and Maybelline, slip on the kind of dark glasses that sell three for a dollar at the Texaco station and tie a scarf over the blondness, and a far too big UCLA sweatshirt (Tits? Tits? In this potato sack?) and the kind of shapeless skirt that would embarrass a Jehovah's Witness, and you disappear, you become nobody

I'm nobody. Who are you?

I'm nobody but I need to be somebody and I need to show them show them all that I am somebody and I need to be loved and need to be somebody's and I need and I need and I need—

V

I take her elbow, feel that tremoring within like a too tightly wound clock spring. She is not surprised that I am here.

I am her need, corporeal, need now made manifest, though I have always been with her.

We sit on a bench. "The crackers," she says. "Whenever I go to a restaurant, I always take the crackers for the ducks. I love animals."

I know.

I know she needs to tell me about her love for animals, needs me to hear about this goodness in her.

"I've always loved animals."

I know.

"Want to hear a funny story?"

She needs me to hear a funny story, needs to remind herself of a time when her life could be safely compartmentalized in funny little stories, mundane events no larger than life and nothing in the least crazy.

"My first husband, Jim, it was when we were first married. We went off on this weekend. He had friends near Van Nuys and they had this small farm. They called it a ranch 'cause everything's a ranch in California, but it really was a farm.

"So we went out to their farm and they were our age, well, Jim's age, he was five years older than me, you know, and we played gin rummy and danced to the radio. We were drinking Blatz beer.

I remember that 'cause it was the sponsor of the radio remote we were listening to, 'Live from the Congress Hotel in Chicago,' with Eddy Howard and his orchestra.

"Anyway, then we went off to bed and it had started to rain and, next thing I knew, I heard a calf outside, it was mooing, you know, and it was so lonely sounding...

"I told Jim we had to get it, had to take it out to the barn."

"He laughed at me.

"I never minded when Jim laughed at me. If that fuckface Tony Curtis laughs at me, if that fly boy even dares, I'll pull his panties up around his neck and strangle him, but I liked it when Jim laughed at me.

"'Babe,' he said, 'don't worry about that calf. Little guy will be all right. He's covered in leather."

Marilyn was silent.

She thought she needed silence.

But I knew otherwise, of course, because I was her need.

She had to tell me—

—the worst, the most tragic and horrible animal story she knew. She needed to tell me *the* story—

"No."

No?

I am her need and a need is patient, patient but insistent. She had no choice, not really: One must acquiesce to need, always, always.

She began to cry then.

So many tears, Marilyn, so many tears so many times.

Then she said, "I had a dog once, Cinders. I was in a foster home then. Cinders was only a puppy, a very sweet puppy, and funny, and like puppies do, Cinders barked a lot. A neighbor got mad about it, just really furious and what he did, I saw it, he picked up this hoe and he chopped Cinders in half. I saw it."

Again, a silence. A needed silence.

"Maybe it was then I started to go crazy."

VI

August 4, 1962
The Brentwood Section of Los Angles

Marilyn Monroe is dying.

Her diaphragm has quit working and her breathing is now all from the stomach. The color of her aureoles is fading. I touch her hand, then her wrist. I can find her pulse but only with difficulty, regular but slow, so very slow and thin. There is a tranquility to her flesh that morticians strive for and never achieve.

She is dying because she needs to die.

And, curious, so curious, I do not understand it but I, I feel no abatement of my selfness, no ebbing away of my consciousness.

I who have never been alive feel no less alive than... Than previously.

I am her need.

And to myself I am becoming an enigma.

VII

You need to hear about the sex, don't you?

I know what you need. After all, she fascinates you, compels your ever so avid interest, Mr. and Mrs. Main Street America:

—you regular fellas at the Tip Top Lounge who with the wisdom imparted by the old after work boilermaker know you'd have her wailing once you gave her the old Jack Hammer John.

—you Lutheran housewives in Michigan who have begun to get the hint from her this hyperbolic persona that is MM: women are supposed to like it, too.

—you, the 13 year old horn rimmed smart boy who's been a whiz with his slide rule but is now discovering there's something about Marilyn Monroe's gyrating buttocks that puts lead in the little pencil

—you, the desperate 19 year, selling ribbons at Woolworth's, just a little orthodonture shy of being beautiful, dreaming of love, dreaming of Hollywood, dreaming of magic

All of you, all of you, I understand your need. How can I not?

So, addressing the topic of Marilyn Monroe's womanhood, I

speak with a degree of expertise, a PhD, if you will.

Marilyn Monroe not infrequently needed fucking and I am her need.

And so, on occasion, I fucked her the way she needed to be fucked, fucked her hard and then harder, knowing she relished the sensation at the spot just above her anus where the testicles go slapslapslap, the hot juices flowing along mounds and fissures, fucked her with her hips doing the comma wriggle bump and pump, fucked her with the exact length and girth and temperature of cock her need demanded at that particular time for that particular fuck, fucked her saying all the amorous vulgarities she needed to hear: You beautiful, wild bitch, you hot cunt, you whore, you sweet pussy, you...

I fucked her.

And so many times, when she came (came because she needed to come), she cried and she cried out, "Daddy!"

I am her need.

> she needed daddy and she needed fucking and she needed home and she needed sanity and she needed respect and she needed dignity and she needed
>
> she needed she was a sucking vacuum she was an endless deep need at the core of the universe she was
>
> she needed limits and laughter and kindness and concern and gentleness and daddy oh god she needed daddy she needed she needed she needed love she needed love she needed love she needed love she needed love she needed love she needed love she needed love she needed she needed she was

All Need. All Consuming Need.
and I am

VIII

August 4, 1962
The Brentwood Section of Los Angles

I am often surprised by all that I know and by all that I do not know.

I have told you that, haven't I? I must be telling you again because it is something you need to know.

I heard the wet rattle within the V juncture of throat and collar bone. It was a death rattle. I had never heard it before (how could I?) but I knew it.

Marilyn Monroe was dying.

She would die and I would be no more.

Then I was startled, that's what it was, I was startled at the sudden slow movement, as her head lolled on the pillow, and white-tinged mucus bubbled at the parched corner of her mouth.

She sat up. It was melodramatic but no less comic and grotesque, like an inexperienced vampire in a Universal Studio's monster film. Her eyes sought focus and found it.

She looked at me. She smiled.

"No," she said. "Not this time. Not ever. No."

I am her need. I have always been her need.

I understood her, understood her even when she did not.

Lie down now, I told her. You need to die.

I know.

I am your need.

And I made her die.

IX

August 4, 1962
The Brentwood Section of Los Angles

Marilyn Monroe is dead.

Her heart has stopped. Her blood no longer circulates. Lividity discolors and distorts her features. You might no longer know who she is.

She isn't.

167

Marilyn Monroe is dead.
And I?

X

A mystery, if you need a mystery.
I am here.
Marilyn Monroe is gone and I am here.
And if I do not understand, then, very well, that is the way of it, I suppose, I assume, I would think, I surmise: who attains full understanding? Jesus, Buddha, Mohammed, Joseph Smith, Mary Baker Eddy, Norman Vincent Peale, Bishop Fulton Sheen...
But I think I am beginning to realize, to know:
you
you are alone in a lonely night and you cannot bear the sound of your own heart cannot tolerate the touch of your mocking breath as it leaves your nostrils to brush your upper lip and the weight of your existence offends you
you
you are at the city's busiest intersection on this busy day and the sunlight that pours down is weighted and cutting and you feel it slice away the flesh slice away your protection slice away all that protects and keeps you hidden
you
you have children and they hate you and you hate them
you are watched all the time watched by secretive men who know what uncle did and know how dirty you are and though they are biding their time for now they will act they will
you are lies covered over with lies covered over with lies and all covering the truth the terrible impossible unendurable truth
you are 52 years old and you still cry for daddy
you have no satisfactions
you have no joy
you (all of you) you are unloved and you are unlovable and you are cursed (all of you forever children alone in the dark) and you cannot try cannot dare cannot hope (all of you the forever lost
you and you and you

168

and you cannot hope and you need you need you need
and you need
you need death
and
I am
your need

BIRD'S DEAD

There's a sign with a tipped top hat out in front.

It's got nothing to do with nothing because this is *The Commodore's Blue Note*.

You walk in. The smoke encircles you and drags you in. Drags you into the music. And there's always music, even when there is no one on the stand. There's a juke box. There's a phonograph. There's a battered to hell upright in the corner – It's Mr. Jelly Lord mainly tickles that one. There's a violin on the wall, supposedly carrying with it a Gypsy curse, but when Stuff Smith comes in and he's feeling *all right*, he takes down that fiddle, says, "Curse of the Romany, I defy you!" and he sets to hard swinging, and though the notes don't always come in tune, the man is pure virtuoso.

Here. That is *right* where you are.

The Commodore's Blue Note can be like staying high all the time.

The Commodore's Blue Note can be like when you are under the lowest.

This is it, the place, the joint, the saloon, the pad, the locale of… hipsters and shysters and mooches and backsliding preachers. And tailgatin' muffaletta chompin' juke jointers and swingers and malingerers and zoot suiters and add in a shouter and a professor and a half dozen unclassifiable unreconstructed originals.

In The Commodore's Blue Note you sometimes find Ben Webster. Ben Webster at the bar, floating on reefer and slugging down Scotch and there is something pinning the eyes that isn't Scotch or reefer and Ben Webster looks for all the world like an obsidian statue of a gorilla. An ugly gorilla. An acromegliac, brow bone bulging, lantern jawed, *low*land gorilla. But did anyone ever play a sweeter horn? Could anyone do that sweep up the register into nothing but breath and heartbreak like Ben Webster?

Ben Webster is the Ugly who plays so beautiful.

However, unless you want your next suit of clothes to be made out of pine, you do not want to insult Ben Webster. You do not want to hurt Ben Webster's feelings in any way, because Ben Webster is *sensitive*. He is a soulful man. He is a man who can all too easily take umbrage.

I saw this once. We were at a rent party. Ben Webster came in, sax around his neck, Scotch fumes trailing him like Mighty Clouds of Glory. And some damn fool, this little bit of a country boy, with his hair all country parted down the center, this hayseed, rube, chicken plucker, happened to give offense to Ben Webster.

What country boy said to Ben Webster was, "Sir, even with that saxophone hanging on the neck, you look like a statue of a gorilla. *Obsidian* " Ben Webster's feelings were hurt. Ben Webster sort of whispered sometimes when his feelings were hurt and he wanted to sound like Dexter Gordon. Ben Webster whispered to the country boy, "I take umbrage."

The he took Country Boy to the window. What he said was, "I am so full of umbrage that I feel like throwing you out the goddamned window."

Well, if you know anything about Ben Webster, then you know for Ben Webster to fool was no different than to do. He threw Country Boy out the window.

Did I mention that we were about fourteen or fifteen stories up?

As I said, Ben Webster was a sensitive man.

You know who else you might find at The Commodore's Blue Note? Damn near *everybody*, that is who. One night in walks Miles Davis with Billy Eckstine. Billy was trying to get back into Miles's good graces because Miles had tried to punch him out over five dollars he had tried to cheat Billy out of and Billy had raised up several major lumps beneath Miles's eyes. (He never hit Miles in the mouth. Billy Eckstine was a good friend to Miles and he also understood commerce.) Now Miles was sulking.

Miles's father was a dentist. This shaped Miles. The offspring of dentists are likely to become architects or abstract painters or Existential Christian theologians. Anything but a goddamn dentist.

On any given night at The Commodore's Blue Note, this could be your—

Roll Call!

Behind the bar. It is *The Commodore*. They call him that because some years ago somebody who claimed to be Wallace Beery gave him a pirate hat. "This here, matey, be the very *chapeau* I was a'wearin' in the movie *Treasure Island*. Now, if you could give me a drink on the house."

Nobody drinks on the house at The Commodore's Blue Note. Forget it. But the Commodore liked the hat. He gave the man who claimed to be Wallace Beery a drink for it. He perched it on his head. "Avast, lubbers," the Commodore would say. "Keelhaul the bilges. Mizzen the poop deck." Even bartenders dream of the sea.

Roll Call: Billie Holiday, here. That gardenia in her hair. Oh, doesn't she think she is the *stuff*?

That is because she *is* the *stuff*. Ethel Waters didn't like her. Ethel Waters said, "She just thinks she's the stuff, don't she? And when she sings, she sounds like her shoes are too tight."

Ethel Waters. This is the *real* Ethel Waters. This is not the Ethel Waters who got to being the Godly Negro Lady for the Billy Graham rallies in Madison Square Garden and The Cow Palace and Comiskey Park and Ecuador and the South Sea Islands. This is the Ethel Waters who starred in *Blackbirds of 1928* and quite possibly coined the legendary bit of advice, "Walk softly and carry a big razor."

Roll Call!

Roll Call!

Roll Call at the The Commodore's Blue Note.

Buddy Bolden?

Present.

Jelly Roll Morton.

Here. Where the hell else has he got to go, now that his career is in the toilet and the hoodoo is on him?

Eddie Condon?

Present and drunk as Cooder Brown.

Bix? Bix? Biederbecke, you here, boy?

Yeah, I'm here... That smile. Jesus, that smile. That smile was so shy and easy, you knew he came from Indiana.

Yeah, Bix is here. He's lost in a mist.

You know who smiles like Bix?

Chet Baker. A man utterly lacking in guile. Mr. Innocence. Right. My ass in two parts. Baker the Faker swiped the smile and about three-quarters of Bix's chops.

Not that Chet Baker smiles like that anymore. Drug thing, you know. He burned some people, you know. People who were called names like The Bear, and Perpetual Scar Tissue, and Emergency Warning Buxton, and Guido and Fat Tony, and Big Tony, and Large Tony, and Tony Kick Your Ass Esposito. What happened was the people he burned in this drug thing – and this is just something I heard, okay? – they got together and knocked every tooth out of Chet Baker's mouth.

It did nothing for his looks.

Of course, with what he had picked up from his father, Miles Davis could have fixed Baker right up, but Miles hated Chet. Miles hated everybody.

And of course, there at the bar, tonight and every night, it is The Detached Cop. He is Webster's size. He wears suits that make you think of Bulgaria. Some nights, he sits and drinks and listens to the music and he weeps. Sometimes someone tries to talk to him. Usually, the Detached cop says, "Get away. I am undercover." You want him to say more. You want him to confess all, become maudlin and confidential. You hope he will reveal, "I am investigating the Lindbergh baby snatch. I am investigating crop circles and Judge Crater and those mysterious strangers and the celebrated rain of frogs that would have been the clincher for anyone except that dumbass Pharaoh. I want to know if Ambrose Bierce and Pancho Villa changed their names and became a tag team on *Wrestling from the Marigold*. I'll sure as hell find out who threw the overalls in Mrs. Murphy's chowder. And who was it played poker with Pocahontas when John Smith went away?"

The Detached Cop never says anything like that, though. I think he's afraid it would make people like him.

Every night, every night, you will find the Two Metaphysical Wineheads at their table.

They are good luck for the joint.

They somehow always have money for Dago Red.

They have discussions which are so laden with insight and all that that the Dali Lama would instantly give them his Rolex and autographed picture of Marilyn Monroe and one of those funky Sherpa hats if he heard them talking.

Consider this conversation:

Man, what time *is it?*

Now.

Yeah, now. *What time is it?*

Now.

Yeah, I say now. *What the hell you think I say? What time is it now!*

Now.

Oh, hell with you. Just drink some wine, that's right.

I will, says a profoundly philosophical Metaphysical Winehead. *I will drink some wine...*

Now.

Thing is, everyone is alive. Everyone who ever was in jazz, everyone. Alive! They're alive, I tell you. 100% guaranteed and bona fide and assured by an electrocardiogram on record.

They are alive.

Right.

Now.

Except for Bird.

Charlie Yardbird Parker.

Yardbird is dead.

That's is why The Commodore's Blue Note is down tonight.

Nobody wants to believe it. Nobody believes it. Paul Whiteman is alive, for Chrissake, and he's so lame nobody even thinks he should be, and Fats Navarro is alive and Bill Evans is alive and Benny Goodman is alive and Robert Johnson is alive.

Robert Johnson. Poisoned and shot and stabbed and chopped up in a cotton baler and with his head caught in a punch press! Acid thrown on him by one old girl, ice pick stuck in his nose, ear, and ass by another, Robert Johnson is alive.

But the word has spread throughout the community.

Bird is dead.

Naw, says one Metaphysical Winehead.

Naw, says the other Metaphysical Winehead.

Bird joking. Bird always one for the jokes.

Bird, naw, he ain't dead.

I hope he is, says the other Metaphysical Winehead, 'cause they done gone and buried him. Oh, my, ain't I a stitch? Ain't I a caution?

Naw, says the other winehead.

It is precisely then...

That a touch of the mystic and unexplainable, of the awesome and of the pure enters The Commodore's Blue Note.

The door swings open. No one sees a human hand upon it.

And if there is no human hand, then there is no human being attached to that no hand and so no human being enters The Commodore's Blue Note.

What flies in is a white dove.

Get it?

A bird comes flying in.

Say what you want about the brilliance of Yardbird, the creative genius, the inspired lunacy, but the man was not always subtle.

Everyone is silent. Even Jelly Roll Morton stops noodling on the battered old upright in the corner of the joint. That's about all he can do these days, about all that gives him comfort. He is convinced that there is a serious hoodoo on him and that is why nobody wants to hear his music anymore. Mr. Jelly Lord's music is called moldy fig music. Moldy oldie. Moldy Mush and Moldy Gramma. Aw, that is stale, that is square, that is... Moldy. The A and R man at RCA told him, "Well, you and your Hot Peppers, you ain't so hot now. So toot sweet, and write if you get work, but I bet you won't."

Whoo! And how's that for a hurt? Whoo! And who was it that just plain *invented* jazz? Why none other than Jelly Roll Morton, and if you don't believe it, just ask him.

But now we are back to smoky silences and a white dove winging its way to the bar. For a moment, it hangs suspended in the air. Some that were there that night swore the dove glowed brilliantly, as though it were becoming a halo, needing only an angel beneath it to complete the religious experience. The Commodore, trying to remember lines his mother and her faith used to inflict on him, thinks The Kingdom of Heaven has come, and he says, in a reverential whisper, "Blow me down."

Then the dove alights on the bar. He is strutting as though he is the literal cock of the walk.

Everyone is saying it, not quite simultaneously, but saying it. "It's Bird. Bird's here. Bird *lives*."

"Horse manure," is what Jelly Roll Morton says.

Now what some folks don't know, because Jelly told a lie or two in his time, is that Mr. Morton's claim to have been a sharpshooter with the carnival was 100% *veritas*.

These days, not knowing if the hoodoo would come at him like a Swamp Dog or a Dhambala bat, Jelly Roll has taken to carrying around an 1873 Colt Peacemaker.

Which is what he yanked out.

He let fly.

And anyone who saw that shot does not dispute the Jelly's claim to have been a carnival sharpshooter. Because in one bang and one burst there is nothing but some splatter on the bar and a feather in the air.

Then Jelly Roll Morton says, "Bird's dead."

He sets the Colt on the piano and, grinning his diamond tooth grin like he has not since being given the RCA heave-ho, he starts in playing "Graveyard Blues."

And there ain't one moldy thing about it.

Dreaming Robot Monster

Boy, was that a dream, or was it!
-Johnny, protagonist of ROBOT MONSTER

PROLOGUE

ROBOT MONSTER: A guy in a gorilla suit and diving helmet portrays Ro-Man, who has come from outer space (or possibly our moon) to destroy all the inhabitants of Earth. Film critic Leonard Maltin described the 1953 film as "one of the genuine legends of Hollywood; embarrassingly, hilariously awful." It was directed by Phil Tucker, with a screenplay by Wyott Ordung.

I saw ROBOT MONSTER in 1954 when it was shown in 3D at the Alex Theater on Madison Street in Chicago. It scared hell out of me.

DREAMING ROBOT MONSTER

OUR CAST

JOHNNY: Eight years old. Slap him a good one and Child Welfare won't call it abuse.

CARLA: Johnny's younger sister, five or six years of premeditated cuteness.

ALICE: Johnny's older sister. Stacked. When she becomes a scientist in Johnny's dream, you don't buy it. Not with a rack like that.

MOM: Mom has problems not even hinted at in the film. (When the films of all of our lives are produced, I think this will also be said of us.)

THE PROFESSOR: *Claims* to be an archaeologist. Commie? Note the accent.

ROY: THE PROFESSOR'S assistant. Quite good looking. *Too* good looking, if you catch my drift.

RO-MAN: Space Alien from the planet Ro-Man, according to Johnny.

THE GREAT GUIDANCE: Ro-man's boss, leader of the Ro-men. As seen on television.

«« — »»

ALICE

Robot Monster was not a robot. That is a misconception. That was the name Johnny, my obnox little brother, gave him, or really, what Johnny called the story.

> ROBOT MONSTER! Credits roll over a background of violent science-fiction and gruesome and subversive horror comic books. Once every kid in the United states read comic books. Good kids read *Archie* and *Little Lulu* and *Walt Disney's Comics and Stories*. Then there were the rest of us.

This explains a great deal.

Oh, he was not of our world. He was *Ro*-man, not *Hu*man – but he was *not* a monster.
He wasn't.
I know.
Alice sighs.

Robot Monster was my brother's dream.

But what of me? Have I no dreams?

I am 11 years older. Do my dreams matter less than those of a juvenile delinquent and socially warped OBNOX of an eight year old boy?

ONE

JOHNNY

Alice is smart, okay, reading books all the time. She's got big torpedoes and I don't care what she thinks, she is NOT the boss of me. I know Alice kissed Sidney Gerstein behind the garage. Sidney's a Jew with glasses and he's a sissy. The Italian guys three blocks over beat him up all the time. That's the kind of guy my sister kisses. A creep.

I tried to tell Mom about Alice and sissy Sidney, but, well, Mom is strange. She never gets mad, not really. You ask Mom "How are you?" and she maybe says, "Hello" or "Tuesday" or "That's just fine." Mom, to tell the truth, is Weirdsville. Not Daffy Duck Weirdsville or Clarabelle Clown Weirdsville. Quiet Weirdsville. Very strange.

Some of the kids at Christ the Comforter say Mom is "like from outer space, man," and then they snap their fingers like beatniks and laugh. Bastards. Alice the Smart says I have to just ignore those "dolts who cannot appreciate or comprehend divergent thinking." Yeah, that's some kind of big tickle, all right. Alice is as full of good advice as a prune is full of pruneiness.

Smarty-smart Alice was not around when everything got started. It was me and Carla. I had my space helmet and Carla had her stupid doll.

(Robot monster got Carla, but that's later. It bothers me. Carla really wasn't all too bad. I don't know what happened to her doll.)

So we were out playing. Mom and Alice had taken us on a picnic somewhere you could call the Valley of Bad Shaped Rocks. It was the kind of place you go on picnics when you're dreaming crazy stuff.

We spread out this itchy old green army blanket on a place that didn't have any big rocks and was only a little bit lumpy. Mom said Dad brought the blanket home from the army. I know Dad was a soldier. Once he let me play with a cigar box full of ribbons and medals. They were neat. Then Dad started to cry for no reason and he hugged me and he didn't say anything and I said, "Men don't cry," and he said, "Jesus wept," which is what you figure one of the nuns at Christ the Comforter would say. Then Dad wrapped his long, long arms around me, and he told me to be quiet, just be quiet, and he said he loved me very much. Then he did his Mr. Monkey face with his lips all pooched out and eyes bugging and made the ape sound that's pretty funny even if doesn't sound too much like an ape.

Dad is dead now.

Mom made the usual for the picnic. Peanut butter and jelly sandwiches. Baloney sandwiches. We had Kool-aid. Kool-aid's cheaper than soda. Kool-aid even tastes cheap.

Some fucking picnic, huh?

So then Carla and I go exploring, I guess you could call it, and I have my Captain Cosmos space helmet and my Zeta12 ray gun that shoots bubbles. Most of the kids at Christ the Comforter want to be cowboys like Hopalong Cassidy or Gene Autry or Roy Rogers. Cowboys are okay or even cool, is what the nuns think, and Sister Mary Loyola is always telling us about how she went to the Catholic Charities Hour radio show in New York and saw Bing Crosby, Bishop Fulton J. Sheen, and Singing Cowboy Bob Atcher. This kid, Billy Svoboda, said he wanted to be Dale Evans and Mother Cordelia smacked him.

I don't know why nuns hate spacemen, but they do. Sometimes I think Jesus was a spaceman who landed here and got all messed up. Next time Jesus comes, He better bring an atomic ray gun.

The Valley of Bad Shaped rocks is bad news for picnics, but it's real good for SPACEMAN because it looks like Mars or some other outer space planet.

Of course Carla wants to play HOUSE.

I tell her no and shut up.

She goes sniffle-sniffle and I'm not sure if she is going to cry or if it's asthma because she's coming down with a rock allergy or something. She yaps some more that we have to play HOUSE.

I tell her to cast an eyeball on all the neat rocks. Cool, huh?

Carla says if I don't play HOUSE she will tell about that time in the bath tub.

I shoot some Zeta12 ray gun bubbles POP right in her eye and she yells and makes like she's going to cry but I tell her she better not so she doesn't but she tells me she hates me and I tell her ask me if I care. (Because I DON'T care. I don't care if everyone hates me. They can all go to hell, but first, let them just take one little minute to KISS my ASS!)

That's when we meet Roy and The Professor. They're at the entrance to a cave, chipping away at rocks.

Roy is young and he's got dynamic tension muscles like Charles Atlas (Charles ASSLESS, that's a joke) but Roy's hair is greasy-curly like he gave himself a Toni perm like a lady. Roy is pretty va-va-voom – if you can say that about a man.

The Professor is saggy with a turkey neck and turkey eyes. (What a turkey!) He turns into my dad (but that's later). He talks in a funny way that's like English but with something stuck on his back teeth and his throat. The way he sounds, well, he sounds like a Red. (But my dad, my real dad, wasn't any Commie.)

I tell them I want to blast them with my Zeta12. You can see they both think I'm just one cute little tyke, a regular little rascal, aw shucks, the bastards. The Professor tosses me this jive about Roy and him: "… archaeologists":

People who try to find out what men were like way back before they could read or write. Then he tells me, *wouldn't it be nicer if we could live at peace with each other?*

Pinko, what'd I tell you? Uh-huh, that's Bolshevik boushwah. Commie prick.

(You go to Catholic school, by the time you're second grade with Sister Mary Loyola, you learn all about the Red Menace. They don't always have Jewish names, either. Communists hate Catholics. Communists torture priests and rape nuns and kill little kids before their first communion. Then kids go to Limbo because of the fucking Communists. That's how it works.)

Then Mom and Alice show up. You can never know if Mom's upset. It's usually like someone's gone over her brain with Johnson's wax (Stay tuned for "The Mom from Outer Space" on the same channel!), but Alice is definitely bent out of shape, because

… Carla and I were supposed to take a NAP right after lunch!

(See what I mean about this picnic? A NAP? Give me a break.)

Roy gives Alice the once-over and then the twice over. Maybe he likes her. Or maybe he's worried she's prettier than he is.

Then, or in just a little bit, Ro-man destroys the earth – pretty much, anyway.

TWO

MOM

Before I drowned, when I was a little girl, I was really quite wild. Yes, I was. It was like my mind was carbonated, filled with this frantic loud and wet buzzing that spread downward, made me vibrate and tingle with wicked energy. And grownups would speak to me, they would always tell me what to do, and I would maybe not quite understand, maybe, I don't know why, but I would maybe get the *idea* of what they were telling me to do – and then I would *buzz-buzz-buzz* not do it and would instead *buzz-buzz-buzz* do the direct opposite, if there was a direct opposite, and if not, I might do something slantwise or catty-corner or at the least, different.

Go to bed now, Mother said, and I took the box of kitchen matches and set the bed on fire and got so close to it that my hair burned. It made a sound that I can think of sometimes but cannot quite hear.

I would sing a song backwards and very loud then, if Uncle Peter or someone asked me to stop, I would start screaming and I could not even stop myself from screaming until I hit someone or bit myself.

Once I tore all the shades from the windows because the spring rollers made this twangy noise that made me laugh and my father picked me up and slapped me on the legs and shoulders and the back of my head all the way down the hall and threw me into the front closet and locked it and I ripped all the clothes from the hangers and peed on the whole pile with that twanging noise inside my head inside my head inside my head.

But then one day we went on a picnic. I still like picnics very much. If you ask me to go on a picnic, why, I will make peanut butter and jelly sandwiches and I will make baloney sandwiches and I will fill Thermos bottles with Cherry Kool-aid and Grape Kool-aid and Orange Kool-aid and we will just go on a picnic, that is what.

The picnic when I drowned was a picnic with my mother and father and Uncle Peter and Aunt Alma and all my cousins and there was beer and a portable radio with Hank Williams and softball and sweet humming mosquitoes and the smell of Lucky Strikes. Then I went down to the lake with my cousins and the next thing that happened was I was in the water.

I went down and down in the water.

I went down slowly. Even though the feeling of slowness was new to me, not part of my life, not the way I was, I was not scared. It was cool and silent and soft in the water and everything seemed to wave all around me, waving silently, and I kept my eyes open and I could look right up through the water and see the sun and almost see worlds far off and after a while the sun froze and everything in my mind froze.

And I thought, *I like this. I like this and this is the way it should be.* I heard a nice sound way far away and it was the slow-stretched sound of the steel guitar on the portable radio. I did not hear Hank Williams and The Drifting Cowboys, just the steel guitar.

I drowned, that's what everyone said. And when they took me out of the lake, and I opened my eyes, and someone yelled, "Jesus saved her," and it was like everything in the world was just light and as perfect as it should be, so I thought maybe Jesus did save me, which is what a Savior would do.

I was not wild any longer. I was slow. I could feel the spaces in between deciding to do something, like waving hello, or blowing my nose, or turning on the radio, and my actually doing it. I could feel spaces when people said something to me and then I answered them. Or maybe I answered a question they had asked before, sometimes a long time before.

I liked being the way I was, the new way.

I grew up.

Tom came along. He was quite a pleasant man and strong. He had very long arms and fuzzy black eyebrows. He walked with a stoop and his long arms hanging. Once he told me when he was a boy other children used to call him "Monkey Boy." He said he used to make himself laugh at them and tell them they were wrong. He was no "Monkey Boy," he was *Mr. Monkey*, and then he'd make this sound like he was a man and an ape.

This is what Tom said to me: "You used to be a nervous girl. But now you're not nervous. You're all peaceful. Sometimes you're so peaceful that people do not take the least notice of you."

"Oh," I said.

"I notice you," Tom said.

Maybe it was sometime later, he asked, "Are you lonely?"

"I don't know," I said.

"I think you are lonely," Tom said.

"All right."

"What if I marry you?" Tom said. "How would that be? You wouldn't be lonely then." Then he smiled. "Mr. Monkey won't be lonely either. Maybe you can teach Mr. Monkey how to be peaceful."

Well, I did marry him. We had Alice and then Johnny and then Carla.

What happened next was Tom went away to be a soldier.

Then he came back.

He was different. He said he had to cry sometimes. He said he had too many bad pictures always running in his head. He said he wanted to really be a monkey and he not a person because people did terrible things to each other, just terrible things, and he said he needed me to hold him and bring him peacefulness and I did.

Then Tom died. One day, when he woke up, he started to cough. He said he was not worried. He said nobody ever died of a cough. But he did die of a cough, you could say, but it wasn't on the day the cough started. It was later.

After Tom died, I got a job at Bell and Howell as "projector tester." (*Projector Tester* are words you can say over and over in your mind, aren't they, like a sweet lullaby about colors or something that tastes very good. They are slow words. I think they may be words that come from outer space.)

Projector Tester is a good job. You have to give new Bell and Howell projectors a three-minute test. If you turn them on and the bulb doesn't pop right away and you can show your film all the way through, then the Quality Control department will certify the projection lamp for a year. If a bulb is going to go, it goes quick:

POP! That is how people should die, I think, only not with the POP!

So here is what I do. I line up 12 just manufactured 8mm projectors on the test table. Then I plug them in to the 12 outlet silver metal electrical outlet strip. Next I click a little reel of film on the upper spindle of each machine. It's the three-inch reel with 50 feet of film. On our newest model, the top-of-the-line Bell and Howell 8mm Lumina, the threading of the film is fully automatic and you never have to touch the film or the filmgate. You put the film's leader here and *zip-click-clich*, the film is automatically threaded!

The 8mm Bell and Howell Lumina also features a retractable power cord and full auto-focus. It is quite a good movie projector.

The test movies are all samples from Castle Films, Inc. (I am sorry, you will not get a sample film with the purchase of the 8mm Bell and Howell Lumina projector. If you wish to purchase Castle films, they are sold at camera stores or may be ordered from the Castle Film Catalog.)

Castle films run three minutes each. I like that. In three minutes, you get the whole story. Some Castle films are in color, cartoons like Woody Woodpecker in *Fowled up Falcon* or travel films like H*awaii: Enchanted Isle* (#9138), and some are in black and white, like the Abbot and Costello films (these are very funny three minute movies and I think I would laugh very hard at them but when I start to laugh, why, I sometimes think Lou Costello reminds me of someone and I get to thinking about who and so I don't laugh after all), and *Chimp's Last Chance* (#855). There are many Castle films about chimps and apes and gorillas: I think it was Tom who told me that chimps and apes and gorillas are not the same except for apes and gorillas.

There is one three-minute Castle film called *Mysterious Dr. Satan*. In it, the hero is the Copperhead and he wears a mask and fights a robot. It was so interesting I even told Johnny about it but I do not think he understood.

When I click the master switch all the projectors show all the movies together on the wall (except for the 8mm Lumina projection lamps that go POP) and Abbot and Costello meet Chilly Willy and there's the chimps and Coney Island and The Three Little Bruins and Audie Murphy and W C Fields and a robot and Lon Chaney the Man-Made monster. It's like a stew of movies on the wall.

Projectors with popped bulbs I put on the FAILED shelf and the rest I pack up and put on the three-tiered cart.

That is what my job is, and now that you know, why, you see why I felt bad I had to take half a day off when the school called about Johnny.

This time it was not just a note home. Mother Cordelia said the school needed to talk to me and that meant she needed to talk to me.

So on Tuesday, I put on my hat and gloves and went to school. Christ the Comforter is a very good school with statues and pictures and flags. Mother Cordelia is principal. When she talks to me, she turns her head in a way that makes me think she will just keep turning it and turning it and it will go around and around and around. "Johnny runs up to the other students and blasts them in the face with bubbles." Mother Cordelia laughs but I don't because Mother Cordelia doesn't look like anything is funny. Laughing is not always about funny. "I guess you could say he's forever blowing bubbles," Mother Cordelia says, "but he's shooting them from that toy, that ray gun."

"Oh," I say. "Well. Then. Yes." That is the kind of thing I say when I need to put words out there but cannot be certain of what to say. It is strange, almost like being underwater, or getting secret messages from outer space, but just then, I can see in my mind Chilly Willy and gorillas and bubbles of light going pop-pop-POP!

Mother Cordelia says when Johnny "blows bubbles at the other children, he yells he is CAPTAIN RAMJET of THE ROCKET REBELS and he will destroy them all with his bubbles of death. We do not like children to make this sort of threat, even playfully. And, frankly, I do not think Johnny is all that playful."

I tell Mother Cordelia Johnny has no father.

"But Johnny has a Father." She points to the Crucifix on the wall by the window. She say, "Johnny's Eternal Father is always with him. Our Father who art in heaven."

I nod my head. *Woody Woodpecker. Mighty Mouse. Fatso Bear. Chimp on the Farm.*

"It's the comic books," Mother Cordelia tells me. "Johnny is obsessed by comic books."

These are Johnny's comic books: OUTER SPACE INVADERS. BEYOND THE GALAXY. DARK DIMENSION 12X. SPACE MONSTERS. BUZZ COREY. ATOMIC MENACE. CAPTAIN RAMJET OF THE ROCKET REBELS. ROGUE STAR. FLASH GORDON. PIRATES OF THE STRATOSPHERE. ROD BROWN OF THE ROCKET RANGERS.

"You must take the comics away from him," Mother Cordelia says. "Get him away from the comic books."

"All right," I tell her.

"No more comic books," Mother Cordelia says, "because you know what is good for him and right."

"Yes," I say. *Chilly Willy is so silly and now the Mt. Everest Woodpeckers return on the Gorilla Show ...*

"I further advise," says Mother Cordelia, "that you have a serious talk with him and then give him ... You. Know. What."

"All right," I say.

"And I advise still further that you give it to him right on the ... You. Know. Where." Now Mother Cordelia smiles.

"All right," I say.

"I am sure ... You. Know. How." Now Mother Cordelia winks.

I know what is right and good for my children. That evening, I tell Johnny and Carla that Alice I am taking them on a picnic.

I like picnics.

THREE

Ro-man set up headquarters and base of operations in a cave in the Valley of Bad Shaped Rocks. (Coincidentally, this was the exact cave site where Johnny and Carla had come upon The Professor and Roy practicing archaeology.) Though he was but a lone warrior, and a hairy one at that, Ro-man had been ordered to destroy all of humanity.

Check and double check, Ro was up for the gig. Ro-man was equipped with a Calcinator ray, a bubble machine, a Televisory Vidscreen and a card table. Wouldn't take much more than that. This was before the Star Wars missile defense system.

No declaration of intent, no cheeseball speeches like THE DAY THE EARTH STOOD STILL. Ro-man royally Japs the planet. Fired up the old Calcinator ray and, brother, that's all she wrote.

Reports via viewscreen that he has put the kibosh on the whole kit 'n' kaboodle. It's a wrap. Case closed, Mabel, and I'm coming home.

That's what Ro-man brags to The Great Guidance, who more or less tells Ro-man, "*Bubbe*, you are so full of prunes." Cram this into your noggin, Ro-man, there are SIX PEOPLE still alive on the planet so let's get calcinating."

Little did Ro-man know that Johnny had been spying, picking up on the two-way interplanetary gas session and bombast between the Great Guidance and Ro-man.

Johnny beat feet back to the ruined house: all that was left was the basement level. Strands of wire buzzing and crackling with electricity – a primitive but effective means of blocking Ro-man's Televisory Probes – surrounded the open air bunker of the last human beings on the plant, who were—

Pop: (who had *been* the Professor but ... Hey, change happens) and

Mom: (ding-dong ding-dong)

and

Carla (ain't she sweet?)

and

Roy, who was now the scientist boy-friend

of

Alice, who had become a scientist in her own right.

And of course ... Here's Johnny!

Johnny threw himself into the sanctuary and says, "I know where Ro-man is. Let's go and kill him."

Alice: Perhaps we *could* find his weak spot.

Mom: Do you think it will rain today? It could. I wish we had a roof. I don't think we have an umbrella and we are not fish.

Roy: Maybe it's ... his ass. We could jam some fissionable materials right up Ro-man's old wazoo ...

Pop: Don't talk like that.

Alice: Roy, your levity is inappropriate. We are confronting certain death.

Roy: Oh ... Alice, will you marry me?

Carla: I thought you were already playing house.

Mom and Pop: Ha-ha.

It was agreed then. Alice and Roy, having in common both science and a penchant for kludgy banter, would wed.

Roy: ... we were wondering how you'd feel about performing the ceremony.
Pop/Professor: You want me to—?
Alice: Oh, yes!
Professor: In that case, let's do it! And I want you to know this is the biggest social event of the year! The whole darn town will turn out!

Pop/Professor is really a big tickle. Har-de-har-har. But okay, if Jackie Leonard he ain't, leave us not to forget he was the cat who, with the invaluable aid of scientists Roy and his own daughter Alice, invented an *ANTIBIOTIC SERUM* capable of curing all diseases, even the common cold.

And upon whom did he experiment with the first injections? Turn around, drop your pants, and a little *shtoch* in *tuchus* for his family and Roy and of course, Himself.

Interesting side effect, one which The Professor had no time to learn from FDA trials. *The antibiotic also provided complete immunization to Ro-man's death ray!*

Which fact gets glommed onto by ... Ro-man.

Ro-Man: Great Guidance, I have discovered the secret of our failure to destroy the remaining humans! Our Calcinator death ray cannot penetrate them. They have been made immune through the antibiotic serum, which I believe is the same as our formula X-Z-A.

The Great Guidance had new commands.

Ro-Man: I am ordered to kill the humans. I must do it with my hands.

≪≪—≫≫

Professor: Dearly beloved, we are gathered here to... Dear Lord, You know I am not trained for this job. But I have tried to

live by your laws. The Ten Commandments ... The beatitudes...
The Golden Rule.

I have always believed in the Brotherhood of Man. I have
always believed that one day, the working peoples of the world
would unite to throw off the yoke of Oppression. The working
class is the class that works and thus, we, the last survivors, reach
out to any other last survivors who might have survived in Russia.

(When you're a Red, you're a Red until you're dead.)

Professor: Father on high, I would like you to give your bless-
ing to Alice and Roy. Even in this darkest hour, we have kept the
faith. In your grand design, there may be no room for man's tri-
umph over this particular evil that has beset us. If by any chance,
we workers of the world emerge in strength and victory should be
on our side, I want You to give a long life to Alice and Roy, and
a fruitful one. But no matter how it ends, Lord, watch over them
this night ... Watch over us all.

Amen.

And now, I pronounce you Man and Wife.

Roy, do you have the ring?

Roy: Why, I didn't think about that.

Johnny said, "Oh, brother." Johnny thought, *Stupid a-hole.
Freame supreme. And he's a swish.*
    Mom took off her own ring and handed it to Roy. "Rings go
around and around," she said.
    Roy: With this ring, I thee wed.

Professor: The only thing to seal it now is a kiss.

They kissed. Johnny asked, "Where are you going on your
honeymoon, Niagara Falls?"
    Roy (laughing): Lad, you are just chockful of scintillating wit.

To tell the truth, we hadn't thought about that.

Professor: Wherever you go – be careful. And I want you back first thing in the morning. After all, there is a war going on! And now, more than ever, I don't want to give up!

Roy: Thanks for everything, Dad. Most of all, for having raised Alice. You too, Mom.

Alice: I'll go get my things, and then we'll go.

FOUR

ALICE

And so, heigh-ho and off I go, a'hand in hand, a'honeymooning with Roy, lah-de-dah, Roy, dunce-in-residence. "Alice," says he, "we really need to talk." A pause, then, "*I* need to talk."

I'd wager a dollar to your Aunt Nellie's discount diaphragm that Roy is struggling with a confession concerning the "love that dare not speak its name" – or even lisp it.

But why should I make it easy? "No, my dear, my darling, my one and only tutti-frutti. What we need is FORNICATION. The future of the human race depends on it. As soon as we find a little out of the way nook or cranny, you're going to jam your beef bayonet into my yummy gummy and ride me like a carnival tilt-a-whirl. We are fucking for the future, Roy, a better bet than US Savings Bonds."

A sidelong glance shows me red-face Roy about to have a cow.

Do the dirty with Roy? Please, My Ain True Love is a Magnificence of Savagery and Intellect. He is Unpredictability and Contrasts. He is Cruelty and Confused Gentleness. Fate has brought him to me and me to him. He's one hotcha-hotcha and I'm totally gone for him. As Blaise Pascal said, "The heart has its reasons which reason knows not of." And as Dale Evans stated, "Every time we love, every time we give, it's Christmas."

So, Merry Christmas to me, as we continue on, Roy trying to talk and me following my unreasoning heart.

Then behind us, Carla calls out. "Roy, Alice, wait for me!" And we stop, turn, and here she comes, cutey-pie in Keds.

Alice: Carla, what are you doing here?

"I didn't get you any presents," Carla says with reach-for-the-insulin adorability, holding out a droopy flower.

"How lovely," Roy says sourly, perhaps thinking of his own pointdexter, likely to droop when summoned to report for duty.

Carla's following us was unexpected, all right, but perhaps it is better this way, I think, as I gush appropriately. "Oh, you little rascal! Thank you very much. Now, you'd better run right on home!"
Roy: Quickly, Carla.

Very good, fly away home, little birdbrain, fly away home.

FIVE

She runs and runs, puffs of dust trailing her. She is afraid now and she tries to think of things that will make her not afraid. Maybe Johnny will play house with her. Maybe Mom will sing her a song: "Chilly Willy cooked in a stew, with a penguin and a monkey and a girl like you." Of course, maybe she will be in bad trouble. Maybe Dad will be mad and yell and spank. Then for no reason she thinks, Maybe this is all a dream. Maybe she is drowning – little girls do drown – and in her drowning she is imagining this.

Suddenly, Ro-man blocks her path. Beneath his dull gray helmet, he has a broad and thick body like the hairiest of apes, although he stands easily erect, not even a hint that he'd feel more comfortable with knuckles on the ground. He looks like his feet hurt badly and you can tell he doesn't want to run because he is more the lumbering than the running type. Ro-man's face (what you can see of it through the misty none-too-clean glass visor of his helmet) is something like Lon Chaney's in *Phantom of the*

Opera, if in addition to his other physiognomic misfortunes, the Phantom had been badly burned in a fire, or had decided to don two silk stockings to rob a currency exchange. Ro-man's space helmet sports one bent antenna and one straight one. Reception is pretty good, considering.

Ro-Man: What are you doing here alone, girl-child?

Carla (sans cuteness): My daddy won't let you hurt me.

Ro-Man: We will see!

It seems she was right to be afraid. She is neither drowning nor dreaming and she is in bad, bad trouble.

SIX

Ro-man contacts the Great Guidance on the Televisory Vidscreen. Ro-man's got plans. Ro-man's got dreams. Ro-man's gotta be cool and just mayhap, Mr. Ro-man, Esq. might have it made in the shade.

Ro-Man: Great Guidance, I have a favorable report. I have already eliminated one of them. It was a simple matter of … strangulation. That leaves four for me to kill.

The Great Guidance: Error again! *Five.*

You can hear the Great Guidance's exasperation: *What's with you, Schmuck? You're coming on like Goof Majorus. You a numbnuts or what?*

Ro-Man: *Four*, well … I have made an estimate in relation to our strategic reserve: The plan should include ONE LIVING HUMAN for reference, in case of unforeseen contingency.

The Great Guidance: Do you question the plan?

Ro-Man: No, Great One. I only postulate—

The Great Guidance implies, *Hold on just one chicken-pluckin' second! Oh, Ro-man, I'm tuning in and the picture is clear! You've gone APE for the female HUMAN, the one with the classy chassis and the outsized nay-nays. 'Fess up, you got a case of the trottin' hots for the babe.*

Ro-Man: I …

Great Guidance: Proceed on schedule! Destroy the others. ALL OF THEM!

Ro-Man cuts the Vidscreen.

Ro-Man (goes all existential a la Hamlet's "to be or not to be," only with more hair and a space helmet: I cannot, and yet I must. How do you calculate that? At what point on the graph do must and cannot meet? Yet, I must.
But I cannot.

SEVEN

ALICE

Believe it or not, despite the rock strewn terrain, we found a small patch of grass, spread out the blanket, and then, just for the hell of it, I surprised Roy with a sudden and fierce kiss.

He did not surprise me in the least. He pulled back, wiping his lips with the back of his hand. "Alice …"

I said, "Our obligation to the future generation is to create it, so let's get propagating."

"Yessss," Roy said super-sibilantly. "I take our responsibility seriously, but it will be difficult, because my natural inclinations …"

"You're light in the shoes? You're a bigger fairy than Tinker Belle? You really love FRUIT cake and NANCY comics and JUDY GARLAND, too? Aw, you nutty nob jockey, you flying flit, you silly shirtlifter, you fucky-sucky Stoke on Trent, I knew you were a ragin' HOMO ever since I first saw you. There's as much chance of my making humpity-bumpers with you as there is my diddling Dwight D. Eisenhower in the window at Macy's during the Thanksgiving Day parade while Mamie farts 'Auld Lang Syne' in three quarter time."

Color Roy confused. "You don't love me?"

I smiled.

Enter … *RO-MAN*!

Enter … My Own True Love!

… who gave Roy such a *zetz* stars orbited his head like in a Woody Woodpecker cartoon. Ro-man said something along the lines of "Alice and I are going steady, pal, so you're cruisin' for a bruisin'"

Ro-man, my Romantic Ro-man!

So that's all she wrote, Roy. Off to the Great Fruit Stand in the Sky. As William Shakespeare had it, "Nothing in his life became him like the leaving it."

"C'mon, Big Guy," I said, and Ro-man picked me up in his great, long arms, My Big Loving Monkey Man, and held me tight against his powerful hairiness as he carried me off to our cave.

«« —— »»

It was easy to lure Mom, Pop, and the Obnox to the cave. Hel-lo, Operator, get me the Televisory Vidscreen of the last remaining Humans on Earth. Ooh, ooh, Mommy, Poppy, the Big Bad Hairy Guy in the Helmet has your poor widdle Alice and I only just managed to get to this communicator while he's recalibrating and recalculating his recalcinator. You've got to rescue me.

And here they come. Mom going woo-woo, Pop singing the Internationale – and the Obnox. (*You tell me your dream/I'll tell you mine.*)

And when they're at the mouth of the cave, Ro-man clunks Mom and Pop's heads together KA-THUNK! (*Nyuck-nycuk-nyuck, you hapless halfwits!*) Ro-man grabs Snotty Johnny by the googler and sets to squeezing.

Takes maybe five seconds, all in all. The three of them lie there, as dead as Adlai (Commie Symp) Stevenson's presidential plans.

And now, I, I and my Strange and Wondrous Love, can begin, Adam and Eve, on this world that is ours and ours alone …

EIGHT

THE GREAT GUIDANCE: You wish to be a human? Good, you can die a human!

The Great Guidance gestures. Lighting shoots from his fingers.
Zap!
Ro-man staggers and falls dead.
Nonplussed, Alice says, "Shit."

NINE

ROBOT MONSTER, DREAMING

Though in many aspects the Anthropoid Ape resembles the Lowland and Mountain Gorillas of Africa, there are marked differences originally noted and recorded by enlightened zoologists of the mid-19th century. The true Anthropoid weighs less than and is not as stocky as his evolutionary underling, the Gorilla. An Anthropoid walks fully erect with no knuckle-dragging and considerably more grace and poise, has a rudimentary but practical language consisting mainly of noun and verbs, and by any measurable scale, is of far greater intelligence than your average maggot-eating, shit-flinging ape.

Which is to say that in their natural habitat and conditions, gorillas are fucking morons and Anthropoid Apes are merely pitifully stupid. If this sounds judgmental, ah, mine is the right: It was my curse to be born Anthropoid. Indeed, from my entrance onto this Earthly plane, was I doubly cursed: Though all was proper for an anthropoid infant from my neck down, I was born with the face of a wrinkled, double-ugly infant human being.

Speculate as you will, and certainly as I often did, there is a simplistic legend among Anthropoids. Yes, now I know about Archetypes and Collective Unconscious and all that, but trust me; with your typical Anthropoid having at best a low double digit IQ, we are talking about a *super-simplistic* mythology:

Once, long ago, an orphan infant human boy was adopted into a tribe of Anthropoids and grew up to be *Tarmangani*: The Great White Ape. He learned from his extended foster family how to sleep safely in trees and flee the claws and fangs of Numa, the Lion, and to keep from being trampled by Tantor when the seasonal mating-madness came upon the tusked behemoth. On his own, he learned the use of a knife (my unimaginative clansmen refer to it as a "hand fang") to read and write English, French, German and Spanish, and, for all I know, how to floss three times a day, use a Zippo lighter, and strum "Whispering" on the tenor banjo.

With smarts like that, Tarmangani soon established himself as King of the Apes. I would assume he suffered an epiphany one day: *I am Ruler of this bunch of hairy, stinky shitheads? I am dying for good conversation, for a seven course meal that includes no fruits, leaves, shoots or grubs, for a dance with a non-hirsute someone of the opposite sex who can waltz or polka rather than stomp around grunting and farting at the ceremonial Dum-Dum."* Intellectually, Tar had gone far above his raising, and so can it be any surprise that he abandoned those who'd taken him in and given him food, shelter, and, on occasion, a backhanded smack to the chops?

It is whispered that Tarmangani will return one day. Myself, I don't care if he does return in glory, riding a white ass though the jungle, while all the assholic anthropoids wave palm leaves and chant, "*Ben Gund Yud* (The Great Leader returns)! Hosanna in the highest! Now there'll be fat larvae in every pot! Huzzah, huzzah, huzzah!" Frankly, once my own brain cells were energized and making connections, putting two plus two together and working quadratic equations on the side, I couldn't buy it: Tarmangani would never come back to this. I sure as hell would not. Not while Howard Johnson's offers 31 flavors.

I mention the legend only as it's thinly conceivable that it supplies a clue as to how I came by my countenance. Genetically, anthropoids and humans are 99+% the same. It is not impossible, methinks thinks me, that Great White Ape grew tired of playing pat his own cake and held his nose long enough to plant his Tarmanganiness into an Anthropoid lass, maybe he got drunk, and then, recessive and dominant genes at work …

Ah, why am I here? Why was I born? What the fuck? Such philosophical questions can and will be contemplated even unto the End Times – and if you come up with the definitive answer, I'll see you get your shot on The 64 Dollar Question.

I know only that I grew up with an ugly human face on top of my neck. Other little anthropoids called me "*Balu Ug Lot*," which translates "Little Baby Ass Face," and my own mother, Gloopit by name, used to wrinkle up her nose, nostrils as big as Oldsmobile headlights, and grunt most un-mommyish phrases.

I was outcast and exile. Oh, I maintained contact with my peers and their elders – my ass was frequently contacted by a foot of a playmate, my head, a fist – but I was the classic ugly duckling, the lonely little petunia in the onion patch, the matzoh ball in the Irish stew.

Until one day … Fate intervened.

Fate! There is no fate. Between the thought and the success God is the only agent. Do you know who proclaimed that? Edward G. Bulwer-Lytton who created some of the worst prose in the English language, perhaps outdone only by his friend and crashing snob and bore Charles Dickens.

I can give you a thousand quotations, pertinent or impertinent. I can build a harpsichord and admirably perform upon it no fewer than 300 Bach Cantatas despite my having fingers like Polish sausage. If you need someone to offer critical thought on cave wall painters or Caillebotte, cite each season's batting average for Monte Stratton, or espouse a credible opinion on why Cyril and Methodius should not be credited with devising the Glagolitic alphabet, good sir, I am your huckleberry!

And how did this happen?

Why, one day in the skies overhead there was a eye searing flash and ear drum shattering explosion. And then, no more than a kilometer from us, an earth shaking impact.

"*Pandar pandar!*" yelled one another.

"*Zu tu!*" shouted another.

And of course, the obvious "*Kreeg Kreeg-gah!*"

"Loud, loud!" and "Big Bright!" and "Beware, danger, danger!" Such were the keen observations of my landsmen.

Please remember, I had not yet metamorphosed into the Einstein of the Anthropoids, but there was a brute force of curiosity within me that overcame my fear.

What had I to lose? My life? As Cesare Pavese has it: "No one ever lacks a good reason for suicide." Human or Anthropoid, both species have an occasional and enviable bent for self-destruction.

Or perhaps I was yet too fucking stupid to know there might be danger involved.

With the cheerful encouragement of the tribe, "Numa will eat you if he can shut his eyes so he doesn't have to look at you," and *"Ngh amba wob at!"* (Don't trip over your little bitty penis), I set off.

I found the wreckage of a flying saucer. (I of course did not know then it was any such thing.) I discovered a grayish dead body, non-anthropoid and *non-zan-mangani* If you are in the *mangani* family, you normally have five digits per hand. This little *pisher* had three. He also had big glassy eyes like some of the bugs I used to find pretty tasty.

And I found ... I did not know what it was, not then, but it was round and gray and like any babbling human toddler or most primitive mammals equipped with hands / paws, I had to try it on.

My head lights up like Coney Island. It is like I'm getting the extra A-Bomb they'd planned to drop on Tokyo if Hiroshima and Nagasaki didn't do the trick.

Epistemological Instant! "What is knowledge?" "How do we know what we know?" "How is knowledge acquired?"

You don't have to send in to the Rosicrucians, amigo. I can testify and proclaim without contradiction knowledge is acquired Just! Like! That! *Zappo-Bam! Bang! Pow! Zoom!* Maybe not the sum total of all Earthly knowledge and that of the worlds beyond, but a damned good bunch for a freeby was contained in the helmet I lowered down over my accursed ugliness (that's a literary allusion, bwah: Gaston Leroux's *Phantom of the Opera*!). I could untangle Tesla and find the Lost Chord, mesmerize the masses and perfect perpetual motion, and even proffer a koan spun off from the last words of Dutch Schultz: "A boy has never wept nor dashed a thousand kim."

Thus I became the intelligent anthropoid with the ugly human face.

201

I fear to remove the helmet. I do not think it would happen, but it is just possible I could revert to my pre-smart state. I could not bear that, to descend to once more being an obtuse pariah.

Because, while I am ever so solitary now, the only one of my kind upon this planet (uberanthropoid!), I dare to hope there are other beings – human beings – who may come to look upon me and discern only my mind …

And if there is such a thing (the helmet does not impart any knowledge of the matter!) my SOUL!

O Joseph Carey Merrick, O Elephant Man, You of Hideous Visage and Victim of a Thousand upon a Thousand Torments, did you not at last find Kindness, did you not come to know Compassion, and to possess companions with whom you might laugh and weep and speak of the Pyramids and poetry and cabbages and kings and all things great and small?

I set forth upon my quest, and Joseph Carey Merrick, you are Inspiration and Companion.

Courage, Friend Merrick whispers, and I take courage, and *Hope*, Friend Merrick whispers, and I take hope

> that
>
> my loneliness might reach out
>
> to touch the lonely
>
> those who carry their own sad and frozen
>
> exile within themselves
>
> that
>
> we will meet
>
> The Lonely
>
> that
>
> we will come to know one another
>
> that
>
> we will love
>
> that
>
> we will love
>
> that
>
> we will love

《《——》》

Note: *Robot Monster* is in public domain and thus I have borrowed some lines of dialogue from the film. My thanks to writer Wyott Ordung, director Phil Tucker, and "N. A. Fischer Chemical Products" for the "Billion Bubble Machine."

Music on the Michigan Avenue Bridge

t's dark, the special dark of the city as it is punctuated by street lights. We see the shoes of the saxophone player on the sidewalk as he is moving right along.

The saxophone player is a man with somewhere to go.

He has somewhere to go tonight because—

—It is Springtime. We have Spring and we have the night.

We have Two A.M. and the city is angles and rhythms. The city is moves and slides and whisperings. You can hear the city breathe.

The city is stutter-starts and staccato tickings. It's the wheeze in the wind and purple after-images and free floating dreams.

The saxophone player is black. He sometimes thinks of himself as African-American. This is America, so sometimes you have to think about that. Mostly, though, he thinks of himself as a saxophone player.

It is the alto sax hanging from its strap that defines him. His fingers are on the keys. He doesn't have to be playing. He is playing when he is not playing.

He is playing the city and its song, because the city is, if you listen, the city is music, it is night music and it calls to you...

If there is music in you.

The saxophone player is on the walk of the Michigan Avenue bridge over the Chicago river. Now he stands near a pillar. Now he leans on the guardrail. Now he closes his eyes. Now he feels the city.

Now he plays.

And the police squad car is approaching.

There is a man in the back seat, huddled in pain, groaning.

He is not what the policemen hear.

The white police officer, driving, says, Hear that?

That is very fine sax.

His partner and his friend, young and black, says, Yeah.

The man in the back seat says, Uh... Says, My nose... Bastards... Says, You hurt me.

The squad car pulls up in front of the saxophone player.

This is a silent moment. Are you eager to talk to a policeman, even if it turns out the cop is only telling you you dropped your ball point pen? Now if you were a black man doing something borderline weirdhead like playing a saxophone at 2 A.M on the Michigan Avenue bridge...

Exit squad car, White Cop and Black Cop.

Saxophone player says, Is there...

White cop says, No problem, no. Heard you. Like the way you sound.

Saxophone player says, I'm not high or anything, if that's what...

White cop says, No problem. Really. You play beautifully.

In the squad car, man in back seat says, Mother Q. Fucker...

Says, Busted in my goddamn teeth...

Black cop says about his partner, He's the one knows his jazz. He says you're good, you're good, y'know.

White cop says, Yeah, you are good. Like Marsalis, you went and listened to the old guys. You're tradition. I can tell.

Saxophone player says, Yeah, I guess.

White cop says, Benny Carter, right? There's a lot of Benny Carter in your music. I can hear it.

Black cop says, Me, I'm not into jazz. Not really. Country is more for me. Clint Black. Travis Tritt. The Dixie Chicks.

The man in the back seat of the squad struggles to sit up. Manages to. Yells, All right, all right! Cut the bullshit! You fuckers had your giggles, now how's about we cut a deal?

The saxophone player doesn't say anything and wishes he were somewhere else.

White cop talks to black cop as though saxophone player is somewhere else. Don't guess that prick understands. Think he's dim, y'know?

Black cop says, Dim prick.

Saxophone player doesn't want to talk but figures he had better talk so he says, Maybe I should leave. You don't...

White cop says, It's all right. It's okay. You just stay here.

Black cop says, It's okay, y'know. You're good. My partner knows jazz. Smiles. Don't you worry about what's in the car. That's Grade A certified asshole. A very bad person.

White cop says, He is a bad asshole.

Black cop says, We'll take care of it, y'know.

Saxophone player does not like this a bit. No, he does not.

White cop says, You play. Do the changes for Bird's "Cherokee." You can do that, can't you?

Saxophone player says, I guess.

Black cop says, Don't worry. Nothing to worry about.

White cop says, Yeah. Bop time. Laughs. Hard bop.

Saxophone player plays "Cherokee," runs the changes.

Wishes he were gone. Wishes he were way the hell away.

Plays changes.

Knows this is seriously bad.

Wishes he were gone.

Cops yank the man out of the squad car.

Cops walk the man, drag the man, kick the man's ass.

White cop says, This way, sir. Concert about to start.

The man says, Fuck you, you fuck. The man could be Hispanic. He could be white. He could be black. His face is bashed in. Dribbling blood is red, dried blood black in street lights, jutting exposed bone, white.

Now the cops handcuff the man to the guard rail.

The saxophone player plays changes. "Cherokee."

Now the police take out their batons.

They begin hitting the man. Snap the sticks into him. They get a rhythm going. Syncopation.

The saxophone player plays changes.

The man screams. A baton smashes into the scream.

Saxophone player plays sheet of sound. Like Coltrane. Yeah, non-melodic thing, up and down, all notes equal, like finding something, like—

Cops use feet now.

Wet and breaking sounds.

Loud breathing. Cops. Not only the cops. Loud breathing.

Plays. "All These Things You Are." "A Train." "Goin' Fishin'."

Plays. "Cristo Redentor." "Cristo Redentor." "Cristo Redentor."

There, shithead! Black cop.

There and there and there! White cop.

Saxophone player plays.

Free jazz. Chaotic counterpoint.

Sound breaking and shattering from the bell of the saxophone.

Sound of the police.

Sound of the city.

Sound collage.

White cop says, Well, then.

Black cop says, Yeah.

Saxophone player cannot play any longer. Doesn't say anything.

Cannot say anything.

Black cop says, Dead?

White cop says, Could be.

It doesn't matter all that much, they decide. They remove the handcuffs. They hoist up what may be a dead man.

Before they toss him off the bridge, the black cop says, Shit, I think we forgot to read him his rights.

There is a surprisingly flat-sounding splash.

Now, there are only the three of them on the bridge, the saxophone player and the cops.

Black cop says, Nothing happened, okay? No big deal. A shithead.

White cop says, It's all right. The man understands.

White cop says, You play beautifully. Really.

Then the squad car is gone.

The saxophone player looks down sees the dark Chicago River, does not know what he thought he might see.

Says, Jesus…

And it is springtime and night and the city is razored angles and thick shadows and he wishes he were somewhere else far from the screaming the screaming the screaming.

Gary A. Braunbeck is the author of 10 novels and 10 short story collections, as well as nearly 200 published short stories in the fantasy, horror, science fiction, western, romance, mainstream, and mystery fields. A ravenous reader since childhood, he rarely ventures outside except when forced to at gunpoint (we exaggerate for effect...but not too much). His novels include the critically-acclaimed COFFIN COUNTY and FAR DARK FIELDS (both set in his fictional town of Cedar Hill, Ohio), and among his short-story collections are THINGS LEFT BEHIND and the award-winning DESTINATIONS UNKNOWN. His work has garnered 5 Bram Stoker Awards and an International Horror Guild Award. He lives in Columbus, Ohio with his wife, author Lucy A. Snyder, and 5 cats who hold him prisoner every day until they are fed.

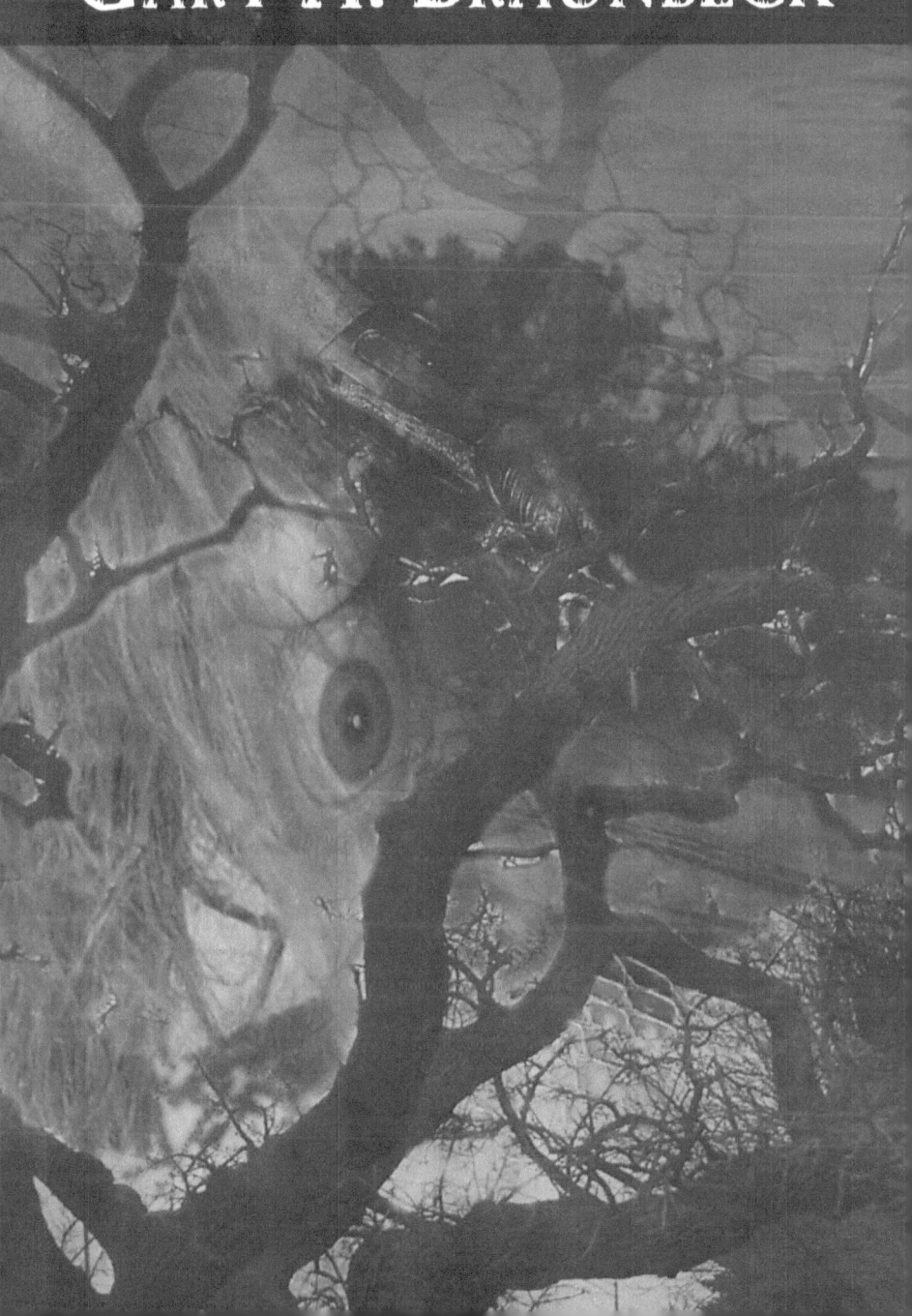

GARY A. BRAUNBECK

Merge Right

Before realizing that he was screwed to the wall, that he was beyond merely lost, that somewhere between 8:45 and 11:00 p.m. the universe as he knew it (or thought he'd known it) had ceased to function under anything even remotely resembling the acknowledged laws of physics, Matt Leigh ventured outside one winter evening, set the urn containing his wife's ashes on the passenger seat of his car, buckled it in place, took a mental snapshot of the home he had shared with her, and drove off to fulfill her last request.

Scatter my ashes at Niagara Falls in winter.

Part of him cursed himself for ever having decided to do it – God, how *lame* could you be? – and then just as quickly realized that Lauren had liked *lame*, had always been something of a traditional romantic at heart (one of the things he'd always loved about her; after all, they'd honeymooned at Niagara Falls), and considering how miserable the last few weeks of her life had been, it would have been a betrayal to her memory to do otherwise.

As he merged onto I-71 and headed toward Cleveland, he glanced over at the urn, felt the sudden tightness in his chest that always preceded a crying jag, and swore that this time he wouldn't allow it to get the upper hand; there had been too many times in the past few months that he'd broken into tears before he was even aware of it, the people around him lapsing into an uncomfortable silence, unable to maintain eye contact because he was blubbering like an idiot. The public breakdowns were bad enough, sure, but the solitary ones were even worse, somehow more embarrassing, because he felt defeated, frightened, alone, and – worst of all – weak. Christ, when he lost it at that memorial service they'd held for Lauren at the high school where she'd taught Science, he thought he'd implode from the humiliation.

There might have been a time, once, not so long ago, when he was a different sort of man, a kinder man, a man of compassion and selflessness who did not feel at all embarrassed or self-

213

conscious about letting his feelings show, about wearing his heart on his sleeve, but then came the baby that was too sick to live and Lauren fell in on herself after the funeral and said almost nothing for a full month until one night she surprised him with a tight hug and a deep kiss and a "I'm going to treat myself to a long, quiet bubble bath," and she did, and that's where he found her a little over an hour later, the remaining foam stained to a sick-making shade of pink, the water a distilled red, her face so calm, so relaxed, so peaceful. Her note, taped to the bathroom mirror, had for the most part been brief and to the point: I'm sorry, Matt. I hope you'll forgive me. I love you. Scatter my ashes at Niagara Falls in winter.

This, followed by something that he hadn't understood at all: *All matter is composed of quarks and leptons.* Written in a different color of ink.

He assumed that she'd written the note on a piece of paper that she'd used to scribble some notes for class. That would be just like her – never waste anything if you can find another way to use it.

Later, he confessed to one of his friends that he'd been suspicious – no, he'd known she was going to do it, and did nothing to stop her. "She was so unhappy," he said. "And nothing was going to make it any better for her. I tried, I really did, but nothing I did or said got through to her."

"Bullshit," said his friend. "You're just trying to find a way to blame yourself for being the one who's still alive."

Maybe that was right. Maybe. But Matt had spent so much time looking into himself since Lauren's death that he didn't know what to think or believe. There were times he thought some part of him was *relieved* that she'd done it. God, how many times had Lauren told him (in those rare instances when they had a conversation lasting more than two minutes) that she couldn't look at him because the sight of him was just another reminder of what they'd lost? He could never bring himself to admit to Lauren that he felt the same way whenever he looked at her, and hated himself for it.

It's too soon, he told himself now. *She's only been gone a few months, it's too soon to do this. Turn around, go back home, and wait until next winter. Keep her around a little longer.*

He reached up and wiped his eyes, then pulled in a hard, loud, snot-filled breath.

Jesus Christ, babe – why? Why'd you do it? We could have gotten through it. I would have done anything to make it better for you, I was just too wrapped up in feeling sorry for myself to notice how much more you were hurting. I loved you so much. So much. Do you have any idea how much I miss you?

If he turned around right now, he could be back home in half an hour. The weather report called for another two or three inches of snow tonight, and New York was supposed to get twice that much. Okay, sure, he'd known this before, but had decided he'd rather try braving the snow at night rather than have to deal with both the snow and traffic. Six hours from start to finish, one way; seven if he took it slowly.

He checked his watch. Not quite 6:30 p.m. The plan was to leave at 6:00 and get into Niagara Falls between midnight and one a.m. He'd booked the hotel room a week ago. He'd get up in the morning, have breakfast, check out, and then walk across the Rainbow Bridge, where he'd scatter her ashes. Matt wasn't sure if it were legal or not, and didn't really care. So what if he had to pay a fine?

You could have checked, he thought. *Another reason to turn around. What the hell good is any of this going to be if you get there and find out it's against the law?*

He shook his head. It wouldn't make any difference. He was just trying to find a way to chicken out. Again.

He looked at the urn once more and said, "Don't worry, babe. I won't let you down, I promise. I just…I can't stop thinking about how *miserable* you must have been, y'know?"

And then he heard Lauren's voice in his head, saying to him the thing she always said whenever his mood turned dark: *You need to think about something funny, Mr. Grumpy-Pants. You need to think about something that will make you smile.*

"Easy for you to say," Matt whispered. "You're not the one who's been left to sift through the detritus. You're not the one who's been left with a list of unanswered questions longer than your arm. You're not the one who…" He bit down on his lip, stopping himself. To say it out loud would be to give it form, to move it from the world of one's private thoughts into the physical world.

Okay, okay, maybe that was a bit existential, but nonetheless, Matt feared that if he said it, if he gave it voice, if he spoke the words, then the terrible thought in his head would always be out here in the world, following him, reminding him that there was a time when he'd told the universe that, despite his claims of relief, he still felt as if his wife had *abandoned* him, had lied to him somehow, and that some part of him *hated* her for it. As long as the thought remained in his head and *only* in his head, then it was safe...safe enough. It was something he could push back, file away, learn to ignore. But once *spoken*....

Deciding that he needed a distraction, Matt flipped down the visor and selected a compact disc from the sleeve mounted on the back, slid it into the player, and adjusted the volume. The disc was one he'd made for Lauren for their last anniversary, a compilation of her favorite Peter Gabriel songs. Though Matt personally preferred the stuff Gabriel had done with Genesis back in the day, he'd come around to appreciating the solo material, thanks to Lauren (although "Shock the Monkey" still got on his nerves no end). He'd promised himself that he'd play this for her along the way.

The disc opened with a live version of "In Your Eyes" – the version Lauren preferred – and Matt found himself humming along. Somehow the song seemed to fit the night outside because it was the perfect contrast; where the song was rich, deep, and warm, the night was bleak, impenetrable, and so very cold. The music, it seemed, was protecting both husband and remains-of-the-wife from the elements.

He double-checked to make sure his cell phone was charging, flipped the visor back into place, and opened a can of Pepsi he'd taken from the small cooler on the passenger-side floor; he'd stocked the thing with sodas, a couple of sandwiches, and some snacks before leaving; this way he'd only have to stop to use the bathroom. The car had a full tank (and had always gotten damned good highway mileage, even in bad weather when he had to drive at a crawl), so he wouldn't have to gas up until it was time to start the trip home.

Somehow he was able to let himself slip into auto-pilot for a little while, becoming just another weary traveler out on the road: moving, moving, moving along. Sometimes this was the best way to do things; just take most of your conscious self out of it and let your body function by rote.

He merged onto I-271 N via exit 220 toward Erie, Pennsylvania just as it became fully dark and the predicted snow was beginning to fall. This was really, truly, sincerely *it* – Put-Up or Shut-Up Time. A little over a hundred miles into the trip. This was his last chance to turn around if he were going to do it.

"What do you think, babe?" he asked the urn. "Keep going or go home?"

He looked at the urn as if he actually expected it to respond, and then realized this was the *second* time he'd spoken to it. That couldn't be a good sign.

Okay, he thought to himself. *If you keep her – it, if you keep it around another year, how sure are you that you're not going to continue talking to it like it's really her?*

"Good point," he said to the urn. "Onward we go, then."

A few miles after getting onto 1-271 he saw the sign telling him to **Merge Right**. So he did, noting that what had been a four-lane stretch was now only three. He glanced out over the concrete divider but saw no other cars traveling in the opposite direction, which seemed odd; it wasn't quite 8:00 p.m.; there should still have been a decent amount of traffic on the road.

Unless the forecast changed and they're calling for a lot more snow than was originally expected. Four or five inches would keep everyone home.

Up ahead, a gray car sat in the emergency lane, its taillights flashing, exhaust billowing into the winter night, sketching odd shapes into the air. Matt wondered if he should pull over and see if the driver needed help – were Lauren still here, *she'd* have pulled over – but then realized that it was exactly under circumstances like these that many serial killers had snatched their victims; no wonder so many people were now wary of a long stretch of dark, semi-empty road. Sure, odds were this was no serial killer, but that's probably what all the *victims* thought when they made the decision to pull over and play Good Samaritan. Didn't those two guys…what were their names? – Henry Lee Lucas and Ottis Toole, right – didn't they claim to have gotten a lot of their victims that way, by faking car trouble in hopes that some poor, unsuspecting Samaritan-type would pull over and offer to lend a hand?

Despite this line of thinking, Matt found himself slowing down as he neared the stopped car. He leaned forward, head turned toward the other vehicle, and tried to get a look inside. The dome light was off, but the illumination from the dashboard lights cast a soft bluish glow over the interior, and as far as Matt could see, there was no one inside the car.

He pulled a bit farther ahead and saw that the windshield wipers weren't going, so getting a better look inside from this angle was out of the question. God Almighty, why was he even doing this? He could see the exhaust, the lights of the dashboard, the flashing taillights, it wasn't like the car wasn't working, so how much of an emergency could it be? Maybe the driver just needed to pull over and check the map, or make a call on their cell phone, or even – hey, *here's* one that should have been obvious – run off into the bushes to take a leak. Matt could sympathize. There had been a few occasions where he'd thought he could make it to the next rest stop, only to find that his bladder had just been messing with him, had just been waiting for the moment when the rest stop entrance was parallel with the passenger door before announcing that, yep, okay, *now* it's time to go with the flow.

He began to pull away when, once again, something made him hesitate. *What* the hell was wrong with him? The driver was just down there in the trees somewhere, writing his name in the snow.

But what if you're wrong? said Lauren's voice in his head. *What if he pulled over because he was having a heart or asthma attack or a seizure or something? What if he's inside, lying across the seat and dying? What if he can't reach his cell phone? What if he doesn't even have a cell phone?*

Matt glared at the urn for a few moments, then looked at the other car once again. *Three minutes,* he thought, checking his watch. *I'll give this guy three minutes, and then it's none of my business.* This seemed practical. The car had been idling here well before Matt spotted it, so waiting an additional three minutes would give the guy plenty of time to finish his business, even if he had to do more than take a leak.

"You're stalling," he said aloud to himself. "And you know it. The guy's fine."

Hell, the guy was probably down there *hiding* in the bushes at this point, wondering what the person in the other car wanted.

The thought brought the week's first genuine smile to Matt's face. He put himself in the other guy's position: it's dark, and he has to pull over to relieve himself, so he sprints down into the bushes to do his business, and when he's finishing up, lo and behold, another car has pulled up alongside his and isn't moving. *Anyone* could be in that car – the police, car thieves, or a pair of sickos who idolize Henry and Ottis. No *way* is he going anywhere *near* his car until the other vehicle is long gone.

Matt almost laughed, then thought of the poor guy down there freezing his nuts off – perhaps literally – and so sped up and drove away, quietly wishing the other fellow the best of luck.

With the exception of the snow – which swirled across the windshield like heavy smoke from a distant fire – the next forty minutes of the drive were smooth and uneventful, if a bit slow due to decreased visibility. Then Matt saw another sign instructing him to **Merge Right** slip into the glow of his headlights, and he did so, and the three-lane stretch of highway became two. Once again – a force of habit, he supposed – he glanced over the concrete divider and saw there was still no traffic heading in the opposite direction, and that's when it occurred to him that he couldn't remember seeing any other cars (aside from the empty one in the emergency lane way back there) since the last time he'd merged.

Maybe the rest of the world was staying in tonight. That was fine with him, were it the case. Just him and Lauren and the road all to themselves.

Okay, that's the third time you've done something like that, thought of the urn as her and not a thing, an object. Knock it off.*

He looked at the urn, reached out to touch her – it, reached out to touch it – pulled his hand back at the last moment, and then touched it, anyway.

"Why'd didn't you talk to me about how you were feeling?" he whispered. "I would've listened. Why didn't you…?"

He stopped himself from finishing the question. Who was here to answer?

Then, two more signs: the first said: **Roadside Emergency, Dial *891.**

The second: **Merge Right.**

What the—? Why did he need to merge again so soon? Now it was down to one lane on his side.

Checking the rear-view mirror to make sure no one was behind him, Matt pulled off onto the emergency lane, put the car in park, removed the TripTik from the driver's-side door pocket, and leaned down for a better look at the map. Maybe he'd let himself drift off a little too much and had missed an exit or something… but, no, according to the map, he was right on track, and wouldn't hit any construction for at least another hundred miles.

He looked up into the rear-view mirror once again. There was still no one behind him. How long ago had he passed that car? Forty, forty-five minutes, right? And he hadn't passed any exits since then, so where was the other guy? Matt had driven enough road trips to know that, for a while, anyway, you tended to share your side of the highway with the same group of cars; not only had he not seen any other vehicles, but the guy that he passed back there should have caught up with him by now.

Oh, Jesus, he thought. *What if the guy really was hurt, or sick, or having a heart attack? What if he really was lying across the front seat and that's why you didn't see him?*

Folding the map back into place, he unplugged his cell phone, checked for the signal, and dialed *891. At least he knew where he was, and how far back the other guy had been.

There was a single ring on the other end, followed by a click!, and then…nothing. Just white noise, a soft static hiss that Matt imagined would be the voice of snow, if snow had a voice. He closed the phone, said, "Shit!", and then opened it again and hit the redial button. This time it rang three times before the *click!* and white noise came in, and just as he was about to close the phone again, a voice came on and said, "If tin whistles are made of tin, then what do they make foghorns out of?"

"What?" said Matt. "Who the hell is this? Listen, I've got an emergency I need to report. I'm on I-271, about – "

"—the only way to get home is never to stop. Never to stop. Never to—"

Matt snapped closed the phone tossed it onto the dashboard. Screw this; he'd get off at the next exit, find a service station, and get his bearings once again. According to the TripTik, there was an exit less than four miles ahead. Hopefully the service station or fast-food joint would let him use the phone.

He put the car in gear and pulled back out onto the highway.

"Jesus Christ, baby!" he said to the urn. "I try to call for help and what do I get? 'Weirdoes 'R' Us! I should've listened to you, baby, I'm sorry."

By now the snowfall was fairly steady; combined with the light wind, it looked as if he were driving on a sheet or slowly roiling fog.

"We're fine, baby," he said to the urn, not looking at it. "We'll get you there, no worries. We just gotta make an extra stop, that's all. Get that guy some help." He tightened his grip on the steering wheel and leaned slightly forward, though why leaning forward would do anything to help visibility, he couldn't say. He'd always done this when driving in bad weather. If nothing else, it lessened the distance between his skull and the windshield should anything happen.

Damn cheerful fellow you are.

Merge Right.

"Fuck!" he made a fist and hit the steering wheel. Less than half a mile since the last one, and still not an orange construction barrel in sight.

He merged, and the concrete divider came closer to his side.

"Sorry, baby," he said. "I didn't mean to swear like that. I know how you hate it."

Three miles until the exit. No problem. He'd maintain, he *had* to maintain, he wanted to do this right, wanted to go to sleep later tonight knowing that he'd done the right thing, that he'd helped another human being before it was too late, and honored his wife's last request. Maybe that would make it easier for him to sleep nights, easier to get up in the morning and face himself.

Two miles to go. He relaxed his grip on the steering wheel and even put in a new CD – Pat Metheny this time. Somehow, Metheny's guitar playing always sounded joyous, and he needed to hear something joyous and hopeful right now. Damn, his nerves had gotten the better of him – and a lot sooner than he'd thought they would.

One mile to go, and he saw the blinking taillights in the emergency lane ahead. This time he would stop, if for no other reason than to see if the other driver was as confused by all the **Merge Right** signs as he was.

And to make sure he's all right, said Lauren's voice. *To check and make sure he's okay. Like you should have done when you realized how long I'd been up in the tub.*

He looked at the urn. "That's a lousy thing to say to me, baby. I always respected your privacy, y'know? I just thought—"

No, honey, you just knew, that's all. You knew, and you just sat there.

"I'm sorry," he said, a single tear slipping from his eye and streaming slowly down his face. "I'm sorry, I'm sorry, *I'm so sorry!*"

This time it was an SUV of some sort, and the windshield wipers were going so Matt had a decent view of the inside, but no sooner had he come to a stop alongside the other vehicle than the wind kicked into a higher gear and the snow became a churning mass of white, so it didn't matter if the other vehicle's wipers were going; the wet snow plastered itself against the passenger windows of Matt's car and blocked his vision as much as did the tears.

He pressed his hands against his eyes and rubbed hard, pulling in his breath to steady himself. *Get a grip, pal; just get a fucking grip already.*

He looked over at the SUV, and then pulled back a bit and blinked his lights, hoping the other driver would see and blink in return; when that didn't happen, Matt hit his horn three times. The driver of the SUV did the same. Matt didn't want to approach the other vehicle without having given the driver some sort of warning.

Reaching into the back seat, Matt grabbed his coat and put it on, zipping up and covering his head with the hood. He dug out his gloves, put those on, took a deep breath, said, "I'll be back in a minute, baby", and climbed out.

The weather reports had called for a low of 27 degrees, but what Matt stepped out into felt damned near arctic. It was so cold that his breath turned to iron in his throat, the hairs in his nostrils webbed into instant ice, and his eyes watered and stung. In the faint starlight and bluish luminescence of the snow, everything beyond a few yards of his gaze swam deceptive and without depth, glimmering with things half seen or imagined. He listened beneath the low, mournful call of the winter-night wind and could detect no sounds save for those made by himself, the purring motors of the two vehicles, and the *thunka-thunka-thunk* of windshield wipers. Everything else in the world might have already died out in this cold.

He raised a hand to wave in greeting as he approached the driver's side of the SUV and realized that the driver had already lowered the window. Matt walked up to the door and offered his hand.

The SUV was empty. Not only that, but the window had been down for quite some time; a thin layer of snow covered a good portion of the front seats and part of the back. Despite the cold, the heater wasn't running, and appeared not have been running for quite some time; the snow had frozen into clumps in places.

Matt opened the door and leaned in, looking into the back seat where he saw a blanketed infant's seat buckled into place. Scrambling inside, he reached back and pulled away the blanket to find that the infant's seat was empty, as well. Jesus Christ – what kind of a moron would bring a *baby* out into a night like this? The taking-a-leak scenario didn't hold up this time, because no one would leave a baby alone in a car on a night like this, regardless of how much they needed to go. Which meant that this person – whoever they were – was out there someplace with a baby.

Matt took a deep breath, feeling the cold slice into his throat, and tried to get a handle on the panic he felt rising in his gut. Okay, maybe they'd had some kind of car trouble – like the heater going out – and they'd decided that, rather than risk the baby's health, they'd call AAA Roadside Assistance and get a ride into the next town. But why leave the vehicle running like this? Dammit, dammit, *dammit* – this made no sense.

He looked around the interior of the car for anything that might be a clue, checking the door pockets, under the visors, even opening the glove compartment, but found nothing to indicate why they'd left the vehicle – or, for that matter, who "they" even were. The glove compartment held no registration papers.

Then he saw the three square buttons over the driver's visor: a GPS system. Sliding into the driver's seat and closing the door, Matt then raised the window and pressed the button with the imprinted phone icon.

After a few seconds, a voice said, "UniStar, how may I assist you?"

"Thank God," said Matt. "Listen, this isn't my car, I found it abandoned a few minutes ago. Whoever was driving this took a baby with them and it's snowing like crazy outside and – "

"One moment please while I confirm your location."

The next five seconds seemed like fifty, but at last the voice came back: "You say you found the car abandoned?"

"Yes."

"We have a fix on your location, Mr. Leigh, and will—"

"Hold on a second."

"Yes?"

"How do you know my name? I didn't tell you."

"I apologize, sir. It's something we do automatically. As soon as anyone calls in, their name, vehicle make, and location shows on the screen. I was just reading the name off the screen. Force of habit."

"That still doesn't answer my question."

"Sir, the vehicle that you found is registered to a Matthew and Lauren Leigh."

Matt stared at the button, then looked out at his own car. "Lady, there must be some kind of mistake. *I'm* Matthew Leigh, and I can assure you I've *never* owned an SUV."

"Perhaps your wife—"

"My wife is dead. She's *been* dead for several months."

"Perhaps this is just one of those odd coincidences you hear about from time to time, Mr. Leigh. Perhaps the owners of this vehicle just happen to have the same names and yourself and your late wife."

Matt didn't like the flippant tone in the voice. "That's not funny."

"I wasn't trying to be funny, Mr. Leigh. Regardless, we'll have assistance to your location shortly."

Matt looked at the baby seat in the back and knew that, despite this bullshit about the names, he couldn't just leave this vehicle if there were any possibility that he could do something to help find a missing infant. "How soon will someone be here?"

"Mr. Leigh?"

"*What?*"

"The only way to get home is never to stop. Never to stop. Never to – "

"*Who the hell are you?*"

There was no answer. He repeated the question twice more, and, receiving no reply, decided to wait it out in his own car. As he was climbing back out into the freezing night, the voice said, "Assistance will be there in five minutes." *Click*.

The wind seemed determined to nail him to the spot – God, the temperature must have dropped at least eight more degrees while he was in the SUV – but he managed to make it back.

"Miss me?" he asked the urn as he climbed inside and closed the door. Removing his gloves, he reached down and turned up the heat, then grabbed his cell phone. Screw UniStar and their promises of assistance and their...whatever-in-the-hell it was that helped them to identify him; he was going to call the police. Punching in **911** he listened for a moment, heard nothing, then pulled back the phone and looked at the screen. *No Available Signal*.

"Horseshit!" he snapped, closing the phone and slowing his breathing. "You can't drive a mile down any stretch of highway without passing a goddamn cell tower these days, and I'm supposed to believe that a little snowstorm kills the signal? I don't think so." He looked at Lauren's urn. "I mean, c'mon, baby – for what we pay for this service every month, I damned well *ought* top get a signal. Isn't that their guarantee? Christ, I'd settle for weir-does again."

He flipped open the phone once again and thumbed in **911.** This time he got results.

"911. Please state the nature of your emergency."

"I found an abandoned vehicle with an empty baby seat in the back. I think the driver and the baby might be lost in the snow."

"What is your location, Mr. Leigh?"

Matt pulled the phone away and stared at the screen. Instead of displaying the time and the number he'd just called, the words **Voice Mail Waiting** were showing.

He brought the phone back and said, "How do you know my name? What the hell is going on?" His only answer was a burst of white noise from the other end. He disconnected the call and tossed down the phone, leaning back against the headrest and closing his eyes.

You're stressing, honey, said Lauren's voice.

"I know," he whispered. "But, Jesus, baby...this is weird."

No arguments here. Out of curiosity, how long had I been up there before you thought something might be wrong?

Matt opened his eyes and sat forward. The UniStar folks knew the location of the SUV and were sending assistance, so he'd done his good deed for the day. The 911 thing…okay, maybe he got one of those stations that automatically pulls up the cell number and the name of the person it's registered to, maybe that was it.

He checked the time and saw that he was over an hour behind schedule. Reaching into his coat pocket, he removed the slip of paper with the name and number of the hotel. He'd call and tell them he was running late, that they were to hold the room. If it turned out there were any extra charges for this, so be it. (Part of him knew this was unnecessary – he'd given them a credit card number to guarantee the room – but another part of him, the part that always worried, the part that always assumed the worst was going to happen, wouldn't let him not call.)

He flipped open his cell phone and saw the **Voice Mail Waiting** message again, and so pressed **OK**, entered his password, and waited for the message to play.

"Sorry we're not going to make it by midnight, baby," he said to Lauren. "But we'll get there. You just relax."

"I'm not worried, honey," came Lauren's voice from the cell phone. "I know you'll get us there eventually. Just remember, the best way to get there is never to stop."

Everything inside Matt's body locked up. For a moment, there was nothing more to the world than the echo of his dead wife's voice.

"To replay this message," came the electronic voice-prompt, "press '1'. To save it to the archives, press '7'. To delete it, press '9'."

Matt pressed "1".

"It's really cold out here, Daddy," said a child's thin voice. "When you gonna get here for me an' Mommy?"

Matt dropped the phone as if it were a hot coal and pressed his back up against the driver's side door, instinctively pulling his knees up and remembering something a Psych 101 professor had said back in college, about how childhood and fear are forever connected in the mind, because even an adult, in the grip of fear, will resort to the fetal position.

On the floor, the cell phone's screen blinked at him as the child's voice kept speaking: "…at, Daddy? It's so cold here. You have to come get me an' Mommy. Please, Daddy?"

Matt pushed out one leg and closed the cell phone with his foot, then pulled his leg back so quickly he heard his knee crack.

A sudden bright light appeared in the rear-view mirror. Turning around in his seat (still keeping his knees pressed tightly against his chest), Matt saw the distant headlights closing in fast.

"Okay," he said, but whether it was to himself or to Lauren, he didn't know and didn't care; for the moment, he need the sound of his own voice to fill the silence.

Silence?

He looked down at the CD player; the Metheny album had been playing when he'd gotten out of the car and he hadn't stopped it.

I always hated Pat Metheny, said Lauren. *All his stuff sounds the same to me after a couple of songs.*

He leaned forward and saw the ejected disc, now snapped in two, lying on the floor in front of Lauren's seat. As he reached down to pick it up, to make sure it was real and not just something brought on by the stress, his cell phone began ringing. He pulled back so quickly that he slammed his elbow against the steering wheel, right smack dead-bang on the funny bone, and the pain shot both up and down his arm as he grabbed his elbow and bent his arm, crying out.

The headlights down the highway were getting much closer now, and his cell phone – which should have switched over to voicemail after the fourth ring – was still going off, insistent, its volume growing louder and louder. He bent down – taking care to keep his throbbing arm a good distance from the steering wheel – snatched the phone from the floor, looked back to see how close the other vehicle was, and answered.

"*What?*" he shouted.

"You're beyond the laws of nature, time, gravity, friction, all of it," said a voice that was a combination of Lauren's soft Southern lilt and the child's tiny whisper. It sounded almost computerized. "Picture two people standing apart from one another on a frozen lake. They're tossing a basketball back and forth between them. Each time one person receives the basketball, the force of the other's throw pushes them farther away along the ice. The two players are the matter particles which are being interacted with, and the basketball is the force-carrier particle which affects them. One important thing to know about force-carriers is that a particular force-carrier particle can only be absorbed or produced by a matter particle which is affected by that particular force. For instance, electrons and protons have an electric charge, so they can produce and absorb the electromagnetic force-carrier, the photon. Neutrinos, on the other hand, have no electric charge, so they cannot absorb or produce photons. Isn't that interesting? I wish I'd gotten to teach some of this to my students…not that they would have paid much attention."

"Why are you doing this, baby?" said Matt into the phone, bursting into tears once again and feeling diminished, inept, and so goddamned weak he just wanted to die.

"*Shhh*, honey, don't get upset," said the voice of his dead wife and child. "All matter, be it the car in which you're sitting or a meteor in space, is composed of quarks and leptons. Both quarks and leptons exist in three distinct sets. Each set of quark and lepton charge-types is called a "generation" of matter – charges +2/3, -1/3, 0, and -1 as you go down each generation. All visible matter in the universe is made from the first generation of matter particles – up quarks, down quarks, and electrons. This is because all second and third generation particles are unstable and quickly decay into stable first generation particles.

"Now, think about something, honey. Imagine that *we're* – little Cynthia and I – imagine that we're a first-generation quark and *you're* a first-generation lepton, and that your guilt, your grief – whatever you want to call it – imagine that it has become so powerful that it's engineered a specific first generation force-carrier which, upon interaction with the first generation quarks and leptons, scrambles them into an instantaneous decay pattern and reduces the object to a harmless spray of subparticles. Do you see?"

"Oh, God, no, *no, I don't!* What're you talking about, baby? Where are you?"

"Right beside you, honey. A bunch of particles in a jar. The Universe is no longer a great mystery, Matt. In fact" – and here she/they laughed – "it's kind of a bore. Everything was always a bore without you by my side to share it with. Even death."

Click!

He had to get out. He suddenly didn't give a flying double-fudge fuck if he got to Niagara Falls or not, or whether or not he found some help for that other car stranded way back there, or if he ever saw another sunrise; all he cared about right now was getting away from the car and the urn and the phone and the guilt in his gut, all of it.

The headlights were almost here, so Matt tossed down the still-active phone, flipped up the hood of his coat, threw open the door, and stepped outside—

—and no sooner was his first leg out of the car with the rest of his body instinctually following that he immediately felt himself *drop* with such suddenness and force that he barely had to time to think *The ground's disappeared!* before his arms were flailing out, hands seeking purchase, and he somehow managed to grab hold of the seat belt that pulled out to its farthest length and then locked in place as he *hung* there, his head at the level of the running board, gripping the seat belt, swinging back and forth, the rest of his body hanging over an endless, seemingly bottomless, black, black, black chasm. He pulled up his free arm and threw it over the running board, trying to grab onto the gearshift, but the first time he missed and almost lost his grip on the seat belt but managed to grab the brake pedal in time, and that was good, yes, definitely, but it wasn't enough because the cold, the goddamned arctic *cold* turned the pedal to fire against his skin, so he took a deep breath, feeling his throat turn to iron, pressed his chest against the running board, and made a second, frenzied grab for the gearshift, and this time he nailed it, got a solid grip around the thing, and began pulling himself up and forward, his legs kicking out and back as if he were swimming, trying to balance his torso evenly between the seat belt and the gearshift because he wasn't sure how much of his weight either one of them could handle and that's all he'd need, for one of them to snap off or tear away, he'd be royally screwed then, no way could he get another grip in time, and for a moment he pictured himself freefalling away from the car, screaming as he watched the bottom of the car rise higher and higher as he plunged down into whatever in the hell waited below – if *anything* waited below – and forced himself not to think about it, just kept concentrating on keeping his weight balanced and his grips firm as he put his shoulders into it, rolling them slowly forward, then back, forward, then back, and soon he felt his hand slide up the seat belt, felt his elbow touch the edge of the running board, and as soon as the first elbow was inside and locked in place the rest was easy, he twisted sideways and lay his left shoulder on the floor, shifting the majority of his weight onto the gearshift and praying that it would hold, and it did, and soon there was his knee coming over the edge of the running board, his hand sliding a little farther up the seat belt, and with a last, painful effort, he got the rest of himself back into the car and onto the seat, still clutching the seatbelt that he at once pulled across his chest and locked into place, throwing his head back against the headrest and pulling in strained breaths, trying to stop his heart from triphammering right out of his chest.

It took a small eternity for him to stop shuddering, and by the time he was able to move again, he realized that the door was still standing open. He pulled his head forward and reached out for the door, gripping the inside handle, and he started to close it, he knew this without looking because he could feel the force he was putting into it, but then he made a big mistake: he looked out.

And what he saw was nothing. *Nothingness.* Only a wide, deep, endless blackness with no varying degrees, not like a normal night possessed, some shadows darker than others, giving it discernable boundaries, recognizable limits, something he could distinguish as being part of the world he knew. No, not this. This was the end of everything, where it all came crashing down, where it all scrambled into an instantaneous decay pattern and reduced everything to a harmless spray of subparticles that were scattered about only to be absorbed by whatever had existed here before the universe had been born.

He *knew* all of this with that odd certainty that every human being experiences at least once in their lifetime, an unbreakable conviction that they and they alone have just realized something that they can never hope to express to others with a tool so pitiful as mere language.

He looked out the windshield and saw the snow-covered highway before him; he looked to his right and saw the abandoned SUV still idling in the emergency lane, its wipers still singing their song of *thunka-thunka-thunk!*, the exhaust from its pipes swirling into the winter air, creating small misty whirlpools that seemed to be trying to resolve themselves into definite shapes.

Matt closed the door, lowered his head, and silently uttered a prayer for safety and deliverance to a God he'd never really believed in nor disbelieved was there to hear such pathetic requests, but pray he did.

And then he did something that he suspected wasn't a very good idea, but he had to know, had to be sure. He pressed the button on the door handle and began lowering his window.

It took only a few seconds for the window to drop halfway down, and that was all Matt needed: through the lower half of the window he could see the highway on which his car was for the moment stopped; but above, in that space where the rest of the window had been, he saw only the blackness of space illimitable, pressing toward him, a few tendrils whispering against the door, curling upward like the darkest smoke, and beginning to spill into the car.

He raised the window a few moments before the first tendril of nothingness could make it inside. From the floor, the voice from the cell phone was still repeating, "...never to stop. The best way to get there is never to stop. The best way..."

The headlights he'd seen earlier were no closer now than they had been before. Matt wondered if the vehicle was moving at all, or if it was only occupying the same space, over and endlessly, while the road below it moved, giving the driver the sense that he was in control.

He looked at the SUV once more as he put the car in gear, and then remembered—

—*jesusgodhowcouldyouforget?*—

—how he and Lauren had looked at an SUV just like this one during the third month of her pregnancy, how she'd convinced him that, with a new baby and all the tons of new-baby-caring-for paraphernalia they'd have to haul around every day, they were going to need a vehicle like this. There was going to be a *lot* of stuff, you know. And if the weather was bad and they needed to take the baby to the hospital, didn't they want a vehicle they knew they could depend on to get them there? And think of all the *groceries* they'd have to buy every week. Don't you think this would be just so *perfect?*

He drove away, mind and body numbed beyond anything he'd ever experienced. He kept driving until he saw the **EXIT** sign up ahead, then the exit, and he took it, and no sooner had he gotten

231

back onto the road than a **Merge Right** sign appeared, then another abandoned vehicle in the emergency lane, taillights flickering, a Ford Escort this time, just like the one he'd been driving when he and Lauren had first been dating, and he kept driving, kept following the directions every time a **Merge Right** sign told him to do so, kept passing other vehicles abandoned in the emergency lane; **Merge Right** – the Honda he'd driven during his last year of high school; **Merge Right** – the Toyota that Lauren's parents had given her for her college graduation; **Merge Right**– and the rusty, damn-near dilapidated Chevy station wagon he and Lauren had once taken for a test drive from a used car lot, just for shits and giggles, and in which, on a crisp autumn afternoon, he had proposed to her, and she had said yes.

Merge Right. Decay patterns. Particles scattering.

He stared at the snow that came spraying forward from the darkness to throw itself on his windshield only to be scattered by the wipers, and he thought about decay, and loneliness, and grief, and responsibility.

He slowed the car and looked into the rear-view mirror, watching as the exhaust danced into the night, combined with the swirling snow, and danced a ballet of form, becoming the faces of every person he'd ever hurt, ever disappointed, ever let down, lied to, betrayed, mocked, ignored, or – worst of all – forgotten about. They danced around his car with a cold grace, and continued to dance around as he inched forward, never touching any of them, until, at last, he came to a stop and put the car in **Park**.

"I knew after about fifteen minutes," he said to Lauren, looking at her, there, scattered particles trapped in her jar. "I knew what you were going to do, and I did nothing to stop it. I couldn't move, baby. I was too scared. I couldn't imagine how I was going to handle it, having to deal with the baby and taking care of you, trying to nurse you back to health, spending the rest of my life worrying that you were going to try it again the minute you were out of my sight, never knowing if you'd ever get over it, the two of us always looking at each other and seeing only the third person in our family who wasn't there."

He turned to face her. "Do you understand?"

I know, honey. I just needed to hear you say it.

"And I still feel like you abandoned me, and sometimes...ohgod, baby… sometimes I really, *really* hate you for it."

Now it's part of the world, that thought of yours. You have spoken it aloud. You have given it form.

"So what am I supposed to do now? How am I supposed to keep my promise to you?"

Leave me here.

"I can't…can't do that."

"It's okay, Daddy," said the voice from the cell phone, once again that of the child, of Cynthia, his little girl who almost was.

Matt leaned over and unstrapped the urn, bringing it to his chest and cradling it with all the tenderness he could muster.

Just open the door and step outside, honey. The ground will be there this time.

"I don't want to leave you."

You're not. You're just scattering some useless particles, that's all.

Matt unbuckled his seat belt and opened the door. True to Lauren's word, the ground was still there. He climbed out into the icy night and stood upon the churning snow that wound around his ankles, holding him in place as the others, the figures of mist and snow and exhaust, continued dancing around his car. He spotted the faces of his own parents among them and whispered, "You two would've made *terrific* grandparents."

He removed the lid from the urn and tossed it into the car, and then, slowly, with great deliberation, raised the urn over his head, turned into the wind, and emptied its contents into the winter night. He did not notice that a good portion of the ashes had fallen into a small pile near his feet.

He climbed back into the car, replaced the urn's lid, strapped it into place once again, and began driving away, closing the door only after the car started moving; he wanted one last breath of the night wind; perhaps some of her still lingered near and he could breathe her in, have her with him forever and always, a part of him, absorbed into his tissue, never to be taken away again.

"Matt?" came her voice from the cell phone.

He leaned over and picked it up. "Yeah, baby?"

"Where are you going?"

"Home, I guess. If I can find the way."

"Honey?"

"Yeah…?"

"You have to forgive yourself first."

"For not saving you?"

"For all of it. For everything. You'll never find your way home if you don't."

He stared out into the snow and darkness, and thought of all the sins, mortal and those of omission, that he had ever committed, all the people he'd hurt, turned away from, alienated, or ridiculed. He realized, with a smile, that he'd been a pretty selfish man for most of his life, and not a particularly *good* man, either. All the goodness, it seemed, he'd been saving for Lauren, and for their child, and what good was it now?

"I don't think that's going to happen anytime soon, baby."

"Then it's going to be a long drive back."

"Tell me about it."

"Remember, Daddy," said Cynthia. "The best way to get home is to keep driving and never to stop. Never to stop. Never..."

And as Matt's car was swallowed by the snow and darkness, a wind came up from the south, softly, with almost no sound, and took hold of the remaining ashes, swirling them around in a final dance before scattering them, one by one, into the night air where they drifted for only a moment before surrendering to the inevitable decay pattern and vanishing into nothingness, leaving only the drifting snow, the sighing of the wind, and the figures of the mist dancers; but soon they, too, began to break apart and scatter, until, at last, there was no sign any of them had ever been there or that any of it had even happened.

But had someone else been there, had they listened carefully, they might have heard the faint, distant echo of a child's voice, urging Daddy never to stop, never to stop, never to stop...

❧

As It Is In Your Head

"O! Keep me from their worse than killing lust
And tumble me into some loathsome pit,
Where never man's eye may behold my body."

– Shakespeare, *Titus Andronicus*, II:3

Like most men whose Quixotic notions of true love crumble into the easy and cynical promiscuity of the failed romantic, Craig Larousse was in no way prepared for the astonishing *beaux yeux* of his fantasy lover when she at last revealed herself; but then, she could have been anything other than the sad creature named Shelly who was next to him in bed and he would have been pleased.

He tried not to laugh as he watched her slip off the bed and glide across the room with something she must have thought to be daintiness. She lit a candle, then turned to face him, untying the belt of her terrycloth robe and smiling as her costume slipped from her bony shoulders and tumbled to the floor. She brushed a thin strand of wiry hair from her eyes and began to caress the tip of a pinkie with her tongue, keeping her small ingenuous gaze on his face.

"This do anything for you?"

"Definitely." It was a lie. With her bony shoulders, shapeless hips, and sagging thighs, she was by far one of the most dismal specimens of femininity he'd been with in quite some time: gray stretch marks over her midsection betrayed the weight she'd gained and then lost; freckles from her childhood had darkened into unsightly splotches; and her chest was sprinkled with disgusting brown moles that formed grotesque patterns.

In the glow of a candle stands the shattered Venus, thought Craig, his mind wandering to the test he would be giving his Mythology class Monday morning.

"I want to do something…different," said Shelly in a throaty whisper.

"I'm game." He couldn't have cared less.

She took a small plastic bottle from her bureau and squirted a small amount of greasy liquid into the palm of her left hand, then slowly doused her skin with the lilac-scented oil as if she were polishing a mirror in hopes that it would show her the reflection she wanted to see. She stumbled over to the bed and began massaging the oil over Craig's body, all the time nibbling and licking his neck.

"Is now okay?" she asked.

"Absolutely."

She smiled through slightly discolored teeth and went down on him in a fumbling burst of passion, biting him only once – which was already an improvement over the last time.

As Shelly labored away at his cock, Craig thought about the test: The Lesser Myths Of Greek and Roman Mythology. Right. What the fuck did any of his students know, or for that matter, care? Not one of them took these myths to heart, not one of them spent their nights fantasizing of a goddess like Venus, one who could make the sex as good in the flesh as it was in your head. Did any of them ever stop to wonder why, as you grew older, the act of physical love became less of a mystery and more of a means to an end? That had, in less abstract terms, been Craig's ex-wife's biggest complaint toward the end of their marriage: *Why can't you be more passionate with me? Half the time I feel like I'm just a third hand to help you jack off.* He would never have admitted it to her, but she had a point, and at times like this he couldn't help but wonder if—

—"Damn," said Shelly, pulling up her head and shaking some hair from her face, "gimme a break, huh? If I try any harder I'm gonna swallow my teeth."

He said nothing.

She crawled up beside him, her fingers tracing circles on his well-defined but hairless chest. Craig cursed himself for not having a go at the blonde who'd been tending the bar; he'd talked with her enough to start the moves, and God knows she'd hinted that she'd be receptive, she would have undoubtedly been better in bed, so what the hell was he doing here?

He stared at the candleglow that bounced and shimmered across the ceiling, forming shapes; images of youth, a first kiss, first sex, the faces of all the early girls…he longed to touch them again, re-shape them, fuse them together like a lump of clay and sculpt them into one perfect lover. He watched as their faces dissolved and reappeared, each time with more clarity and substance, coming closer until they split apart like magnified atoms and spun away in a cataclysm of yellowish light, leaving behind only the eyes.

The eyes.

Stationary and unblinking, the candleglow formed two eyes that looked down on him with frightening desire. He held his breath, his heart triphammering against his chest as the glow spread farther, outlining the ghost of a face that smiled at him with a thousand secret flames of ineffable pleasure.

There was a sudden movement below his waist and Shelly stopped massaging his cock and pulled her hand away.

He tore his gaze from the face for only a moment, but when he looked back, it was gone.

"Is there some problem?" snapped Shelly.

He wasn't sure if there was petulance in her voice or not and right now he didn't care; that face was gone because of her. Something in him had awakened during those few brief moments of communion and he wanted it back. More than anything, he wanted it back.

He touched Shelly's hair; it felt like an old Brillo pad. He forced a smile onto his face to make her feel special. Girls like her needed to feel special even though they weren't and never would be. At one point in his life he would have been angered at the idea of a man pulling on a woman what he was about to pull on Shelly, but that point had been left in the dust long ago; now he'd become an expert. And prided himself on this maneuver.

"There's no problem, baby."

Shelly pulled away. "Don't lie to me." She lifted the sheet to cover her tiny breasts. "You were fine earlier, the first time, and now you turn into cotton candy. I don't mean to sound bitchy but…well…it tends to make a woman feel…I dunno…ugly and undesirable."

Undesirable. What a goddamn joke that word was coming from her mouth. How could she sit here in front of him with her marks and her moles and her bony shoulders and try to make *him* feel guilty? How could she do this after that face? How fucking *dare* she.

"Answer me one question," he said coldly. "Why aren't you beautiful? You're not even pretty."

Her face drained of color. "I didn't mean anything by it, honest. I just...I don't know what's wrong all of a sudden. I don't know what I can do to make you...oh, *fuck*! I'm sorry, but I just...I can't keep competing against memories of other women every time I'm with a guy, y'know? I'm sick of having sex be just a one-shot wonder and I can't...I can't..." She pressed her chin down into her collarbone, previewing the double chin that would hang around her neck someday.

"Don't cry," said Craig. "I'm warning you, don't." In her face he could see the traces of the hurt left behind by other men before him. He felt no guilt over adding to this damage, though some part of him whispered that he should. Someday Shelly would be just another unhappy wife who lived in just another unhappy house that was too small and too untidy, who went to church and sat in the back with a husband who didn't like her very much and kids who didn't listen to her. Maybe she would wear a scarf around her head to hide the prematurely graying hair. Maybe people would feel sorry for her. Maybe she would join a community group who sponsored bake sales and parking lot carnivals to raise money for charity.

Maybe he didn't give a fuck.

He climbed out of her bed and reached for his pants. She lurched forward and clutched at his arm.

"I'm sorry," she said. "I didn't mean for it to—"

A sudden fury unlike any he'd ever known before took hold of him; he threw down his pants, whirled around, slapped her arm away, then grabbed her by the shoulders. "You really don't get it, do you?"

Her eyes welled with frightened tears and that, almost as much as the candleglow face, aroused him.

He tightened his grip. "You think it all has to be romance and candlelit dinners and poetic declarations of undying love. Try again, sister! Those sensibilities were buried along with Jane Austen and all you're trying to is resurrect the dead. Take it from me

– I found out long ago that you're better off settling for a good, sweaty fuck than searching for a soulmate who can hold you hand with tenderness."

"P-please...you're hurting me."

He pulled her up onto her knees so that her face was less than an inch from his own. "Even now you don't know what you want out of this, do you? All you know is that you want something more than what you've got and that you'll spread your legs and grunt and scream and squeal if it will help you pretend that you're closer to finding it." He thought her arms might snap off like pieces from a porcelain doll pulled from a dusty trunk in a darkened attic.

She shook her head, her eyes pleading. "I just want it to be special, Craig, that's all. I don't expect for a night like this to change my world, but is it...is it so stupid to think that maybe it'll make it seem less lonely? Isn't that enough for it to...to mean something?"

Mean something.

With those two simple, harmless words, she released a monster that had been lying dormant inside Craig since well before his divorce, one born of anger, disappointment, heartbreak, loneliness, and unfulfilled desires; this monster made its right arm into a bettering ram that slammed into her jaw, flipping face-down onto the mattress.

The monster wasted no time; it was firm and erect.

It knelt behind her, wrenched apart her legs, and rammed itself deep inside. She howled in agony but the monster didn't hear; it was looking into the candleglow face that had re-appeared, running a moist, promising tongue over its full lips. The monster pumped on, going deeper, rocking the bed and slamming the headboard rhythmically against the wall. There were noises, terrified noises, pained noises, sub-human noises; there was struggling, clawing, biting, thrashing; there were horrible words screamed into terrified ears, savage acts that snapped the bed supports under the mattress and drew blood. Among other fluids.

And all the time the perfect, loving, seductive face stared from behind its luminous veil; smiling, laughing, moaning, promising.

Soon Shelly was far too damaged to be of any further use. She fell off the bed with a heavy, wet noise and dragged herself over to a darkened corner where she shuddered and bled and whimpered like some thrashed animal while the monster that had once been Craig Larousse stood clutching a torn section of bed sheet in its hands.

"You are really something," it said. "Pissing the bed like some goddamn three-year-old watching a horror movie." It heaved the ruined sheet across the room. It fell over Shelly like a shroud.

The monster that had once been Craig Larousse collapsed onto the remains of the bed and lay staring up into the candleglow face. Something about it struck immediately at the core of his dead heart. It and it alone held the promise of all that he'd been missing. A forgotten, decayed part of him had been revitalized and he would not be deprived of tasting more.

Shhhh, said the face. *C'mon, baby, close your eyes.*

He did. The candleglow passed through his eyelids to warm the corneal fluid, washing over him, pulsing through his veins, turning his blood into a warm summer rain in a place where he walked through the playgrounds of his youth, dreaming of a beautiful princess he would one day rescue, knowing all the while that no woman would ever want him with equal measure.

Behind his eyes the face drifted closer to the newly-awakened part of himself and the two slowly but inexorably coalesced. He felt weightless, freed, and renewed as two soft hands reached beyond the candle smoke to take hold of his own, lifting him higher into a dream corridor upon whose gauzy walls like a movie screen replayed all the women from his life: there was Diana and her crooked front teeth; Linda, his ex-wife, came next, with her lustrous brown hair that she would never let him touch because she was afraid it was falling out – but she could do things with her tongue that should have been illegal; Lori, then, with her small body and lifeless red hair, bent forward on her knees and begging him to fuck her hard in the ass; Kate, next, all blonde hair and big bones, licking his shoulder just before she reached it and then squealing like the pig she was when she finally came—

—others, after that, their faces clear, their bodies lacquered in sweat, their names forgotten, their aromas enfolding him, reminding him that he'd taken some small part of them every time he'd slipped out in the middle of the night while they lay sleeping, leaving not so much as a note, a touch, a kiss, or a pleasant memory behind.

None of them compared to the woman before him; eyes of bluish-gray, breasts that were neither too small nor too large, full and ripe, with engorged nipples that begged for the tip of his tongue, a mouth that was full and moist and pleaded for the taste of his cock, and a sweet, pink cunt that was already heavily lubricated.

She pulled him closer, becoming finite as Shelly and her pathetic surroundings faded away, leaving him suspended on a bed of darkness where he could see only this magnificent, succulent candleglow goddess.

I'm gonna burn you, baby, he thought.

Never in his life had he been so consumed by such wrenching hunger. She stroked his erection with a moist, velvety tongue as her finger slipped smoothly and deeply into his ass, probing, pushing, making him all the harder.

She pulled her mouth away and whispered: "Remember the time Linda asked you to tie her up?" You liked that, didn't you?"

He arched his back and began to cry out but she choked him with her tongue, her body coiling around his. She pulled out her fingers and began pumping his erection.

"And Lori," she said. "All the time howling 'Fuck me in the tail!' That really got you hot, didn't it?"

"...oh, yeah..."

She straddled him, her wet thighs sliding against his own as she met him thrust for thrust, throwing back her head and shoving her engorged nipples into his mouth; he sucked at them hungrily.

"You're right about romantic love," she purred. "You always... God, yes!...you...

ungh...always were..."

He tried to stop the eruption that was rising inside of him but she was so good...so damned good...

"...love can...oooh, baby, fuck...fuck *harder*...that's it...love can only bring heartache and sorrow, this way is so much easier... so much better...so much...God! *GOD, YES! DO IT! HURT MY PUSSY! HURT IT!*...this way is *so much better*..."

She bucked and shuddered, and when he finally came, when he finally felt everything inside of him explode inside of her, years of frustration and desire undimmed as his juice shot up until she was so full that it began to run in rivulets from between

241

her legs, dripping over his balls. She dug her nails into his chest as her body shook, the soft groan in the back of her throat rising into a shriek, then a deafening scream as she rammed downward, pushing him deeper, crying out his name again and again and again.

When it was done he fell back, sweating, breath heaving, onto their bed of night.

"I'm so glad you finally let me out," said his own personal Venus. "There's so much I've wanted to return to you, so much pleasure I want to give back." She rose onto her knees before him, her body ripe and wet and glistening with sex.

He started to roll over but something had closed about his wrists and ankles. He tried to move but he couldn't get to her, couldn't touch her, couldn't taste her. A hot wind burned against his exposed flesh and he shrieked. He looked down and saw that his legs were chained apart, exposing his cock and balls to the night. He tried reaching down to cover them but the chains and manacles that held his arms were even stronger. Something hard and jagged scraped against his back and drew blood. He turned his head and saw that he was chained to a rock.

Chained to a rock.

Like fucking Prometheus, he was chained.

Venus giggled.

"Now the *real* fun starts," she said.

A large lump appeared between her breasts and began to fill with a thick, milky liquid, drooping down past her navel and toward her legs, expanding; light blue veins crisscrossed under the oozing flesh and it touched the ground and began rolling toward him, stopping at the base of the rock. Venus threw back her head, her chest heaving, her body rippling with an orgasm that she seemed to be sharing with the growth. She took a deep breath of the whirling, dark, fiery air and leveled her gaze at Craig.

"Do you know whey you never find it as good in the flesh as it is in your head? Because you forgot that the most erotic thing you can offer to a woman, in bed or out, is imagination. That's why none of them ever responded to you the way you wanted them to – because there is a difference between imagination and just fantasizing. And only women understand this. Few men are willing to learn how to tell the difference."

She leaned forward and bit one of his nipples, sighing. "But you don't have to worry about that now…"

The growth began to pulse from within.

"…because I'm here for you and I've got more than enough imagination for the both of us…"

The surface of the growth cracked open with a thick, wet, sickening pop! as something meaty and fluid seeped out.

"…I'm all your lovers, baby, rolled into one…"

The meaty fluid congealed as she spoke, its stench forcing bile into his throat and mouth.

"…and I'm gonna burn *you*, lover."

The congealed mass exploded outward and upward, spewing a fount of blood and intestines and fire. So much fire.

Venus screamed, the sound shattering Craig's composure and wrapping around his heart like strands of barbed wire. The manacles dug in deeper as the wind increased, searing his flesh with its heat and tearing away his reason shred by bloody shred. He shut his eyes against Venus's laughter but it would not go away, would not stop, would not lessen. Only grow louder, becoming the voices of a thousand women. He struggled against the chains until he felt his bones starting to snap under the strain. He tried to breathe but the thick, putrid smoke clogged his lungs. He opened his eyes and stared in horror as the hair on his body turned red, then yellow, then shriveled up to vanish in a cloud of stinking black vapor.

A shadow fell over him.

Tears burst from his eyes but evaporated before hitting his cheeks.

The thing towering over him was Shelly and Linda and Kate and Lori and Diana and all the nameless others, fused as one within a phantasm of flesh and flame; they were of one body, with one massive torso and two wide, thick, tree-like legs that shuddered with the anticipation of feeling his cock plunge between them—

– but each face was separate, jammed in with others like photos in a collage; a hundred malformed hands reached out toward him. Inside, fire pumped through their veins as they shimmered and grew larger, their hair burning down to the roots and vanishing like strips of paper tossed into an open furnace.

The pain was immeasurable.

243

Craig wished that his mind would just crumble but knew it wouldn't; they would make certain that the last string of his sanity would remain intact so he would be aware of every exquisite second of their coupling.

The thing reached down and lifted something long and shiny from the ground, strapping it around its waist like a log-sized dildo.

Hands came down, searing his flesh as they flopped his cock over to the side, exposing the soft, vulnerable area between his erection and balls.

"Is it true," asked the Venus-thing, "that all men who are sexually frustrated secretly wish that they had a vagina of their own?"

"...ohgod, no, please...*pleaseGod NO!*"

"Don't be afraid," whispered the collage of fiery faces. "It only takes a little imagination."

Bargain

*"Then wilt thou not be loth
To leave this Paradise..."*

– John Milton
Paradise Lost

The night grew silent, an almost majestic silence, as if every living thing was holding its breath for fear of breaking the purity.

As the silence became deeper, so did the darkness, allowing a massive shadow to detach itself from a corner of the night and move unnoticed over the city, past every building, every house, every church, over the farmers' fields and the woodlands, until it reached the north and south forks of the Licking River near Raccoon Creek. Here, the North Fork marked the community's eastern boundary. In this spot the county began to gradually slope from the Mississippian bedrock it rested on to the much trickier Pennsylvanian bedrock. Shale lay under the surface of the topsoil from the west where sandstone began mixing in.

A small tributary of the Licking River formed in this spot, and it was here that the shadow hovered as still as the point of an ancient divining rod. This sixty-acre plat had always been extremely weak; the ground here was known to often simply collapse without warning, half-swallowing barns, outhouses, even the corpses of abandoned cars rusting in the nearby automobile graveyard. This was not a place many visited anymore.

What better spot, then, for a certain corner of Hell to open one of its back doors?

Beneath the clear, still surface of the tributary, its surface made almost turquoise by the moonlight, lay a series of small, evenly-spaced hollowed boulders, each with a translucent sheet of isinglass covering the top. Inside each of the hollowed objects – which, upon closer examination, the shadow saw were not boulders at all

245

but leathery eggs – huddled a clay-like lump; some were shapeless blobs, others vaguely humanoid in form; some were skeletal, others so corpulent their bodies could barely be contained; still others were mere hand-sized, featureless fetuses. All lay with knees pulled up against their chests, dark, sunken eyes staring up blankly at the draping algae and bodies of insects floating on the surface.

The shadow slumped closer to the surface, whispering *Awaken* to any of the figures who could hear.

A set of tiny fingers broke through the gelatinous cover of one egg and began pulling apart the shell, sections snapping off and flaking away until the featureless fetal face poked through, followed by two pink arms, hands moving slowly through the water as the Unfinished Soul pushed free of its prison and swam through to the surface. It pulled itself onto the ground, crawling toward the tip of the shadow.

The shadow reached out and helped the Unfinished Soul to stand.

I need a guide, little one, whispered the shadow. *A debt is being collected tonight.*

Lift me up, said the Unfinished Soul. *It will be my pleasure to show you the way.*

The shadow poured over the figure, ink spreading across a sketch, until it vanished completely.

Do exactly as I say, whispered the Unfinished Soul.

The shadow began churning in the air; slowly, at first, curling wisps of smoke from a forgotten cigarette, growing thicker, its speed increasing, soon twisting itself into a funnel and dropping low.

The ground rippled, then began sinking inward with heavy, dry sounds as the shadow threaded itself into the center of the chasm like string through a needle's eye. Sections of earth spun outward as the shadow-thread drilled deeper, finally disappearing beneath the surface. The ground shuddered, jumped, then grumbled. The remaining eggs in the tributary swirled like flecks around a drain before vanishing down the chasm.

In the heart of the shadow, the Unfinished Soul glanced upward, just once, out of curiosity, and saw the moon vanish behind a blue-tinged night-cloud, then re-emerge a few moments later to reveal it was no cloud at all, but something much more solid – a balloon.

Beneath its death's-head body and the glowing fire within, his hands gripping the flying wires of the basket, a young man who could no longer remember his name watched as the chasm grew wider. As he stared into the pit he saw a ring of trees emerge around the perimeter – fingers of the dead pushing upward through forgotten grave-soil – and stood helpless as the balloon moved downward, toward them.

The trees were well over thirty feet tall, each with a thick trunk resembling that of a cactus, only black. The branches of each tree were obscured by heavy onion layers of bleak blue leaves that collectively blossomed outward to form human faces, each turning upward to stare at him through milky eyes containing no pupils, each face twisted into a tight, pinched expression of concentrated grief. As the wind passed through the trees, the faces opened their mouths and moaned; deeply, steadily, mournfully: the sound of cumulative anguish.

The young man felt tears welling in his eyes, and wished he could say something to ease their pain. After all, he recognized every face.

A strong gust of wind howled, snatching the balloon from within the ring of keening trees and hurtling it into the gale. It bounced across the night sky, turning, dipping, rising, caught in the thermals. It ebbed across roads, spun down streets, and arced over buildings, its cast-off rope whipping back and forth as it was tossed into the pocket of a wind that pulled it down until the tip of the rope touched the sidewalk. It scooted along until it reached an old but noble-looking house where a single dim light burned in the downstairs window. The balloon moved with great care, positioning itself so that the young man was given a clear look inside the window.

Murky light from a glowing street lamp snaked across the darkness to press against the glass. The light bled into the room, across a kitchen table, and glinted off the rim of a glass held by a man whose once-powerful body had lost its commanding posture under the weight of compiling years; he was now overweight from too many beers, over-tense from too many worries, and overworked far too long without a reprieve. Whenever this man spoke, his eyes never had you; this much the young man watching from the balloon recalled with morbid clarity. His father's eyes were every lonely journey the young man had ever taken, every unloved place he'd ever visited, every sting of guilt he'd ever felt; he stared into his father's eyes that never had you, eyes that only brushed by once, softly, like a cattail or a ghost, then fell shyly toward the ground in some inner contemplation too sad to be touched by a tender thought or the delicate brush of another's care. You'd think God had forgotten his name.

Albert lifted the glass to his mouth. The cool water felt good going down, washing away the remnant of the bad dream. He drained the glass, sighed, then went to the sink for a refill. He was thinking about his days as a child, about the afternoons now forgotten by everyone but him, afternoons when he'd go to the movies for a nickel and popcorn was only a penny. He thought about how he used to take his son to the movies all the time when his son was still a boy, how much fun they always had, and Albert longed for the chance to do something like that again, something that would put a bright smile on his son's face and make himself feel less of a failure. His son was now a great success, and Albert was still what he'd always been, a factory stooge, a worker on the line. He tried to remember how long it had been since he and his son had last spoken. Seemed a damn shame, it did, the way they never talked anymore, and his son living just the other side of town. Why hadn't the boy called in so long?

Albert stood at the sink listening to the sounds of his wife sleeping. Janice snored loudly, and though it used to get on Albert's nerves, he now found the sound comforting. He didn't know how he'd be able to face the rest of his life if she weren't by his side. She was a marvel to him. After all the mistakes he'd made – and, God, he'd made a lot, no arguing that – her respect and love for him never lessened.

Albert raised the glass to his lips and found that he was smiling.

The balloon rose higher, then, toward a window on the second floor, giving the young man a chance to look in on the sleeping form of his mother, and smile; even from outside, he could hear her snoring. *Sawing logs like a lumberjack*, his father used to say.

The keening trees had perfectly captured the faces of his parents, as well as the others.

The young man reached out his hand but stopped just short

of placing it against the glass. *Would it do any good if you knew how sorry I am?*

As if in answer, the wind kicked up once again and the balloon was swept away, up and over the house. It rode the breeze above the roofs of the town until its nearly-imperceptible shadow fell across the head of a couple climbing out of a car and running toward another house, one the young man recognized all too well, as he did the couple; their faces, too, had been perfectly reproduced by the keening trees.

The balloon hovered, unseen by Patricia and her husband, Richard, as they rushed toward the front porch of the house. Patricia had been trying to get in touch with her brother for the last week and had finally given over to panic when she'd called Mom and Dad to find they hadn't heard from him for a long while, either.

"He's probably out of town or something," Albert had said to her. "He's been real...busy lately, what with the company taking off like it has."

The explanation wasn't enough for Patricia, who insisted that Richard and she make the two-hour drive from Dayton to Cedar Hill.

Patricia pounded on the front door, calling out her brother's name and getting no response. She began flipping through her keys until she found the spare door key her brother had given her last year when he'd bought the house.

"I don't know if just barging in like this is such a good idea," said Richard.

"Don't start with me again," said Patricia, slipping the key into the lock. "I don't care how great things are going for his company, you *know* how bad his depression can get when he doesn't take his meds. He pulled this disappearing act the last time he went off them, and it damn near killed him."

"I still think you're panicking over nothing."

"I hope so, Richard. I truly hope you'll be saying 'I told you so' to me in a few minutes."

She got the door opened but Richard stepped in front of her.

"Let me go in first, okay, hon? He might...y'know...have company or something."

"*Goddammit*, Richard, I'm not going to worry about—"

"Just humor me, all right?"

Patricia exhaled, then nodded her head. "I'll wait here. But not for long."

Richard went inside, leaving the door half-opened.

The young man in the balloon wanted to close his eyes, wanted to cover his ears with his hands, wanted the balloon to leave here right this second because he didn't want to see or hear what was about to happen when—

"*Jesus!*" shouted Richard from inside. "*Oh, good Christ – PAT!*"

As if propelled by the volume of Richard's shouts, the balloon caught a thermal and glided farther on, reaching the banks of the Licking River. The thermal expanded and the balloon lowered its basket and passenger into the waters, the currents carrying it to the junction of the north and south forks.

It bounced off a section of jutting rocks and spiraled upward, pulled into a pocket of churning wind being sucked into the deep chasm in the center of the field.

The keening trees blinked their milky dead eyes and cried out again; louder, this time, and with a deeper anguish. The young man felt their cries chew through him as the balloon hung suspended over the chasm of collapsed earth.

The balloon's tie-off rope began lowering itself. The rumbling from deep inside the chasm became a whistle. Small sections of hillside crumbled away, giving way to increasingly larger sections sliding toward the chasm and pouring over its edge.

The chasm grew wider. More ground collapsed. The whistling was replaced by the sound of a million rocks cracking apart from the center. The tie-off line then pulled taut, a fisherman's line at last making the catch of the day, and the balloon began rising, pulling the thing now attached to the end of the tie-off rope.

An ornate kiosk that might have been a belfry poked up, followed by curling arches that formed the overhang of stained-glass windows where stone gargoyles sat underneath.

A tug, another gust of wind, and the tie-off line snapped tighter, tugging with all its might.

The bulk of the rising church was pulled free of the membranous sac beneath the soil. The young man looked down and saw the world he'd known – as well as those he'd never know – unfurl before him like wings of a merciless predator.

He saw mountains crumble, the sky change color, and the seas give up their dead.

He saw himself watching a television screen that showed him watching a television screen of himself watching another screen where film of a funeral was shown to him as he watched. He watched his soul grow wings and take flight. He watched himself grow older. He watched himself become a baby once again. He watched himself never being born.

He watched himself being born a thousand times in a thousand different places.

He watched his soul's wings catch fire and plummet downward into the Pit.

He watched as everything shifted and changed and faded into shadows, only to be replaced by other, firmer worlds; there were skies filled with fire and songs to be sung; there were ships and seas and fields of green; there were races being born, becoming children at play, growing up, growing old, dying, becoming ashes, blowing away; he saw his own ghost walk through these ashes and stand over the bones of a child who had once been him, and he wept at the sight, at the wasted potential; he saw the bones rise up and grow skin, replacing the ghost of himself, growing up to become young and reckless, grow strong and virile, healthy and pink-cheeked, suddenly a child, a baby once more, a seed in the womb of its mother who snored too loudly, spinning back in time before starting over once again, clicking off the television remote of the funeral scene and struggling to his feet, old, ancient, his grey hair thinning, back bent, legs thin and weak and unstable, wishing for one last kiss from the wife he never had, then hobbling off to a lonely deathbed to lay down, close his eyes, and disintegrate into vestiges of flesh that blew away to land in a field of ashes where the next ghost of himself stood weeping over the bones of a child....

The church shook off the dirt and began to glow from within as candles were set aflame. The doors were unlocked with a loud, creaking groan, and thrown open.

The Dust Witch stepped from behind the doors and gestured up toward the balloon, the bones in her arthritic index finger cracking as she curled it forward, then back; forward, then back: *Get yourself down here, now.*

The balloon lowered. The Dust Witch took hold of the tie-off line and wrapped it around one of the gargoyles. The basket touched ground, and the young man climbed out, slowly, with much hesitation and even more sadness.

Around him, the keening trees turned their faces downward, screaming.

He touched his lips, then pulled away his fingers to look at the blood covering them; then he reached toward the back of his head, surprised at the size of the exit wound.

He smiled, shrugged, and looked at the hag standing before him.

"A belated word of advice," said the Dust Witch, taking his hand and leading him through the doors into Hell. "Whenever you sell your soul, don't sell it so *cheap*."

...And When It Is Decided That The War Is Over

"...and for those of you who might not have been born yet, in September of 1945 the General Headquarters of the Occupational Forces issued a statement so flat and emotionless in its content and intent that it still leaves one absolutely speechless. This statement – I can't remember the exact wording, it's been well over half a century and I was only five years old at the time, but my uncle, Robert Pearson, was a correspondent with CBS and so had access to a copy of the report, which said, in essence, that those civilians of Hiroshima and Nagasaki who were likely to die from A-bomb afflictions should be left to die. The official attitude was that people suffering from radiation poisoning were not worth saving, and that any attempt to do so would be an inexcusable waste of time, money, and medical supplies. What was understood but of course unwritten was that the General Headquarters of the Occupational Forces did not want to risk the lives of U.S. military personnel by sending them into the quote affected areas unquote. They were just beginning to understand the wide-ranging effects of what had been done, of how long those effects were going to last, and how they had, in their zest to end that damned war, unleashed their version of Frankenstein's Monster on the entire world. Perhaps calling it 'Oppenheimer's Monster' would be more precise, but I never agreed with that, not entirely. I had the privilege of interviewing J. Robert Oppenheimer in December of 1966, shortly before his death a few months later. I was 26 years old, it was my first really important assignment, and put me 'on the map,' as the saying goes. Even then, he could not stop himself from railing against the 1954 hearings that resulted in his security clearance being revoked.

"The man who is now in referred to as the 'Father of the Atomic Bomb' was, in his own way, broken by what he had helped to create. His outspokenness against the bomb before, during, after the hearings is well-documented, and I have no doubt that those records – now in the form of computer files – are tucked securely away on several hard drives scattered about through the dozens of underground cave bunkers where the men and women who once governed us are now making their preparations for when it is decided that the war is over. Those computer files, like those whose duty it was to assemble and organize them, are safe and sound, along with those three thousand U.S. citizens who were chosen for their skills, or their knowledge – or were among the seventeen-hundred-and-fifty who were given a place by lottery drawing. After all, while it's all well and good to have the politicians, the doctors, the physicists, the scientists, poets, writers, newspersons, composers, actors, painters, and others without whom American culture would vanish from the face of whatever will be left of the Earth, there must also be a place for those who perform the invisible tasks that the others cannot be bothered to think about. There must be a place for the cooks, for the dishwashers, for the construction workers, janitors, plumbers, maids, electricians, the butchers, the bakers, the candlestick-makers...

"I was told by the technicians who helped me to set up this broadcast that the network has picked it up for a national feed, so there may be millions of you watching me right now...or maybe no one is watching. I don't suppose it matters, since everything is being recorded, stored away on digital files, preserved for posterity...or maybe not. I have no idea if this broadcast will be saved or even remembered, I have no idea how long the electricity is going to hold out, but I will not stop talking to you until the choice is taken out of my hands.

"If you'll look behind me, you'll see that I am standing atop a television station building in a typical, bland, white-bread Midwestern city. You can see the roofs of houses in the distance, just past the section of now-deserted freeway. The panic is over, the rioting has stopped, the looters have taken all there is to take. If my calculations are correct – and I base these calculations on those issued by the Pentagon – then I have a little over thirty-six minutes before the first missile strikes the air force base a few dozen miles from here.

"Do you like this tie I'm wearing? I actually spent five minutes this morning choosing it. It is the tie I wore when I made my first news broadcast over fifty years ago. My late wife knew how to take care of such things – ties, shoes, suits, all manner of clothing – and it seemed only appropriate that I wear this tie for my final broadcast. The morning of my first broadcast, Carol – my late wife – chose this tie for me. I do this for you, my love, my heart, and hope that you can hear me, wherever you are. You've no idea how happy I am that you are not here to witness these final minutes of the human race – the human race that has been abandoned above-ground, I should clarify. The human race who didn't have enough money, education, talent, or skill to rate a place in one of the underground bunkers. The human race that has been left to face its own extinction with the same matter-of-fact dispassion that deemed the survivors of Hiroshima and Nagasaki not worth saving. I never thought I would say these words my love, my heart, but I am so grateful for your being dead right now. I don't know if I could have found it in me to...

"I'll get to that in a few minutes. Right now, I want to talk briefly about how all of this came about – not only for whatever historical record of this broadcast may or may not remain, but for my own...understanding, if that's the correct word. I *still* can't believe that we, as a race, allowed this to occur. To destroy the world because one nation tried to help another that was starving to death by the millions each day. Until seven months ago, most of us had never heard of Zuhirain in east-central Africa – or if we had, it was just another poverty-stricken, disease-laden, revolution-wracked Third World sink-hole where starvation and sickness were a way of life.

"Our late president, James Ryan, as you'll recall, sent in ground troops when anti-government rebels blocked all ports in and around Zuhirain and began using anti-aircraft guns on any planes that attempted to drop medical supplies and food. As a result, nearly half a billion dollars' worth of food and medicine was either being sold on the black market, distributed among the rebel camps, or simply left to rot and expire. The UN Peacekeepers were having little-to-no effect, even when combined with U.S. ground forces, and so President Ryan had little choice but to send in even more troops, much to the ferocious outcry of the public.

"Remember what he said a few days before his assassination? At a press conference one network reporter who, judging from his manner, wasn't breast-fed as a child kept asking Ryan the same question over and over, changing only the words: 'Why does the U.S. have to go in there and help the people of Zuhirain?' And in what was in my opinion the greatest moment ever in a presidential press conference, Ryan gave that reporter a look that could have frozen fire and said, 'Because no one else is, and I don't know about you, but I find it a little difficult to sleep at night knowing that a minimum of fifty thousand people will die of starvation and disease while I'm sawing logs in a soft bed with a full belly. Now sit down and shut the hell up.'

"Less than sixty hours later an assassin's bullet silenced Ryan forever, and our government was shuffled around into the hands of madmen who took swift and decisive action, you have to give them that much. There was no hesitation.

"I liked Jim Ryan. He was a moral man who had the misfortune of allowing his morality to sometimes override his political savvy. I well remember the famous line that many credit with winning him the presidency: 'All problems confronting the human race are and always shall be at their core *moral dilemmas*, matters of conscience, human decency, and compassion; they only become *political issues* when someone or a large group of someones can gain wealth, power, fame, or real estate – preferably all four – by exploiting them.'

"How right he has been proven. Except who will buy the real estate when it is decided that the war is over? Who will buy any piece of the scorched and razed land that will greet them when they finally emerge from their underground havens and walk out into sunlight again? Who will even have the money, wealth, fame, and power – illusions that they have now been revealed to be?

"I have seen too much war in my lifetime. Yes, some of these wars were called 'police actions,' 'border skirmishes,' or 'peace-keeping missions,' but when bombs are dropped, villages and cities reduced to rubble, when bullets are fired that take the lives of men, women, and children, it's a war. And it is not kind, despite the debated irony of that famous poem.

"I remember, when I was covering Vietnam, standing with a film crew on a road outside a Montagnard village that had recently been bombed. The surviving villagers were stumbling and crawling away from the destruction. A few of them had managed to find wagons in which to place their dead or wounded. One old woman was pulling such a wagon, and her strength struck me then as it does now as the kind of superhuman strength one finds in oneself during times of war, for inside this wagon was a young man or perhaps fifteen who was using a sewing needle and some kind of terrible thread to try and stitch up the chest and groin of a child – I couldn't tell if it was a boy or a girl, only that it was a child. The child's innards were spilling out, and the young man was trying to hold them in place with one hand while he used the other to push the needle and thread through the child's flesh.

"The child was still conscious and screaming, but it did not try to move or push away the young man's hands, as if it understood that he was trying to save it. Both were covered in blood and burned skin, their clothes – what remained of them – still smoldering. But what stays with me above all else is what happened when that child saw us as the old woman pulled the wagon passed. Its eyes widened, and the expression of anguish on its face softened for just a moment, and then...excuse me...and then...*dammit*!

"...and then it *smiled* at me, one of its small, ruined hands rising up from its blasted body to point at the camera. It understood that it was being filmed, that it was going to be on television. Somehow that knowledge – however the child had acquired it – took the pain away for just a few seconds, and it waved at the camera as the wagon was pulled by.

"That footage was never aired, and it was my fault because I was in tears...not unlike the pathetic spectacle you're witnessing now. But that was Vietnam. Since then I've witnessed similar scenes in the Gulf, in Israel, Nicaragua, Afghanistan, Iraq and Iran, I've seen the 'dying rooms' in the mountains of China where sick and deformed children are abandoned to suffer a slow, miserable, lonely death, I've seen bodies floating in rivers of blood and intestines through the center of Rwanda, I've seen corpses piled as high as the sun in El Salvador, and I have seen too many screaming, wounded, terrified children running through bomb-blasted streets crying for their mother, or their father, or brother, sister, *anyone* to come and hold them, to make them safe, to take away all the pain and fear and make everything all right again...and I am here to tell all of you who might be watching that *this time*, this time there is no making everything all right again. For those of us left above-ground, there remains between fifteen and ninety minutes of life, depending on where in this country you live. California is gone, as is Utah and Nevada. Was anyone there to record *those* screams, I wonder. Is anyone there to open their arms to the radiation-charred children who are crawling through the debris, crying for someone to come and hold them? And when it is decided that the war is over, will those children, should they still somehow be alive, find it in their war-ravaged hearts to forgive? Or will forgiveness be nothing more than an abstract concept to them, like freedom and compassion and God?

"Forgive me for raising my voice like that. It won't do to have my final minutes spent with you remembered for my having done nothing but scream. For over fifty years you have – if I am to believe the Newsweek poll done a few years back – looked to me as the 'voice of reason.' A reasonable man would not scream at you, not with so little time left, so, again, please accept my apologies.

"I came back here to the city where my career began so that I might see my daughter, my son-in-law, and my grandchildren. They were so happy to welcome me into their homes, even knowing how terrible things had become. My son-in-law, you see, was not one of the people deemed 'of use' for the bunkers and caves and mine-shafts where now America functions and will continue to do so for years to come. My son-in-law, you see, is a factory worker whose only 'useful' skill is cutting saw blades. My daughter is, by choice, a stay-at-home mother. I could not possibly be more proud of either of them, or of my wonderful grandchildren. They took me into their home at this worst of all possible times and made me feel a sense of being loved again, of being needed, of being *necessary*.

"They didn't know that I had been offered a place in the bunkers, in the caves, in the mine-shafts of America Below. They didn't know that I had told the military officials who came to 'collect' me that they could go straight to Hell – which should be easier for them, since they'd be so much closer to it than I. I had watched these same officials literally pull a physicist away from his wife and children, telling him that they were not 'on the list,' that they were 'acceptable losses.' I watched these officials knock that physicist unconscious because he refused to leave without his family. And I watched as his family, screaming and in tears, chased after the vehicle into which he was thrown.

"When it is decided that the war is over, perhaps it will also be decided that there is no such thing as an 'acceptable' loss. I don't know where that physicist's wife and children are now. Maybe they're watching this broadcast, If they are, I want you to know how sorry I am that the government and the military in all of their collected wisdom somehow found it 'acceptable' to offer a place in America Below to an old newscaster in his seventies who's dying of cancer, rather than allow you to remain a family.

"My daughter and her family did not know about my cancer. Nor will they. You see, my doctor is an old coot, like me, who knows there are better and more peaceful ways to shuffle off this sad mortal coil than to be consumed in slow degrees by a disease that leaves you without any dignity in the final hours. And so my doctor, he gave me something. I don't suppose it will matter much to tell you about it now. What he gave me were two vials of Potassium, enough for several sixty milli equivalent doses. Death is instantaneous and painless when it's injected.

"This morning, before leaving to come here, I left the vials and the hypodermics in the refrigerator, and I left a note for my son-in-law, explaining the dosage amounts. If he loves his family as much as I hope he does, he'll do the right thing.

"I showered, shaved, chose this tie from the three I'd packed, and came here to the roof of this local television station. The sentimentalist in me, the little boy who believed and embraced the idea of God and Heaven and Peace Eternal, hopes that my daughter and her family are with Carol at this moment, and that there is no more suffering, no more pain. As sad as I am that they are gone, I feel not one bit of regret for my actions.

"So in these last few minutes, let's not talk about what is or what was. Let's talk about what's to come – much later. Let's talk about what will happen when it is decided that the war is over, shall we? This is Lowell Douglas Pearson, broadcasting from not-so high atop your favorite local television station, and it's time we spoke directly and honestly.

"Can you see it in your imaginations? The day when the nuclear winter is past, when the radiation levels have dropped to an 'acceptable' level, when the sealed solid-steel doors of the American Below are opened and the survivors walk into the new day?

"When it is decided that the war is over, they will all embrace one another and shake hands and kiss each other's tears away. When it is decided that the war is over, they will pour one another celebratory drinks and organize parades. When it is decided that the war is over, they will gather in public places and sing happy, spiritual songs, even if it is raining or well above ninety degrees. They will feel good about themselves and all they've managed to protect and save, because feeling good will be the first step toward doing good when it is decided that the war is over. And they will believe in doing good, just as J. Robert Oppenheimer and everyone who worked on Fat Man and Little Boy believed they were doing good. 'It's good to feel good,' they'll say. 'It's good to *do* good,' they'll say, then all join hands and sing 'Shall We Gather at the River' or 'Teach Your Children' or 'Michael Rowed the Boat Ashore.' Their pets will eat only organic food along with them when it is decided that the war is over. And all of their artists, all of their composers, their philosophers, their poets with their visions and their novelists constructing new visions and all their lyrical essayists who have been busy scribbling or typing or recording their thoughts and memoirs, all of them will rethink their stances and outlooks and viewpoints when it is decided that the war is over. And their leaders will all assemble and say to one another, 'This must never happen again,' while their assistants secretly gather the sticks and stones that will be needed to fight the next war that no one wants to think about but knows is coming.

"And what of us, we who will never savor the joys and safety of America Below? We will be the bodies they have not seen and so do not speak of as they step into the light of the new day. When it is decided that the war is over we will still be here, mud, rot, dust, bones, sleeping peacefully beneath the soils of a ruined land, and the survivors will hear our bones crunch under their feet and smell the faint scent of our charred flesh and, perhaps, a few of them will imagine that they can still hear our final cries wafting by on the breeze, a paper cup tumbling in the wind when it is decided that the war is over.

"But we'll be beyond all of that, you, your families, and I, because when it is decided that the war is over we will not be the ones in need of forgiveness, or comfort, or a way to fall asleep at night without the faces of the dead marching across our memories.

"I don't know how much time we've got left, so I'm going to tell you the thing you most need to hear, the thing we all want to hear, the only thing that can perhaps be that warm hand reaching out of the smoke from a death-stinking battlefield to pull you in and enfold you in understanding arms. And maybe, just maybe, when it is decided that the war is over, some part of this broadcast will remain, and they'll know that we who were not part of America Below spent our final minutes caring for one another, soothing the fears of our children, giving thanks that our loved ones would not leave this world alone.

"So come closer, my family, my friends, all of you. Come closer and look into my eyes and listen to the sound of my voice as you kiss your wives and husbands and brothers and sister and children and grandchildren. Listen to me, listen to the sound of my voice.

"Don't be afraid, everything's all right, it will all be over soon. Don't be afraid, everything's all right, it will all be over soon. Don't be afraid, everything's all right, it will all be over soon. Don't be afraid, everything's all right, it will all be over soon. Don't be afraid, everything's all right, it will all be over soon. Don't be afraid, everything's all right, it will all be over soon. Don't be afraid, everything's all right, it will all be over soon. Don't be afraid, everything's all right, it will be

✥

More Great Titles from Dark Arts Books!

Rough Cut, a novel by Brian Pinkerton (2017 reissue)

Synchronized Sleepwalking, a fiction collection by Martin Mundt (2016)

The Dark Underbelly of Hymns, a fiction collection by Martin Mundt (2013 reissue)

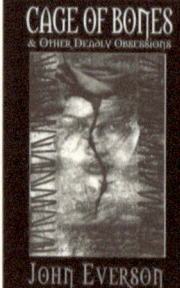

Cage of Bones, a fiction collection by John Everson (2013 reissue)

Vigilantes of Love, a fiction collection by John Everson (2013 reissue)

The Crawling Abattoir, a fiction collection by Martin Mundt (2013 reissue)

Four-Author Anthologies only from Dark Arts Books

Discover amazing new fiction from our critically acclaimed original anthology series!

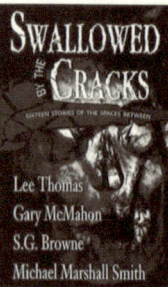

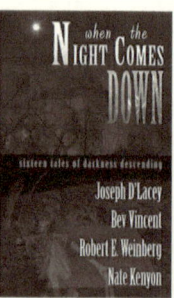

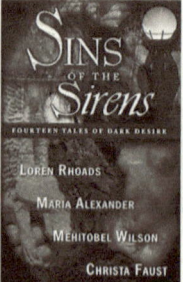

Visit www.DarkArtsBooks.com